The tent-flap moved.

"Message from the King, sir," said one of his own tent-guards.

Dewar lifted his eyebrows, nodded once; the guard stood back and admitted Luneté.

Dewar studied her. "May one ask," he said after a moment, "what you're doing here? Or must one draw conclusions from one's perhaps excessively creative and lively imagination?"

Luneté's cheeks reddened brighter than the winter cold had left them. "I have been worried," she said. "My huband has not written."

"Otto is not a diligent letter-writer," said Dewar.

"Not when things aren't going well," she agreed, looking away, and then looked back. "So you are surrendering," she said.

He sighed. "He is."

"Why?" she whispered, a hot hard word.

"Because it is the prudent thing to do," Dewar said, leaning back in his chair. Because it is better than losing everything."

"You couldn't lose."

"Otto could lose," Dewar said. "Madame, I am not in the business of giving advice, but I submit to you that Otto has a long life ahead of him in which to plot, scheme, and fight, never mind the portions of it which he would spend with yourself, and were he executed now it would put a serious blotch on that rosy future."

Luneté drew her breath in, the blood fleeting from her face, ivory in the darkness. "It will kill him," she whispered.

"His chances are better there than if he continued here," Dewar said, lighting the pipe off the candle and puffing smoke around his words.

"I mean the dishonor!" cried Luneté.

Dewar gazed at her over the candle and smoke. "Otto's honor seems rugged and durable enough to withstand a compromise," he said. "He knew the odds when he started the game, Luneté."

**Other Books by Elizabeth Willey**

*The Price of Blood and Honor**
*A Sorcerer and a Gentleman*
*The Well-Favored Man*

*forthcoming

# A Sorcerer and a Gentleman

Elizabeth Willey

A TOM DOHERTY ASSOCIATES BOOK
NEW YORK

A SORCERER AND A GENTLEMAN



Edited by Teresa Nielsen Hayden
Cover art by Charles Vess

A Tor Book
Published by Tom Doherty Associates, Inc.
175 Fifth Avenue
New York, NY 10010

Tor Books on the World Wide Web:
http://www.tor.com



ISBN: 0-812-55047-1
Library of Congress Card Catalog Number: 95-14725

First edition: August 1995
First mass market edition: July 1996

Printed in the United States of America

0 9 8 7 6 5 4 3 2 1

*To the Reader*

"For herein may be seen noble chivalry, courtesy, humanity, friendliness, hardiness, love, friendship, cowardice, murder, hate, virtue, and sin. Do after the good and leave the evil, and it shall bring you to good fame and renown."

—Caxton

# 1

IT IS A PROVERB OFTEN QUOTED but seldom applied, that all a gentleman needs to travel is a good cloak, a good horse, and a good sword. Indeed, given the style and comfort in which those on whom society bestows the appellation "gentlemen" usually travel, the picture of a well-dressed, handsome young man on a fine horse, armed with a blade housed in a long silver-chased scabbard, the end of which protrudes from his full-cut sea-green cloak with its shoulder cape flaring in the haste of his travel, would inspire a beholder to identify the gallant as anything but a gentleman. "A highwayman," one might say; or, on a closer look, "a special messenger for the Emperor, who dwells in this great city here in the distance"; or more cynically, "a rake fleeing the city on account of his debts and his mistress's husband"; or any of a hatful of titles might one append to this picture, before "a gentleman" be suggested.

And that one would be instantly derided as inaccurate.

For, look! This man has no baggage but the saddlebags on his horse; he is alone, without a single servant to attend him; moreover he is on horseback rather than in a carriage with the fine horse ridden by his lackey; and furthermore, he is plainly galloping, as may be seen from the billowing of his cape and the elevation of his horse's hooves, and his hair is blown about and his clothing disordered by the exercise. Lastly and most tellingly, it is night-time in the picture, as the swollen moon breasting the horizon and a few stars show, long after sundown, a time when any true gentleman would long since have been snugly established in his chosen inn for the night with a good dinner and a bottle of wine.

Thus do many antiquated proverbs suffer derision when they venture into the harsh environment of the modern world. Can he truly be a gentleman, though he ride swiftly, at night, away from the security of the city, alone and armed?

Only the rider knows. He is quite secure about his own estate, and perhaps is now observing to himself that he is the very picture of that proverb mainly quoted nowadays by gouty earls at the fireside deriding the softness of the younger generation, who travel with everything but a wine-cellar and purchase and consume one as they go. (The earls suffer amnesia regarding their own pasts and curse the present gout whilst recalling fondly wines of bygone days.)

He has no question in his own mind as to what he is, and if you were to ask him, he might tell you without hesitation.

You could not ask him. He was already gone by the time it occurred to you; his horse swift and his purpose clear, he went left at the crossroads on the hill where the moon cut a black shadow beside a kingstone. His first goal was to pass that crossroads at that time, exactly as the moon was clearing the horizon and casting the kingstone's shadow as a pointer down the road he took. When he turned, he faded from sight, as if he rode into a fog bank when there was no fog there at all.

# 2

"ARIEL!"

"Here, Master!"

"The full moon's rays are requisite for work I plan tonight. Dispel these scudding clouds without harsh wind or undue storm, that the rising lunar light may fall unfiltered on the world."

"All of it, Master Prospero?" Ariel asked, dubious.

"This part where I am," Prospero clarified, not unkindly. "Let us say, the eastern region of this continent, including this island. All night."

"The breath of your order shall be gale, good Master," Ariel said, and left with a gust of wind, racing east.

Prospero's black-lined blue cloak flared and rippled with the Sylph's passage; his dark hair stirred; the island's trees soughed and whispered among themselves, then calmed. From his place by the mighty tree that crowned the island's hill, he gazed over the river to the east and saw Ariel's rippling wake pass over the landscape, out of sight, purling and streaking the fat gilt-shouldered clouds. Now he took his silver-wound staff and struck its bright heel on the ground three times.

"Caliban!" he called.

"Aye," grunted a voice beneath his feet. The stone roiled and rose: a torso; a rough head coarse-featured; a square slab-body and hard arms textured like fine-grained unpolished granite. Caliban squinted in the beating midsummer sun.

"Here at this living tower's roots I'll have a basin sculpted in the stone whereof it grips," Prospero said, lifting his staff and then setting it down, "a hollow which is spherical, circularly exact, such that the diameter be measured from here—" he struck the stone with the heel of the staff and paced—"to here at its broadest point below the surface of the ground, and such that its opening be from here—" and he paced again— "to here."

There was a perplexed silence, and then, "Ah. Like an orange with the top cut off to suck at it."

"Even so."

"That will fill with the waters of the Spring that rises here in its middle, Master—"

"Even so."

"Ah." The black stone over which the tree's roots ran and into which they had forced their way rippled as Caliban moved. "If it's a well you'd have me delve, Master—"

"No well, but a bowl, which shall cup the Spring's unstinting flow for my night's work."

"The basin shall be scoured as you command, Master."

"Be finished ere the sun sets," Prospero said, "ere the sun's disk is a fist's width above the long horizon, for it must fill, and I've preparations to complete."

"Aye, Master." Caliban sank into the stone, which hissed and heated with his hasty passage.

Prospero watched as the stone began to move. The rest of his preparations were made; the stage was being set; there remained but one vital piece of business before the hour of his sorcery came. He left the hilltop and its great tree and went down a footpath, winding through the straight trunks of high-crowned trees and along a rocky outcrop, until he came to an end of the cool-shaded wood. A garden lay before him in casual beds and terraces, clumps of fruiting trees and clusters of exuberant blossoms, and at its farthest end he descried a bent back and a mill-wheel of a yellow straw hat radiant in the sun.

A neat gravelled path led him to the gardener.

"What cheer, daughter?"

She sat back on her heels, grubby and smiling, dark curling tendrils falling from under the hat to nourish themselves on her damp neck. "I suppose you want strawberries," she said.

"Were they less sweet and thy care of them less fruitful, I'd have none," he replied, smiling, "so 'tis a tribute to thy own hand that I have devour'd so many; they are the very heart of summer and their goodness nourished of thine, therefore must I love them as I love thee. But nay, 'tis thee I'll have. The heat's great, the day wears long; thy labor's never done, and as well ceased now as ever. I bid thee lunch with me."

"It's early," she said.

"Not untimely so," Prospero disagreed mildly. "Go thou, bathe and dress; I'll look to the meal, and we'll meet on the green where the table is. Take our ease as the wise beasts o' the wood do when the sun is fiercest on the flesh."

"It *is* hot. Yes. We must have strawberries, though—they'll rot if we don't eat them, and the idea of cooking even more jam . . ." Her voice trailed away.

"Well enough. Hast thy basket?"

Prospero picked the strawberries with her, though they both ate any number of the winey-ripe ones as well, and carried them off while she ran ahead to fetch clean clothes and a towel. He had already made some preparation of the meal, and now he finished and laid a cold roast pheasant, poached fish, a salad of peas and tiny vegetables dressed with vinegar and mint, a dish of hot-spiced grain with raisins, and a pyramid of fruits out invitingly on his huge dark table, its single-slab top upheld by the wings of two carven birds of prey which clutched lesser earthbound creatures in their brass claws. The table, as was their summer custom, stood outside beneath a spreading tree on the little lawn before the small scarp wherein lay his cave, its thick door open to the soft air.

He was just opening a cool bottle of sweet white wine when his daughter came up the path that led to the river, bathed and fresh-gowned in gauzy green. Prospero set the bottle down and watched her approach, approving and appreciative. Her tailoring skills were simple, thus all her dresses were little more than smocks, ribboned and laced to fit: indecent in civilized society, but charming here in the wilderness.

"In such heat," she said, "the forest is a better place to be. Tomorrow, will you hunt with me?"

"What of thy garden?"

"Oh, well, as you say, 'tis never done."

"No ground to shirk," he chided her gently, and poured wine for her.

She curtseyed slightly, as he had taught her, and took the cup. "Thank you, Papa. It was you who tempted me from work with swimming and a lovely luncheon; you can hardly blame me for wanting a holiday."

"I blame thee not at all. Come, all's ready, and my appetite as well."

"This breeze is good," said she. "It is nearly cool here, in the shade."

They ate side-by-side, looking down the slope below their tree and table, which she had planted with flowers and small trees. When the cold fish and meat were gone and the fruits being picked at leisurely, Prospero turned the conversation abruptly from the flowers.

"I have in mind to make some alterations in our life," he said.

She set down her wineglass and tilted her head to one side, puzzled. "Alterations?"

Prospero leaned back. "Long ago I told thee, Freia," he began, "that I am a Prince in my own realm, far-distant Landuc—a Prince, and should be King, but that my brothers conspired against me and denied me my rightful place."

"I remember," she said.

"Dost remember? 'Twas many winters past, and we've not spoken of't since. For it displeaseth me to chew it over."

"I do remember," she said, "for you told me of your friends there, and of beautiful Lady Miranda, and of the great city and the Palace gardens."

"Thou rememb'rest, then, that my pompous brother inflated himself from King to Emperor 'pon his accession to the stolen throne."

She nodded.

"Thou rememb'rest that I told thee 'twas not finished." His eyes were like high grey clouds with the sun behind them.

She nodded again, wary of his intensity.

"Time's come," Prospero said, "for me to make my move

'gainst that false popinjay and knock him down. I've labored long here and elsewhere, setting my plans in slow motion, and now the hour is nigh for swifter action."

"What are you going to do?"

He seemed not to hear her. "To move that action shall require changes here. I warn thee now; I've spoken of some to thee ere this, and I saw them little please thee. Yet change cannot be denied."

Freia tensed, straightened. "Why not? Why shouldn't we live as we have, here, you and me and your sorcery and my garden and things? I like this. Don't you?"

"I like it well, wench, but a man cannot sup on strawberries all the days of his life," Prospero said. " 'Twill change, I tell thee, and we'll change too. My idleness ill-fits my nature, and it must end and this idyll withal."

She shook her head, contrary. "This is perfect, just as it is, and there's plenty to do and I'm not idle. What are you going to change? What is lacking? Why shouldn't we stay the same?"

"Freia, Freia. Think'st thou that I was always as I am today? Wert thou? Nay; I've bettered thee, hast said it thyself. What thou art today, is what I've made of thee; my daughter, a lady, and soon a princess: bettered again." He had taken her hands in his and held them as he held her gaze.

"I don't want to be a Lady or a Princess! Why do you want to be a Prince, or a King? Aren't you happy here?"

"Freia, 'tis more than a thing I wish to be. 'Tis what I am. This place is comfortable enough, were I but a sorcerer, but I am not. I did not choose this place to be comfortable in, but to labor, and my labor here draws near completion; the fruits of my patience come ripe, e'en as thy garden beginneth with hard work and small shoots, then groweth to savorous maturity. And thou, thou didst not choose this place; 'tis all thy world, I know, and though thou'rt content enough here solitary 'mongst thy fruits and flowers, I know the little discontents that shall fret thee to aversion in morrow-days. Better to remember thy garden-isle fondly later than to hate it."

"I love this place, I always shall, I love it as it is," she said, heart-wringingly. "Please don't change it. Please. What are you going to do, Papa?"

"We must have a city, Freia, walled and strong—"

"No!"

"—and bridges o'er the river, therefore great numbers of hardy men to build—"

*"No!"*

They stared at one another. Freia's expression of stubborn determination mirrored Prospero's, and Prospero's hands tightened around hers balled into stone-hard fists. "Darest thou contradict me?" he snapped. "I'll not countenance it; the world moveth forward, be thou retrograde as thou wilt. It must happen, Freia, and it shall, and thou'lt see: 'Twill like thee better than thou think'st."

The Prince of Madana, Heir of Landuc, lay on his bed fully clothed and stared at the white-and-blue scrolled ceiling.

Something had happened to him last night. It was something unpleasant. He was dressed, and that was wrong; he never slept in his clothes—he would sooner go naked to dinner. His head ached. Shreds of dreams still clung to his thoughts: suffocating dreams, drowning dreams, entangled dreams of nets and sticky webs.

"Sir?" someone said.

The Prince turned his head and saw the concerned faces of five people who stood at his bedside. They were all leaning toward him, eyes wide, and the same expression of relief and rejoicing washed over all five.

"Doctor Hem," said the Prince, wondering what was wrong with him.

"Tell the Emperor and Empress," said Doctor Hem to the footman beside him, who hurried out. "Yes, Your Highness," he added to the Prince, smiling, bowing.

"What's that stink?" The Prince frowned, swallowing and beginning to sit up.

"No, no! Do not rise, Your Highness, the crisis is only just past; do not rise, lest the balance of humors be disrupted again," cried the Doctor, and made him lie down again.

"What the blazes is going on? What's the matter?" demanded the Prince, grabbing the Doctor's arm.

The door banged and the footman cried hurriedly, "His Majesty Emperor Avril—"

"Silence," said the Emperor impatiently, entering, and glared at the others as he did. "You. What are you doing here? Nothing? Out! We know you, you're Hem's boy. Out."

They got out, all but the Doctor and the Emperor. The Emperor glowered at his son from the side of the bed.

The Prince thought he'd much preferred the gratifying audience now departed. He played a filial note, cautiously. "Father, am I ill?"

"Perhaps you can tell us. You've been asleep like this since we don't know when."

"What?"

"What have you been smoking? Drinking, perhaps?" demanded the Emperor furiously. "With whom? Some bastard you dragged in off the street—"

"Your Majesty," said Doctor Hem hurriedly, "still the balance of humors is very delicate and it would be best not to—"

"Silence. Well? What have you to say for yourself?"

The Prince stared at his father, confused, and shook his head a little, and sat up again. Hem started forward to stop him and retreated at the Emperor's look.

"Tell us," said the Emperor, arms folded, glowering at his son, his eyes like coal.

"I don't remember," the Prince said, shaking his head again.

"Don't remember?"

The Prince rubbed his temples.

The Emperor hissed through his teeth with impatience. "You came in at the tenth hour yesterday with someone your chamberboy identified as Harrel Brightwater—"

"Brightwater," the Prince said. "Yes. That was. . . . We met at the armorer's. Bellamy's."

"Not for the first time, in all likelihood," his father said sarcastically, and noticed the Doctor again. "Get out. We'll call you if you're needed."

Doctor Hem left, bowing. He had served the Palace for long enough to know how his service might best be extended.

When the door had closed on him, the Emperor went on with the beginnings of a fine rage in his voice. "Josquin, we have had enough of—"

"We dined here," the Prince said, ignoring him, rubbing his temples. "I remember that. Chess first, dinner. Talked about fencing. Horses. We had one bottle, didn't even finish it, the new stuff."

"It is surprising that you remember that much. What else did you have?"

"Nothing. Nothing. Just . . . We sat after dinner with the chess-board again. . . . Let me think. Nothing. Didn't smoke anything. Hm," he muttered, still rubbing his head. "It's—he threw something."

The Emperor, who had listened with mounting anger, said, "Threw something!"

"I didn't see what it was."

"Threw you, more likely—"

"Father. He . . . Where is he?"

"He left, in your coach. Your standard treatment for your catamites after you—"

"Father." Josquin's headache was worse than ever. He ground his teeth and pressed his palms to his temples. "Throwing," he said, "I was standing . . . He followed me in. I set the candles down. He— I turned around and he threw something."

"Threw what?" asked a new voice. They both glanced at the door, where the Empress stood; a pair of attendants hovered behind her straight, slender back at a discreet distance, listening for all they were worth.

" 'Cora, don't—" began the Emperor.

"Jos, what happened?" She joined them, quick but graceful, and sat on the edge of the bed.

"I don't know. He—he threw something. I remember

. . . I felt dizzy," whispered Josquin hoarsely.

"What did he throw?" the Empress asked softly.

"Nothing. He had nothing in his hands. Nothing. But he threw something. It . . ." Josquin put his hand over his face. "Like that."

"How could he throw nothing?" she wondered, frowning.

"How . . . ?" the Emperor began, and stopped. "Nothing," he repeated.

"Yes."

"He shall be arrested and questioned," decided the Emperor, and opened the door. A few words to his ever-handy secretary Cremmin, and he returned.

"My head is splitting," Josquin said to his mother.

"Poor dear. Doctor Hem will have a powder for it."

"It may unbalance me further," Josquin muttered. He disliked Doctor Hem intensely.

"If he has none, my maid Mellicent will," said the Empress, stroking his forehead. "Who was this man who threw something at you, Jos?"

"Glencora, leave it for now."

"No. I am very puzzled as to how throwing nothing could make Josquin sick."

"Having nothing thrown at him."

"Exactly. How could it make him sick?"

"Was I sick?"

"You wouldn't wake up," she said gravely, and pressed his hand.

"Oh," said Josquin.

"Who was he?" the Empress asked.

"A . . . friend."

"One of his good-for-nothing prancing pickups—"

"Father, he—"

"What is his name?" the Empress interrupted.

"Brightwater. Harrel Brightwater."

"One of the Anburggan Brightwaters? I don't remember any Harrel among them," she said doubtfully.

"Doubtless some bastard," growled the Emperor. "What do you know of his family?"

Josquin thought and shrugged. "Don't know, really. He

seemed a gentleman. We never discussed it. That's women's business," he added in a tone tinged with contempt.

"What *did* you discuss?" the Emperor asked through clenched teeth.

"Cards. Horses. Swords. He has an eye for good weapons. Ask Bellamy. He bought a sword from Bellamy yesterday; I fenced with him in Bellamy's yard and he beat me. As good as the best of Uncle Gaston's students."

"If he has studied with Gaston—"

Josquin shook his head. "No, I asked him about that. I don't think he has. He would have admitted it, I think."

"Hm. So you know nothing of his origin."

Josquin began to contradict him and stopped. "No. Come to think . . . No."

"Were you ever in his rooms?"

"No."

"Hm. We shall have to investigate further into his movements and associates. In the meantime you are confined to the Palace and grounds."

"What! Why?"

"Because you display abominably bad judgement in your activities outside them." The Emperor left; his absence made the stifling room seem cooler.

"I suppose it could be worse," Josquin said. "He could have confined me to my apartment. What *is* that stink?"

"Hem was burning incense, I expect," the Empress Glencora said, wrinkling her nose, and rose and went to the windows, opening them, waving her hands in the air, which was warm and still today. The incense hung in the room like a veil. It smelled, Josquin thought, like burning bananas flambéed with cheap cologne and quenched with piss.

## —3—

THE BASIN WAS COMPLETED IN GOOD time. Prospero stood over it as it filled with splashing water from the Spring, which arose at the foot of the great tree and which soaked again into the hilltop after running over the stone.

The first battle of his war he'd won with guile. Freia slept, her senses fogged by his gentle postprandial sorcery; he had borne her heavy with dreams to her bed and laid her there, and she'd not wake until morning came. He looked up. The dusky sky was still fringed with clouds to the west; the massive, swift-rising wind driven by Ariel had torn them to shreds and swept them away.

In the south above the tree-canopy Prospero saw the first blue-white star of the evening. He stared to the east and discerned, in the deepening line of darkness, the first orange-gold sliver of the moon beyond the sea. The wind that had ruffled his hair and snapped his cloak died. The world was still.

"Master, it's done," whispered Ariel.

"Bide," Prospero said.

He bent and dipped his hand in the water, brought it to his lips and tasted the jolting freshness. Invigorated, he smiled and, as the moon with gravid dignity rose from her bed, lifted his staff and began to Summon the powers at his command. A light swelled from the water in the basin and from the Spring as he stirred and shaped the force that slept there. It grew into a spindle, four threads of which wove and knotted around him and four others of which began curling, turning with the spindle, reaching out and away through the trees and silver moonlight.

The best of his sorcery always seemed like a dream to him afterward. This had that stamp, the inevitability and perfection of every act, every word, every event at once foreseen and occurring. Prospero's staff hummed and trilled in his hand, and around him the stillness of the world, into which his voice rolled like the very music of the night sphere that turned overhead, brightened with the light of the moon and rustled with life. He knew, as he worked, that this was going to go very well.

"By this hallowed Spring I stand and by it I command all of its nurturing; all that row in the limpid air, all that are borne in the soft water, all that earth and stone engender, all that spawn in the constant flame; here to the heart of the world I Summon ye, here to the Source of your existence, here to me above the Source, gather ye air and water and earth and fire, gather ye within the Bounds I draw by this hallowed Spring . . ."

The arms of power swept outward, stirring like the wind but moving nothing, reaching and gathering. The darkness around Prospero began to fill with rustlings, movements, warm bodies and cool, tense and quick breathing.

The Air Summoning brought birds large and small, lone and mated, who crowded into the branches of the tree behind Prospero, to the north of the Spring. One brilliant dovelike bird with butter-colored feathers and a bright golden crest boldly settled on his shoulder and nestled against his cheek a moment before joining the others. Prospero did not leave off his Summoning, but he smiled.

The Water Summoning included a few great white-winged birds who settled awkwardly on the ground before the Spring; there were splashing and swishing sounds from the night-dark river that ran around the island, just to the south.

The Fire Summoning netted nothing; within the reach of Prospero's spell there were no Elemental or Essential creatures of fire, for the Spring was antithetical to Fire. So east of the Spring was darkness.

But the Earth Summoning drew as many of its kind as that of the Air. West of the Spring, first on a rocky bare patch exposed in the light of the moon and then filling the wood that stretched down over the island to the water that surrounded it, assembled creatures unnamed with horns and claws and hard feet and soft, with long teeth and flat, with bodies of every description adapted for every use. From the forests that overspread the round-shouldered hills came the animals, hopping or sliding some, bounding and leaping some, pacing with aloof dignity or, sun-eyed, stalking through the undergrowth, plunging fearlessly into the river and swimming to reach Prospero. The forest itself shivered and woke, altered by the tendril forged of the Spring and Prospero's sorcery that curled through it and then held steady, encircling and Binding the Summoned.

Arms upraised, Prospero paused, lit by the light of the moon filling the water and shining out more brightly than the moon herself, who hung just at her fullest as Prospero completed his initial Summoning.

He lowered his arms slowly, barely breathing, wholly sustained by the Spring. His eye fell on the foremost of the animals who crouched, unafraid but overawed and worshipful, to the west. It was one he knew well, a furry, broad-shouldered, blunt-eared creature of long and lumbering body and thick black claws who had dug his burrow by the very Spring. The animal's nose twitched. It rose on its haunches to look at Prospero from bright black eyes, its coarse black-and-brown ticked fur still dusted with the earth of its run.

Prospero bent and cupped water from the shining basin, which overflowed now; the Spring was tentatively exploring a little water-course down the hillside. The water gleamed golden in his hand. The sorcerer poured it onto the unflinching animal's head, starlet drops falling.

The moon, imperceptible to any but the sorcerer, was turning from full.

"Born of earth, be born again a child of Spring and moon and man," Prospero said in a low, deep voice, and the water plashed into the coarse fur; the animal dropped to its fours, shook dust away, and its body flowed and took on bulk below the serene, benignant countenance of the moon; and where the animal had fallen, now a man knelt, sitting back slowly on his heels.

Prospero and the man gazed at one another. The man's expression was bemused. He blinked, then smiled, then shook his head again. He was naked. His dark skin held hard muscles and drops of water glistened on his hair. His merry face was bearded and his square hands lay on his legs.

"I am yours to command," he said, in a rippling language that had but once before been heard in the world.

"Bide," Prospero said, and returned his smile.

The man inclined his head and settled back on his shins. He watched as Prospero repeated the transformation with a dun-furred, lean, sharp-clawed, stump-tailed animal who came to drink at the Spring from time to time, and this one tossed his head and shouted from a mouth losing fangs and acquiring lips and a joyous, fierce smile as he became a man.

"Master!"

"Bide," Prospero said again, and as the moon proceeded above in her pirouette with grace and precision, he worked his sorcery on the earth-creatures. When the moon was a good ways down the sky, he turned to the birds, and with the invocation, "Born of air, be born again a child of Spring and moon and man," he touched them with the ever-replenished water of the basin and they became men and women, dazed, smiling, wide-eyed with wonder, looking at their hands and feet and abiding Prospero's command.

The eastern sky took on tints of rose and the moon hovered in the west. Prospero worked over the children of the waters, and he stirred his staff in the basin to make a cloud of light and water which rained down on those who had assembled in their element. In their odd new form they splashed and waded, stumbling, onto the island and crowded it with their number.

The sky brightened. The moon lingered over the horizon. Prospero looked around himself at the quiet, waiting people he had created and nodded. It had gone well.

With a stir of air, the cream-gold bird came to his shoulder again. Soft feathers brushed his cheek. Prospero lifted his hand and brought the bird down, admiring. There had been none other like it among the rest; he had forgotten to make sure—

"There's an instant left yet, and I'd not leave thee, pretty friend, behind," he said, and stooped to the water. He cupped his hand and reached, but a dark streak sliced through the surface before he touched it.

It was a snake, a black, thick-bodied, long reptile which had its hole among the roots of the tree; ofttimes he'd seen it basking on the rock, and once it had frightened Freia badly. Dwelling near the Spring, even swimming there, it had become more than mere serpent, intelligent and sorcery-sensitive. Now it reared up on the bank and sought to fix him with dawn-yellow eyes.

He was not such a simpleton as that: to invite the serpent to his company. Even his daughter, innocent fool, had wit to shun it. "Nay," he said, and swiftly scooped water up to plash the golden bird and speak the words of change.

Under his hand, which lay on her shoulder, just as the moon's rim touched the horizon, the bird became a woman with long, fine, straight hair the color of the first mellow moonlight of the previous evening and eyes warm and honey-brown. Prospero's breath caught in his throat; he stood, forgetting time, regarding her.

"Thank you," she said, gravely.

"Be welcome," he whispered, and bowed.

The snake hissed and rose higher, a vanelike flap of skin to each side of its body undulating.

"Nay, insidious Tython, I know you," Prospero said to it; "you have tarried too long, waiting in your hole; that low form shall be your house for eternity, and in earth your dwelling, for you did not come forward with the rest. The time is past. I shall have the last be the best." And he smiled at the woman again.

The snake glared and twisted, rippled into the water.

Prospero took his hand from his last creation and with the proper words released the force which had poured through him for his labor of transformation. As it drained away he shivered, weary now and hollow. The sorcerer, without sorcery, was a hull without meat. He swayed.

A hard grip closed on his elbow. Prospero opened his eyes and looked to his left. The first of his new-made men supported him. On his right, the second stood poised, watchful.

"I must rest," Prospero said.

"We will wait for you," his man said. "You have done much. You have made the world."

"Nay . . . nay. Only changed it. Where . . ." Prospero looked around him. The fair woman was gone.

"She would not wait," said the second.

"She is free to go where she list." Prospero smiled a little. The second man lifted the sorcerer's cloak from the ground and hung it around his shoulders.

"We will wait for you," said the first again.

Prospero nodded and sat down at the tree's foot. He closed his eyes and leaned back, then looked around him again and lay down to one side. The Spring splashed and jingled softly. There was a soft susurrus of breathing and heartbeat, of quiet waiting, all over the world, waiting for him, but Prospero, exhausted, hunched in his cloak and slept.

Prince Josquin, mallet on shoulder, selected his next shot. His aunt Princess Viola had had the croquet lawn and an impeccable formal garden emplaced many, many years before, wheedling them out of her father when she was in particular favor for some forgotten reason, and she made use of them erratically for garden-party amusements. The Princess was sympathetic to her nephew and had arranged today's entertainment specially for him, and also to spit in her brother the Emperor's eye, because she had invited a considerable number of people who would not usually have received invitations to Palace functions.

"It's almost as good as billiards," said Earl Morel's son, who was not among these this year.

Josquin stared at him, astonished. "I'll take billiards any day."

"More people at croquet."

"As I said."

"When did Your Highness weary of society?"

Josquin chuckled. "Not exactly that. For mixing and meeting, croquet serves very well, but for a game—" He bowed to the Countess of Roudé, who had taken her turn at the other side of the lawn, and made his own shot.

"Oh, I'd have to agree with you there; no comparison possible. —I understand Brightwater is either fled or dead."

Josquin kept from starting or showing particular interest. "I'd heard something of the sort. Dead? How dead?"

Morel's turn was up; he aimed and overshot his wicket. "Dash. Well, there was a devilish fire in rooms he kept at the Broad Shield—I'd no idea he had quarters there, but evidently he did, besides living at the Greenhead. Double life, eh? Anyway the fire—it's quite something to see the building—it burnt everything but the nails and there's not an eyegleam of him now."

Balls clicked together, jostling at the center wicket.

"Great shame if it's so. Smoking in bed, perhaps," Josquin said. "He had an eye for horses." He strolled toward his green-blue ball for his turn.

Morel laughed ruefully. "Yes, you won quite a lot on his pick."

"I was pleasantly surprised by that. I'd never have chosen Bezel's nag myself, but it was worth the flutter. Has he run her lately?"

Morel's first love was cards and his second was the track. Josquin had channelled the discussion away from Brightwater, a subject on which he knew Morel could have no further intelligence than the Emperor.

Which was a pity, Josquin thought, nodding as Morel recounted a race, because he'd like to hear more about Brightwater from somebody, sometime, somewhere. Harrel Brightwater was not the sort of fellow to smoke in bed and burn down an inn. The Prince stared at the lawn, a little chill running down his back as he thought of Brightwater's slow-starting smile and his brilliant blue eyes, his sensuous low voice, his hard-muscled broad-shouldered body when he was fencing coatless and loose-shirted in Bellamy's yard—

"Your Highness," interrupted Lady Filday, "I sue you for mercy and beg that you will not send my poor little ball off to go bushwhacking in the pansies when I have only just escaped them."

Josquin banished Brightwater, thinking he'd trade a year with all these people for half an hour with him alone, and made her a pretty reply.

The game and party proceeded languorously. It was an unusually warm day; the guests murmured over the temperature with little energy for genuine indignation. Josquin circulated through the crowd, greeting everyone, wearing his official-function manners. Pity Aunt Viola hadn't invited some of the wilder fellows. There might have been something to break up the tedium. She did mean well, though, and it was better than reading trade statistics, and watching certain of the nobility reacting to certain of the guests was better than a play. One enterprising gambler had calculated handicaps for all the ladies present and was surreptitiously collecting wagers, beside the gentlemen's punchbowl, on their performances at croquet. Lady Filday was doing unexpectedly well, to the pleasure of one of her nephews.

The Emperor and Empress were not in attendance. Avril rarely deigned to grace his siblings' parties; today the royal couple sat in a first-floor parlor shaded by a grove of the most ancient trees on the grounds, which must not be cut or pruned. It had been a preferred room of his father's, but the Emperor disliked it because the trees made the room dark and made him uncomfortable with their age and size, and so he used it only when the weather made it expedient, as today. The parlor had a small terrace outside onto which opened tall windows. In shirtsleeves, eschewing formal clothing, the Emperor lounged in an armchair and read Brightwater's dossier.

The Emperor of Landuc retained an agile and able staff of spies, gossips, sponges, sneaks, ears, and eyes. With only three of these set on Harrel Brightwater's trail, directed by the indefatigable Count Pallgrave, he had in hand within three days a thick sheaf of notes regarding the still-absent Brightwater's life in Landuc.

Brightwater had departed Landuc through the city's Fire Gate at a quarter past the sixth hour of the night on the night that Prince Josquin had fallen into an unexplained stupor. He had appeared to have arrived on some vessel the previous autumn, but his name was on no passenger list; he had owned no baggage but a haversack. His funds had apparently come from selling a Spinel Street jeweler a trio of large pearls, an exceedingly fine diamond, and a pair of rubies. He paid all his bills on time. He had interests in rare books, maps, charts, astrology, alchemy, and history and he was, according to the merchants at the Broad Shield where he had roomed and dined daily, a courteous man who could converse intelligently and with interest on many subjects but who also had seemed clerkish and unworldly. They had pegged him as a noble's scholarly younger son come to the city to seek a Court position; he had never spoken of kin or country to them, and they supposed him without estate or local relations. The Emperor frowned. A gentleman, even if he has no estate, has family—indeed, cannot be said to exist without it. There was no Harrel to be found on any branch of the Brightwaters' family tree.

Only late this spring, after spending autumn and winter in a hermit's routine of books and study, had Brightwater taken up a social life. The Emperor had tailor's bills, descriptions of clothing, dates. The last item was a finely damascened straight sword from Bellamy's; that same morning, the day of his midnight departure, Brightwater had picked up in person (suspicious in itself—he had no valet) a new travelling cloak at Gamtree's, winter-weight and winter-styled, of the finest blue-green double-woven Ascolet wool, a peculiar garment for summer's hottest days. The earliest order was for a pair of stylish suits from Gamtree, and a week later Brightwater had bought his fine horse. A few days after boarding the horse at an hostler's, he had moved to a more-costly less-sedate inn, the Greenhead, and had paid in advance for two months' lodging, though he had kept his place at the Broad Shield as well and had divided his time between the two. The Greenhead innkeeper knew him as a man of informed and expensive tastes.

Brightwater had promptly made a place for himself as a regular card-player and dicer and had appeared to be setting determinedly on a rake's progress downward, seeking out the stews and gambling dens. He won more than he lost. Earl Morel's son had introduced him to Josquin at a card table in one of these loose-knit clubs. Josquin had taken to him at once, but the night the man dined with the Prince Heir in the Imperial Residence was the first time he had been in the Palace.

The Emperor reviewed this and nodded thoughtfully. The man had studied Josquin's movements, gotten in with his crowd, gotten close to him, and struck.

But how and why? The Prince Heir was alive and well. He

had suffered no obvious ill effects from his night- and day-long nap. What did it mean, that Josquin had seen him throwing—nothing?

The Emperor growled and rose, pacing, impatient with the puzzle. He had no illusions about Josquin. The boy was clever enough but too lazy to think, and this was a direct result of that. It was time for him to take on more responsibility, to be forced to think. He was wasting his time in Landuc, his time, his allowance, his body—

He passed, in his restless circuit of the room, the divan on which the Empress was reading letters of her own. She wore a gold-embroidered opal-green dress of very light silk, and with her fine blonde hair and pale skin, the effect was cool and wintry, belied by her languid, deliberate movements. Glencora, who had been reared in worse winters than this summer, coped with the swelter instinctively.

"Avril," she said, finishing a letter.

He grunted.

"Are you thinking of sending Josquin away?"

"Yes."

She folded the letter, her wide eyes on his light-red head. The Emperor felt the pressure of her gaze but did not look back at her. It was a contest of wills of a sort.

"Do you have some destination in mind?" she asked.

"Yes."

"May I ask what it is?"

The Emperor said nothing.

"Avril," she said a little severely, setting her narrow chin.

"Tyngis," he said shortly.

"No!"

"Yes."

"At this time of year! Avril!"

"Exactly. Winter is coming."

"They do nothing but drink from dawn to dawn there and there is nothing to do but that. Do you think that will improve him?" the Empress demanded. "I agree that he must do more than dissipate himself, but Tyngis has nothing to offer."

"Clearly you have a preferred destination already in mind

and we shall have no rest until we hear it," the Emperor muttered.

"Send him to Madana."

"He has spent too much time in Madana. He will do nothing but more of the same there." The Emperor curled his lip at the thought of Madana. Josquin had passed his boyhood and youth in Madana, and his father blamed all of his present character flaws on it.

"I do not think so," the Empress said, folding her delicate hands with precision. "In the past he has been there and behaved very creditably. You surely remember that he even managed to jolly around Sagorro."

"Because he's the same stripe of wastrel as our son, only older."

"He jollied him into signing that treaty."

That was true. The Emperor grumbled wordlessly and finally looked at the Empress. "Madana," he said.

"Yes. My cousin Iliele could host him."

"Iliele?" The name was utterly unfamiliar. The Emperor shrugged; his wife was related to half of Madana.

"She has a daughter, Avril."

"Do women think of nothing but marriage? Josquin is not marrying your cousin's daughter. Indeed if he doesn't mend his ways it will be difficult to talk anyone into having him."

"Don't be silly. He's our son," the Empress said firmly.

"True." The Emperor shrugged again. "So your cousin has a daughter on the market and she wants Josquin to look her over."

"You don't understand," the Empress said, exasperated. "They'll be having many social events, parties, outings, what you will—don't you see? It's a very good set of people, but they're the independent Eastern landowners—"

The Emperor comprehended. He smiled slowly, narrowly. "Glencora, you are a very marvel. By all means let Josquin go to East Madana. His drinking prowess will awe them into supporting us more openhandedly, he can win them over with his dicing and cards, he can escort his umpteenth-cousin Iliele's daughter, and if we are extremely fortunate he'll lose his virginity to the girl."

The Empress blushed and glared at him.

"East Madana it is," the Emperor said. "Yes, things are quiet in Tyngis. It will do him good to go south for the winter."

## — 4 —

DRAINED OF SORCERY, PROSPERO DREAMT OF death.

Prospero's dream-self ran leaden-legged through mighty colonnaded trees of a forest—perhaps the forest that surrounded his island of safety in the Well-scourged wastes—pursuing glimpses of Freia fleeting through the trunks, chasing her with sluggard feet, pursued himself by a consuming darkness that drew closer and closer to his back, devouring the world. The darkness was blood-stained, blood-black; he had made it himself, and it would destroy him as it would destroy all around it, but if he could but reach Freia there might be some hope. . . . He never caught her; when the darkness reached his neck he'd wake breathing rapidly, his heart rattling in his breast, recalling that he'd had the dream more than once before this, turning, sleeping again.

Now he darted with dream-urgency through the dark trunks, and this time the dream was different. Freia was going more slowly; he saw her between two trees ahead of him, and though the destruction he fled was on his heels he thought he could catch her. She paused, looking away, and he drew near; she went forward, and he followed, passing betwixt the two trunks.

They were not trees, but columns. He stood in his own hilltop tomb in Landuc between two pillars supporting the portico, lichen- and vine-covered stone festooned with dark wild grapes hanging in clusters, the sepulchre foully whited by generations of nesting birds. It was a masterpiece of neglect, Avril dealing superficial insult because he was incapable of real injury; Prince Prospero flourished yet, for the

Node of the Well's power that rose here still pulsed through him where he stood gazing toward the approach that led to the ivied arch over the stair down the hill.

With dream-suddenness, someone stood there in the archway. Prospero stepped forward.

The visitor approached slowly. Prospero's leadenness had left him, and now he was in command of himself, thinking with exactness and lucidity. This was a portentous dream; that they met at his tomb signified that they two were deeply linked, and Prospero must assure that later he would know who this man was, what he was. The man was a stranger now, but Fortuna would cast them in one another's paths. Prospero felt his blood within his body surge and reach toward the man, and he knew: a near connection.

"Though we meet at my tomb, I am not dead," Prospero said.

The visitor nodded.

Prospero looked penetratingly at the young man; it was plain to see that he was a man of oceans, rivers, waterfalls, alive and active. The visitor's face was intelligent, his eyes an uncommonly pure and brilliant blue. The Well leapt bright in him, contained and channelled: he was a man of powers, then—but Prospero was a sorcerer, accustomed to binding power. "I lay upon thee this geas. Thou shalt seek me until we meet, and when we meet shalt thou tell me thy name and lineage that I will know thee."

The fellow seemed disoriented, studying Prospero, perplexed.

"Safe journey," Prospero said. "That which brought thee here will bear thee safely away." Behind the young man, Prospero's late father Panurgus reached for the youth's arm and spun him around, and they vanished as they turned; Prospero turned himself, back to his suddenly-enlarged tomb (as high now as a temple), and saw Freia small and forlorn in her pretty green dress, standing between two massive stone columns. Prospero started toward her, but the dream dissolved as he did.

Beneath the tree that stood beside his life-soaked Spring, Prospero turned and drowned his dream in deeper sleep.

* * *

Josquin's valet had packed everything. In order to allow him to do it, the Prince Heir went a-hunting with his uncle Prince Herne and his aunt Princess Evote, and a large party of others, while the work was underway. When he returned he observed approvingly that efficient Orle had finished.

One small case was on the bed, as the Prince had instructed. As his valet began filling the bath, Josquin opened the case. He took the keys to his desk from his pocket, opened the desk, and froze.

A very unpleasant frisson went through him.

He began dumping things out of the desk onto the floor, pulling out drawers and rifling them carelessly, feeling all the while a deadly certainty that he would find nothing but stationery, pens, old notes and invitations, creased and stained IOUs, seals, nibs, ink-bottles, calling-cards, bills, pencils, sealing-wax, pocket-sized memorandum-books. . . .

When the desk was emptied, he looked in the waiting case on the bed. Then, pale and sicker by the minute, he bolted from the room.

He hurried through the Palace to the Emperor's apartment. His father was dressing for dinner and frowned at the unseemly interruption.

"What is this?" snapped the Emperor.

"Leave us," Josquin ordered the valet.

The valet looked at the Emperor, who frowned more and nodded. He left.

"They're gone," said Josquin, sitting down on the bed.

"What's gone?"

"My Map. My Ephemeris."

The Emperor whitened. "Gone? How could they be gone?"

"Not in my desk. I've got the key. Only key," Josquin whispered.

The Emperor looked at the clock. There remained a quarter of an hour before dinner. "We'll go to your rooms."

They hurried there. The Emperor looked at the mess. "You found it thus?"

"No. No. I, I came in from hunting with Herne. Saw that

Orle had done the packing. He'd left this case as I'd told him to; I meant to put the book and the Map in it. I unlocked and opened the desk and saw they weren't there. I searched."

The Emperor glared at his heir. "When did you last use them?"

Josquin shook his head. "Two and a half years ago at least. I went to Brutt with Uncle Fulgens. I haven't looked at them since."

"When did you last open the desk and see them?"

"I— Hm." Josquin sat down at the desk and closed his eyes. "I took out some cards last month, and they were there then. Yes."

"Last month," the Emperor repeated quietly.

"I'm not in the habit of looking at them daily!" Josquin cried defensively. "Who—"

"Most likely we know who."

"Brightwater?" whispered Josquin, horrified.

The Emperor strode out.

Within Prospero's cave there stood two beds, one at each end of the long room. The one was high, carved and deep-curtained, its panels rich with broidered allegory and arcane signs; the other was low, a simple white cot half-hidden behind a screen painted with woodlands and hills, screened from the chill stone of the cave wall by an arras depicting herbs and trees of many varieties, none local. The fireplace was empty and cold, bare of ashes, and two high-backed chairs stood, unoccupied, to either side of the hollow hearth. All around were shelves and cupboards of dark wood, carved or inlaid with geometrical patterns, burdened with heavy books and parchments and things of metals, wood, and stone, with locks and seals and knots to ward them from curiosity.

A sweet, velvet-warm breeze stirred through the cave, rustled the dried herbs suspended from the roof, rippled the arras, and left.

"Tricksy wind! Leave Mistress sleeping," Caliban roared from the bushes beyond the lawn.

"Ho, wouldst thou teach me my errand?" Ariel jeered, and he rattled down leaves on Caliban. "Mind thy netherworld affairs, and I shall not hinder thee."

"Master set me here," Caliban retorted, "Master bade me wait for Mistress."

"For Mistress, for the Lady! Small wonder then she dreams yet, that must see thy ugly face when she wakes. Thou hideous man-mock, thou crude sculpture!"

"Wicked wind-thing, nothing! Lady talks to me of flowers."

"She will not look on thee, travesty! For thou art foul to look on, deck thee with flowers as thou wouldst."

"Ladies like flowers!"

"What, dost liken thyself to a flower, thou lichen-crusted relic of failed Art?"

"Master made me!" bellowed Caliban. "Master made me, this form is his making!" He swatted futilely at Ariel, and Ariel hissed mockingly though the fronds and leaves and sped away, uncatchable. Caliban subsided, grumbling, sinking halfway into the earth in the darkest shade he could find; the daylight pained him, but Prospero had commanded him to bide here on Freia's waking, and Caliban must obey.

Within the cave, the wind's stirring breath on Freia's face had stirred her sleep. She sighed, murmured wordless sounds, and opened her eyes a crack. The creamy background of her screen was bright; thus it was day, and she might rise without fear of interrupting Prospero at his night-work. She pushed the bedclothes down and rubbed her eyes and head; groggy, foggy, her thoughts were jumbled. Such dreams she'd had—she might tell Prospero, for they'd been vivid and strange.

Freia stood, stretched, peered around the painted screen and saw no Prospero. She padded out, barefoot beneath her drifting smock, yesterday's gown unbound, to wet a cloth and splash and wipe her face and eyes, waking. Her father's bed was empty. Prospero walked the isle, no doubt, or groomed the horses or did any of the thousand things to do outside the dim cool cave on such a shining day, and she had slept longer than ever was her wont in summer.

Freia went out and stopped, her ear struck by the sound beneath the birdsongs. There were not as many birdsongs as there ought to be—why, but a single one, a dull-chiming bell-bird, rhythmically stuttering its tedious note.

"Good-morrow, Mistress—"

"Quiet, Caliban. I'm listening." Frowning, she tilted her head and strained for the sounds: murmuring like water, odd barkings now and again—something like wind and water and rustling leaves all together, a new sound under the sun. The sun pierced her thin smock and glowed on her skin; there was no wind. She opened her eyes and looked down on Caliban, perplexity on her face. "Where is Prospero? And whatever are you doing here?" Caliban shunned daylight, shunned visibility; he was Prospero's diligent laborer at some task Freia knew nothing of, deep beneath the earth, and he never left it save at Prospero's command.

"Mistress, Master bade me wait here for you and tell you he wishes you to wait here for him. Could you tell me again of the flowers, Mistress, the mountain-flowers—"

"Why should I wait here?" Freia asked the world generally. "This is not a day for staying within. I'm going hunting," she said firmly.

"O, Mistress, do not go!" Caliban protested, but she had returned to the cave, and he might not enter there.

Sandals, tunic, leggings—she would go bare-legged for now, but in the undergrowth she'd need cover. Freia dressed and braided up her hair, packed a leathern bag with leggings, salt, dried apples, and bread, put her knife at her belt, and took her bow and arrows from their pegs behind the door. Prospero had not come, and she would linger no longer here.

Caliban called to her as she left the cave again. "O, Mistress, Mistress, bide the Master, bide, he commands it," he said in his gravelly voice.

"Caliban, I will not. I said I would hunt today, and I shall hunt, and you may remind Papa of that when he seeks to scold you for my leaving. He was supposed to hunt with me. Go back to your own tasks that he set you and he won't be angry."

The noise was still there, the birds still quiet. Caliban grumbled unhappily behind her as she set off along the path that would take her to the upstream end of the island. From there she would paddle the tippy little coracle to the mainland.

The strange sound grew louder to her ear as she went. Suspicion stirred in Freia's thoughts; Prospero had said he would change things, and she feared he had done that, had worked some sorcery to alter the island. He'd made her sleep before when he had great sorceries afoot, things he did not wish her to witness (not trusting obedience to conquer curiosity). There had been a midwinter night she'd slept three days, waking famine-hungry to find Prospero irritable and short-tempered; he'd never told her what he'd done then, but thereafter she had encountered queer hooved and horned little people, shy and difficult to approach, in the surrounding forest, and other, stranger things of blended natures. This overlong night's sleep smacked of such sorceries, and Caliban's relayed command to her to wait at the cave for Prospero was novel. Ever before she had had liberty to go where she liked.

Prospero, then, had done something, Freia decided, trotting along the footworn path. But what might it be?

She pulled up short as the path came out into a bit of meadow where they pastured the horses from time to time, seeing before her the unbelievable answer to her question.

The crowd of people standing and sitting and lying in the long grass, playing with flowers and laughing and talking and becoming acquainted with themselves and one another, the crowd of strange voices and odd faces and nude bodies pale and dark, the crowd fell silent and stared back at Freia.

A breeze gusted past her and rippled the grass that the people had not matted down, passing up the hillside in the hard, hot sun.

Freia, tense and wary, continued along the path slowly,

her gait stiff, looking with distrustful dismay at the faces and bodies of the intruders.

They surged, following her, whispers swirling through them. A hand reached for her. Freia flinched from the alien touch; the hand dropped away. They crowded around her but let her pass, slowly, moving nearer and farther, all of them jostling to look at her.

Freia began hurrying. They parted, still following her, too close, too many; the heat and sweaty smell of their bodies was overwhelming, the sight of their hands and hair and torsos and faces a dizzying mosaic. A hand brushed her arm; another touched her braided hair, and then there were many touches, light inquisitive fingers feeling her leather tunic, her bow, her body. They whispered, said with strange words things she understood: "Soft . . . hard . . . tail . . . mane . . . claws . . . breast . . . hide . . . smooth . . . soft . . ." in a torrent of puzzled collective exploration. They were too big, too many, too intent on her; Freia panicked, pushed, bolted.

They shied, running away in a mass—or some tried to. The meadow became a churning disturbance, and there were cries of pain and fear as others were jostled roughly. Freia shoved and shouldered her way through them, touching bodies, bodies, bodies, hair and skin and limbs and softness and hardness, and she shut her eyes and put her fist forward—clutching her bow and quiver to her with the other—and bulled blindly ahead. They shouted, words she didn't listen to, jumbled noise among the jumbled bodies.

She struck something coarse and hard, not skin; it grabbed her and she screamed and twisted away.

"Freia!" Prospero shouted, seizing her wrists, dragging her to him. "Stop this! Thou'lt frighten the folk."

"Let go!" Freia screamed.

He shook her quickly; she was panicked, though, and Prospero must drag her out of the press of bodies, shouting over her head at them until they parted meekly and left space for him to lead his struggling daughter to the trees' shade. Prospero hugged her, wrapping his cloak around her despite the heat, hampering her movements as he would net a bird to confine it.

"Freia. Freia! Hold, hold—I did bid thee abide my return, girl, and thou'rt paid for impatience. Freia! Look on me."

She did, wild-eyed.

Prospero nodded and gazed into her eyes. "Now calm thyself," he said. "There's none here will harm thee. Thou hast given them worser fright than they have given thee."

"What are they?" Freia whispered, looking from Prospero to them. They stood, watching, their faces serene and interested.

"They are people, my people," Prospero said proudly.

"I don't want people here! Why did you bring them?"

"These folk have been here all their days," Prospero replied, "and they've as firm a right as thou to live here, for I have made them of the native creatures of the place. I shall not brook thee quarrelling with them, Freia: they, like thee, are made to dwell here, and—"

"There's no room for them!"

"Pah, they'll build houses for themselves, and a better for thee and me as well, a dwelling fit for men."

"Then there's no room for me," Freia declared. "Let me go!"

Prospero released her wrists, though he still held her arm loosely. Frowning, he said, "It is my will that they be here, and my will shalt thou not shake! Whither goest thou so furnished?"

"Hunting! You said you'd hunt with me today," Freia reminded him.

"I've much to do amongst the folk," Prospero said, "and I gave no promise to course the wood with thee—"

"Then I'll go alone," Freia said, and she slipped from his hand and darted from him, from the people, into the trees.

The Emperor, oddly, did not seem to blame Josquin particularly for the theft—at least, not to Josquin's face. He bid him a fair journey in the morning without visible rancor.

"He must be angry," muttered Josquin to the Empress.

"There's nothing to be done for it now, dear," she whispered back.

Josquin knew better. His father believed firmly in the efficacy of revenge.

When the Prince Heir had gone in his coach to the dock where his ship waited, the Emperor went to his private office, told his secretary he would have no disturbances, and locked himself in.

He drew the red brocaded draperies closed and went to a black-lacquered writing table which stood against a wall with a large, convex Mirror over it. From the locked drawers of the table he took a number of articles, setting them on its polished red marble top, and then from his pocket a smallish, heavy leather packet which he untied. It held an assortment of peculiarly-shaped Keys.

Selecting one, he put the rest away and seated himself. A quarter of an hour was spent in arranging the apparatus correctly and consulting yellowed sheets of handwritten notes; then the Emperor touched a candle to the oil in the glossy brass firepan which now stood beneath the Mirror. He chanted in a furtive undertone.

The glass brightened; it took on an insubstantial depth and appeared to enlarge itself somehow, to iris open on a fog, although its shape and size were unchanged.

Shortly, the glass cleared and the Emperor faced not his own image but that of another man, head and shoulders taller than the Emperor, broader and darker, frowning slightly as he rubbed his sleeve on a spot on the glass into which he gazed. Two long-flamed candles in knots of brass stood to either side of his Mirror, sparking reflections in his gold-brown eyes.

"Avril," said he, and then, as an afterthought, "Your Majesty."

"Gaston," the Emperor said, "we have trouble."

Prince Gaston nodded. The flames swayed.

"Josquin has buggered us all. He picked up a hot one and we're properly burned."

"This I have not heard."

The Emperor snorted. "Why, how surprising; Viola knew

of it. Our son, in his usual way, took up with a man calling himself Harrel Brightwater. The man's no member of the Brightwater clan . . ." and he told Gaston of what had followed.

"You believe this man to be some degree of sorcerer," said Prince Gaston slowly.

"We fear it is so."

"Yet he cannot have been to the Well of late."

"No. Not the way it is now." A gnawing worry bit the Emperor afresh: since their father King Panurgus's recent lingering death, the Well that was the world's heart had been dark and deep-withdrawn, not leaping with sheets of fire. The Emperor took it as a personal slight. The Well had obeyed Panurgus's slightest whim, the Fire shifting and changing as it sustained the world, as the King had willed it. Panurgus had left no instructions on how to tap and command the Well, and the Emperor had refrained from experimenting with the thing, a failure he suspected everyone of whispering about.

"An he hath not been to the Well, there'll be but scant good he get of Map and book," Prince Gaston said. "They are of no use; he cannot reach the Road without passing the Well's fire, though he know where the Road lieth."

"He knew *something*. At the least he knew where to look, and although Josquin is a fool he has told no one where he kept them. Nothing else is missing."

"His servants?"

"They are being questioned, but they have all been here a long time."

"And are still there."

"Exactly. No sudden departures."

Prince Gaston rubbed his chin and leaned back in his chair; the Emperor's flame swayed toward the Mirror, toward him. "I know not what might be done to remedy this, brother," he said finally. "On the one hand: 'tis done. On t'other: perhaps could be undone, but if so I know not how. You seek him?"

"Still. Yes."

Prince Gaston appeared to be thinking out loud. "Without having passed through the Well's Fire, he cannot leave Landuc on the Road. He must conceal him, masked by an assumed name, a disguised face— Ah. The horse."

"The horse?" the Emperor repeated.

"You said he kept a horse. A good animal?"

"They are looking for the horse too. Yes, it's harder to disguise a beast than a man. That is what is bad, Gaston: he has vanished from the Empire."

" 'Tis possible one of the others hath sponsored him. The wards Panurgus set are old, belike weakened, failed." Prince Gaston said this reluctantly; it touched on a charged subject.

"We thought of that. Oriana, Esclados—unpredictable and untrustworthy, all that sorcerous lot are." The Emperor shook his head. "But it makes no sense, for in that case he needn't steal Map and Ephemeris. He'd copy his sponsor's."

"True."

"It could be Prospero," the Emperor said.

The Prince shook his head slowly. "Why? No doubt he could disguise himself, but why wait, why befriend Josquin? If he lacked Map and book, he could slip in and take them. He knoweth the lie of the Palace as he knoweth his arms, his legs. It's not reasonable that the thief be Prospero."

"Perhaps Prospero sponsored this so-called Brightwater, then. He has been too quiet."

Prince Gaston forbore to point out that the same objections applied to Prospero as to any other sorcerer. "He may have quit his claim."

The Emperor slapped the table with his hand, glaring at Prince Gaston. "Hah! Don't play the fool, Gaston. You don't like facing him, but he will never give it up until he has been defeated and killed. You have managed the one and never the other."

"I saw him deeply wounded last time. 'Tis possible he died," said Prince Gaston, "elsewhere."

"We haven't seen his corpse."

Prince Gaston nodded slightly. "Nor heard of him."

"Nor heard anything." The Emperor tapped his fingers

quickly, once, in succession. "Golias hasn't been heard of, either," he said, his mind skipping to other bad old news.

"'Tis lamentable we lost his trail in wild Ascolet. I'm more certain of his return than of Prospero's. Yet it hath been years, Avril."

"And their tombs are empty," said the Emperor. "It has not been time enough." His hand tightened into a fist.

# — 5 —

THE TWO CLOCKS NEVER AGREE.

The constructions are a marvel of the sorcerer's Art. One tells the time in a place so far removed from this one that the nature of the creatures who live there is fundamentally different. The other tells the time at a place very far away which can be found only with difficulty, but yet is more attainable than the first.

Their ticking never synchronizes. They chime out of order; sometimes one will ring a single hour to two or three of the other's; sometimes they ring midnight and dawn together. The spheres and circles, beautifully and precisely etched on metal and glass, move around and around one another in motion as perpetual as the Universe—or rather, Universes. Standing on their black table at one side of the room, the clocks collect light coatings of dust, which are regularly removed by a quick hand wielding a soft old flannel cloth, and they reflect sunlight, moonlight, starlight, and the light of the more and less earthly fires made by the hand which dusts them.

On the wall over the clocks has been engraved and painted an elaborate analemma for telling local time, along whose curves sun and shadow progress through the year. Beneath the analemma, a grey slab of slate covering the wall is covered in turn with small and large chalked notations. The center of the room is occupied by a polished black table, its mirror-slick surface adorned with curious looping, stretching, curling designs set in fine lines of gold like spiderwebs mixed with cyclonic swirls and radiant bursts. The design is partially obscured by sheets of parchment and paper and papyrus, by curled scrolls of smoothed bark and thin metal sheets finely scratched with notations, but enough is uncovered to show that the lines have two foci at opposite ends of the long table's top.

Close examination would show that some of the designs on the table's surface also appear in the engraved circles and spheres of the clocks.

The door is of triple-thick and cross-grained dark wood, reinforced with iron bands shaped like arms reaching from one side to another so that the hands grip the hinges. It stands ajar, and one can see that it lets upon a small landing from which descends a narrow stair. The stair is lit by a skylight above it, and now, at high noon, a patch of sun skylight-shaped falls straight down upon the landing, a doormat of light.

Beneath the skylight, to one side, hang three glass globes, like those which formed the spheres of the clocks. One has a bubble; one is infinitesimally thicker on the bottom than on the top; and the third has the beginnings of engravings upon it, one of which contains an eyelash-fine line imperfectly curved. These are inadequate to become parts of clocks, but sorcerers are thrifty and do not willingly discard even broken apparatus after having invested so much of their time and themselves in its making.

Today the two clocks look like soap bubbles. Freshly dusted this morning, they sparkle as they move in harmony with the different pulses they measure, until the sun that falls on them is briefly interrupted by the graceful flight of a folded piece of paper.

The paper glider whisshed as it landed on the gold-inlaid black-topped table in front of a dark-haired, young-looking man in a finely pleated blue-green silk shirt. He was folding another paper glider out of a sheet of closely-scribbled paper decorated on both sides with large, definitive X's. He launched this vessel with a flick of his wrist and watched it spiral up and up and then plunge nose-down into the floor from about five meters' altitude.

"Bah," he said, and collected an armada of paper from the floor and doorway. Returning to his table, he smoothed them out again and put his head in his hands.

"I am a charlatan," he grumbled, and pushed the whole stack of papers away. "I ought to hang out a shingle and go into business, peddle love potions and wart removers to benighted villagers," he went on to the empty room. "I've studied geomancy, hydrology, pyromancy, lithology, astronomy, mathematics, alchemy, logic, and botany—I've learned them all and more, all the pillars of the Great Art. None has mastered the Art as I have; none has travelled as far as I, and I believe there is none living who has stood to both Fire and Stone. But look at me! Were this insoluble the cosmos could not exist. I find no error. None! The cosmos *does* exist—this is the base of philosophy, truth fundamental, a sine qua non!—and thus *I'm* in error. But *where?"* he cried, and slapped the papers with his hand.

The clocks moved.

The sorcerer glared at the clocks. It was the clocks which had first caused this unexpected detour in his programme of research, which had begun years previously with an ungentlemanly but necessary violation of hospitality. They were wrong: a tiny, tiny error, like all errors of the sort, had cumulatively thrown them off by varying orders of magnitude, and they were useless. He trusted his craftsmanship enough to say that the clocks were capable of keeping time correctly; the error's root was that the forces they measured were not behaving as they ought. They were being bent and distorted, rather than flowing in the prescribed currents.

Understanding that there was an error and then calculating how great it was and how it increased had occupied him in his lonely octagonal tower for nearly twenty years. He had been confident, as he began, that he would discover some simple fault in his calibration or calculation, but there were no mistakes: the clocks ran correctly and the times they kept were wrong.

It was remarkable that they ran at all, but he wanted them to be right. He had come here to live in peace and quiet, to occupy himself with building ingenious devices and elegant apparatus and using them, to invent new ways of doing and new things to do, and now he was confounded by a flaw in the very foundation of his premise. He could ignore the flaw and develop his skills further—it did not affect most of his activities—but the idea of leaving the problem unsolved galled him. Arrogantly, yet accurately, he believed himself uniquely talented and blessed with ability in all the worlds, and since only he knew of this problem then only he could solve it. Indeed, he ardently desired to solve it.

It defied solution.

The checking and re-checking of his figuring was making him a little mad, feeding the righteous anger he was beginning to feel at the Universe for not operating the way he thought it should. He had gotten back into the habit of pacing agitatedly, a habit he had been glad to lose somewhere after his childhood; he granted the most trivial of doubts and possibilities serious consideration day and night; he could no longer divert himself with music, books, or poetry. Now he went up and down beside his table, from window to blackboard, not really thinking of anything but his own vexation.

When both clocks chimed at once, it was too much; he flung himself out of the workroom and stomped down a flight of stairs, through a library to a door which led to another flight of stairs. At the bottom were some pegs on which hung a few pieces of clothing and a bench with a couple of pairs of boots under it. He doffed his slippers, donned a nondescript grey-brown coat and tough brown boots with thick soles, and went out through the door beside the pegs. The commotion in his head had grown too cacophonous to be contained in the tower.

Outside, it was a fine day, brisk as late spring was apt to be. The nameless long-thorned flowers which grew in abundance at the base of the tower and some little distance up its sheer sides were setting buds. Seemingly blowing in the breeze, they drew back from him and from the doorway, clearing a path through their thicket of tough vines and finger-long thorns. The sorcerer stood for a moment on his doorstep, inhaling and looking around, and then set off in no particular direction.

He returned as the shadows were filling the valleys. The stairway was dark, but lights leapt up in iron sconces when he opened the door and crossed the threshold. He sat on the bench and put on his slippers again slowly, hung up the coat, and then shuffled into the kitchen, tired after a day-long trek up hill and down dale but still—still with the same load of mind-bending, world-distorting problems he had had before.

However, he thought, at least it would be easier to sleep when he was this tired. He hadn't cheated; he'd rambled all day, drunk water from a stream when he was thirsty and jogged on, ascending, circling, and descending the straight-shouldered mountain nearest to his tower in its bowl-like dell. He rummaged in his cupboards for dried fruits and vegetables, bread, a cheese, and ate an uninteresting but filling supper.

When he had cleaned up the kitchen and put everything away, he started out and tripped on a small three-legged stool which was hidden in the shadow of the table. He was a tall man, but agile, and he would have recovered but for the stool's getting under his other foot as well. It rolled; he staggered and grabbed the table with an "Ow!" of surprise, and his head struck the side of the stove as he was thrown backward.

The lights in the kitchen burned tirelessly.

Upstairs in the workroom, the clocks whirled and spun slowly.

The man on the floor groaned to himself and rolled onto his side, holding his head. There was blood on his hand—he'd cut the scalp, and he was glad it hadn't been an eye he'd hit on the iron stove. With crabbed, uncomfortable movements he rose and saw the stool. One kick sent it crashing into the opposite wall.

"Oohhhhh . . ." sighed its victim, and tottered to a trapdoor in the floor. Beneath it in a hidden drawer was ice, chips of which he dropped into the dishrag and held to his head as, one-handed, he closed the icebox again. When he had risen, the stool came in for another kick back toward the door. He started toward it for a third and picked it up instead, an incendiary spell on his tongue.

It had been a long, difficult spring, the culmination of long, increasingly frustrating years. He was a little mad, but only a little, and the idea of taking vengeance on the stool suddenly appeared to him to be as ludicrous as it was. He laughed and shook his head, then hefted the stool to toss it in the corner. It landed, rolled, and lay on its side. He gave it a small kick to upend it and turned to leave the kitchen, still cooling his bruised head.

Then he stopped and looked at the stool carefully.

He bent and picked it up again, staring at it, a frown coming onto his face.

"Three," he said.

The melting ice and blood began to run down his neck into his collar.

"Three," he whispered reverently, and set the stool carefully in its proper place beneath the table.

The blackboards were covered with smudgy numbers, lists, and diagrams drawn freehand over everything else. The table was clear save for a few small, oddly-shaped counters, placed on certain parts of the engraving which covered its top, and a trio of instruments. Papers and books were stacked on every other flat surface—beside the clocks, on the windowsills, on the shelves, on a chair. A delicate scale made of some fine-spun transparent stuff clearer than glass stood in the center of the table; a thing that looked like a windmill growing out of a compass of the same delicate crystal stood a foot or so away from it. Its feathery vanes were spinning lethargically. Another, identical device was on the other side of the table, pointing in a different direction, also moving but more slowly. They would have been invisible but for the reflected light flashing from them as they turned.

The clocks twirled and precessed in degrees.

The workroom was empty. On the bed in the next room,

the tower's occupant, half-undressed, lay on his back snoring softly. His previously clean-shaven face had accumulated a short beard. His mouth was slightly open, and his hands were slack on his chest, where the laces of his shirt lay untied in his fingers.

A partly-eaten apple had rolled onto the floor at his feet. The exposed white flesh had become brown; the peel was curled around the bitten area.

A square of sun progressed along the wall and across the carpet and then along the wall again before he moved.

"Uff," he exhaled, and drew his legs up onto the bed, crawled to the pillows, and lay down with his face in them. From the workroom, the soft chimes of a clock sounded. He chuckled before falling asleep again to descend into an old dream.

He walked away from the burning Well in its eight-sided white wall and wandered in dream-fashion through gardens, until he came to the Royal Tombs and found himself standing in the ivy-choked arch that led to one. He ascended the mossed and crumbling stair behind the arch and found at the top a great tomb.

A tall man, bearded, by his bearing powerful yet clothed austerely, emerged from the tomb's grapevine-overgrown portico. The grapes were ripe and purple. "Though we meet at my tomb, I am not dead," he said.

The dreaming sorcerer nodded.

Now the stranger walked toward the dreamer, down the weedy walkway of the tomb's approach, and stood before him. "I lay upon thee this geas," he said, and he moved his hands and spoke slowly, and the force of the Well flowed into his words so that they became one with the world. "Seek me until we meet, and when we meet shalt thou tell me thy name and lineage that I will know thee."

The sorcerer looked into the man's eyes, which were bright grey like clouds, not cold but kind and grave, and the geas fell, settling on his life and altering it.

"Safe journey," the man said. "That which brought thee here will bear thee safely away."

Something tugged the sorcerer deeper into sleep, deeper than dreams, and he sighed and turned unknowing.

When the sorcerer rose from his bed, he bathed and dressed, then went down to his kitchen and prepared a hero's breakfast. Having eaten well and tidied the room, he climbed up to his bright workroom again and stood, arms folded, contemplating the table.

The twin vaned compasses, which he had designed and built in his fury of enlightened insight, still pointed in two different directions. However, the lines along which they pointed intersected in an area nearly devoid of the markings etched into the table's glossy black surface.

"I have you at last," he whispered to the table, uncrossing his arms and leaning over the place where the lines intersected. "There: wherever *there* might be."

The sorcerer took from a shelf a single-dish scale with a polished ball of flawless rock crystal suspended where the pan would be. This he placed on the table, changing the location by fractions of millimeters many times, until he was satisfied, crouching at eye-level to the tabletop and squinting at the vaned compasses, sighting from it to them. He straightened and reached for one of the compasses, touching it lightly. A golden line sprang from it, running back to the center of the diagram, where the scale swayed and steadied itself, and more lines sprang out from the counters placed here and there on the lines, finally hitting the second compass. A new line arced from both compasses now and struck the crystal sphere, which bobbed, and the sorcerer reached into the lacework of the spell and adjusted the sphere's placement again and again until the ball filled with light of its own and a new network of lines sprang into being over the old, very pale and fine.

He took his hand away and looked at the tabletop, which lit the room now, and then opened a glass-fronted cabinet to take out a long slender sliding-rule with six moving bars and peculiar scales engraved on it. With this he sat by the table for a long time, calculating, writing in a leather-bound book.

One of the clocks chimed with an almost apologetic note. He snorted softly and murmured "You're next" to it but did not look up.

Thus he passed the day and the night, then slept awhile and worked again, measuring and calculating and plotting in his book, seized by an inspiration of genius and knowledge and revelling in the possession. This phase of his labors bore him through the waxing and waning of summer in the mountains around his tower. In the autumn, he found his apparatus to be inadequate to his vision and passed the winter, and many seasons following, designing and building a substitute for his tabletop covered with fine lines. It required that he leave the solitude of his tower several times to travel and obtain materials. He was exacting about the composition and purity of everything he used and could tell at a glance what were the qualities of a stone or spool of wire.

The old table was retired to the kitchen with honors; for the sorcerer loved kitchens and respected them. A new, larger, more detailed—and round—table took its place. The sorcerer sat looking at it, pleased, for some little while when he had it arranged; and when he had looked his fill, when he had fully savored his accomplishment in its creation, he rose and left the table, left the cunning whirling clocks which were now correct and now were three in number, left the glassed cases stuffed full of the tools of his trade, and, wearing his long sea-green caped cloak, he locked the tower behind him and set out on a great journey whose ending he could still only dimly forecast.

## 6

THE SORCERER STARTED ACROSS A LOW-ARCHED stone-and-plank bridge, lifting his hat to wipe his forehead, and stopped halfway to the other side. Sweet-noted bubbling dawnsong pealed from the thick-grown forest around and above the bridge's stream; early sun glowed through pale new greenery that fringed the branches over the stream, which was at spring flood, chuckling and gurgling around boulders. The water was deep and the current swift, catching and discarding flotsam as it pushed along the rocks. The steep banks were impenetrably thicketed to the brink, chewed by the turbulence so that knots of roots and stones hung half-exposed over the water, festooned with trailing white- and purple-flowered weeds. A red-headed bird whizzed out of a tree to sit on a slender branch, doughtily repeating his high-pitched spring challenge. The sorcerer gazed at the sight with a pang of appreciation, forgotten hat in hand, leaning a little on his black staff.

"It is just as well to stop, sometimes," he murmured.

As he stood, filling his eyes with the moving water and light, he heard the rhythmic, disorganized sound of a troop of horses approaching from the direction he'd just come from. The sorcerer put his hat on slowly. Brigands? As he travelled, he'd been warned many times against the gangs of armed robbers who peregrinated through these Pariphal Mountains south of Ascolet, but he had yet to encounter any.

They came around a shallow curve and down the slope that led to the river and pulled up, forming into ranks as they did. Twelve threes, armored and dressed uniformly: uncommonly well-accoutered brigands.

"Hey! You!" yelled a man in a red cloak in the center of the front rank. "Move!"

The sorcerer's heart sped with instant rage; no one commanded him thus, like a lackey, a peasant. He half-turned toward the mounted men.

"Get your bloody ass off that bridge," shouted the red-cloaked man.

"You find something objectionable in other travellers using a public bridge?" retorted the sorcerer, drawing force up through his staff, flexing his hand around it.

"Captain," said a slight rider beside Red, "there's no need to quarrel—"

"We're wasting precious time, your ladyship. Get moving, tourist, or be over-ridden!"

The sorcerer's eyes hardened. He shifted his grip on his staff and muttered quickly as he brought it down hard on the bridge, stepping back from the center toward the bank.

The piers shivered. The stones of which they were built tumbled down into the stream, and the thick wooden planks fell with them. The rumbling and crashing of the wood buried the outraged shout of the commander and the growls of his men.

The sorcerer stood on a small platform of wood remaining on the opposite bank, three planks still fixed to the first stone pier of the bridge. The stream's banks were sheer and the water deep, turbulent around the boulders. It would be difficult to cross without the bridge.

"Shocking that the Emperor's gold buys such shoddy work," he observed, the fires of anger and power still in him. His staff hummed in his hand, a note only he could hear through his palm.

The horsemen were tense and silent.

The red-cloaked man urged his horse forward a couple of steps, moving, trying to see under the traveller's dark-grey hat. He raised his right hand.

The other lifted his staff, waved negligently, and scattered the rocks up- and downstream with splashes and cracking sounds. For good measure, the sorcerer threw a geas of repulsion on the debris of the stream for as far as he could in each direction. It would be impossible to stack them now. Any new bridge must be built of other stones.

The red-cloaked captain swallowed. He stared across at the man in the sea-colored winter cloak, who chuckled and turned and walked quickly away into the wood.

"Otto," whispered the woman.

"Son of a bitch!" Otto lowered his hand, realizing he had nearly exposed himself to great awkwardness, a fool's mistake, in his anger. He chided himself. It wasn't time for that. Too many explanations.

"Who could that have been?" she asked.

"We'll have to ford here." He sat staring at the stones for

three breaths, then turned and called the order to move ahead, adding, "Watch your footing!"

They didn't see the man on the road after picking their way across the stream, which at once relieved and worried Otto. He had simultaneous urges to kill him for wrecking the bridge and delaying them (though it was some comfort to think that Ocher too would be delayed by the missing bridge) and to grab him and ask how the hell he'd done it. On the third hand, if there could be one, Otto thought he could live the rest of his life happily without running into him because he'd challenge the bastard if he did—

"Otto," the lady said.

"Thinking."

"Ocher will believe you destroyed the bridge."

"Let him. It'll occupy his six brain cells with something new."

"But he'll file a complaint against you. On the Emperor's road, that's a crime against the Crown." She was genuinely worried.

"Well, in that case I have a lot of witnesses to say I didn't do it. Including you, my lovely abductee." He grinned reassuringly.

She laughed. Ottaviano laughed with her, but not long nor hard. It was a bad start to the day.

The summer had been dry, after a dry spring and a warm, snowless winter. Prospero had left the weather to itself, for in the preceding seven years he had done much weather-working, and it was tasking to constrain the natural patterns for very long. He had other things to occupy him, drilling and instructing his army of men, taking them step by step through formations and maneuvers. The drought was no great inconvenience; the river still ran, and his folk got from it their drinking water without difficulty. Nonetheless, he used the occasion to have teams of men sink wells, pounding through the soil and rock, in certain auspicious locations where he divined that water would be easily reached. They toiled unwillingly until their first bubbling water-strike, which delighted and heartened them so that

Prospero was hard-put to dissuade them from driving holes all through the forest and the cleared fields.

The fields by the riverside (where a few years before trees had reached over the water) were brown early in the season; crops must be irrigated by hand and with quickly-built pumps, and Prospero released men from laboring on the first stone building of the town to aid the women and children in watering the sapling orchards and the fields of grain.

Seven years had his people dwelt by the riverside; seven years of changes had they wreaked under his command, and seven years of change had worked on them. There were long-houses now, communal places where the folk lived together; in the beginning Prospero had tried to segregate the sexes and had given it up, though men and women labored at different tasks in different places. He was amused by his own dismay at the easy manners of his people, for they coupled without inhibition when the notion struck, and that was often. Though some were pair-bonded from the beginning, the idea of matrimony made little headway here. They had not even a word for it in their rippling, lilting, Spring-born tongue. They all appeared to be mostly free of jealousy, which was well, because few were inclined to fidelity and none to chastity.

The first child was born less than a year after Prospero's night of Spring-fed sorcery, and so many others hard after that Prospero could not recall which of the many it had been, nor who the mother was. The place had teemed with smug, big-bellied women and then with squalling infants. This occasioned delay in Prospero's plans; he ruefully adjusted them to accommodate the nurturing of a sizable population of children. The men who were not paired to women were largely uninterested in the infants, although many of them were visibly annoyed by rebuffs from the preoccupied mothers.

Prospero had not expected a sudden crop of brats, but indeed that was the natural consequence of the vigorous amorous activity. After the initial explosion, births came in a more even scattering, most frequently in autumn. None of the children wanted for sustenance or attention, and the score or so whose mothers had died in childbed and soon after—for with births came the first deaths—were adopted and nursed by foster-mothers, without need of Prospero urging it.

In the third year, Prospero became aware that many of the women had formed into close, clan-like associations, based around the farms, and that some of these groups mostly spurned the company of men—though not all, for the women bore children still. The men lived in a military structure Prospero had shaped, gradually imposing more and more organization on them as he taught them the use of weapons and supervised them in the heavy clearing work of preparing land for the women to farm. Yet some of the women's clan-groups included men who worked the fields and gathered wild food with the women, and Prospero gave up trying to comprehend the shifts among the settling population.

He cared not, Prospero decided, what their sexual customs were, so long as they did his bidding in more important things; their nature was still half-bestial, and so he glanced over the grappling in furrow and forest without censure. As long as they avoided violence and none were forced, as long as they accepted his rule and served his plan, they might associate in whatever ways pleased them. Prospero's only qualm was for what Freia's reaction might be when she returned and was exposed to the cooing and rutting. Surely such unbridled and flagrant activity would stir her own covert desires. Though he had no ready plans for her marriage, he would not have her make her own. She was his own blood, after all, of noble and particular genesis, not to be squandered on the first lubber who might catch her eye and tumble her. Therefore he spoke of her to them as different and other, an object of reverence as Prospero himself was, aloof and untouchable; no playfellow, but a mistress, a lady.

For himself, his attention was focused on other matters—although he sought without success for the woman who had been his last-made creature. She had gone wandering, as some of the folk had; she returned briefly in the third year, in the arms of another woman, and Prospero shrugged to himself wryly and pushed her from his thoughts. A voluptuous blonde called Dazhur, his first-shaped female creature, made no secret of her interest in bedding Prospero; his courteous refusal piqued her vanity and heated her desire, and she displayed herself invitingly to him whenever possible. But Prospero was cautious of such entanglements, and Dazhur's lust came to naught though she sought year in and year out to slake it.

Seven years had passed, and Freia had not returned from her hunt. On full-moon nights Prospero Summoned visions of her in a golden basin full of the Spring's water, to watch her as she cooked her meat, paddled in dark waters, or slept curled beneath sky or bough, all unaware of his spying. Healthy and solitary, she roamed through mountains and in thick, saturated tropical forest: far north of the Spring. She would return. Prospero could wait. She had bolted before when their opinions diverged and, drawn back to him by her own nature, she had always returned, had always reconciled herself to his will.

Freia was seldom in his thoughts, but occasionally, as today, everything brought her to mind and he wished she would return; seven years was as long as her longest journey before this, surely long enough. The weather was oppressive. Her abandoned gardens withered in the drought. He had neglected to have them weeded or watered: the folk did not come to the isle unless he bid them.

Prospero walked through crumpled plants and flaccid leaves in a searing red dawn, uneasily sniffing a hot, dry wind. It was a wild wind, none of his calling, and it smelled of cinders and smoke. There had been great numbers of wood-elk about for the past few days, other beasts too, and bloated corpses had floated by in the river. Prospero suspected fire, struck by one of the hail-throwing thunderstorms in the mountains and borne through the wood on the wind, high Elements allied against the lowest.

The wind sucked the moisture from his lips and eyes. He wiped them. Perhaps he should raise a storm of his own to batter the wild ones down, to counter them before they reached here. Such raisings had frightened Freia, and he recalled with melancholy fondness how she would rush to his arms for comfort when he returned to the cave from the Spring's hilltop, having stirred a fine storm to blast and blow. Then he must hold her, but he would stand in the open doorway, mentally critiquing the storm's thunders and lightnings whilst soothing her terror.

Prospero reached the stones at the upstream end of the island and sat on one. Someday he would have a proper boathouse here, with proper boats, not this clutter of crude canoes and coracles; proper civilized gardens, too, green and groomed, not the wilderness resulting from Freia's desire to plant some of everything and her inability to keep it all tidy. Cool shade he'd have, and fountains; grapes and roses on arbors, and soft lawns.

Prospero mopped his neck; he wore only a thin shirt on his back, but he was sweltering. The water was busy this morning. As he sat, a quartet of the native spotted otters came out of the water nearby, looked insouciantly at him, and poured their long bodies into some hiding-place among the stones. Logs had piled up at this end of the island and were snagging flotsam in their limbs and roots. Prospero saw a tree-trunk, its roots wrenched from the earth, floating silently past in the hot morning light, and another, and dark shapes he knew to be animal corpses. Yes, there must have been fire, far upriver, and now the river bore the debris to the sea.

"Papa," he heard, a panting voice at the water's edge where the otters had been, accompanied by a splash and a slosh.

"Freia?" Prospero jumped to his feet, some part of him unsurprised.

"Papa," she said again. Freia it was, dripping wet and sagging onto the ground. She wore only her scant hunting tunic, no leggings, not even an arm-brace, and she was barefoot; and as Prospero made his way to her he saw that she was bone-tired and somewhat singed. There were blisters on her left arm and a long angry burn on her left thigh, and her legs were laced with scratches. Her hair was burnt unevenly on the left and back.

"How now, Puss," was all he said, and he bent over her, half-lifted her to her feet. She nodded, wobble-kneed, and let him lead her from the water. He patted her shoulder. "Wert caught in the fire?"

"I couldn't get away. I ran and ran. It's horrible. Papa, Papa, it's all flames, all the wood, and the animals run, and the poor little Satyrs, and the birds cannot fly fast enough—" She coughed, shaking her head. "The river is full of death," she said. "I thought I could float with the logs, but the flames falling, and the animals—" Freia sat down again, on a long rock this time, shivering in spite of the heat.

Prospero sat beside her. " 'Tis a dry season," he said, "and some lightning-strike in the mountains hath sparked the blaze. It will devour until it meeteth its own flank, and there die, self-poisoned." An infelicitous metaphor: he thought of Panurgus, of the flash of fire and blood as he was wounded, dismissed the thought.

"Please, Papa, please, make it stop?"

" 'Twere best I not tamper overmuch with it," Prospero said. "There's a natural rhythm to these things best left unchallenged. Such fires are not unknown; they've come beforetimes, though thou hast never seen them, and they serve to scour the forest of deadwood and choking brush, making place for new growth. I'll not hinder it, Freia. I know it pains thee, but I'll not stop the fire 'less it threatens us here."

She stared at him. "Why won't you stop it? How can you let it burn all the forest away?" and she coughed again.

He stood. "Come now. Let's feed thee and salve thy scorchings."

"How can you?" Freia's reddened eyes accused him. She wiped at her face and stayed seated.

Prospero sighed and sat again. He took her right hand in his left, pressing it. "It likes me little, Freia, but I cannot mend all that's amiss in the world. Yet what's amiss with thee, can be mended." After a pause, "Hast been long from home," he said.

"Are *they* still here?" Freia asked, looking significantly at the clearings on the banks, the boats drawn up, the long-houses.

Prospero nodded. "Aye, they are here. I would no more send them from the place than I'd send thee. Less, indeed." He watched her face change, open heart-ache. "Freia," Prospero said, leaning toward her, "thou hast that which none other hath, my blood. Thou'rt mine own and there's none like thee. Dost compass the difference 'twixt thyself and these others I have made?"

Freia looked down at their clasped hands. He took her left hand also, holding them both between his now.

"Puss," Prospero said, pressing her hands, "I do love thee; art dear to me as only mine own child could be. Yet thou canst not have me all thine own, no more than the wind may blow only on one tree or the rain fall on one stone. Must share."

"There's too many of them," she whispered. "They're a, a herd."

"Thou hast not seen a group of men before," Prospero said, scenting victory. "They startled thee, I know; thou art likewise strange to them. Aye, they're many, but withal my concern for them is balanced by my love for thee, and thou'lt receive full measure of thy entitlement."

"Why did you make them? Wasn't I good enough?" Freia asked, looking up at him.

Prospero smiled at her. "Good? A flower fresh-budded hath more of evil or hatefulness than thou. Leave jealousy, lest it canker and corrupt thee. Good enough? I am pleased with thee; thou art made to please me. I made them to serve my purpose in ways beyond thee, in matters where I would not hazard thee. Sooner would I build a wall of blossoms than spend thee on such wholesale work as I undertake with them."

Freia gazed at him, perplexity in her face. "Then what do

you want me to do, Papa? Why am I here? I'm no use to you. What should I do?"

"Do thou obey my bidding, and be of good cheer, and keep thy duty uppermost in thy thought," he told her. "Do as thou hast ever done, as a daughter ought, and thou wilt be ever near my heart."

Ottaviano, his lady, and his men arrived in the large chartered town of Peridot as the town gates closed, having pushed five miles further than kind usage of the horses and the spring-muddied roads would have permitted, and, Otto reckoned, leaving Ocher at least ten miles behind them, stranded in one of the far less hospitable villages through which their road had taken them that day.

Their feeling of safety died when Ottaviano selected one of Peridot's three inns and found that a large chamber had been reserved for Luneté. Otto asked how this came to be, and the landlord explained that a gentleman had bespoke it for her.

"What *gentleman?*"

"Put him down, Otto! Was he a tall man with a blue-green cloak and a black staff?" Luneté interrupted.

"Yes," whispered the landlord. "He's out—sir—my lady—back soon now I daresay, sir—"

"I'll—be—blowed," Otto said, and apologized to the landlord in cash. Then he, his lieutenant, and his betrothed put their heads together.

"Third time's the charm," Luneté suggested, smiling despite Otto's glowering face.

"Charm, my left—" Otto interrupted himself. "This is the third time he's been right where we're going. Last night and yesterday afternoon, not to mention yesterday morning at the bridge. He's following us."

"Sir, we've got to get rid of him. He may be reporting to Ocher," Otto's lieutenant Clay urged.

Luneté said, "Ocher wouldn't have such a man working for him. Indeed, I don't think such a man would work for Ocher." Clearly she thought him too elegant to be associated with the gross Baron of Sarsemar.

"What do you think he is, then?" Otto snapped at her impatiently. "An eccentric nobleman fond of walking alone? A wandering student? A bard with expensive habits and a long purse? Coincidentally bound for Lys, just as we are?"

"Would a spy reserve a room for me?" To Luneté, the answer was obvious. The spy would betray himself by showing too much interest in her if he did that, and so no spy would.

Otto began to frame his own answer to this question and said instead, "I'm checking it over before you set foot in it."

"Do it now, please. I believe my head begins to ache."

They proceeded upstairs without further conversation, Otto carrying the small bundle that was her sole baggage. His humor was not improved by his discovery, on opening the door, of an unseasonal yellow rose in a slender glass vase on the table. Behind a screen waited a basin of steaming water strewn with rose petals, and the fire had pleasantly overcome the spring chill.

"Oh, lovely!" exclaimed Luneté, and brushed past him.

"Lu! There could be—"

She shook his hand off. "Otto, you're being very silly. I think you're jealous."

His jaw slackened; he gaped at her, taken off-guard by the accusation. "Sky above me! We're running from half an army, toward a war, and you think I'm jealous because this, this crazy rich vagrant is following us?"

"Yes," she said firmly, taking her baggage from him. "If you knock on the door in an hour and a half perhaps we'll have dinner together. Au revoir."

The door closed behind him.

Otto stood with his back to it, fuming, building up a good head of steam, and then growled deep in his throat on his way down to the public room.

There he was, talking with a well-dressed merchant in the common room. Ottaviano ignored him and had a mug of good dark beer until the merchant had left, with many courtesies, to join his fellows at table in a smaller room on the other side of the inn. There were few locals in the inn yet, and they were loitering at the counter. Otto ignored the stranger a few minutes more and then suggested to Lieutenant Clay that the men should go into the inn-yard and run through an hour of drill, to limber them up after the riding and keep them at peak readiness.

When his men, grumbling, had left the inn, Ottaviano walked up to the stranger, who was now reading by the fire in the early spring twilight, at his elbow a table which held a candle, a pewter plate of tidbits, a glass of red wine, and a bottle. Otto observed that he wore high black riding boots and clothing of good but not ostentatious cut and quality, displayed by a full, bluish-green cloak thrown back over one shoulder; the light showed gold on his dagger's pommel and his sword-hilt, and a very nice emerald pendant dangled from his left ear.

Ottaviano glared down at the stranger. "Who the hell are you?" he demanded in a low voice.

"I beg your pardon," said the man, lowering his small black book. "Are you addressing me?"

Otto belatedly alerted his senses for nascent sorceries and locked his gaze on the other's. The guy might try another spell. If he did, Otto must disrupt it or avoid it.

"Yes, I am," Otto said softly. "Don't get cute."

"I have been called many things, but never 'cute,' " said the other coldly.

"I believe you. You're tailing us, or me, and I find it very, very annoying, buster."

The sorcerer looked at the man leaning over him. The fellow plainly wanted to pick a fight. He thought he'd deny him the satisfaction of it. "You have an overrated opinion of yourself if you believe that, sirrah. I have no interest in you at all."

"I find that hard to believe, considering the number of times I've seen your face lately."

"Believe anything you like, by any means," said the other, indifferently.

"I'd also like your attentions to my fiancée to stop," Otto said.

"You have confused me with someone else," the sorcerer decided, and raised his book again.

"I don't think so."

"You think?" the sorcerer muttered, and it took a few seconds for the insult to register.

Ottaviano reached for the sorcerer's wrist, but a slow, sticky resistance engulfed his hand. He tugged back at it. He couldn't free himself, and he realized he had been snared and immobilized by a protective spell—one he hadn't sensed in the slightest degree.

"I can leave you like that all night, you know," said the sorcerer, not lifting his eyes from his book.

"Where are you from? Noroison?" Otto whispered, cold seeping into his extended arm through his fingers. There was no one to see his odd position; the room was still empty.

"Yes."

Otto had intended the question sarcastically; he had expected any answer but that. "No shit."

This statement had no possible reply that the sorcerer could conceive. He reread the sonnet. He couldn't decide whether he liked it or not. The conceit was not novel, but the interesting way the poet had broken the meter in the concluding couplet—

Meanwhile, Otto tried to free his hand again. No success, and he was numb to the shoulder. "Uh, look, if you don't mind, we should either finish this conversation—"

"We aren't having a conversation. You're swaggering and making an ass of yourself. If I release you, you shall cease this buffoonery."

"You just happen to be going everywhere we're going."

"It appears so. Unfortunately. The journey becomes rather dull when one sees the same faces again and again."

"Where are you going?"

Silence.

"All right, your business. It's rather unusual to see anyone from Noroison around these parts."

The sorcerer glanced up, and Otto noticed that the man's eyes were a remarkably intense blue, even in the dim light.

"I suppose so. You'll speak of this to no one."

"Yes," said Otto, automatically it seemed, his mouth agreeing without consulting his thoughts.

"Excellent."

Ottaviano's hand flew back; he staggered off-balance for a moment, then walked away from the sorcerer without another word, massaging his arm.

Noroison. That put the wind up Otto, left him cold long after his arm was flexible and sensate. Was it possible? One of the legendary bogeymen, here: not far from Landuc and the Well itself. How had he crossed the Limen, King Panurgus's sorcerous screen between cold, ancient Phesaotois and burning, younger Pheyarcet? Had that outermost Bound begun to weaken, after the King's death, as the Well had faded and drawn inward? Otto pushed that question aside for more immediate worrying.

The stranger was probably a spy, and certainly a sorcerer, as all the people of Noroison were reputed to be. He was not spying on Otto personally, but on things in general. Otto's doings, however, would form part of the spy's stock in trade, and Otto thought he objected as much to that as to the attentions to Luneté.

Yet there was pitifully little that he could do about the man. Killing him outright, considering the command of sorcery he'd demonstrated so offhandedly, would be difficult. He was protected and wary. Otto wasn't so foolish as to get himself into a sorcerers' duel.

Stepping out the stableside door into the damp spring twilight, Otto folded his arms and leaned against the wall, scanning his surroundings automatically, longing in vain for tobacco or anything smokable. His hand, in his pocket, found his special red-handled folding pocket-knife. He took it out and began whittling a twig of wood he picked up from under his feet, making it into a spiralling screw-shape. The thuds, grunts, shouts, and clashing of his men's practice session came from a paddock behind the inn, homey sounds.

A sorcerer, travelling alone and inconspicuously. It occurred to Otto that this could even be long-silent Prince

Prospero, titled the Duke of Winds; in which case Otto thought he would like to know where Prospero was going and why.

The door rattled. "There you are," Luneté said, smiling at him.

"Here I am." His irritation over the sorcerer was balmed by Luneté's conceding to seek him. Ottaviano folded his knife away.

"Are you awaiting an assignation of honor, sir?"

"I was awaiting a brilliant idea, but I think the odds of one visiting me just now are low. I'll accept your brilliant smile instead," and he smiled back at her.

"I was afraid you and that fellow would have brought the building down by now," she said, dropping the courtly tone to match him.

Otto considered asking her to make herself agreeable to the stranger, thereby to try for more information. He reconsidered. The man had already taken too much notice of Luneté.

"Did you find anything out about him?" Luneté asked, interrupting the thought and slipping her hand through his arm.

"How did you know— No. Yes. In fact I did."

"Being . . . ?"

"He—" and Otto's tongue froze.

Luneté waited politely.

"Son of a bitch!" he exclaimed, regaining command of his vocal cords and realizing what had happened.

"If you keep calling him names like that, he'll get really annoyed, Otto," Luneté said, sighing.

"He's—" and Otto found he couldn't tell her what had been done to him either. He gurgled incoherently. "I'm going to break his ribs bone by bone," he gasped.

Luneté stared at him in alarm, took his shoulders, and shook him slightly. "What's wrong? What's wrong?"

Otto, breathing slowly and hard now, commanded himself to calm down. There was no point in raging like this. He'd been bagged as neatly as any coney could be, a geas slapped on him to tie his tongue and lock his throat when he tried to speak of the traveller being a sorcerer from Noroison. Humiliating, it was, and infuriating. He knew just when it had been done, too: when the other had said "You'll speak of it to no one." And done so well Otto hadn't even suspected it.

The subtlety and force of the sorcerer's workings were impressive. Otto had felt nothing of them, though they had seized him and settled on him while he was wary of just such measures. There were few, or no, sorcerers so able in Pheyarcet, and none in Landuc, a lack due to the late King's and now the Emperor's vigorous discouragement of the Art. Who could he be? The Well, nearly inaccessible after King Panurgus's death, was supposed to be banned to new initiates—a ban that could be evaded, Otto knew, but still—

"Otto?"

"I'm all right, Lu."

"You didn't look it." She still stared into his face, but took her hands from his shoulders. "You looked ready to choke."

"I'm all right now. Just a—spell." Otto smiled to cover his dismay. "I think I'll stay out of that guy's business. No point messing with a strange magician when we've got a war to worry about." Could the Emperor have bargained with a new sorcerer? But this wasn't the time to consider that problem. Luneté came first.

"I'm glad you've changed your mind," she said, and squeezed his hand, pleased that he'd dropped the quarrel. "Come up for dinner."

After their meal, Luneté allowed Otto a single chaste kiss on her hand before closing and barring her door for the night. He bowed, smiling, over the hand, and they played their customary question-game:

"How long, my lady?"

"Four weeks, five days, and six hours," she replied, smiling also.

"It gets longer every day," he muttered, straightening. At times there were disadvantages to being a gentleman.

"It does not."

"It will take infinitely long, madame, for first we must live halfway until then, then half the remaining time, then half what is left again—"

"I've heard that before," she said, folding her arms demurely, smiling, "and I didn't believe it then and I don't believe it now. Four weeks, five days, and six hours, sir."

"Good night, Your Grace. I go to lose a few hours in oblivion, counted off by the clock of my heart." He thumped his chest theatrically.

"Good night, Otto." With a last smile, Luneté closed the door, then leaned against it and sighed, pressing her hand to her breast. Four weeks, five days, six hours. There was no point even thinking about it; that only made the waiting longer, she chided herself. They would ride on toward Champlys in the morning. Then it would be four weeks, five days even, and she did not believe the time could ever pass quickly enough.

## 7

PROSPERO'S FOLK WERE INDIFFERENT TAILORS AND seamstresses. Their clothing, when they wore it, was loose-draped and little decorated, pieced together from scraps of whatever cloth was to be had. Cloth was scarce; Prospero had brought in bales of woollen and linen stuffs, but there was none woven locally, and no native material save leather, mostly used for winter boots and garments worn by those who hunted.

Freia, gowned, beribboned, and sandalled, her scorched hair sheared evenly and curling as it dried, trotted stiffly beside her father as he took her to meet one of the men. She looked at the stained and frayed wool and at the coarse leather on the people carrying water to the irrigation trenches of the fields. "I can make better clothes than they do," she observed, almost smug, to Prospero, "and you said I'm not very good at making clothes."

"No need for thee to be so," he said. "For them, 'tis the early work of their novice hands, and I doubt not they'll better it in time, with experience and material. But material's in short supply. Soon I'll fare forth to the wider world for purchase of such goods as those, and other things needful to carry out my plans."

"They could make cloth from the tossflowers," Freia said.

"Tossflowers?" Prospero said.

"The tall yellow flowers on the black stalks have long threads in the stalks," Freia said. "They stick together. I made a fish-net, and ropes, and my belt, and a map when I was in the north. I showed you my belt this morning."

Prospero paused and looked at her acutely for an instant, then walked on. They met black-bearded Scudamor, and the Prince made Freia known to this man, his first-shaped and now his Seneschal. Prospero had Freia tell Scudamor of the tossflowers, and later that day the Seneschal set people to collecting the plants. Freia was shy of Scudamor, wary of all the new folk; she half-hid behind Prospero to talk to the Seneschal in a near-whisper, and the tactful Seneschal never looked at her directly, but at her feet, or the sky, or the grass.

Then Prospero took Freia in tow again, and with her hand on his arm or holding on to his pocket he led her to where his Castellan Utrachet and three others were making bows and arrows. But Freia murmured that she used a better wood than that the Castellan had, and the Castellan and his helpers trotted off into the forest to find it.

"Why are they making so many bows? Surely they do not all mean to hunt?" Freia asked, following Prospero along a muddy track between fields where trees had stood before she left. Her trees: the cultivated fields looked wrong to her eyes, and she tried to see only Prospero, narrowing her vision to his back, his hat, his broad shoulders dark-clad.

"Time comes when they'll be needed," Prospero said. "I have chosen my time, and I shall strike down the usurper in Landuc. There's much work to be done here before then: we'll have fletchers and smiths, bowyers and armorers, ropemakers and weavers, sailors and carpenters, all manner of trades among us soon."

"Why?"

Prospero stopped, dipped a drink of water from a bucket by a stone-sided well at the meeting of three muddy paths. He offered her the wooden cup. "Why? Why, maid, think'st thou that Avril will return my stolen patrimony for th' asking? Though I'm the rightful ruler in Landuc, he's had long years—why, longer than thy memory runs—to drive out or murder all contrary to him: my friends, my agents, my subjects. Even Lord Gonzalo, that Panurgus consulted in any matter of law of the realm, is banished for his service to the truth, his lands baldly stol'n, little left him but his daughter fair Miranda. Avril is a fool, and a fool's arse is ill-seated on the throne of Landuc. The realm suffers for't."

Freia had listened to this, understanding not all, and waited when Prospero concluded for a further conclusion.

"But, why?" she asked again, when nothing further came.

Prospero dipped water, drank again. "The realm's the mirror of the king—"

"The, the sailors. The smiths. The foundries. Why those, Papa? Are they driven from Landuc?"

"Nay, miss, Avril in Landuc hath armorers and smiths aplenty. And I have none. Therefore do I prepare to arm me, to arm my men, to dispute false Avril's claim."

"With him?" Freia asked.

"In war," Prospero said, exasperated, "in battle, Freia, art wood-headed yet? In war I'll face his men with mine, and I'll conquer them by force and sorcery, drown 'em in blood if need be; possess the city, depose the usurper, and claim my throne. In war." He shook his head at her and started off again.

Freia stood, understanding at last, and then hurried after him, catching his arm. "Here—"

"There. Hast lent ear to one word of mine in a thousand, 'tis patently shown." Prospero shot her a quick grey look. "Very natural art thou indeed. Come now. I'll tell this to thee slowly once again, and this time I'll hear thee say it back to me. We go to war with Landuc, that I may be King as is right."

"But, Papa, why? Aren't you happy here? You have people now; nobody is killing anybody—you told me it's wrong to kill people! Won't your people be killed too? They don't have any quarrel with these Landuc people! Won't they kill you? Please, Papa—don't go to Landuc and have war. Everything is good here. Will you not stay here and be happy?"

They had halted again amongst a terraced patch of vegetables; women and children were hoeing and weeding at the far end of it, out of earshot, peering up curiously at Freia.

"Thou hast as much sense of honor as yon cabbages," Prospero declared, scowling blackly at Freia, "and as much knowledge of policy and sorcery. 'Tis right that I make war 'pon Landuc, by any means to hand; I'm the King, by right of blood, for the King died without naming another heir, rather murdered himself and fouled the Well with his death. Say naught of these matters thou dost not understand! The world's wagged amiss since that Avril insinuated himself upon a throne too great for him, beneath a crown too heavy. The Orb and Scepter are idle in his hands. The Roads ravel, the Bounds unbind; the very vigor of the world spends itself, useless, in the wastes. I, I have all the powers and every right to take it from him, to rule the place better than he, witling princeling, can. He's no scholar, no sorcerer, knoweth naught of the Well: he's unfit to rule. Now give me peace indeed: thy questions are a very battery of foolishness. Hearken to me, cease thy larking, thou'lt learn all needful to thee in good time."

Ottaviano roused Luneté and his men an hour before the spring dawn, as the sleepy folk of the inn and village were stumbling through their waking chores. Then he hurried back to his room and finished dressing, shaving hastily but painstakingly, re-using the basin of water he had just put to a wholly different purpose. The water glimmered faintly, but with reflected candlelight, not the trapped light of the morning star, and it showed no image of Baron Ocher of Sarsemar nor his men, only Ottaviano and his razor and soap.

It was stupid to waste the time, Otto thought as he

shaved, but a stray piece of his father's advice had gotten stuck in his head and he'd never been able to ignore it.

> *Assume,* Sebastiano had written him, in the letter stained on one corner with his blood, *that in any confrontation you will be killed, and, when possible, prepare yourself to present a dignified and gentlemanly front to the world in death as in life. Keep cleanliness foremost among your habits. Let your attire be neat and not ostentatious. Let your nails be clean and pared, and your boots well-soled; let your face be shaven, or, if you should wear a beard, let it be washed and trimmed neatly as your hair, without extraneous matter or perfumed oils. Let your person be as free of flaws as is in your power to assure, bathed and dressed in such a way as you would not be ashamed to lie upon your bier, and then go forth and conquer any who oppose you . . .*

"Shit," Otto said, and emptied his basin out the window.

A moment later it flew back in and splatted him in the face.

"Hey!" Dripping, he looked out, knowing what he'd see.

A cold and disdainful face glanced up at him for an instant from beneath a grey hat.

With a sharp, tight-lipped inhalation, Otto turned red, pulled his head back in, and slammed the window shut. He was sure that this guy was working for Ocher, no matter where he claimed to be from, for his habit of following them around was disturbing and his methods of getting to their next stop before they did disconcerting. A Ley-path, Ottaviano knew, ran from Stonehill in Sarsemar to the Shrine of Stars in Lys, but it was weakened by disuse: there was a newer road, and riding on the road was easier than following the old Ley up hill and down dale. Otto supposed that old King Panurgus had probably meant to supersede the Ley with the new road, perhaps forge a new Ley; but he had died of Prospero's wound before completing the work, and his son Emperor Avril had made small progress on any public-works projects.

Picking up his saddlebags, Otto left the spartan chamber which had fallen to his lot—a quarter the size of Luneté's, which had, gallingly, been located right next to the stranger's—and went downstairs. The men had slept above the inn's stables, and, had Luneté not been along, Otto would have been with them; but she preferred him to take an inn-room rather than a common bunk.

His men were assembled in the stable-yard. Luneté, flushed with excitement, held her horse Butterfly off to one side.

"Ocher's on our ass," Otto told them. "We have two goals: delay Ocher so Lady Luneté at least gets over Lys's border, behind Champlor's city walls, and get there ourselves. We'll hurry, but I expect him to overtake us and we'll have to fight. I also expect that we can beat him. Everybody got that?"

They "Yes, sir'd." He told them to mount and they swept as a body out of the inn yard and onto the road for Lys at a gallop.

As ever, the strange sorcerer was nowhere to be seen on the road, and Otto wished he'd lose himself or get his throat slit by the bandits who worked the woods hereabouts, though such an end seemed unlikely for so able a man. Luneté rode now in the center of the line of his armed men and they were quiet and alert.

Clouds closed overhead as they arrived at a crossroads where a rutted path from the market town of Semaris joined theirs to Lys. The intersection's chipped-nosed kingstone was neglected, mossed on one side and the ground bare before it. There were no signs of passage of any other large group, which comforted Otto somewhat: he had feared Ocher would have cut through Semaris. What Otto had seen in his scrying-bowl had not been clear as to just where Ocher was, only that he was near. Perhaps the Baron of Sarsemar had turned back, accepting inevitable defeat.

Would *he* turn back? Otto asked himself, and answered,

No. Not with Lunetè and Lys at stake. Not until he had lost everything trying.

The forest was still, without bird or animal sounds to break the murky silence. A sweet warbling birdsong was a relief. Lunetè looked overhead for the brown-backed idler, but did not see it, which was not remarkable; the new-budded leaves were plumper here in the lowlands. Another sounded a few minutes later, followed by a challenging note from across the road—the idlers are territorial birds—and a fraction of a second later Lunetè heard other sounds, a clink and a thud, and then Ocher's men were racing out of the wood to either side, along the cleared area toward them, and Otto was shouting commands to his men. They spurred their horses and managed to fly out from between Ocher's closing lines. Lunetè crouched low against her Butterfly's neck and rehearsed Otto's plan in the event of attack: she and four picked men who rode before, behind, and beside her were to flee onward and take refuge at a prearranged location; Otto would deal with Ocher and follow.

It occurred to her that Otto might be killed. She had never thought of that before, and she was seized with panic on thinking it now. She would not leave him to face Ocher and death alone—she could fight at his side—

Idiot, Lunetè interrupted herself, and he'd be killed trying to protect her. Best to stick to the plan.

They were still outdistancing Ocher's men, and Otto yelled something. She tried to see ahead, but the ranks of men and horses blocked her view.

"Splitting off now, m'lady!" the man next to her shouted, and she nodded; the others were parting now before them and she and her four escorts pounded through the line that, even as they passed, was re-forming and preparing to meet Ocher; she looked for Ottaviano but didn't see him, which lack twisted around her heart with her fear that she might never see him living again. And then what would she do?

* * *

The sorcerer dismounted to collect a certain herb he had noticed at the roadside, which was valuable for its topical anaesthetic quality when prepared correctly. He heard the horses approaching and sighed to himself. His horse, which he'd bought this morning on seeing the excellent animal in the inn's stables (left as payment by a valet's straitened master), pricked his ears and looked back toward the approaching mass of men and horses.

Five riders shot by at racecourse speed, and the sorcerer recognized them as belonging to the group whose route lately had coincided with his own. Wondering what was toward now, he rolled the leaves in his handkerchief and mounted again. The sorcerer urged his horse among the saplings that edged the forest.

The rest of the red-cloaked, belligerent captain's force came along more slowly, passed, then wheeled about with drilled precision and took on the look of a formation.

They were about to do battle, the sorcerer realized, but with whom—brigands? And it puzzled him that he had not been attacked, for a lone rider is easy pickings. He worked a small spell to make himself less noticeable, a veil blended of air, light, and darkness, and he watched down this straight stretch of road as the red-cloaked captain's troops and the pursuing force, which bore a device of red tower, approached one another.

They were outnumbered three to one at best, thought the sorcerer, and he acted without thinking further.

Ottaviano yelped and hauled his horse up as the earth in front of him erupted. One of his men banged into him, wrangling his horse for footing and balance—on the left, luckily, his sword sliding off Otto's shield—and shouted curses came from every side. Horses whinnied shrilly, panicking. There was dirt flying up in the air, rocks, dust—

Coughing, choking, Otto shouted a retreat order to his men, and they complied, disorderly but prompt.

The dust was settling, although the ground in front of them still boiled in an unnatural way. It seethed, as the surface of a stew or overheating custard does; it rumbled in many keys, the sounds of stones grinding together; it hissed and threw friction heat. The air above it shimmered as on a hot, dry summer day.

Ocher faced Ottaviano. Otto could just see his moustaches beneath his helm's nosepiece across the thirty-foot-wide breadth of this no-man's-land. They glared at one another.

"You bastard puppy!" screamed Ocher. "You birth-damned unclean dog . . ."

The sorcerer listened, smiling, and saw the five riders returning at a cautious pace. He nudged his nervous horse out of cover without lifting the spell that veiled them and walked the horse until he was at the verge just opposite them where they had drawn up to the rear of the others. As one of the men went up to ask his fellows what had happened, the sorcerer rode toward the small party, undoing his concealment as he went. Someone was bellowing at the unsettled edge of his earthen barrier. Occasionally, an unseen tree crashed in the forest as the disturbance lengthened.

The men with the lady drew their weapons and surrounded her as he approached, but she spoke and they reluctantly put up their blades and moved aside.

The sorcerer and the lady in riding clothes regarded one another. There was some shouted conversation going on now over the seething earth.

"What did you do?" she asked. "It was you, wasn't it?"

"I? Do?" The sorcerer blinked innocently and smiled, tipping his head to one side. His hat hung at his back, suspended on a cord.

Luneté's heart did three backflips and landed somewhere near her liver. "Uh," she said, and smiled also. He *is* a magician, a wizard, thought Luneté distractedly, but her smile was still there and so was his. He was so young! And so handsome. She'd thought wizards were centuries old—

The sorcerer lifted an eyebrow. "Your party appears to be in disarray," he observed. "Perhaps it would be best to regroup and continue on your way, madame."

Luneté couldn't stop smiling. "Is that what you advise,

sir?" His eyes were an uncommon shade of blue. And he was quite tall, taller than Ottaviano—

"My advice is always worth its price, madame."

"What price will you ask for this advice?" she asked him, collecting herself.

He shrugged, smiling still. "I do not engage in trade, and you have already returned more than its value, madame," he said, bowing from his saddle, and he flicked his left eyebrow again and turned away, nudging his horse toward the re-forming line of men.

Ocher was trying to circumvent the disturbed, moving section of ground. Otto turned his horse to prepare for the assault and saw the sorcerer.

"Son of a bitch!" he exclaimed. "You!"

The other man smiled. "Is he trying to flank?"

"Looks that way," Otto replied tersely.

"Mm, he'll fail," decided the stranger, studying his handiwork. "It would be wisest for you to go on your way, Captain."

Otto stared at him and then saw Luneté, who was gesturing urgently in apparent agreement with the stranger.

"What did you do?"

The magician shrugged.

Otto stared at him again, narrowed his eyes, and then shouted an order to fall back to his men. Shouts of dismay were coming from Ocher's troops, mixed with the sounds of more crashing trees and the screaming of an injured horse. Ottaviano cleared his throat. "Thanks," he said.

The magician shrugged again.

They studied one another.

"Our paths seem to coincide," Ottaviano said after another moment. "Want to ride with us?"

The sorcerer thought about it. "I thank you for your offer," he said, inclining his head. "I will join you after completing some business which that rude fellow's arrival interrupted."

Otto wondered what in the names of the stars it could be, but he nodded and turned his horse, shouting "Fall in!" When he glanced back half a minute later, he saw that the man had dismounted and was picking plants by the road, ignoring the simmering ground twenty steps away.

Half an hour later, the men muttered as the magician's horse overtook them and then matched their pace at the head of the troop. They were on a pleasantly wide stretch of road, its sides guarded by tall, slender straight trees just coming out in bud. Beyond the trees lay fields of turned earth, black beneath the grey sky.

"Why, hello," said Luneté, smiling.

"Good afternoon, madame," replied their newly-acquired companion, inclining his head.

"Hello," Otto said, "you finished your—business?"

The corner of the other's mouth lifted in a half-smile. "For today."

"I am Luneté of Lys," said Luneté, "and this is Ottaviano, King of Ascolet."

"Countess Luneté of Lys," Ottaviano corrected her, nettled by her openness.

She shrugged. "Oh, well, yes."

The magician managed a graceful bow to her, from horseback—no mean feat. "I am honored to make your acquaintance, Your Grace, Your Majesty."

Ottaviano heard mockery in his tone, but again Luneté spoke before he could.

"Please call me Luneté."

Their new companion smiled at her, bowed again, and said, "Dewar," indicating himself.

An outlandish name. "Pleased to meet you," Ottaviano said.

"For a change," Dewar said, catching his eye.

"For a change," agreed Ottaviano. "May I ask why you did that?"

"Did?"

"Blew up the road."

Dewar shrugged. "Certainly, you may ask," he invited Ottaviano, without a trace of sarcasm.

Duckshit, thought Otto, and said, excruciatingly nicely, "Why did you blow up the road?"

"To get to the other side?" Lunété suggested in a light, lilting voice.

"Because it was there?" wondered Dewar, and chuckled. "I don't know, Your Majesty. It amused me to do it."

Otto inhaled, giving him a hot look that was just a degree removed from a glare. "I don't like being on the receiving end of favors from strange magicians—"

Dewar interrupted quickly, hardly thinking, "Then you are in luck. I am a sorcerer."

"—sorcerers because it can be notoriously expensive."

"Wise of you. However, I did you no favor," Dewar said.

Lunété looked at the road and felt her cheeks grow warm. Ottaviano shrugged, not noticing.

"I am not familiar with the kingdom of Ascolet," Dewar said after a short silence, "although I believe that one of the sons of Panurgus held a barony of that name, at one time . . ." and his voice trailed off invitingly. It had, at least, not been mentioned in his guidebook, but the book was years old.

Ottaviano looked at the road now. "Long story," he said curtly.

"Prince Sebastiano was Ottaviano's father," Lunété said softly.

"He is dead."

"Yes," she said.

"You seek to claim your patrimony, then?" Dewar asked, and something in his tone made Otto glance at him again. He wasn't condescending now; he looked interested, his brows drawn together, his voice serious, not mocking. This was, thought Otto, the stuff that spies were supposed to find out.

"Something like that," Otto said. "As I said, it's a long story."

"But it can be shortened," Lunété prompted him in an undertone.

"In short, yes," said Otto.

"Following Prince Sebastiano's death, the Emperor declared the barony extinct and took Ascolet as Crown territory," Lunété explained.

"Ah," said Dewar. "Avril the Usurper."

"I don't care how he got his throne," Otto said. "He's a son of Panurgus, he was there when the old man died, he's been able to keep it, and he can have it. I don't give a damn who reigns in Landuc, but Ascolet is mine."

"Yet if your father was a Prince of Landuc—" Dewar said.

"His mother was Queen of Ascolet," said Otto. "By blood, not marriage."

"I do seem to recall some old tale of that species," murmured Dewar, exhuming gossip and scandal from the back of his memory. Assassinations, land-grabs, marriages of convenience—

"You seem to know a fair bit of ancient history," Otto remarked.

"It is not terribly ancient," Dewar replied. "So Lys allies herself with Ascolet to seek independence from the Well-wielders?" It was an innocent-toned, though leading, question, accompanied by an amiable smile and nod to Luneté.

"Not exactly," said Luneté, a delicate pink again.

Ottaviano recalled referring to her as his fiancée to the sorcerer—a stupid slip. "In a manner of speaking, yes," he admitted. "We, ah, the other is an incidental thing."

"But the armies of Lys are well-spoken-of," murmured Dewar.

"Justly so," Otto agreed.

"On the other hand," Dewar said, as if thinking aloud, "plainly someone objects."

Luneté blushed deeply. "It's not what you think," she said.

"I'm not sure what I think it is," Dewar said, amused, glancing at Otto to check his reaction. "On the one hand, someone objects; on the other, unless I have been gravely deceived, we are travelling to Lys, not from it."

"It's a long story," Otto said.

"Best kind," replied Dewar, overmatching his terseness.

"What are you doing up around these parts?" Otto asked.

"Travelling."

"I always thought sorcerers had hooves, tails, horns, and yellow eyes," said Otto.

"In all truth, some have," said Dewar, and he turned his attention from Otto to Luneté. "Champlys is reputed a fair city."

"It is indeed lovely," said Luneté.

"I have heard high praise spoken of the Shrine of Stars," said Dewar courteously.

"It is the most ancient Shrine of Stars anywhere in the Empire," Luneté said, "for King Panurgus founded it first of them all and placed it in the care of my ancestor Urs, the first Count of Lys."

Ottaviano held his tongue and listened as the two discoursed politely, across him, about the attractions of Lys and Champlys for the better part of an hour.

"You're familiar with Champlys and Lys," he remarked to Dewar finally at a convenient break in the conversation.

"The place is of some renown," Dewar said. His Madanese guidebook had assured him of it.

Not so much as all that, thought Otto. "Have you visited there before?" he asked.

"No," said Dewar.

"What brings you there now?"

Dewar shrugged. "I travel for my own reasons, sir, and sometimes I am hard-put to find one for travelling where I do. I might say, that Lys lies between my last location and my next, and certainly that is sufficient reason for going there."

"So you're passing through?" Otto suggested.

Dewar met his eyes and slowly raised his left eyebrow. "My time is at my disposal," he said blandly. "I tarry when there's something worth tarrying over."

"Lys may not be a salutary spot for tourism just now," Otto said.

Dewar's expression did not change.

"I hope things do not go so far as that," Luneté said, trying to break the tension.

"So do I," said Otto.

The sorcerer shifted his gaze to Luneté. "A lady's wishes

should be granted whenever possible," he said, and inclined his head to her.

Ottaviano clenched his teeth and looked ahead. They approached a crossroads with a milestone for Champlor. Beside the milestone was a watering-trough for horses and oxen and a fount for human travellers which overflowed to fill the trough. At the other side of the crossroads, hard at the edge of the road, was a man-sized pillar of rough-dressed hard white stone, a kingstone topped with a good likeness of the late Panurgus. It was in better condition than the Semaris crossroads' stone. This image looked toward Lys, not smiling but with a benign expression.

"Whatever else one may say of Panurgus," Ottaviano said, "he maintained the roads."

"You are a fair-minded man," said Dewar.

Ottaviano ignored this, turning to inform Clay that they would stop to water the horses.

"We seem to have lost Ocher, sir," Clay said.

"I doubt it's permanent," Ottaviano said, "so make the halt brief."

"Yes, sir."

Ottaviano dismounted; Lunetė got down also before he could assist her and led Butterfly to the trough. Clay, having passed the order on to the men, asked his commander where he intended to halt next. Otto drew Clay to one side, watching Lunetė and the sorcerer. They were talking, he stroking his horse's neck, she nodding.

"I'd planned on stopping in Champlor," Ottaviano said to his lieutenant. "However. I don't trust this sorcerer, although I'd rather keep an eye on him than not."

"Maybe it would be best to push on to Champlys, then?"

"Maybe."

Clay looked over the men, nodding. "If we'd had to fight Ocher, sir, I'd say no, we couldn't do it. But as it is . . ."

"With a feed and a rest in Champlor instead of a night, they'll make it."

"The horses have been ridden long, but not too hard. Easily, we'd make it, sir."

"We'll go on," decided Otto.

"And when you arrive in Champlys—"

"We arrive. What do you mean?"

"The sorcerer," Clay said, his eyes narrowing a little.

The sorcerer had turned away from Lys and led his horse across the crossroads. He appeared to be addressing the pillar, bowing and gesturing, and the men were carefully and uneasily not watching him. Luneté was, though. Dewar knelt. Ottaviano saw him pouring from his wineskin at the base of the pillar and nodded to himself.

"Oh. Him. I don't know. They're tricky bastards. I'd just as soon he jogged along, but I have a feeling there's damn little I might do to encourage it." Ottaviano shrugged slightly. "I suspect that if Ocher attacks, he'll find the place less interesting than he thought, and if he sticks around—" He shrugged again.

Clay nodded. Ottaviano moved away, leading his horse to the trough.

A light, misting rain began falling as they left Champlor, which was a small, fortified city on the border of Lys and Sarsemar. The rain became more determined in the last ten miles, and the horses' hooves splashed through puddles on the road.

Dewar, who by his sorcery needed no light to know the road, carried none; a soldier riding beside Ottaviano bore a torch. By its light, Dewar glanced from time to time at the other, picking up a new detail of his bearing or face each time. He was perhaps a hand's-breadth shorter than Dewar, neither bulky nor slender, and quick in his movements—mirroring quickness in his thoughts. Dewar considered that Ottaviano had acted rashly toward him, but admitted to himself that, were he indeed a spy of Ocher (which seemed to be what Ottaviano thought he was), Ottaviano's handling of him was shrewd enough. By picking him up, Ottaviano exerted a certain control over his movements.

Dewar's curiosity was engaged by the situation into which he had ridden. His knowledge of Landuc's local politics was spotty. Who was Ocher? Why was the Countess of Lys fleeing him, with Ottaviano's assistance? What would they do in Champlys, and would it be worthwhile to stay and watch this play itself out? And he thought also that he would enjoy talking more with Luneté, or flirting with her to amuse them both. His travelling was without timetable; he could linger a few days or a month and cement an acquaintance that could prove useful later. Surly Ottaviano might object, but Dewar had the clear impression that his influence over the lady was something less than iron-banded. He glanced at Otto again; their eyes met, for Otto was studying him with the same surreptitious intensity.

"I thought sorcerers hate the rain," Otto said, feeling caught out.

Dewar raised his eyebrows. "Your Majesty, show me a man who will indifferently stand out in the wet and be soaked to the skin, and I will show you a man who is at least half an animal. Probably a sheep."

Ottaviano blinked, then smiled, then laughed softly. "Touché."

Dewar smiled and looked away, suddenly liking Otto for all his bluster. He caught sight of a milestone at the roadside in the dull torchlight. "Five to Champlys," he observed. "Or fifteen."

"Five. I know where we are."

Dewar nodded and sighed to himself, settling in for the last handful of mud-weighted miles.

Luneté left her place in the middle of the troop of men and rode forward to join Ottaviano as the walled city of Champlys became vaguely apparent before them in the rain and darkness. She nudged her horse between Otto's and the sorcerer's and smiled at them both, unseen in the smoky light, but the smile colored her voice.

"Welcome to Lys," she said.

"But I thought we had been in Lys for some miles," Dewar countered.

"Champlor has been part of Lys for not more than a hundred and fifty years," Otto explained. "It was somebody-or-other's dowry."

"Ah," said Dewar, "from Sarsemar . . ."

"It came from the penultimate Baron of Yln, actually,"

Luneté put in. "He had five daughters, none of them inclined to religion. Champlor went with the youngest, who was a spendthrift and a burden to her family. Unhappily she died just ten years later of the wasting disease, which annoyed the Baron greatly—but it was too late to get the city back, because it had passed to her husband, my father, by the terms of the marriage contract."

"Which is why Yln today is so much smaller than it used to be," Otto said. "There's a moral there."

"Don't dower your daughters with real estate," said Dewar. "But he is hardly the first to learn that the hard way."

"Hmph," said Luneté.

In spite of himself, Otto chuckled.

Behind them, Clay yelled an order to shape up; they were half a mile from the city gate now. Luneté glanced back at the sodden line of men and shook her head slightly—they looked as if Ocher had beaten them soundly and harried them home. But at least, she thought, nobody was killed. Otto managed it all very neatly, and the sorcerer Dewar's fortuitous intervention came in time to prevent the one potentially lethal confrontation they had. Ocher must be apoplectic with frustration. She smiled to herself and lifted her head in the rain, which had lightened to a drizzle, as they drew near the gate.

The standard-bearer blew three lamentable notes on his horn. "Open for the Countess of Lys!" bellowed Ottaviano at the watchtower.

"Who calls without?" cried back the watchman, querulous.

"Shsh," Luneté said to Otto, and raised her own voice and her face to the tower, pushing back her hood to be clearly seen in the torchlight. "It is I, your Countess Luneté of Lys with my escort come from Sarsemar, and if you do not know me, you are a fool," she called.

"Aye, m'lady," called back the watchman, and some wet minutes later the gates swung outward, admitted them, and closed behind them.

Dewar began edging away from the party as Luneté

leaned down and spoke with a man who stood with a torch inside, under an archway. Luneté, however, had kept her eye on him, suspecting that Ottaviano meant to tell him to begone, and called, "Wait, Dewar."

Otto sighed and wryed his mouth in his hood.

"At your ladyship's command," Dewar replied.

"Your company has been a welcome diversion on the road. Accept my hospitality, I beg you, and permit me to offer what comfort may be found in my house to you for your courtesy."

Dewar smiled and inclined his head. "Your Grace could not have bethought herself of a more welcome nor a more generous offer," he said.

Luneté smiled at him and returned to her conversation with the man, which concluded half a minute later. She nodded to Otto and nudged her horse forward; Dewar came up on her left again, Ottaviano to her right, and Otto's men followed as they clopped and splashed through the dark town, past another arch, through a wide market-square, up a modest hill to a modest castle, where they were received.

# 8

TWO MEN SIT IN A TAVERN where the lighting is bad and the clientele worse. They are in the back, at a table barely big enough for their forearms and steins, but of a perfect size to lean head-to-head and dice, as they are doing.

The room's low ceiling is simply the floorboards of the second storey, supported on timbers as thick as a big man's thigh. It is stained from above and below in a free-form mosaic of blood, urine, beer, wine, water, and smoke-circles. There are names, initials, and occult signs carved into the crossbeams, so many that the beams are nowhere square. The corbels and braces at each wall-end of each beam were decorated early in the inn's history and have been acquiring a patina of adornment since; some have become buxom figurehead-like women (some with additional heads where their breasts should be); others are fantastically Priapic expressions of wishful thinking (around these are carved many exhortations and insults); and fully half are deformed gargoyles and sheila-na-gigs. The broad-brimmed plumed hat of one of the two gamblers hangs from a set of male genitalia at half-mast over his head, getting smoked by a greasy lamp below. The walls are sparsely adorned by such lamps, whose chimneys are dirty and wicks ill-tended; they have black-striped and greyed the graffiti-laced walls with their soot over the years, and the few tiny high-placed window-panes are nearly opaque from their accumulation of grease-cemented smuts.

But little light is desired by the patrons for their pursuits. The drinkers, both sullen and boisterous, prefer the dimness and fug to bright clean air; the prostitutes working the crowd, or being worked in the corners and booths, consider the bad light an ally; the host saves pennies on oil; and many gamblers' stratagems are covered by the shadows. The gambling between the two men at the small table in the rear, however, is as clean as a pair of loaded dice on one side and a touch of sorcery on the other could make it.

Unlike the other gamblers, those two make little noise; the movements of their hands and coins is nearly automatic, with only perfunctory emotion expressed at a win or loss. Both are well-armed and both wear heavy leather jackets with no device; they both have well-broken-in boots and bulky, weatherproof, weathermarked cloaks in nondescript tweeds. One wears his sword across his back and the other at his side; the former, very dark but with bright cold grey eyes, is bearded and the latter, brown-haired and blue-eyed, approximately clean-shaven.

"This offer of yours is a little strange," said the brown-haired man, resuming the conversation after a meditative lull.

"So may't seem," his companion murmured, "yet my client, though peculiar, is able to afford such whims." He dropped the dice back into the wooden cup they were using as a shaker.

"I'd like to know what your client gets out of me and my

men heading in and raising hell. I'm suspicious of a deal this sweet."

"Captain Golias, I shall emphasize: nothing granted for nothing done. 'Tis required to do real damage, to face true opposition."

"I'm being used as a cat's-paw, then, and I don't like it."

"There's no need to engage; indeed 'twere counter to the purpose. Ride and harry."

"Decoying. Decoying. They'll be after me pretty damn quick."

"An it please you, take Vilamar for the winter," said the man, shrugging. "Catch them by surprise, and you're well-set for a long siege."

Golias studied him: aquiline nose, elegant short beard, tanned face, callused hands clearly accustomed to lifting more than dice; yet his speech was of the Court, the old Court of Panurgus's days, and his arrogance fit his speech. The captain was perturbed by his inability to place the man's face in memory, and a prickling consciousness that the other was not what he seemed made Golias cautious.

"This sounds like a load of shit to me, and I'm not touching it without hearing the full story first," said the captain. "From the man who's hiring." He was beginning to guess who the employer might be: there were few nobles alive with a long purse and a long grudge who could locate the captain in his chosen refuge.

"You may hear it from me, but if you refuse the commission afterward . . ." The dark man's voice dropped ominously.

"Oh?" said the captain softly.

"Aye," said the other.

They stared at one another.

"So why have someone attack Preszhëanea? Grudge?" tried the captain.

"Of a sort."

"Against someone specific?"

The dark man's eyes were low-lidded, and they watched the captain's hands. He lowered his head slightly.

"Some Court feud," speculated the captain.

"Your charge is to damage the towns and roads as greatly as possible and then to withdraw to some local fortress and stay there," said the dark man.

"To trash the place and leave," said the captain in an undertone.

The other smiled slightly. "In a manner of speaking."

"Preszhëanea specifically? Vilamar in particular?"

"Ere you'll know more, we'll discuss the contract."

The captain nodded. "You know my usual terms. Nothing usual in this job. Four times my usual rate for it, considering the disadvantages."

"I'm prepared to offer double your usual terms. The sole unusual clause would be that you'll continue your . . . efforts until you receive word to stop. There is no other object."

"And surrender? Three times my usual, then."

"Done," said the other, his voice ringing through Golias for a moment. "Nay, to withdraw to safety and there wait. 'Tis understood that you may not be in position to do so at once, but must do so as soon as 'tis feasible."

"For example, hole up in Vilamar or one of the other little cities."

"An it please you."

"*Triple* pay for this picnic. My, my. This is an expensive feud."

The dark man's left eyebrow flicked up and down. "Indeed."

"You're saying, you want me and my men to head into northeastern Landuc and do as much damage there as we can until we receive orders from your boss to stop?"

"In summary, that's correct."

"Pillage, burn crops, violate shrines—"

"As it please you. Those are the usual activities of an attacking army."

"I could do a lot better with a goal."

"There may be further word of ends, later. You are the means."

"And the pay schedule? With no clear destination . . ."

"This quarter in advance. Thereafter, you'll be paid for the coming quarter on the first."

"My, my. Fringe benefits?"

The dark man smiled. "They're what you make of 'em."

Captain Golias chuckled. "And transportation? Just how are we supposed to get back to Landuc from here, my friend?" he asked, his smile disappearing, leaning forward. "It's a long, hard Road."

"I believe you can arrange that yourself, as you arranged your transport here," said the dark man quietly.

The captain's eyes narrowed. He considered taking exception, and reconsidered. Triple pay. There was no point losing the contract, and he could indeed arrange his own transportation from the Eddy-world to Landuc.

"Your men will follow you?"

"Oh, yeah. The hard part will be convincing them the job's for real." The captain tipped the dice, which had sat idle several minutes, over and over on the table with his fingertip. "Your boss wouldn't mind," he asked, "if I used the opportunity to get a little personal business out of the way, I take it?"

"So long as it interfered nowise with his own works and purposes."

*His.* Bullshit, thought the captain. With a closed, pleased expression, the captain nodded a few times and then smiled gradually. "You've got yourself a deal."

## ⸺ 9 ⸺

DEWAR STOOD ON THE BALCONY OUTSIDE his bedchamber in the castle of Champlys, looking down. He was a small distance back from the lichened balustrade, so that he was not obviously looking at the couple on another balcony one floor below him; he hadn't intended to do so when he came out for a breath of air before leaving the provincially comfortable chamber where he had spent the night. But the sunlight glinting off Ottaviano's reddish-blond hair and the sparkling sound of Luneté's laughter had drawn his notice, and he wanted to study them in this unguarded moment.

Ottaviano wore a purple cloak today, gold-bordered. His back was to Dewar; he leaned over the Countess of Lys, who was seated with her breakfast before her on a low table. The Countess wore turquoise and red. Dewar could see no servants with her. She was laughing at something he had said, shaking her head, now shaking her finger too. Together, they made a colorful splash on the sober old grey stone balcony.

Before she looked up and saw him, Dewar stepped back inside. The Countess's laughter bubbled to a halt, and the songs of the birds in the courtyard below were audible again. Dewar folded his arms and looked up at the blue, blue sky revealed by the passing of the night's rain, considering what he would do now: go on his sorcerer's business alone, or pause here in this pleasant place, Lys, and dance at a wedding.

The Countess, Luneté, left the balcony after her breakfast. Though the day was pleasant, the weather was still cool for lingering outdoors once the sun had moved away from that side of the building, and at any rate she had business to attend to. Ottaviano, with her authorization, was working with Lys's Marshal to organize an army to oppose Ocher, who had paused to collect a larger force. She had sent the announcement of her betrothal out with the city's criers that morning, and to do so had given Luneté a delicious thrill. There was no turning back now. Once everyone knew, there was no way to change it.

Thinking of that thrill, smiling to herself, she walked to the Fiscor's office with Laudine, her maid, and went in.

The first clerk who sat at a high stool in the Fiscor's office was also the one who answered the door, ran errands, and announced visitors to the Fiscor when he was in his office. Now he wrote busily in a ledger while the Countess's dark little maid awaited her lady's pleasure on a bench by the door, turning her fan around and around in her fingers and looking at the three clerks, one after the other, from beneath her lashes. From time to time, the first clerk, who was closest to her, would feel her gaze on him and just twice he lifted his own eyes to meet hers for a fleeting instant. She smiled, each time. He blotted his book, each time.

The Fiscor spent the morning reviewing certain accounts with the Countess, who wished to be assured that the funds she and Ottaviano anticipated needing would be available at once. She gave directions for getting more cash—for what, she did not say, save that there would shortly be demand. Although she was not yet of age, the Fiscor had heard the announcement of the upcoming wedding, and he had decided that, legal or not, the Countess's word was law.

"I am thirty-six days from majority," the Countess said to him as she rose to take her leave.

The Fiscor nodded.

"I know that it is not lawful for me to command my own affairs yet."

The Fiscor smiled. "Your Grace," he said, "I have lived within the law all my life. If living within the law now were possible, I would. However, I cannot, in good conscience, do so. And in the end, a man's own conscience judges him more harshly than any monarch can."

Luneté, who had meant to offer him an opportunity to resign and leave Lys if he wished, smiled. "Thank you, Sir Matteus."

He smiled also, embarrassed. "Although your guardian was appointed by the Crown, Your Grace, I was appointed by your late father. I consider myself his humblest servant, and yours." He bowed deeply.

"Thank you, Sir Matteus," she said again, softly. "May the Well favor your loyalty. Good day. Please keep me informed about the money."

"Yes, Your Grace." He bowed again and opened the door for her. She left his office and the first clerk hopped down and opened the outer door for her, bowing deeply. Her maid swept out behind her.

The Fiscor's offices were in a relatively recently-built black-and-white tiled corridor, which had a shallow gallery on either side where there were benches. Winter tapestries still hung between the galleries' high, narrow windows. The pillars were spirally striped black and white, and the tapestries were mostly in shades of red: an outdated fashion since the death of King Panurgus, but homely to the Countess's eye. She started down the corridor, meaning to go to her own rooms and send for certain burgesses of the city to inform them in person as to her intention of marriage and the probable consequences.

She paused, however, seeing a tall man in blue-green and green-blue standing with his back to her studying one of the tapestries in the right-hand gallery. He turned and smiled frankly, then approached her and bowed.

"Good morning, Your Grace," he said. "I wish to thank you for your hospitality."

"Good morning," Luneté replied, and, though it felt oddly intimate to address him nakedly by first name, added, "Dewar."

He smiled again. "You are much occupied with business, I know, but I would steal a few minutes of your time today."

"The theft of time is a grave thing to contemplate," Luneté said, beginning to walk again and nodding to him to join her. "Once stolen, it cannot be returned."

"True. Yet the victim can often be compensated in other ways, even to the point of welcoming the theft," he suggested.

"The compensation's value must in such cases be well in excess of the time's, then, for time is a precious thing to all mortal creatures," Luneté said. "We have a fixed allotment which cannot be increased."

"The theft of time, by and large, cannot account for nearly so many of the days lost from a lifetime as time wasted and time squandered on trivial things," Dewar said drily.

"It is often difficult to determine what is trivial and what is significant until time is nearly out," Luneté countered.

"Thus I must offer you, for the time I'd steal, something of enduring and evident value," he said, and smiled at her again.

Luneté could not but smile back. She felt her face grow warm. She was engaged to be married, she thought; she should not be flirting with this man. He was a sorcerer. There was no knowing what he really wanted in Lys.

"Sorcerers are not known for gambling," she said. "You must have something which meets those criteria already in your mind."

"I do," he replied. "And if it does not meet those criteria in your mind, I shall do my utmost to refund your wasted time."

"This is uncommonly generous of you," Luneté said, "and I shall strive to assay the value of your compensation as justly as humanly possible."

"I thank your ladyship for double kindness, then: for enabling the theft and for your justice in judging the thief. In return I shall offer something few victims of theft receive: the boon of naming the time."

As they talked, they had left the black-and-white checkered corridor and crossed through the central hall of the castle, ascending a flight of stairs at its back and arriving outside Luneté's solar. Luneté had stopped; Laudine hovered a few steps behind her mistress, watching the sorcerer with evident dubiety.

Luneté hesitated, then suggested that he join her at the eighth hour for a light luncheon in the garden. Dewar bowed and thanked her again and took leave of her. The Countess watched him go and then went into her apartment.

Laudine tried to catch her mistress's eye. The preoccupied lady, however, went to her writing-desk and sat down, ignoring her maid.

"Madame," said Laudine finally.

"Yes?"

"Is it true that that man is a sorcerer?" Laudine asked.

"By his own admission, Laudine. He is clearly a gentleman as well."

"Handsome," Laudine said, in an undertone, going to the window and looking out.

Luneté shrugged. "He speaks agreeably," she said.

"Have you need of a sorcerer, my lady?" asked the maid.

Luneté turned and looked at her, raising her eyebrows.
"No," she said. "But a gentleman who makes himself pleasant is welcome everywhere he goes."

Through a glass, Prince Prospero watched his daughter watch the town.

She was sitting on her heels on a felled tree at the edge of a stump-littered clearing, half-hidden in the tree's foliage. He could see the end of her bow above her shoulder, see the leather band that held her hair more or less in order, see the line of sweat trickling through the dust on her throat; her mouth was set in a line, her brows wrinkled in a frown, and her demeanor was that of the animal which intends to have a look, then move on.

The objects of her suspicious glare, a party of men apparently resting from the midday heat of the early summer sun, lounged and chattered tensely at the other end of the clearing. They were unsure what to do, and so they pretended—badly—that she was not there, that her brilliant and unrelenting stare did not discomfit them, and that they were going to go back to trimming the tree's branches and cutting it up as soon as they had rested.

Prince Prospero frowned. She was wild; rather, she had become feral. He'd had her domesticated, at least he had thought so, and he had been caught unawares by the revival of her solitary roving habits. She'd run for seven years after he had shaped the people he needed, and run again three days after her return from that long absence, yet not so far as before. For an hour or a few days or most of a winter, Freia would sidle back in, wary and weatherbeaten, bearing some gift of game or gathered fruit. She'd rarely acknowledge with look or word the hundreds of folk, denying them. It always ended: she'd take offense at some little matter and fly. He had not wished to hobble her and keep her forcibly with him, trusting time to tame her; yet soon he must lead his army into Pheyarcet, and he intended that she sit in governance in his absence and carry on his works in the town. He had told her this, yet still she preferred the forest.

It was enough; it was too much. Prospero put the glass back in its case and walked down the bare-sided steep hill where he'd been watching for a stone-barge on the river. He could not fathom Freia. Though she had no art for dissembling and showed all her thoughts in her face, he could not pierce her moods and fits of temper to see what stirred them, nor what spurred her departures and returns.

He picked his way through a pasture and over a fence, and the folk at the edge of the clearing saw him now—and he saw the other thing they'd seen that he could not see from his hilltop: an animal behind Freia, hidden in the green.

Freia noticed him. The animal—a bird, he saw the beak, of gigantic size—tossed its head, rustling the branches, and he recognized it. A gryphon, by heaven's veil; he had seen few enough of them. It might be a favorable portent.

Freia shifted on the tree-trunk, waiting for him to come near.

"How now, daughter," Prospero said. "Hast seen fit to be seen." Freia said nothing, but her expression altered: he had stung her thin skin. Prospero sighed, softened his voice. "And I am pleased to see thee," he concluded.

"You were not here. I came back, and you were gone, they said."

"That is half a year ago—nay, more. I travelled away some days, and returned. 'Twas business that concerns thee not. Thou wert wiser to have waited for me here."

Freia tossed her head back. "I had business too. I went to meet someone, because I had promised her I would do that."

Prospero, briefly dismayed by her "someone," was reassured by "someone's" sex. It would be educational for Freia to spend more time with the women here. "So thou hast made a friend of one of my people? That is well," he said.

"She is nothing like them. I don't like them," she said.

"They have done thee no offense."

"They cut down the best trees," said Freia, and Prospero heard real grief in her voice. "You let them."

"I commanded them."

There was a long, cold moment.

"I found this animal," Freia said, "and I brought her back."

Prospero said levelly, "Do not allow thy gryphon to prey upon the folk here. I command thee so."

"Of course not. I'm going to give her a pig," Freia said firmly.

"Nay, no pigs, nor cattle—"

"Why not? They're not people."

"They're for breeding and working and eating in winter," he said. "Let the gryphon hunt her wild meat."

"She is hurt, and I promised her a pig," Freia said. "I promised."

"The pigs are not thine to give," Prospero said, folding his arms, "that thou knowest, for I have told thee. Now leave this game and come—"

"Not without my gryphon. She's mine, I found her, and I said she would have a pig here. There are many pigs. I counted forty-four. She can have a male pig and you still will have pigs to breed."

"The pigs belong to the folk here, not to thee," Prospero said, his patience fading.

"Then I will ask them," Freia said, and she stood, walked along the trunk of the tree, and jumped down. "Chup-chup-chup!" she called, clapping her hands, and the gryphon's head withdrew into the green shade. A disturbance, and the animal pushed through the bushes, snapping at them with that terrible beak. It—she, Prospero corrected himself—looked briefly at Prospero with an unnervingly intelligent gold eye. As she emerged from the trees, wings protectively tucked tightly against her back, Prospero realized he had underestimated her size. He had never seen such a large one.

Freia had a plaited leather halter around the gryphon's beak, head, and neck. She tugged on the lead-rope and the gryphon, favoring her off hind leg heavily, hopped after her, toward the little group of people on the other side of the clearing. Her wings, Prospero saw, were restrained by a fibrous-looking rope, made by Freia, and one wing was splinted.

"Freia—" Prospero began.

Freia threw him a quick, brilliant glance and looked back to the people.

They were backing away, murmuring. One stood his ground, and Freia went to him and stopped an arm's-length away. The gryphon halted and settled into an uncomfortable half-crouch.

Scudamor and Freia examined one another. Freia's bow and her little leather knapsack of gear, her short leather tunic and the knee-high leggings she wore, made her appear a wild woman of an explorer's dream before black-bearded Scudamor, who wore a simple muddy-white sleeveless smock, belted up above his sandalled legs for ease in working.

"Welcome, Lady," said Scudamor.

"This is a gryphon," Freia said. "She's Trixie."

Scudamor looked at the gryphon.

"I promised her a pig, and Prospero says the pigs are yours," Freia said.

Scudamor looked at the gryphon still. She had pulled her head in, sitting hunched.

Freia looked at Scudamor, and then Prospero heard her say a very small, soft word that gave him all hope for the future.

"Please," Freia said.

Scudamor said, "The gryphon favors her leg."

"Yes."

"She cannot hunt," Scudamor said.

"I hunt for her."

"Let us go to the pigs," Scudamor said.

" 'Tis not needful—" Prospero began, and Freia drew in her breath, and Scudamor said mildly, "To give the Lady's gryphon a pig is a good thing." He nodded, as if to himself, and turned and walked away. Freia tugged the gryphon's lead gently and the gryphon rose and limped with them.

"Be damned," muttered Prospero, confounded. Well, let them give the beast a pig, and when her leg healed they'd have no pigs at all in eight days.

But the gryphon ate her one pig, and then no more, for

Freia hunted for her; she hopped after Freia devotedly, and Prospero realized when the gryphon's feathers and fur began to shed and grow again that this was a youngling, coming only now into bright mature plumage. He did not know how young she might be, but she was growing larger as she fledged. Trixie had apparently decided Freia was her foster-mother, and Freia, who had never shown inclination toward pets, poulticed and bandaged and combed and fed her assiduously.

"Belike," Prospero suggested, as Trixie pulled strips of meat from a wood-elk Freia had shot and rafted home to the island for her, "belike thy gryphon were better encouraged to hunt for herself." He feared the day the animal's health returned.

"She cannot fly," Freia said. "Her feathers are half-out. I told her she mustn't eat anybody here, or the pigs or the new ones."

"Sheep."

"They don't look very nice to eat. They're all hairy."

"That's wool, wench, and thou hast seen it 'fore this, in thy garments." And he told her about wool. Freia thought that cutting the hair off the sheep was a strange occupation, and suggested that waiting for them to shed would be easier, but Prospero forbore to expand upon the minutiae of husbandry.

"Anyway Trixie won't eat them; I said she mustn't," Freia said when Prospero had risen to leave her. "Papa—"

He waited.

"I asked the men who were making the ship, the big one, if I could not have some of the iron ropes—"

"Chain, Puss. It is chain, or chains."

"Chains. So that is what chains look like. I had wondered. —They said I must ask you."

"What wouldst thou with chains?" Prospero asked, guessing.

"For Trixie."

"Wilt not let her fly when she's mended?"

"Yes, I will, but . . . she must have better harness. The

leather is thin, and she doesn't mean to break it, but it breaks."

"Ah. Hm. Well, there is little to spare. Do thou wait, and tell them I have said thou mayst have any excess, but only when they have completed their work. 'Twill not be long—five days, or six; they labor with good will."

Freia nodded. "Thank you, Papa."

Dewar used the hours between his meeting and his appointment with the Countess profitably. He went into the town and found a tavern where he eavesdropped and gossiped, learning as much as he could about the Countess and her affianced. At the eighth hour he met a page as he emerged from his room at the castle, and the page led him to a sunny, pleasant bower in the garden where the Countess's maid and the Countess waited by a table laid with covered dishes on a yellow cloth, beneath a tree which was seasonably adorned with clouds of white flowers and sharp, impossibly bright-green new leaves.

"Good afternoon, Your Grace." Dewar bowed.

"Good afternoon, Dewar. Laudine."

Reluctantly, Laudine withdrew to a bench some distance away and sat down to a piece of needlework, and the page was also dismissed to skip off back to the castle.

"Please be seated."

"Thank you, madame."

"I seem to recall asking you to call me Luneté," she said when he was beside her.

"I would not seek to presume on the informality of fellow-travellers," he said, "but to willfully disoblige you would be far more presumptuous. Luneté, then."

"Thank you. Would you care for salad?"

"Allow me. It is kind of you to grant me this interview today. There are a great number of things clamoring for your attention after your absence."

"I am curious," said Luneté. She *was* curious, and his talk was delightful. With his courtesy and address, he made her feel as if she were the Empress Glencora herself.

"And so am I," said Dewar. "You see, I am not particularly informed on local issues. I wondered why you and the King of Ascolet were pursued by Ocher of Sarsemar." He had acquired some inkling of the business in the tavern, but wished to hear the tale from the lady herself. The town had begun to seethe with preparations for some kind of battle; Dewar had glimpsed Otto leading a column of pikemen.

"Oh," said Luneté. "Ah." She sipped some wine. "Well, it is complicated. In effect, Ottaviano kidnapped me."

Dewar raised his eyebrows, watching her over the rim of his heavy old-fashioned goblet.

"In effect," she emphasized. "Baron Ocher was appointed my guardian by Emperor Avril on the death of my parents when I was a child; he was no particular friend of my father, but when he petitioned for the position, the Emperor granted it to him. The terms of my parents' will and the custom in this area have kept him from assuming real power over Lys; I have lived here sometimes, in Champlor sometimes, and in Sarsemar sometimes, but in Sarsemar more than anywhere. When I was sixteen Ocher petitioned the Crown for permission to wed me. He was denied. I am told this was probably through the interest of Empress Glencora. My mother Sithe of Lys was a lady-in-waiting of Queen Anemone, and she knew Princess Glencora in Landuc. The Baron lately has made every effort to—to woo me, although I find him entirely disagreeable. I refused and made myself as unpleasant and unmanageable as I could, while keeping close ties in Lys. Ottaviano was a captain in Ocher's service who maneuvered himself into the position of escorting me as often as possible—" She smiled, her cheeks flushing red for a moment.

"I see," Dewar said, also smiling. Parents, guardians, friends, lover—forces that acted on other people, but not on sorcerers. It was an engaging change from his usual work. He envisioned Luneté's story as spheres circling spheres, colliding at times.

"I did not know he was Prince Sebastiano's son at first."

Another sphere, its orbit tangent. "I daresay he's kept that very quiet. If the Emperor had known of such a potential troublemaker, he'd have had his throat cut."

"Oh," Luneté said, and she paused before continuing her tale. "My twenty-fifth birthday is four weeks away. Sarsemar, for reasons of his own which I cannot fathom, recently decided to use force to make me consent to the marriage after all. If I marry as a minor, you see—"

"Your assets pass to your husband. Lys." Dewar nodded. Territory was something of importance to everyone, even here in Pheyarcet where there was only one ruler over the Well. If Luneté was Lys, then she must act for Lys first, always.

"And if I marry as an adult Lys remains mine. Yes. I couldn't let that happen to Lys. I am the last of Lys blood; only the stones have been here longer. My great-grandfather was made a knight by King Panurgus in the War when he conquered Proteus and seized the sacred Well from Noroison. Lys is part of me; I belong here. It would be a betrayal of the very soil to let Ocher or another rule here while I yet live." Luneté straightened slightly. Her voice rang with pride.

Dewar smiled. "So you ensured this did not happen."

Luneté nodded tautly. "Ottaviano rescued me and we fled Sarsemar. That was when we met you. We contracted our betrothal before we left. Ocher knows about that, because Otto made the captain of the guard in the place where I was held sign the agreement as a witness. Now all we have to do is hold Ocher back until we are wed."

"A pretty tale, madame. I presume you have selected for the wedding the most auspicious day you could as closely as possible following your twenty-fifth birthday," Dewar said. The system would stabilize, he thought, around this new twin planet, Luneté and Ottaviano, and all would go on, with them and around them, comfortable and foreordained.

She relaxed, smiling back at his smile and humorous tone. "But of course."

"How delightful. So Ocher, if he comes to war, shall be attempting to seize your person, or, failing that, to kill Ottaviano."

"Or to keep us apart on that day. Anyone could guess

which day we chose; it was the best one in the calendar for a month, Otto said. I wished to petition the Crown to remove Sarsemar from his position as my guardian for the balance of my minority, but Otto thinks that such a petition would be refused. It might even end with Sarsemar being given me by the Emperor, and then Lys would no longer be mine but his, my family's blood erased by his. Besides, by the time a messenger rode to the Emperor in Landuc and returned, I would be of age—so we may as well do as we will. I know it is right."

Dewar began to ask why, and stopped. "And Lys's army remains yours," he said softly. Even in Noroison, the men of Lys were famed for their fighting skill and spirit. He had forgotten an element in his mental model: Ascolet, Ottaviano's Ascolet, Ottaviano's territory. As Luneté sought to preserve Lys, so must Otto burn to hold Ascolet—but Ascolet had been taken from him by the Crown. Dewar's pang of recognition and sympathy surprised him. It was an old story in Phesaotois, and an old story here in Pheyarcet too; in the end, everything came down to land, and the Source.

"Yes. If Sarsemar promised additional men to the Emperor, the Emperor would be sure to give me to him."

"While Otto will use them against Landuc."

"We haven't agreed on that yet. It depends on what Sarsemar does. I will not leave Lys vulnerable."

"Wise of you." Luneté's explanation bridged wide gaps in the gossip Dewar had collected this morning. The Emperor would be very annoyed to find the armies of Lys suddenly turned against him on behalf of Ascolet—if that was what Luneté intended. If Ottaviano refused them, he was a fool, and Otto did not seem a fool. "The Empress, you think," he said after a moment, "takes an interest in you."

"I have never met her; I have never been to Court. But Mother knew her. People here said, when Baron Ocher was refused me when I was sixteen, that the Empress must have done it."

"The Baron might have had tacit Imperial approval for his recent plan to marry you against your will, then," Dewar remarked, and poured more wine for both of them. "If the Emperor desires Lys under Sarsemar but did not wish to arrange it openly, he might have let Ocher know that this would be overlooked."

"Ye-es," agreed Luneté slowly. "I suppose he might."

"You can count on it not being as simple as it looks, when monarchy is involved," Dewar said.

"May I ask, Dewar, why you take an interest in Lys suddenly yourself," Luneté said. "There is a saying about sorcerers and simplicity."

"I've heard it," said Dewar. "I am curious."

"Curious?" she said, when he did not elaborate.

"Yes. Or perhaps I should say, I was curious. Now I am interested."

"Interested?"

"I find Ottaviano's case against the Crown compelling," said Dewar. "I would like to see him succeed in it."

"You would?"

"Yes," he said. "I have every sympathy for his undertaking. I understand that people in areas like this would regard a sorcerer's attention as more a threat than a possible benefit, but mine is benevolent."

"Benevolent," repeated Luneté.

Dewar nodded, holding her eyes with his. She had wide, bright brown eyes with straight, barely-curved brows over them; they dropped from his suddenly and a wash of color went over her cheeks.

"However," Dewar went on, "it is very difficult to demonstrate mere goodwill."

"You helped us yesterday," Luneté said, aligning her silverware precisely. "For no reason." She glanced at him from under her lashes.

"That made Ottaviano less than happy," Dewar said, "and more than suspicious."

"He is worried," Luneté said softly.

"You are too."

"Yes, of course."

"If an occasion arises," he said, "in which I might be of assistance to either of you, it would give me great pleasure to grant any aid in my power. And lest you concern yourself over with what fee I might burden you in return, hear this: I do not sell my sorcery."

Luneté looked up at him, still high-colored, and said, "You are not anything like a sorcerer, or not like the ones I have heard of."

"Of what sorcerers have you heard?" Dewar asked. The general ignorance of the Art in Landuc was appalling.

"Oh, Prince Prospero, let's see, Esclados the Red, Lady Oriana of the Glass Castle, the Spider King, Neyphile, Foul Acrasia—"

"I see. An unsavory collection." Dewar sipped his wine. "The scorn heaped on the Art here is deserved, if those are its most noteworthy practitioners." They were of undistinguished repute in Noroison. Lady Oriana was the only one worthy of serious thought, and she had been but a minor sorceress before supporting Panurgus and leaving Phesaotois—and had not, after all the travails of exile, become his consort. "I am of a more retiring and scholarly bent than any of them, having deliberately cultivated a certain . . . distance between myself and my peers."

"I'm afraid it's not very usual to even meet a sorcerer."

Dewar smiled crookedly. "If one were wise, one would not wish for such a meeting. It is usually dangerous, or at least unhealthful."

"But I am glad to have had the opportunity." Luneté smiled at him again. "How did you happen to be travelling that way?"

Dewar selected a pale gold-white pear from the tray of fruit—last fall's, but still good—and peeled it carefully as he spoke. "I am looking for something of interest to me." His head was tipped back and he addressed the fruit through half-closed eyes.

Luneté watched him peeling the pear with undue attention. "A known thing? Or just something to amuse you?"

"I know its characteristics; I do not know precisely where it is to be found."

"Oh," Luneté said. "Is it rude to ask such a question?"

Dewar's left brow quirked. "It is not sorcerous etiquette

to ask such a question other than to annoy the questioned party. However, you asked without intention of offense, and so I answered. Be warned I'll say no more of it."

"I beg your pardon—"

"Granted already." And he smiled at her, that broad, brilliant smile which through some curious trick of perception Luneté felt at the base of her spine.

Luneté smiled and blushed a little again. "So you will be leaving soon."

"I have no fixed itinerary," Dewar said. "If you are uncomfortable with my presence in your house or your demesne, I shall not impose a moment longer on your kindness—"

"I didn't mean that at all," Luneté interrupted him, leaning forward. "No, no. You are welcome as long as you care to stay, and I say so sincerely."

"I still don't know," replied Dewar, smiling merrily, with such a mischievous, teasing look that Luneté laughed outright.

# — 10 —

ARIEL HAD GATHERED A COLLECTION OF fallen leaves, bright-colored and dark, all different, and whirled them up and down in a column, rattling them on the ground as they struck, then spiralling them up again in a circle. There were wild winds and gusts about, too, swooping up drifting leaves and grasses and blowing them against the stone and wooden walls of the buildings clustered at the bank of the river opposite Prospero's island. Ariel had cleared the weather for Prospero last night, and the morning was a hard, cold bright one, the mud stiffened with frost, the grasses and stubble bleached into winter. The hard ground was good for men to walk on, Prospero had said. The cold air kept them moving briskly. When Prospero commanded, later, Ariel would move them briskly in their ships.

The men who must travel that day were arranged in neat

square patterns over the tide-bared beaches a few miles from Ariel's sporting-place, at the mouth of the river. Carrying their weapons and packs, they had marched there in rows and columns in the infant hours of the day and had begun embarking there, row by row, orderly and in good time, climbing into boats, shoving them off the beach, and rowing out to their moored ships through the calm sea, a forest of masts bobbing offshore now with faces turned shoreward below the rigging. Another crowd stood apart from the array of men, a compact mass of women, a few men, and children. They were quiet; there were no cheers, nor marching music, nor banners nor parting shouts, a silence which bothered Prospero. An army should set forth in good heart, he thought, should bear with it the confidence of its home, and these gloomy faces were no meet farewell.

Prospero stood apart from both these groups, watching the embarkation with one eye, the other on his daughter and his Seneschal before him.

"I am loth to leave thee, Scudamor," said Prospero, "yet must I, and think not that 'tis for any lack in thee; rather for thy strengths that will guide the folk here in the work I must leave, unfinished, in thy charge." Prospero had left behind a handful of adult men. The oldest of the boy-children, grown now and sprouting beard-fuzz, were in the army; the others stayed, with the women and girls, to carry forward (slowly, Prospero knew) the project of the city walls under Scudamor's direction.

"Master, I shall not fail you."

"Do not. I know thy ability; let not thy will fall short of it." He looked piercingly at Scudamor, who was square-bodied and dark-bearded, dignified in loose belted robes of blue-grey wool and an undyed grey woollen cloak. Satisfied, Prospero glanced over the handful of others who hovered some few paces away and fixed on Freia.

Her oppressed look and silence angered him; she had infected many of the women, and some of the men, with her worries about his enterprise before he commanded her hold her tongue, but the damage had been done and doubt sown among them where only confidence had flourished before.

Now she stood like a road-pillar, wrapped in a stained old cloak and a fraying shawl.

"Freia."

She tore her gaze from the boats and ships and said, nearly whispering, "Don't go, Papa."

He made a sign to her, to follow him apart from the others, and they walked over the loose sand to a serpentine, silvery trunk of driftwood. "Thou knowest better than to oppose my will, daughter," he told her, looking down into her eyes.

Freia stared up at him an instant only, then turned her face down, away. She nodded.

"Do not abandon these folk, whom I leave in thy care. Ill to them shall be ill for thee."

"I don't want . . ."

"What now?" he demanded sharply.

"Papa, please don't go. I cannot imagine you not here. It's so far away. What if you cannot come back?" Freia looked up at him again, so pleading, so sad, that Prospero was softened: he knew her devotion to him was bone-deep, blood-strong, despite her youthful rebellions and tempers. This time, he left her behind, for an indefinite time, and she was frightened.

"How now, Puss. I must go, and I shall go." Prospero squeezed her shoulder. "Hast thou not coursed unmarked, unseen wildernesses, faced beasts never met by man before, brought thy gryphon to heel o' thy will and heart alone? This time must thou be brave enough to stand thy ground: to stay here. Thou'rt strong in body, strong in mind, too strong to tremble at my leaving thee for a time. I have gone away before, and returned: and so shall it happen again."

"When? How long?"

"I do not know," he said, "but if my plans fall out as I intend, ere two winters come again to Argylle. But do not reckon overmuch on that, Freia: for the Well is disturbed and all runs warped and unruly from it, so that time is crooked. When I've claimed the Orb for mine, there'll be urgent tasks to complete and vows to fulfill."

"Will you not let me go with you? Please, Papa. I will

bring Trixie. I will help you if you want me to. She's very fierce; she can fight for you. And I can help, can't I?"

"No," he said. "No. I command thee, Freia, to stay here. Do not seek to follow me, do not try to send thy gryphon after me."

"I found her for you, Papa . . ." Freia's voice failed her. Her disappointment and frustration brought tears to her eyes. "I kept her *especially* for your war!"

"I thank thee. It was most generously done. But a dozen gryphons, fierce though they seem to thee, will not make Landuc quail. 'Twill take more familiar threats. I have my plans already, and no call for gryphons." He veiled his amusement; truly, it touched his heart that she had gone to such labors for him. "And while I am gone, do thou attend to the folk here, be good, be a Lady as I have taught thee. Promise me."

Too dispirited to argue, Freia said, "I will, Papa. —Are you going to bring her here, Lady Miranda?"

"Mayhap. 'Tis early for such plans. I'll not tempt Fortune by such speculation." Prospero turned away, watched a group of soldiers clambering into a rowboat and pushing off.

"Papa." Freia put her hand on his arm.

He looked at her; her face had changed from uncertain child to watchful woman, as sometimes happened of late. She was maturing at last, pushed out of long childhood by the pressure of the times, Prospero thought. When he returned, he must see about settling her. There were men enough willing here, but he harbored better plans for her. "Puss."

"My friend Cledie— I told her about Miranda, and she wondered, we wondered, if you brought her here, would she not miss her family?"

Prospero had never yet met Freia's friend Cledie, who was one of the folk who had wandered into the forest in the first few days after the transformation. Freia mentioned her name only occasionally. "There's but her father left her, Freia, if he lives yet."

"Then if you brought her family, her father then, also,

you would not need to go away to Landuc again, would you?" Freia's head was cocked to one side, her eyes missing no nuance of his expression.

Startled, Prospero stared at her, at once annoyed and charmed. "Thou'rt transparent yet in thy persuasions, little diplomat," he said, with a rush of tenderness. He bent and folded her in his arms, then lifted her, a strong tight embrace: she was dear to him, he knew it in his heart. "And I shall not promise thee anything of the sort, but I will not wed without thee knowing of't, I do promise that."

Freia sighed when he put her down, resigned. She had not expected any argument to turn aside Prospero's plans, but she had wanted to try, hoping (she knew) vainly for a miracle.

Prospero watched his men embark. Freia stood beside him, her hands tucked through his arm, hugging it. When the time came for him to go, climbing into the last boat, she kissed him on both cheeks and was kissed, without tears; as brave, Freia thought, as Lady Miranda could ever have been.

The Emperor of Landuc waited to receive a guest with whom he had had, in all the time of his reign, no previous dealings, and with whom he would have preferred to have none. He sat in the Small Formal Reception Room, attended by only his six highest ministers, Count Pallgrave, and also Cremmin, and waited for the herald to come in and announce her. A winter-toothed autumn wind rattled the tall windows; the Emperor, disliking the clatter, turned to his secretary and told him to see that the windows did not rattle in the future. Cremmin bowed and made a note.

Her arrival was precipitous and unexpected, but this was characteristic. She came, the messenger had said, in a chariot drawn by black goatlike animals with long horns; the messenger had preceded her to the Palace by minutes, and the Emperor had instantly broken off his audience with the new Ambassadors to be sent to two tributary nations in Pheyarcet, away on the Road. He had rushed into a more formal robe and rushed to the formal room with his Lords of this and that, Count Pallgrave, the rival Barons Broul and Cashallar, and his brother Prince Fulgens, who had been in the conference with him.

There were very few people for whom the Emperor would rush to do anything.

"Lady Oriana," the herald said, bowing deeply, knee bent.

Lady Oriana, tall, cloaked from head to foot in ice-blue satin and white fur, entered slowly and stood, examining the Emperor with eyes the color of her cloak.

"Greetings, Your Majesty," she said.

"Welcome, Lady Oriana," he lied.

Her mouth moved very slightly: perhaps a smile, a Sphinx's smile. Conscious of the effect she created, she moved forward a few steps. "Your Palace has grown since your accession," she commented. She had not received an invitation to the attendant festivities, a conspicuous discourtesy after her close and extensive dealings with the late King.

The Emperor inclined his head, accepting it as a compliment. "As has our Empire," he said.

"And in much the same way. Yes, Landuc is larger now than when Your Majesty took the Orb of Pheyarcet and the Scepter of the Well; it is larger than in Panurgus's day; but it is not so large as it was a few days since." Her smile widened very slightly.

"What does this mean, Lady Oriana?" the Emperor asked, showing no concern.

She looked from him to his courtiers and her eyebrows moved a hair's-width upward. The Emperor narrowed his eyes.

"Your journey," he said, "has doubtless been arduous; some refreshment perhaps would be welcome. Let us retire to a more congenial place for such a collation as might please your ladyship."

Oriana's smile widened as she bowed her head fractionally in agreement. Cremmin, at the rear of the assembled peers, scurried through the back door to carry out the Emperor's implied order. The Emperor rose and left the throne, bowed to the sorceress, and offered her his arm. She was half a head taller than he, and looked down at him with that same weighing, calculating expression before setting her hand very lightly on his arm and accompanying him through the side door.

They went to the Gold Salon, three doors down the white-and-gold corridor. The Emperor dismissed the peers with a glance; Pallgrave began to follow and was given a pointed glance of his own, so that the Count stopped abruptly in the doorway and backed out, graceless, to close it. Within, the Emperor seated the sorceress on a sofa upholstered with gold-flecked red velvet and took a gilded chair at right angles to her.

"It is never wise to ask a sorcerer what is meant," Oriana said, still scrutinizing him, "unless one is prepared to know the answer."

"Your comment begs for clarification, madame."

"My comment," she said, "would, to some, require none."

"To say to an Emperor, that his Empire is not so large as it was a few days past, is to either insult him or tease him," the Emperor said, leaning back. "Clearly you have some information about the realm for which you think we would trade with you."

"Your Majesty has, of course, let it be known that you will not deal with sorcerers. If you verily have no interest in my information, which I flatter myself is of the variety in which monarchs generally take great interest, then there is no need for clarification."

The door opened and three liveried servants entered and set out, with efficient haste, trays of canapés, cold meats, and fruits, three chilled bottles of various light wines and one of a heavy sweet red. During their half-minute intrusion, neither the Emperor nor the sorceress spoke.

The Emperor suggested one of the wines and, on Lady Oriana's slight nod, poured glasses for them both. He was on the horns of a dilemma: he did not like sorcerers, did not want to do business of any kind with them, but Oriana's abilities to divine and see and foretell were legendarily accurate, and Panurgus had used her. If she knew something about his Empire—something about it shrinking or being smaller—it was of acute importance that he know what it was, the sooner the better. The Well might do anything, in its present sullen state.

Yet, he thought, anything to do with his Empire would certainly come to his attention. What value could he place on having the information sooner? She had struck hard and peculiar bargains with the late King Panurgus, and the Emperor preferred to remain out of the webs of sorcery, unencumbered by vows, outside interests, and hidden clauses.

"Madame," he said, "one must distinguish between curiosity and interest. We are curious about your remark. We have, however, no interest in and no intention of transacting any bargain for further information related to it or any matter."

Lady Oriana lifted her bright coppery brows slightly. "Very well," she said, and sipped her wine.

The sorceress departed an hour after arriving. She drove her black beasts from the Palace to the Gate of Winds and passed unchallenged through that portal of the City of Landuc. Veiled and hooded, she smiled to herself as she went along a Ley and made her way to the Road at a Blood-Gate. She had had her information for two days, but had delayed her journey until she knew she would be able to enter and leave Landuc quickly. Today was a favorable one for travel; many of the Gates regulating the Road were passable, and so she made good time, spinning along in her chariot. She gave no notice to the faint outlines of superimposed cities and hills, forests and oceans, villages and wastes, as they slid past; her black beasts, blinkered and accustomed to such use, pulled the chariot and hurried their hooves along to the broad plain where Oriana dwelt.

The Castle of Glass was surrounded by a deep, glittering empty moat and a high, slick greenish wall ornamented by pale hollow objects whose empty eyes looked out in every direction from the Castle. In the milky-white paved courtyard, two sere and wrinkled men took the chariot and beasts from their mistress, bowing obsequiously.

Lady Oriana refreshed herself on entering her residence, then went to her highest workroom, where a tall mirror stood in a pivoting, swivelling silver frame. The mirror, curiously, was not smooth; its surface was rippled, composed of many small, rounded lenses, and it was not silver, holding instead fragments of scenes, of colors, of shapes caught among the myriad lenses. The mirror was a relic of the early days of Pheyarcet, forged before Panurgus had utterly dominated the Well; it too looked out in every direction from the Castle.

She performed certain necessary preliminaries and looked on the scene it showed her: the Emperor Avril and the Empress Glencora in a box at a theatre.

Oriana dismissed the image for another.

This showed her a city beside a grey, stormy sea. Outside the city walls, a plain stretched, and on the plain there was encamped an army. In the city's harbor, ships rode at anchor, a great navy, and from their masts fluttered banners bearing a device which was not the silver octagon on crimson usually seen on Landuc's vessels.

The image burst apart into prismatic shards. Oriana started back, alarmed, and began a sweeping gesture with her hands.

"Ah. Lady Oriana," said the man whose image coalesced to replace that of the city and harbor. His mouth, framed by a neatly-pointed dark beard and moustache, smiled, yet there was no coloring of the smile in his voice. He wore a plain blue-black doublet without jewelry or ornamentation, and his bearing and expression were those of authority.

"Your Highness," she said, collected again, and curtseyed, perhaps mockingly.

"'Ware thy step, fair Oriana," said the man. He was seated before a dark drapery, a detailless background which gave no hint of his location. "We've rubbed along harmoniously in the past. 'Twere regrettable that I be forced to some measure we'd both find painful to dance."

She laughed. "Your brother is a fool, Prince Prospero."

"That's debatable, depending on which thou speakest

of," Prospero said, drawing on a pipe whose bowl was carved and painted to resemble a curling-horned ram.

"As long as your brother is a fool," Oriana replied, disregarding the other's unconcealed contempt, "we two, you and I, may continue in our present courteous relations. I will tell you a thing, Prince Prospero: I would rather see the Orb and the Well in your hands than Avril's; Pheyarcet prospers not in these days of his lame, blinkered rule."

"That reined you not from calling on him," murmured Prospero, fixing her with his eyes.

"He is a fool," she said again.

"He refused to cheapen Empire for sorcery."

"Yes," she admitted.

"I could have told you 'twould be thus." Prospero smiled. "Ill-judged of him." He looked at her for a long half-minute, saying nothing. "Last time," he said, exhaling smoke, " 'twas Esclados played Pandarus, tendering tidings to Avril—tidings which he bought from you, for Esclados can barely see his own face in a mirror."

Oriana's eyes narrowed. She began to speak and stopped.

"This time," Prospero went on reflectively, "you'd sell without his agency. Thy fair-faced flattery offends me, O Lady who dwells in the Castle of Glass, and it reminds me thou'rt treacherous as a Salamander unbound." He put the stem of his pipe between his teeth again.

Oriana smiled tightly. "I will also remind you that I keep my word," she said.

"That is true. When you are bought you are bought, an the fee be high enough and cunningly entailed." He blew a ring of bluish smoke, which tinted itself rosy slowly as it dissipated.

"I would be pleased to conclude some bargain with you which would serve us both advantageously," Oriana said. "For example, to know how you detected my Summoning of Vision toward Ithellin."

He snorted, smiling unamiably. "Doubt not that you would that, yet I'd not purchase privacy at such a rate. I compliment you on your subtlety and efficiency, Lady Oriana. Your work presses at the very boundaries of our

Art, o'ershadowing them. However, mine presses at other boundaries. 'Twere regrettable for your Art to stunt mine. I think they cannot be consonant."

The sorceress's expression was a mask of blandness. "You decline to deal with me?"

"I mislike to allow any such knowledge as your spells gather."

"I have never broken a contract! Do you imply that I would?"

Prince Prospero shook his head, holding the pipe and looking into its bowl. "Nay. I'll have none—not even you, dear, honorable Oriana—to know how I fare and whither and when."

Oriana lifted her eyebrows. "Oh?"

"Naturally, I'd not say that had I no means of enforcing it," he said, drawing on the pipe.

"Oh?" repeated the sorceress, coldly. "You challenge me?"

"Alas, no. I've struck aforehandedly. Wilt find it laborious and taxing now to use thy Mirrors for the duration of the war, madame. I apologize for the discourtesy, but I remind thee that thy past intrigues leave me scant ground to build trust with thee." He gestured, a wave of his hand, and the Mirror misted and dimmed, then cleared and showed Oriana only her own haughty visage.

She commenced at once another Summoning of Vision. But the spell was only words—when she Summoned the Well to it, the Well flowed weakly, an insufficient power to act on the words and structures. The Mirror of Vision misted, but the commands she had uttered slipped away and did nothing.

Oriana rose and left the room, hurrying to another chamber at the top of the Glass Castle's glittering keep, and there sought to find what Prospero had done—a barrier to the Well's flow, she suspected, such as the late Panurgus had often shaped, though she had never known how such barriers were made. All that day and the night through she labored vainly to fathom what spell he had laid about her and found no trace of any. At last, hissing a curse on the

Duke of Winds through her teeth, she went down again, and vented her frustration other ways.

Dusk had come early, or so it seemed; low, thick clouds had swept in and by their shadow advanced the season to its darkest. The Imperial household's lamplighters hurried through the Palace of Landuc, touching flames to wicks and hearths against the sudden night and cold. Yet the clocks had not struck the first night-hour, and so the gates of Landuc stood open and traffic still pressed through, some with torches and lanterns swinging and some merely benefiting from borrowed light. A city's lamplighters' guild is not so easily moved to respond to circumstance as those bound to the Emperor, and so the main thoroughfares were dark, even those leading to the Palace, and everywhere called voices uncertainly for misplaced associates and streets. "Loto? Your pardon, sir; he has an orange coat as well. Loto! Come up here, sluggard, we are scorching late!—Fire and Flame, this may be Chandler-street, but 'tis snuffed for all I can see of it.—Chandler's one down, my lord!—Mistress Sigune, may I offer this lantern and my arm?—My purse! My purse!"

A lightless messenger, riding up the dim and jostling road on his post-horse, saw his goal illuminated before him as he approached: windows sprung lit from obscurity to outline the wings, the towers, the walls, and then the lanterns were lit at the very gate he neared, a sight that heartened him to haste. The stone archway glowed with the Well's promise of haven and help. He fumbled at his neck for his pass-token.

"I've come from Ascolet," he told the lieutenant, as the lieutenant took the token from him and examined it. "I must see His Majesty at once. There's war."

"War? In Ascolet? Do the goats rebel?" asked the lieutenant. "Sir Strephon, isn't it?" He returned the pass-token.

"Yes—Chard Pirope! Lieutenant Pirope, I should say. How came you here? It's no joke, Pirope; there's blood shed already and my father's in great danger. I have messages for the Emperor."

"Then you'll have to see him, won't you? You, you; escort

Sir Strephon to His Majesty's presence with his news of revolting goats! And you can ask for me at the officers' barracks tomorrow, Stuffy."

Ten minutes passed, and the swarthy youth's hoarse breath puffed the flame of the lamp on the Emperor Avril's desk to and fro despite the chimney. His face was chapped with cold and wind.

"You have further news?" asked the Emperor curtly. He handed the letter over his shoulder to Count Pallgrave, scowling at the young man. "Where is our Governor, your father? He does not say."

"He feared I'd be taken, Your Majesty. Didn't write it. He is in Cieldurne now if all has gone well."

"The fortress."

"Yes, Your Majesty."

"With how many men?"

"He had about one hundred twenty when I left, Your Majesty. They were going to split—leave forty to hold the manor and distract the attackers while the rest went with him to Cieldurne. He counted on gathering allies, reinforcements, on the way; but, Your Majesty, in Verdolet I saw men mustering to go, they said, to the King, and they quizzed me roughly about my destination. My lord father may have met opposition on his way to Cieldurne if the countryside rose so quickly, and my mother was with him and sisters—"

"And eighty men of his household and in the Crown's service," said the Emperor. "Pallgrave, his token."

"Sire." Pallgrave handed the token back to the young man, a ring on a stained blue ribbon. It was one the Emperor had given the Governor-General of Ascolet, Earl Maheris, on appointing Maheris to the office.

"Count Pallgrave," the Emperor said, "Sir Strephon is our guest; let him be accommodated. Sir Strephon, we see you have travelled long and hard. You shall attend us again later."

"Yes, Your Majesty," Sir Strephon said, and bowed, and left the room with a footman to whom Pallgrave muttered something.

The Emperor scowled at Sir Strephon's back, recalling Oriana's remark.

The Emperor's next messenger arrived an hour later, in true darkness and just before the night struck, after His Majesty had spoken with Prince Herne and ordered him to begin preparations to take part of the standing army to Ascolet. This messenger was in worse condition than Sir Strephon, an older man with tattered clothing and battered gear. He rode his weary horse to the Palace gates and demanded entry of the guards there, who denied it to him.

"I've important tidings for the Emperor!" cried the messenger.

"We had one of those already today," said the lieutenant on duty. "You rode a little too slowly." The guards permitted themselves small smiles.

"I've come from the West! It's about the war," the man shouted, furious.

"The war's in the East," Lieutenant Pirope said.

"Idiot!" retorted the messenger, who was tired and overexcited, having lost three days on the wrong roads. He had circled the city without approaching it, misreading the signposts and kingstones, passing the same places again and again until he thought himself cursed. "My message is for the Emperor about the war!"

"You're drunk," said the lieutenant. "Get out of here before we arrest you."

"Holy Sun!" cried the messenger. "You'll be sorry if you keep me a minute longer when the Emperor hears of it! Ithellin is fallen!"

"Ithellin?" said one of the guards. "I'm from Ithellin! It's in the West, Lieutenant Pirope—"

"I know where Ithellin is!"

"Fallen how?" demanded the guard.

"The Dark Prince of the Air—"

"Don't say it!" cried the water-boy, who had been bringing the guards' supper when the man arrived. The superstitious among the guards brushed their arms and breasts in warding gestures to avert the attention of evil sorceries.

A shocked silence hung over the courtyard for a moment, and then the lieutenant said, "Dismount and come with me."

Count Pallgrave fixed the second messenger with a cold look as the man doffed his coat, a waistcoat, a jacket, and another jacket beneath. He produced from the inside of his innermost waistcoat a folded parchment document. The Count took the damp, sweat-stained letter gingerly, unfolded it slowly, and handed it to the Emperor with a bow.

> *To His Right Royal and Gracious Majesty Avril the Emperor of Landuc and Ruler of Pheyarcet Salutations from his Loyal and Devout Subjects the Master Guildsmen of Ithellin which is chartered a Free City under the Crown. We cry to Your Majesty for Assistance as is promised in our Charter in our Affliction of War which hath come upon us of a Sudden in the IIII Month of this Year the XXIII of Your Majesty's Long Reign. For on the Night of the Dark Moon in this Month we found our City surrounded by a Force which overpowered our Defense which could be but meagre being unready for Attack and having no Warning previous of Same and within the Day following were presented with a Choice of Death or Surrender by the Attacker whose Force battered the Gates of the City and was prepared to breach the Fortifications which have been a Protection to our City since its Founding. Upon which Presentation the Guild Council conferred and Elements within the Council who spoke Treachery and Treason against Your Radiant Majesty prevailed upon Reason to prostitute herself for them in persuading others of weak Conviction and flawed Morals that Capitulation to the Attacker who styleth himself Prospero rightfully King of Landuc—*

"Scorch his soul!" snarled the Emperor, with an inner wrench, and read on.

*—and in consensus unwillingly did we endorse this Treason against Your Majesty with the private Conviction that a live Ally serveth better than a dead Partisan. Thus do we present ourselves to Your Majesty as ready to carry out any Order which you might send by Courier or by Pudlock who beareth this Message to Your Majesty and hath sworn Blood-Oath to see its Delivery. The Number of the Army which lieth now without our Walls is Ten Thousand or greater and a Boy of sharp Eyes hath espied others unnumbered in the Wood which lieth beyond the Commons and the Number of the Vessels which to our Knowledge bore the Force hither is about Fifty but cannot be counted exact on account of Movements. We have heard Rumor of other Assaults and Victories at Methalin and the Seat of the Governor of the Province but Nothing hath come reliably—*

The Emperor snorted and paused at the proverb evoked there *(Indeed, the only thing more reliable than Nothing is Trouble)* and finished.

*—from either of those Places and so we take the Tidings with Salt. We do send this Petition to Your Majesty to invoke our reciprocal Duty of Assistance from the Crown in time of War as stated in the Charter of our City in the V Paragraph II Sentence and send also Assurance of the Support of those loyal to Your Radiant Majesty the Rightful Emperor of Landuc in the Name of the sacred Well. Signed this VI day of Bluth . . .*

There followed a half-dozen names and seals. He handed it to Pallgrave. "Verify the seals," he said.

Pallgrave murmured "It shall be done, Sire," and bowed.

The Emperor looked at Pudlock, the messenger. "You rode here directly, rather than to the Governor?"

"We had word, Your Majesty, Sire, that the Governor was dead, Sire, and it seemed a bad chance to take. I rode to Prendile, Sire, and took ship from there to Roysile."

The man had been uncommonly swift. Thirty-five days in winter—he must have had favorable winds behind him all the way along the river, his bad news borne on the cold blast from the West that had been frosting Landuc unseasonably. He could have gone overland to Chenay (the city where the Governor of the southern province of the same name dwelt), but to do so would have taken nearly as long as the ship voyage.

Prospero, at last. The Emperor had always known his older brother would return to recommence his battle for the throne. If Gaston did not defeat him this time, a fatal defeat, he would come again, and again, and again. This time there had better be no mistakes, or the Emperor might get him a new Marshal. The Emperor's jaw tightened. "You may go," he said to Pudlock, and "Cremmin!" as the man left, escorted by the lieutenant.

"Sire," said Cremmin, from his table near the door.

"Give the messenger from Ithellin sixteen crowns and suggest he join the army."

"Yes, Sire."

"We are not to be interrupted save by Prince Herne."

"Yes, Sire."

The Emperor Avril rose and went through a tall door into his private office, where he seated himself at the writing-table before the convex glass and performed the Lesser Summoning of Vision and Sound for Prince Gaston.

## ⸺ 11 ⸺

IN A LONG ROOM HUNG WITH maps and weapons, with three narrow-slitted deep-silled windows at one end and none elsewhere, two Princes planned war for an Emperor.

Prince Gaston, the Imperial Marshal, and his brother Prince Herne stood at an octagonal table of old dark wood. On it, covering the eccentric webwork of antique curlicues, scratches, and gouges which made it an unsuitable writing surface, a large map lay unrolled and weighted. They were placing counters deliberately, allocating forces, moving them, exchanging them, considering possibilities of weakness and strength. Over their heads above the table hung four yellow-flamed oil lamps in thorny black baskets, four flames per lamp; the flames cast a clear mellow light over the map and put sparks in Prince Gaston's hair and shadows in Prince Herne's tendrilled curls. Beyond the lamplit table, the walls and floor were dark and the windows hollow.

"If he has taken Ithellin, then he will next proceed up the Ithel River," suggested Herne.

"Too predictable," Gaston said. "Certes he'll move men there, but 'twill not be hard to dominate the region. He'll not waste any bulk of his force on't. Nay. The question foremost in my thought is, whether he be indeed in the West in Zeächath—or in Ascolet." And his finger tapped the Pariphal Mountains and drew a swift curving line along their length and northward, straight to the City of Landuc. "Think thou like Prospero, not like Herne, and recall his strategies afore this. His works are subtle, indirect, yet apt to his need. He blows hot and cold, here and there; ceaseless movement veils his central purposes. He's mutable, and in his mutability dwell both his strength and weakness. For I do believe that betimes his own deeds surprise him."

"We need fresher tidings," Herne said. He folded his arms and studied at the table. "Hm. Gaston, there was some rumor—very recent—about Lys."

"Lys?"

Herne grunted an affirmative. "You recall Red Bors of Lys—he died in that battle against Golias, with Sebastian. Lys's army turned that one for us. I can't think what I heard, but it was about Lys."

"Lys," Gaston said to himself. There, extending from the forested foothills of the Pariphals across the Plain of Linors, lay Lys, an inconsequential kingdom in bygone days, now a bucolic County.

Herne nodded. "Lys. It's too much of a coincidence, that we have trouble boiling up there and hear something or other from that backwater."

"The men of Lys fight well. I'll draw upon them 'gainst our opponent in Ascolet."

His brother frowned. "You think Prospero could be there?"

"I questioned Sir Strephon. He said that the men he met mustering did so in the name of the true King." Gaston picked a half-dozen counters up and weighed them in his hand.

"Prospero right enough. Odd. Ascolet's never been partial to him nor any but their sheep and goats."

"He'll have struck some bargain with them. Yet there be no grievances to my knowledge. 'Tis but another Crown province." Gaston placed three tokens near the City. "Hath ever Avril studied reviving that Barony?"

"No. I mentioned it to him once—I thought to reward my man Sir Anguran with at least a Baronetcy. Avril said it's as extinct as Sebastian." Herne snorted. "Anguran has nothing still," he said.

Gaston nodded and tapped a pass on the map. "He'll hold this ere I arrive, an he be Prospero," he murmured.

"You'll go to Ascolet?"

"Aye. The terrain's like to my Montgard. I'll bring men hither. An this be Prospero, shall want the best force available to me there; an it be some other, and Prospero in the West, then shall I put this down and join thee. Thou'lt take the mass of our forces with thee to Zeächath."

Herne pounded his fist into his hand. "That misbegotten sorcerer. I'll take his head off when I see him."

"That's no man's prerogative save the Emperor's, and methinks even he would hesitate to exercise it," Gaston said coldly.

Baring his teeth briefly in a humorless grin, Herne paced beside the table and watched his older brother allocate the army.

That night at the Emperor's semicircular high table, Prince Herne said, "I heard some news from Lys, but I can't recall now what it was."

The Emperor set his spoon down with a frown. Empress

Glencora, with a serious expression, sat a little straighter and watched him. Princess Viola took on a knowing look, and Princess Evote's mouth settled in a thin line. Prince Gaston continued with his soup without reacting.

"Your memory is usually not so poor," Evote said, and lifted her spoon to her lips.

"Well, it was *minor* scandal," said Viola. "Nobody took any note of it. Lys—really." She shrugged Lys to oblivion.

"Nobody with half a brain," the Emperor said caustically. "Lys. Yes, there was news recently. Why do you inquire?" he asked Gaston.

Gaston shrugged.

"Then it can wait," said the Emperor, "until we have supped."

And the meal resumed, with Viola unusually quiet as she strove vainly to recall particulars of the forgotten gossip from Lys that might hold secret significance.

Afterward, the Emperor collected Herne and Gaston with a nod and led them to his private office.

"Are you intending raising troops from Lys?" he asked point-blank.

"Aye," Gaston said.

The Emperor nodded.

"Something wrong there?" Herne half-asked.

"We hope not," the Emperor said. "This will be a test of whether anything has, as you put it, gone wrong. You recall that Bors and Sithe of Lys left one surviving child, a girl."

"The son died hunting," Gaston said. "I recall no girl."

"There was a daughter, much younger. Bors took his wife back to Lys when she was carrying, rather than stay here, although Panurgus wanted them to stay, Bors was a favorite—you know how he was. The wife died of childbed-fever, although the girl lived, and then Bors was killed. Thus the girl became a ward of the Crown, and the Crown appointed Baron Ocher of Sarsemar her guardian."

" 'Tis old business," Gaston said. It came back well, old Court feuding and jealousies, and not wholly as the Emperor told it. Avril himself had been the reason Count Bors had left Panurgus's Court, risking his King's displeasure. Bors had left in solidarity with Prince Sebastiano, Avril's and Gaston's bastard half-brother, whom Avril had manipulated into a quarrel with their father through ceaseless plotting, picking, and politicking. Less than a year later Sebastiano was dead, Bors was dead, Panurgus was dead. . . . The Fireduke remembered the truth of the business, far better than Avril would ever want anyone to do now that he had gotten his desideratum, the throne. Gaston blinked slowly and attended.

"Our concern was to secure Lys, because the armies of Lys are a useful tool. We had discussed with Ocher the possibility of his son marrying the girl, but Ocher himself was interested in her. He petitioned the Crown for permission when she turned sixteen and came out of first minority a few years back. Ocher had been . . . aggressive and we were pleased to deny Lys to him for the nonce."

"That incident with the Free Port," said Herne. "He's a braggart but a good soldier."

"A little too good. We had rather not have Lys's armies under someone with such obvious ambition to aggrandize himself and his lands. We have had other nibbles of interest in Lys and the girl, but we put them off because none was right, and we had no other good candidate for the place handy."

Gaston thought that he would not leave such a vacancy long open. Avril had always been too grasping.

"All very well," the Emperor said, pacing, "until last summer when we had tidings from Ocher. The girl, what's-her-name, eloped with a captain in Ocher's guard who was no fool at all, for he ran straight from Sarsemar to Lys with her and wed her on the first day of the appropriate auspices after her twenty-fifth birthday."

"Ah," said Gaston. "She came of age." Girls always did. And Avril's grasping hand had clutched nothing this time, lost its grip on the scion of Lys: tinder quickened at the touch of the match, become intangible flame.

"Exactly. We do not trust Sarsemar, but now there is a complete unknown down there. Ocher tried to get the girl back in time but failed and was beaten out of Lys soundly."

"It could be just as well," Herne said. "Recognize the new Count and give him some small favor, and he will perhaps serve better than Ocher."

"Perhaps. There's no doubt that the fellow has his own ambitions. Men don't do things that risky for the hell of it." The Emperor stopped in front of a locked cabinet and opened it. From a drawer he took a stack of papers and looked through them. "Here. Her name is Luneté. The man's name is Ottaviano. No family information—probably he's just a soldier who presented a more handsome face to the girl than Ocher's."

"They waited till her majority," Gaston said.

"So we said." The Emperor looked up inquiringly.

"Probably no coercion, then," Gaston pointed out.

"That means she rules, not he, since she inherited before the marriage," Herne said, understanding. "If he wanted power, he'd have taken her without waiting."

"Or he's a fool," said the Emperor.

"Hath the Crown recognized her?" Gaston asked.

"Yes. Ocher informed us of the abduction, so-called—she was still a Crown ward when that happened and he had to, or we'd have had to remind him of his obligations. He wrote again and informed us that he had failed to prevent the marriage after skirmishing in and around the Lys-Sarsemar border. The abduction was an offense against the Crown, but since it wasn't strictly a rape—they were formally betrothed before the man took her out of Sarsemar, very clever—the Crown took no action against them. Here," he picked up a paper, "she informs us that she has taken the title of Countess of Lys and cites her rights to it and so on, taking an administrative-oversight tone. As if we had forgotten to confirm her in the office. There was little we could do about it; we don't want to make a difficulty where none is needed. We sent back a confirmation of her right to the title and a request that she present herself at Court at her earliest convenience in order to be vested and to take the oaths."

The Emperor's plans were a sticky web of threads; Gaston saw them all. Avril now waited to see what sort of fellow the girl had taken, waited to see what she would do, waited to draw them into his influence. "Which she hath not yet done," Gaston guessed, leaning back in his chair and crossing his legs at the ankles.

"No. With winter coming, we suspect they'll not attend Court until spring unless we command their attendance."

"What's the husband's name again?" Herne asked.

"Ottaviano."

"Madanese?"

The Emperor shook his head. "Out of Ascolet. Ocher had nothing good to say about him, but we cannot be surprised by that."

"The sum is that we cannot be sure of Lys," said Gaston, "and there is war in Ascolet."

"Lys probably knows that," Herne said. "I say that we inform Lys that her men will be required by the Crown."

"As simple as that," Gaston said, studying his feet.

"Her husband can't be too stupid," the Emperor said. "He'll jump at the chance to distinguish himself, more likely. Quite a promotion, from soldier in Baron Sarsemar's service to Count of Lys."

Prince Gaston and Prince Herne were at their map again, discussing contingency plans, when a footman interrupted them with a request from the Emperor for their immediate attendance.

They collected their notes and locked the room, both being of untrusting and cautious disposition. The Emperor was in his private office again, and he was in a foul temper.

"Read this," he said curtly, and threw a letter at Gaston.

*Unto His Gracious and Radiant Majesty . . .*

Gaston skipped five lines of titles and honorific flattery.

*. . . from Lord Esandor Frett, His Majesty's Governor-General of Preszhëanea, salutations. I have sent this by the swiftest courier available to me and hope that it reaches you without delay. Word has*

*lately reached Eälshchar that there have been attacks in the southwest border region, by a substantial and well-organized force of men. Although reports varied widely, I have been able to ascertain that the force is quite large, 2000 to 2500 in number, and well-equipped. They have struck (to my knowledge) at four smaller villages (of 20 to 50 hearths) and a market town of 2600, Viddick. All have been looted and fired, and many of the residents were slain, taken as booty, or impressed into menial servitude.*

*Report of these attacks is causing high alarm in the area. I have dispatched the locally-posted Twelfth Regiment of the Army of Landuc thither, in accordance with the CXXVI point of my commission, but I am certain that a single regiment will be hard-put to defend an area so large from a mobile and opportunistic attacker.*

*There have long been difficulties, as Your Majesty is aware, with brigandage in the area known as "Outer Ascolet"; the incidents, however, have been in the south and west, particularly in the Pariphals along the Plain of Linors near Sarsemar. Preszhëanea is not prepared to meet or repel such assaults. I petition Your Majesty for reinforcement of the Twelfth Regiment with at least one other and for investigation, on the Ascolet side, into this assault. I have sent queries to Earl Maheris, Governor-General of Ascolet, and have had no reply. The messengers may have been taken on the road.*

*Awaiting your reply with great concern, I am . . .*

Gaston looked up from the letter, which had been written in haste and featured blots and crosses. "More trouble," he said, passing it to Herne.

The Emperor sneered. "Very astute, Marshal. More trouble."

* * *

"Oh, dear," said Luneté of Lys to herself, but aloud.

"Bad news, madame?" asked her maid, Laudine.

"I'm not sure," said Luneté, folding the parchment and tapping it against her chin. "Is the blue gown ready?"

"Yes; shall I bring it?"

"I'll want it tomorrow," Luneté said, and she opened the letter again. Rising, she walked to the window and reread her letter.

Laudine watched her, seeing her anxiety, and asked again, "Is it trouble?"

Luneté sighed. "We had foreseen something of this sort," she said, "and I—I simply quail somewhat at what my answer must be. That is all: the nervousness before the leap."

"This year has been full of leaps and bounds," Laudine said comfortingly, coming to her side.

"Yes, and we have landed on our feet every time so far."

"Because each time you have considered the jump ere you made it, and planned your way," the maid pointed out, "with circumspection and due caution each time. As for the leap of marriage, it's always blind; there's no way to know what comes with that."

"Indeed," and Luneté wryed her mouth, "that's small comfort. I do not like the chasm now before me."

Laudine looked at her inquiringly, and the habit of a lifetime made Luneté speak on.

"I must deceive my Emperor, who is my liege lord," said Luneté, "and I cannot help but think it a bad start and a rebellious one to a lifetime I had rather fill with harmony and goodwill."

"He calls for troops?"

"Yes, in such a way that I believe the intent would be to use them in Ascolet, under Prince Gaston. That is news also: the Fireduke is sent against Ottaviano."

"He did not expect it?"

"It did not seem likely. He thought the Fireduke would rather be sent into the West, to quell the disturbance lately arisen there. —My answer to this is ready-crafted, but still it mislikes me to turn coat against Landuc."

"It is not really against Landuc," Laudine said.

"It is. They will see it so. If Otto fails—"

"He cannot fail," said Laudine confidently.

"One would think you his wife." Luneté smiled, pleased by Laudine's loyalty.

"My lady, I have seen enough of men to know that that one is not lightly to be put down. If they have sent the Fireduke to do it, they are fools, for even he will not prevail against the men of Ascolet and Lys if they go, in their fatherland which they know well, fighting for a King in whom they have all faith and against one who robbed them."

Luneté nodded. "That's true," she admitted.

"He has planned it well, madame, you yourself have told me so: the winter will be his strongest ally, and if it be severe then the Fireduke will find himself doused and shivering."

Luneté laughed. "As the unwelcome troubadour below the balcony, eh? But with snow and ice. I am a silly girl to think about this now, Laudine. The decision was made, the plans laid, long ago, and we cannot now deviate from them. Send for Barriseo and I shall dictate my reply."

In the Pariphal Mountains south of Ascolet, autumn had come and fled. It never lasted long, not like the lazy, slow-ripening, heavy-fruited autumns of the plains where time poured by at the indolent pace of thick honey. The Pariphal autumn flickered through the high, sharp sides of the snow-topped heights hastily, preferring to linger on the hospitable lowlands, and only gave the mountains perfunctory attention in all phases. Snow flew in the air while the small yellow pemmefel fruit, sweet though seedy, hung still on the trees, those freezing which had not already dropped to become winy mulch for future sprouts or been eaten by the birds and beasts.

Dewar was standing by just such a tree at the edge of a mountain meadow, his heavy blue-green cloak thrown back over one shoulder despite the sandy white snow which scoured his cheeks and hissed in the twigs. It had dewed his dark beard with tiny droplets and whitened and then dampened his hair. His companion, in a red cloak, had a cocked bow in his hands and was watching a thicket upwind of them. The sorcerer was eating his way through a handful of chilly, honey-sweet pemmefel.

He was just crunching down on his last pemmefel when the other released the bow. The arrow hissed in the air and thudded into a russet-furred mountain buck's side, just behind its left foreleg; the animal leapt up, crashed out of the thicket, and staggered twenty or thirty paces across the meadow before it collapsed.

"It's not dead," observed the sorcerer. "I hate that about hunting."

"The last blow?"

"It ought to be clean."

"You're too squeamish, Dewar."

"I'm not looking forward to this war, either," said Dewar, picking another pemmefel, and he followed Otto to the deer. He bent and offered the fruit to the animal, pushing it into its mouth. Its jaw closed convulsively on the pemmefel, its eyes glazing. "Drink the untongued beast's blood, O Earth," he said, watching the hunter slash the buck's heaving throat. "You'll have better soon—"

"Knock it off," Ottaviano grumbled.

"It's a famous poem," said Dewar, smiling.

"Are you going to help me with this?"

"I'll help you carry it. I'll even help you carry it by finding a pole we can sling it on. Unless you had planned to put it over your shoulders like a proper vision of the Mountain King."

"I'll pass. My back is killing me after that workout yesterday. Where did you learn to throw like that?"

"Postgraduate research. I'll fetch a pole."

Otto watched his companion go and hack a sapling from the edge of the thicket whence the mortally wounded deer had run. Dewar trimmed the trunk roughly with a few cuts and then walked back, whistling, whittling off branches and brown leaves. The snow had stopped, but the thin wind still pushed the dry yellow grass back and forth.

"Somehow when I suggested *we* go hunting I had something else in mind," Ottaviano said drily.

"You suggested that I accompany you, and I have; it is more rewarding than hunting idle words and overheard rumors. This has been very pleasant. We have also had an excellent view of the Viden Pass all day, which we hope to be occupying tomorrow."

"The next day, probably, with this storm coming. The valleys may have deeper snow; it'll be slower travelling."

"We're well ahead of the Fireduke. It doesn't much matter." Dewar pared his sapling.

"You said he isn't in Landuc. Is he on the Road?"

"I told you: I cannot know. Prince Herne travels west, gathering levies as he goes. I'd give something precious to know what's up out there."

"Something big."

They looked at one another for a few seconds.

"If it's big enough," said Dewar reflectively, leaning on his trimmed tree, "they may summon troops from Lys."

"I expect to hear any day that the Emperor has done just that, to use either here or there. Since the Marshal is away, I'd bet he wants them when he gets back. The Fireduke keeps an army or two of his own in reserve, in that stronghold of his."

"If I were an Emperor, that would make me nervous." Dewar cleaned his knife on his pants leg.

Otto took the tree from him and began lashing the buck to it. "He's tame. No ambition along those lines. I've never understood why; he could've had it any time—"

"Since Panurgus's death—or before it. And he has not. So we must consider Prince Gaston to be a man who is either too smart to desire to rule or too self-effacing. Princes are seldom self-effacing." He sheathed the knife.

"He's not stupid, certainly. If Prince Herne is going west that means Prince Gaston is coming here, and frankly I'd rather face Prince Herne."

"Then go west."

"Funny man."

"You could," said the sorcerer, smiling a little. "There is

plenty here to keep Prince Gaston busy without you."

"The rebellion will die without me."

"Ah, but I did not say rebellion, did I."

"What I hate about you sorcerers is that you all talk in riddles. You know something new?"

"Something I had previously not seen as what it really is." The sorcerer bent and hefted the sapling, which bent with the buck's weight. "One—two—three!" On the third count they both lifted it up onto their shoulders and settled the burden comfortably.

"Tell on. If you're going to."

"Have you ever heard of a man called Golias of Charbeck?"

The pole crashed to the ground. Otto had dropped his end, spinning to face the sorcerer, who perforce put his down quickly too. The deer lolled on the frozen snowy grass.

"Golias? What about him?"

"So you have."

"Yes."

"Ah. Recently?"

"What do you mean?"

"I'm asking whether you've recently had any business with him," Dewar said.

"No. I'd thought he must be dead."

"No, he's not dead."

Otto demanded, "Then what about him?"

"We'd better keep moving. The snow grows heavier."

"Dewar, in three seconds I'm going to get pissed off—"

"I thought your back was bothering you. What do you know about him?" Dewar crouched down and took the pole in his hands again, his eyes crinkling with suppressed amusement.

"Why do you ask?"

"Curious."

"Curiosity has killed more than cats."

"As a sorcerer, I am well able to take care of myself. Tell me of Golias. Lift."

They heaved the carcass up again, Ottaviano smoldering.

Then he laughed. "You're like a little boy, you know? You have to have your surprises—"

"It's an endearing trait; I cultivate it. Golias, Otto."

"Well, how's your history of the turmoil around Panurgus's death?"

"I do know that Golias shifted from side to side in there. Seemed like he had it in for everyone and they had it in for him at the end."

Otto led the way down the meadow, picking his footing and his words. "My father died fighting him."

"Ah."

"My father Sebastiano was good friends with him. Golias knew Count Bors of Lys first, somehow; I'm not sure just how. Bors was friendly with my father, too. Golias's mother was one of the Palace women—he said a lady-in-waiting to Queen Anemone. Panurgus futtered around with her for a while, the usual thing, and then when she got pregnant blew her off. Had her sent off to one of those little retreats and informed her he'd no intention of making her Queen, which apparently disappointed her so much she ran away, off to the West, and hid and nursed her baby and her grudge until she died when he was in his early teens. They lived in a cottage; she had sold a lot of jewelry to get money, when she first ran off, and they used that to pay rent and they had a cow and poultry and pigs. She did some spinning and whoring and Golias did everything else. When she died, Golias took what money was left, which wasn't a little, and bought himself some good armor, a sword, a shield, and some lessons. He wasn't going to herd cattle and swine around for the rest of his life; he knew who he was, that he was the King's son, and he meant to make his mark in the world."

"A romance," Dewar commented. "I'm rapt. Go on."

Otto snorted, chuckling. "Yeah. I think maybe he romanticized it a little and sanitized it a lot. So Young Prince Golias—of course he didn't call himself that—went out into the world, sword in hand, and joined the Army. He liked the life, the travelling, and he found he had the charisma and talent to lead men. Much more to his taste than following livestock. He went independent and became a mercenary, recruited a company pretty quickly and got experience fighting in smaller wars, not in Landuc. That lasted about fifteen, twenty years, I guess. Then he distinguished himself in the Flange War by a lot of heroic deeds. All according to schedule. Unfortunately he didn't get the degree of distinction he wanted from that, though he did get the Well's favor by being knighted. In the last naval battle, he'd taken fifteen of the Flange ships, and he was naive enough to expect King Panurgus to be more grateful.

"Some people say it was Queen Anemone's doing that he wasn't. Golias slogged up to Court to be knighted and afterward announced his lineage to the King. The King denied it and laughed him out of the place. Anemone had borne many sons to him—he liked Queens who had boys, as Diote found out the hard way—and was high in favor and had a lot of powerful relations, friends, and supporters, and I'm sure the last thing she wanted to see was a bastard getting on equal footing with or precedence over her brood, like Princes Gaston and Herne. So Golias wasn't believed, wasn't permitted to bathe in the Well's fire, and was publicly humiliated."

"Not merely a romance, a cheap romance. Thrilling. Of course, Panurgus knew he was telling the truth; he was a sorcerer, and truth lives in the Well. Curious that he should endanger himself with the denial."

"Of course he knew. Stupidly, Golias's mother, I forget her name, hadn't bothered to get anything in writing about it, and the King could deny it up, down, left, and right, because there wasn't any way to prove it."

"There are ways," murmured Dewar.

"Say, this is a good way to distract me from the fact that I have the heavy end of this damn buck. Golias was incensed. He went back to his company, who believed him, and they were peeved too because they'd all figured on riding his coattails to the top. Since the Flange War was over, there were a lot of loose blades around, and Golias recruited them and headed toward Landuc.

"He had gotten friendly with Bors of Lys and Prince Sebastiano during the Flange War, I guess. They had supported him in his petition, and they were angry when Panurgus threw him out. Esclados was the last bastard the King recognized, and maybe he'd had enough of his old sins coming back to haunt him. He'd exiled and disinherited Prospero over his sorcery, and Prospero had already returned to attack the King on that account, and he'd come damn close to killing him. Maybe that famous wound was getting to the King and he was starting to think about an heir, and the second-in-line of the eligible Princes, Fulgens, is by nature unsuited to command the Well of Fire— Anyway, that's all old gossip, and the upshot is that Sebastiano persuaded the King that it would be worthwhile to recognize Golias. Panurgus agreed to acknowledge him, but refused to give him any titles or privileges. When he sent Sebastiano to Golias to say this, Golias got even angrier."

Dewar nodded, unseen. Otto seemed to have remarkably detailed knowledge of the business; perhaps Sebastiano his father had told him of it. How old was Otto? As a son of the Well, even unfired, he would change but slowly. "I can see how things could get complicated quickly."

"Yeah. One of those five-hundred-thousand-line epics full of blood, treachery, royalty, and stinking politics. In the end, of course, Panurgus unleashed Prince Gaston, who had been off somewhere flexing his muscles for a rematch against Prospero, Prospero raided Landuc again, and Golias lost everything."

"Except his life and his wits."

"Right. He took those off somewhere along with a king-sized hatred of Landuc, and if you're hinting that he's back again—"

"Sebastiano died in one of those battles, didn't he."

"Yeah."

"On whose side was he? He was Golias's friend—"

"He tried to stay out of it," Otto said. "In the end he fought under Prince Gaston. Had to. He was sworn to uphold the King and all that crap. He and Bors of Lys both."

Dewar, at the other end of the pole behind Otto, nodded again. The account he had heard had pointed out that

Sebastiano hung back, nearly losing the battle with that hesitation, and had claimed that the two bastard Princes had been planning to join forces and turn on favored Gaston. Dewar had also heard that Golias had taken refuge in Ascolet after the final battle over and within the Landuc city walls. However, it was understandable if Otto preferred not to discuss that side of the tale, and Dewar did not wish to overburden their still-fledgling friendship.

"So," Otto went on, "what about him? That's what I know."

"I had the impression you were personally acquainted."

Otto shook his head quickly. "No."

"Oh. Sorry. Well, he is somewhere to the north of here, burning and pillaging in southern Preszhëanea."

"Son of a bitch," Ottaviano hissed.

"He has confined himself to Preszhëanea thus far, and not intruded into Ascolet proper."

"How do you know this?"

"I know things."

Otto snorted. "Yeah. Well, that's very interesting."

"I'd wager, though," Dewar said, "that the Emperor and his Marshal do not know it. They know, that is, that they have trouble there, but not that it is Golias."

"Hm."

"Indeed."

"That's very interesting," Ottaviano said again. "I'll have to think about that."

"I thought you would. The tale was well-told, by the bye."

"I rushed it a bit because we were getting close to camp, and here we are. Ah—don't mention this elsewhere, naturally."

"Naturally."

They carried the deer carcass through the camp, past piles of packs and small tents where off-duty soldiers mended their gear or huddled knitting beside small, smokeless fires.

"Dewar, what's your cut in this?" Otto asked when they had set the kill down at the feet of a cook and started back to Otto's quarters.

"I prefer the haunch, roasted but not burnt, basted with wine and gravied with mushrooms," Dewar replied.

Otto rolled his eyes. "Come in here." He lifted the flap of his larger, floored tent and mock-bowed; Dewar returned the bow with grace and without seriousness, and they went in. Otto uncorked a half-empty bottle of wine. "You know what I meant."

"I know what you meant, and the answer I gave is as meaningful as any. I've said it before: I do not sell myself. I wish to see you win this war."

"Why is that?"

Dewar shrugged, smiling slowly, and lifted his cup. "Victory, Your Highness."

"Victory."

They sipped. Dewar made a face. " 'Tis better mulled."

Otto banged his cup down. "I don't know what to do with you, Dewar. You ambled in a little too nonchalantly, you hung around all summer and helped chase Ocher out of Lys, you're tagging along on my personal war, and all you want is bed and board? Come off it. Sooner or later there's going to be a price to pay." He examined his companion as if something in his face or clothing would change and tell him what that price would be.

"I hope not," Dewar replied. "However, if you do not trust me, I will leave. And I will not be joining Prince Gaston, either. I have plenty of other affairs to look into."

"You're a hell of a sorcerer," said Otto. "Why hasn't anyone heard of you?"

Dewar shrugged, cleaned the fingernails of one hand with the other's. "I *am* modest."

Otto made a rude noise.

"Come, come, Otto. Why this, now? Because it comes close to an acid test?"

"You're too good to be true! Speaking of cheap romances and threadbare fairy tales—sorcerers, hotshot sorcerers who can rearrange a mountainside with a couple of words and a thump of the staff, do not just waltz in out of nowhere and offer to help out rebellious would-be Kings—"

"Certainly they do. The stories get started somehow,

Otto." Dewar grinned, then laughed. "What *has* gotten into you? I would never have thought of it that way. Did you train as a skald sometime?"

Otto sighed. "Put yourself in my shoes, Dewar."

"I do," Dewar said. "I think: I am a military man of no small ability fighting a hugely superior force. I think: I need all the help I can get. A man volunteers his services. He serves well. Do I refuse?"

"Put that way, no. But you've stripped out a lot of little details. Like, I don't actually know anything about you."

"All I know about you is what you have told me," Dewar said, "and more importantly, what I have seen. If I did not think you were worth the trouble, I'd be on my way months since."

They stared at one another, eye to eye, a mutual challenge.

Otto broke the silence. "All right. Let one thing be clear between us, though: If you turn coat on me, if you're playing a double game, if you betray me in any way—I'll never rest until I have your skin on my wall."

Dewar smiled and shrugged. "Fine."

Otto stared at him a moment longer. "Fine. Have another drink."

"No, thank you. I have work to do, but be assured I shall be done when the venison is."

# — 12 —

A MAN HAD RIDDEN TO LYS with a letter, and now he rode back to Ottaviano's camp in the dry, hard ice-wind. Snow had not fallen in Ascolet in nearly a month, not since the Fireduke had led his soldiers there. This unusual drought was attributed by Otto's army to the force of the Well, but they did not take it as an ill omen for their defeat, because it worked as much to their advantage as to Gaston's. The messenger was a shepherd, native to the area, and knew the cliff-walks and hidden paths well, and the Marshal's men that prowled everywhere around Ottaviano had not seen him, nor even scented him.

His sturdy mountain horse was weighted with a chest and two heavy bags. He gave the pass-words to Ottaviano's patrols, when he chose to meet them near the camp, and he went, as he'd been instructed, straight to the uncrowned King of Ascolet's tent and there delivered himself, with a grunt, of the burdens and, with a salute, of a letter.

Ottaviano opened the letter first. A weighty lump of wax made a clumsy wrinkled blob at the bottom; scratching with his pocket-knife showed metal—a coin? No, it was a ring. He read.

> *Right well beloved husband, I recommend me to you, and knowing your urgency I shall dispatch this letter and your man Hedel as soon as he may be rested and freshly horsed. I send to you again the pledge-ring I gave to you on our wedding-day, which you sent to me by your man that I might know his message to be truly from you. I do sadly charge you to find some better way for us to know our letters, for this is no meet way to use a token of my love. Your letter brought me great joy as I had not had since tidings of the Prince Marshal's coming to Ascolet reached me. My joy is greater still that I may help you speedily to conclude your business, and that you may bring it twice as swiftly to the best end, Hedel carries with him in gold double the sum of money you asked of me. Let there be no word of loans and interests between us. Though you have need of men I can provide you only the coin to hire them, for a rider from the Marshal has borne to me a message, saying that in the Emperor's name he will have me raise men for him, and I dare not serve him falsely. That some did volunteer to go with you I can conceal, yet I mislike that any of Lys should enter this war, and I shall delay as I can, for I would no more see Lys blood spilled than yours. I pray that you will make haste to victory and that we shall soon sit at table and*

*dine together. It must happen for the truth of the Well is in your cause. I have no leisure to write half a quarter as much as I desire and I pray that you will wear my ring, while yours is fast upon the hand of your wife Luneté Countess of Lys.*

Ottaviano read but halfway through this letter, then threw it down and hastily opened the two metal-bound leather sacks and the coffer Hedel had brought him.

Golden royals lay there, sleek and cold to touch, some new that bore the Emperor's head, some old with the hawk-nosed glare of King Panurgus, three glinting piles of money, enough to hire the whole of Golias's company. Ottaviano, grinning, began laughing softly to himself, and he plucked a coin from each bag and one from the coffer and tossed them in the air, one after the other, pinging them with his thumbnail and dropping them back in their piles.

After several minutes of quiet glee, he recalled there had been something about the Marshal in Luneté's letter, and he took it up again and finished reading it. She had taken the ring-sending entirely in the wrong way, which irked him, but by the Fire she had come through with money and information and the intangible but important aid of time. If she could keep Prince Gaston waiting for the levy from Lys just long enough for Ottaviano to send for and plan with Golias, then she was worth a dozen rings, a different gem on each, one for every finger and two for her ears.

Ottaviano closed up the bags and the coffer again. He'd have the paymaster count the money while he drafted his second letter to Golias. And the Fireduke would get a singe-ing he wouldn't forget.

The uncrowned King of Ascolet fairly jigged from his cold tent out into the camp to find Dewar to tell him the news, stuffing the letter inside his jacket.

Prince Gaston, the Fireduke, stood with his hands out-stretched. Beneath them leapt flames. When the wind died down, they came almost so high as to lick his palms, but never quite managed it, and the Prince Marshal never flinched back from them. He was staring into them, thinking hard, and his captains were doing similar things, some crouched, some with their backs to the fire, some rubbing hands over it, some scooping cups of mulled wine from a blackened pot that squatted at the edge of the coals. The Prince Marshal was not fidgeting. When the wind blew, he stood and let it go around him; when it stopped, his cloak fell back to his heels unregarded.

His captains around him respected the Marshal's mood and did not address him directly. They talked among themselves, businesslike and low, reviewing parts of the day's battle and praising or blaming the actors. There was little to blame. The Marshal's forces were superb.

But Prince Gaston had met a nasty shock today on the battlefield, and he was considering what he could do to prevent it happening again. The Fireduke did not like surprises. He especially disliked them when they happened in war. Although he accepted his own fallibility and had years ago come to terms with the fundamental imperfection of all human endeavor, the day's discovery was a thoroughly unpleasant thing to have found out with no warning, no prefigurement in any of his intelligence.

The flames shaped all with moving light, flowing shadows; and ceaseless wind pushed the flames to and fro. The golden-glowing Prince crossed his arms.

This surprise could cause Landuc to lose the war. His opponent, eight days ago revealed to be Sebastiano's son Ottaviano, styled King of Ascolet, was not badly placed now. He had more local support than before; he was handling the areas he controlled very generously and they had no sense, to see how it would change if he won and took Ascolet from Empire, losing wool-buyers and grain-sellers. He was young and rash, but he showed a canny mind. Gaston wondered what Otto had paid for the sorcery that had cost Gaston blood today: a hundred lives. Surely it had not come cheaply. What paid and how? It might be a weakness.

Flanked like a greenhorn. Gaston's fists clenched. He

would not be fooled again. If Ottaviano's men could move under cover of illusions, invisible to the Marshal's scouts—then Gaston's scouts must work harder. Sorcery could be countered with vigilance; this he had learned against Prospero years before.

If this so-called King of Ascolet was indeed, as Ocher claimed, the man who had wed the young Countess of Lys, Lys might rise to support him; the Lys levy under Gaston's command fought reluctantly now, for some of their own had already volunteered to fight for Ascolet—nominally, treason, but difficult to prosecute when they had done so before the levy. Lys and Ascolet shared a border—but that was irrelevant at the moment. Lys was not in league with Ascolet. Whether Ascolet was in league with Prospero or not remained to be seen.

Ottaviano's sorcerer added another unpleasant dimension to the war. Gaston would have to tell the Emperor they needed a sorcerer. If the Crown wanted Ascolet's uprising put down and Prospero conquered too, the Crown would have to meet Ascolet's forces evenly. It was too easy to waste too many lives thus.

The Emperor would not like it. He, or Pallgrave, would insist that the Empire could not afford it, that the Fireduke must continue without a sorcerer. However, another loss such as that day's at Erispas would require half an army again of him. The Empire could not afford that either, with Prospero pushing Herne eastward.

The Fireduke flexed his bare hands slowly in a shower of sparks; some landed on the backs, to lie burning there, unburning, not even scorching a hair. He shook them off.

He ought to be in the West, not here. Prospero was the greater threat. Avril should see that. It was a misallocation of forces. The Empire should make an agreement here and let the Fireduke drive the rebellious Duke of Winds back from the shore to the ocean again. The Emperor could recognize the boy as Baron. Prince Gaston suspected he'd take that. Political rhetoric aside, it was more than he had now and he would not have to fight so hard for it. Youth was impatient. Ottaviano might leap at the chance.

A nephew here, a brother there. The Prince did not like fighting blood-kin.

The Fireduke nodded to himself, spun on his heel with a nod to the circle of men and a quiet good-night, and went to his tent.

There he opened a locked iron box on the table. From it he took things that clinked and chinked softly against one another, things that gleamed in the lamplight. He poured oil in a long, flat bronze dish from the chest, sat down, drew the lamp a little nearer, and took a light from its wick.

Moments later he faced his brother Avril's image in a sheet of flame.

"Your Majesty."

"Good evening, Gaston. Or is it?"

Prince Gaston shook his head.

"What now?" the Emperor asked, sharply, not hiding his annoyance.

"Our nephew hath worked a trick which I must applaud for its cleverness, Avril, as must you. By all evidence he hath hired Golias."

"Golias!"

"Yes."

The Emperor's eyes narrowed and he breathed slowly, hard. Gaston sat as calmly as he had before.

"You've beaten him before," the Emperor said finally.

The Marshal nodded. "If 'twere but Golias, my plans would not be perturbed. However, together he and Ottaviano, as I judge by the fight Ottaviano hath fought afore this, are more able than either is alone. And 'tis not Golias alone who aids Ottaviano. I took heavy losses today at Erispas. As I pursued Ottaviano, Golias swept in from a wood my scouts had reported empty and did great damage. Truly I was baited—Ottaviano's forces turned and engaged me as Golias hit, a perfect trap. Golias had lain low there, concealed by sorcerous working."

"Sorcery!" snapped the Emperor. "You're certain it's Golias?"

"I am certain. I took two of his wounded and put them

to question. It is Golias. Ottaviano hath a sorcerer as his ally, but they know little of him save that he worked the spell of concealment on them. Golias is using the same banner as before, also."

The Emperor said a hissing word. Gaston ignored it.

"I must have more men to continue against both; Golias hath a large force and fresh, and I, though I have done well thus far, have been here a while now in severe weather. I fear they will cut my supply lines—although, were I Ottaviano, I'd have sent Golias to do that at once rather than throw him directly at me. 'Tis a flamboyant gesture, a young man's tactic."

"Cripple you, then jump."

"Aye."

"We cannot send you more men now. Herne needs them against Prospero. He advances rapidly."

Gaston held Avril's eyes through the flame. "Then do I recommend that you make an accommodation with Ottaviano and send me to face Prospero with Herne."

"No."

"An you make the place a barony again, give it to the boy, he might accept it and be satisfied, and I'll take him to the West 'gainst Prospero."

"Landuc does not yield," the Emperor said through gritted teeth.

Prince Gaston said mildly, "Landuc yields naught. Landuc takes his fealty. He becomes a vassal."

"And we still have that jackal Golias around. Maybe we'll say conditionally yes, Gaston—we'll make peace with Ottaviano for Golias's head."

"To whom would you extend this offer?"

"We're joking."

The Fireduke said nothing.

"Or maybe not," murmured the Emperor, and sat back, biting his lower lip. His eyelids sank. "Hm. Hm. Then what do we have. Dead Golias, live Baron of Ascolet, a bunch of loose mercenaries you can pick up . . ." He began to smile. "Ah, Marshal. You are not quite subtle enough. A dead man cannot be made to live, but a live one can be killed. We will grant Ottaviano, son of a bastard, the Barony of Ascolet. We will pardon Golias. We shall set thereto a condition: that they shall both with their armies, including those of Lys which are due to us from the imprudent Countess of Lys, oppose Prospero under your command."

Gaston said nothing again.

"We are now not joking," the Emperor said drily.

"I misdoubt how steadfast Golias's hirelings would be 'gainst such opponents as Herne faces."

"Surely the bait can be made very attractive. Every man has his price."

Prince Gaston did not speak, but he shook his head slightly.

"Except you, we all know."

The Fireduke was thinking about it. "'Twould be in them to turn on us and demand more at first opportunity," he said at last. "However, if thus is your will, 'twill be done so."

The Emperor scowled. "We hear little enthusiasm, though we have solved your problem for you, Marshal."

Slowly, Gaston shook his head. "It will serve—perhaps. 'Tis Golias I mistrust. The boy's young. He'd come to heel with a dram of coaxing, meseems—soft words, small favors . . . pity he's married."

"We have no daughter, appearances to the contrary, but we see what you're getting at. Make him Baron, recognize his connection to Landuc, treat him like one of the family. Hell, he is one of the family if he's Sebastiano's son. Glencora can tickle him round. She knew his mother Cecilie and Sithe of Lys—she was one of Anemone's women—and she could use that as an in with what's-her-name. Lys. The only question is when we'd find the time for such folderol. It would be best to get him over there sooner, rather than later."

Avril never changed, thought Gaston. "Well, I will put the proposal to him."

"Let us consider this yet two days more before you do," the Emperor decided.

"Very well. Yet your consideration will cost the Empire

blood. Let your thoughts hold that also." Prince Gaston inclined his head slightly. The Emperor still had not addressed his second concern. "And the sorcerer?"

"Well, we'd be pleased to throw him at Prospero too. Whichever one got blasted, we'd be ahead. Have you seen him?"

"Nay. Nor have I had success finding out who he is. He must be one of Ottaviano's captains, or feigning so; but they are many and they hail from different quarters, thus none knows much about the rest. My spies have given me scant ground on which to found a surmise, and the prisoners know little of use."

"The idea of a sorcerer getting into such a war is disturbing," the Emperor muttered. "They're all supposed to be under oath to the Well, the Crown. They're not supposed to be able to oppose it."

Gaston waited.

The Emperor shook his head. "We cannot afford a sorcerer. If you wish to hire one, the Empire will sanction the contract but will not be a party to it."

"I see," Prince Gaston said.

"An Emperor cannot make the kind of bargain one of them would want to strike. We cannot engage in that kind of commerce."

"As you will, then. I do not have time to seek one out and negotiate, nor could I delegate such an important task. I will wait for your word on the other business."

# — 13 —

IN AN ANCIENT HOUSE SURROUNDED BY titanic gnarled trees which shade and darken every window, a man whose hair and beard are the color of snow warmed by late golden sun sits reading a letter in a deep, comfortably-cushioned armchair which has assumed the imprint of his body through long use. His slippered feet are propped on a little stool embroidered with roses and a motto—"Vere veritatem servire"—and his elbows are accommodated by cushions similarly decorated by the same hand. On his long, thin hands are three rings: on the left hand, middle finger, a plain band with a lock of brown hair braided around it; on the right third finger, a gold signet ring engraved with the wearer's arms (five roses in a wreath); and beside it, on the middle finger, a plain, heavy silver ring with a dark-blue cabochon stone. The autumn sun enters the red-curtained windows and angles down onto the brown carpet in heavy, dust-laden beams.

The man's light blue eyes are on the letter, which he holds within eight inches of the end of his nose. His brows are slightly raised with the effort of focusing; his expression is mildly bemused. On his lap lies a handsome book bound in tooled red leather whose spine is a little misshapen, a little frayed at one end; on the floor lies brown wrapping paper and oilcloth and a tangle of string in which the book had been packed. The letter is pleated in many small accordion folds.

A woman stands at one window, looking out through the bare branches of a tree at the gardeners raking and sweeping the lawns.

"Father, what is it?" she asked softly after a long, thick silence.

"Eh," he said. "Eh. Come see." Slowly, he lowered the letter and let her quick fingers snatch it, her sharper eyes racing over it faster than his. The sun tinted her smoothly knotted hair, which was the color of a winter morning, and to her fair cheeks came the bright hue of emotion.

"Here," she whispered.

"Not even near," her father said. "Not even near. But more here, than elsewhere." He chuckled drily. "Hah. This shall be fun. I am sure he is ready this time."

"Last time he moved too quickly," said the woman softly.

"Anger does that to a man," he said. "Act in haste, repent at leisure. Yet may one consider well and still repent at leisure."

She lowered the letter and looked at him, a line dividing

her brows. “We have done nothing to repent of,” she said. “I regret nothing, would regret nothing had it been much worse.”

“So dost thou repent at leisure with me,” said he, but smiling.

“What shall we do?” she asked.

“Do? Nothing.”

“Nothing!?”

“Not a blessed thing. Think, Miranda: He knoweth his work. Were there any aid we could render he would ask.” The man walked slowly to the window where she had stood in the sun and stood as she had watching the gardeners. “Another winter upon us,” he said. “Ah, we have had better fortune than most. Beort, beheaded. Chargrove, poisoned. Tebaldo and Truchio, hanged. The others . . .” He did not finish.

“They will all be vindicated,” she said, lifting her chin.

He nodded, his back to her, his mouth turned down. Though their tombs be hammered to rubble, their bodies limed in a pit-grave, would their souls rest easier, vindicated?

Outside, the gardeners removed the leaves from the lawn lest they decay and mar it.

Miranda read the letter again, her eyes devouring each word and taking on fire and intensity of purpose. “If I were a man!” she cried, dropping the letter and striking her palm with her fist. “He would have taken me with him—”

“Nay. He would not,” said her father. “He went alone because he must. We understood. Wert thou a man, belike we would have ended as the others.” This was an old argument, familiar to both of them, and he sighed a little at its reiteration.

“I know,” she said wearily. “I know. Father, I am sorry to plague you. I hate this inaction. It is *worse* than being dead, being thwarted so, and the waiting, the waiting that has gone on, and now we have only a few words in a letter which may be no more than rumor.”

He shook his head. “No. This is true tidings. I feel it

. . . in my bones." His hand, unseen by her, clenched around the heavy silver ring.

"It is good of Fidelio to send the news. He takes a great risk each time," Miranda said. "Someday I shall thank him. Someday *he* shall thank him."

# — 14 —

THE STEEP SIDES OF THE PARIPHALS are solid grey rock lightly coated with scree and, below the higher perennially-iced peaks, moraine. The gentler slopes of loose matter provide support for any number of trees large and small and for broad meadows drained by whimsically twisting streams. The mountains' lower flanks are cut by water-graven sheer-sided canyons, whose floors form natural livestock pens for the Ascolet herdsman and a brutally limited field of battle for an army.

Otto had baited Gaston into such a canyon, one which sloped gradually and whose walls were, at first, far apart; Golias had attacked the Fireduke there, and the Fireduke had turned and fought his way out, a purchase not cheap but necessary. Now Imperial soldiers were scattered along the canyon rim, bivouacked and firing bolts at the Ascolet army when it showed itself and sometimes when it only betrayed its presence by movements in the brush and sapling spinneys. Gaston himself lay with more soldiers some little distance away, in the frozen floodplain of the Parphinal River where it had scooped out a valley for itself—a canyon again, but one with maneuvering room. A drovers' road to Erispas, unpaved but wide-trampled, ran above the river and, three miles upstream where the cliffs drew together again, a narrow five-arched stone packhorse bridge arched over it, out of reach of the meltwater floods.

Secure from the bolts and arrows of the Empire's sentries, a bareheaded messenger carrying a green bough rode along the drover's road, then up into the canyon, and slipped out of sight in a cluster of high-topped evergreens.

Among the trees, Ottaviano and Golias watched the big-chested bay horse trot toward them with tall Dewar in his bright cloak on its back. When he arrived, Otto held the horse's head as the sorcerer dismounted.

"You're not going to believe this one," Dewar said, grinning.

"Try me," Golias said. "He wants my head, and then it's all pardoned."

Dewar shook his head, grinning still. "Better than that."

Otto handed the horse's reins to a groom, murmuring "You're welcome" to himself with a sidelong glance at Dewar. "Let's go inside, shall we?" he said aloud.

They walked to Ottaviano's tent. Ottaviano turned and said "Well?" softly as soon as they were inside.

"The man has imposing taste in wine," Dewar said.

"Everybody knows that," Otto said. "What else?"

"He is imposing in height as well."

"Dewar, knock it off. What did he say?"

"I thought I'd start with things you'd recognize as true, to enhance the improbability of his proposal. Here you are: If you and Golias will haul up and trek off with him to join Prince Herne in his defense of the Holy Homeland against Prince Prospero—"

"Then the rumors are true!" exclaimed Ottaviano. Golias snorted.

"I said they were," Dewar said coolly. "I also said it worked to your advantage. If you will do this, you, Ottaviano, become Baron of Ascolet, and you, Golias, are pardoned and named Prince; you both are permitted to bathe in the Well's fire, taken into the familial fold, and bygones go by the board." Dewar smiled slightly. "I think there is not much flexibility in this offer. The Marshal indicated that several times, subtly; he murmured that the Emperor's clemency should not be tested."

"Baron of Ascolet," muttered Ottaviano.

"My first thought on hearing that, Otto, is that it is no less than your father had."

"That is true," Otto said. "For Golias, pardon."

"Which is no small thing, considering how they feel about you," and Dewar nodded to Golias.

"I don't give a black shit what they think. Anything else?"

"Not that he spoke of then. That may be the one item for which we can negotiate more: land for you."

"I'd settle for cash."

"You might not be able to get that. Wars tend to leave governments long on good intentions and short on coin."

"Cash on the nail," said Golias. "What do you want to do, Otto?"

"I'll have to think about it."

Golias snorted. "He's offering this now because he'll take heavy losses and probably lose."

"I do not tell futures," Dewar said, bowing slightly.

Otto leaned back and drummed his fingers lightly. "I'd rather have it be an independent country again," he said. "They will think I've sold short. I'll think I've sold short. For the privilege of facing down the man the Emperor fears more than anyone alive."

"Is there a deadline?" Golias asked.

"I said you would tell him tomorrow at the same hour and so on whether it be acceptable or we desire more time in consideration. If we attack or move in the meantime, he will consider that a refusal and hostilities go on as previously scheduled."

"I wonder if he's stalling for time," Otto muttered.

This hadn't occurred to Dewar. He lifted his eyebrows. "Why?"

They looked at one another and then at Golias, who, a veteran of war with Landuc, was most familiar with the opponent.

Golias said, "Reinforcements."

"Not that I've seen," Dewar said. "I wonder where they'd come from. They seem to be throwing everything to Herne. Rightly, too; Prospero is a greater danger, though distant."

"Then he wants to finish this up and head out after Prospero," Ottaviano decided. "Hm." He slouched further down in his chair, tipping it, and propped his feet on a chest. "Is there any advantage to us in continuing to fight here, now, if Gaston really wants to leave?" he asked, half-aloud.

"Prince Gaston isn't going to walk away from the fight," Dewar said, shaking his head. "*Think* of what people would say."

"No, no. I'd never expect that. Maybe if Prospero marched on the capital, Gaston would evaporate for a while and come back later," Otto said testily. "I wonder . . ." His voice trailed off; he took his oblong red folding knife from his pocket and began tapping it against his left palm. "Prospero," he said in an undertone.

Golias poured wine for himself. "It's to Prospero's advantage that we delay Gaston here," he said.

"It is," Dewar said. "No doubt he's very grateful to you."

"How grateful do you think he is?" Otto asked his pocket-knife, cleaning a bit of grit from its handle with a fingernail, then opening the knife and beginning to clean his fingernails.

Dewar chuckled softly, shaking his head.

"What's funny?" Otto asked.

"I think it sounds like a good question," Golias said. "How grateful is he? Can he beat the Emperor's offer?"

"You just send round and ask him," Dewar said. "Do you think he doesn't know about you, about the war here? Of course he knows. If he were interested in prolonging it, you would have heard from him, or from a proxy." He glanced at Golias for a moment. "Have you?"

Ottaviano looked up from his knife, his attention caught by the sharp note in Dewar's voice. "Have you?" he echoed, when Golias said nothing.

"Not lately," Golias said. It was true; he had heard nothing from Prospero for the past twenty-five days. Twenty-five days ago, he had received payment in advance for the coming quarter's mayhem, a shaggy pony trotting up to him with four bags of well-muffled coins in its panniers. Golias had counted the coins, had slapped the pony and sent it trotting back wherever it came from, and a few days later had entered into contract with Ottaviano—at the rate of pay Otto had agreed to, which had been one and a half times Golias's last.

Otto had been somewhat surprised by the answer, but Golias had pointed out that the costs of doing business, for the independent man, had increased steeply.

"What did you hear and when?" Otto asked.

Golias gave Dewar a look of unveiled dislike. "I've worked for him," he said.

"Doing what?"

"That's confidential, Your Highness," Golias retorted.

"So it is," agreed Ottaviano, nodding. "I beg your pardon. I didn't mean to pry." Otto admired the underhanded, yet open, way in which Dewar had just made him aware that Golias's interest, after all was said and done, was in staying alive and getting paid for it, not in settling; had warned Golias that he knew more than Golias might like about the mercenary's business affairs; and had pointed out courteously that deals struck with Prince Prospero were unlikely to benefit anyone but Prospero. Dewar, one of these days, would make somebody a hell of a Privy Counsellor.

"Don't see any point getting in touch with the Duke of Winds, now that you put it that way," Otto said, frowning a little. "If he wanted to exploit this, he'd have made an offer. Maybe what he wants is to face Prince Gaston fast—before he's had the expense of a drawn-out fight, before he has to spread himself out holding territory." He thought, trying to second-guess Prospero. Prince Gaston was probably much better at doing so. Ottaviano began fiddling with his pocket-knife again. "What was it the Marshal said about the offer, Dewar?"

"That the Emperor's clemency should not be tested. Those were his words," Dewar said. "I suspect strongly that the corollary is that, if you refuse now, there will be scant clemency later. Clemency does tend to decay, if not plucked promptly."

Golias grunted. "Clemency. Yeah. We get to go fight for Avril, instead of ourselves."

Dewar shrugged. "Fighting and causes and so on aside," he observed, "they are much alike, being baron of a large and powerful barony owing fealty to an Emperor and being king of a relatively small and poor kingdom neighboring the same."

"Alike?" Otto said. "What about the small clauses of fealty, requiring me to go fight Prospero if the Emperor tells me to?"

"Oh, well, that," Dewar said. "I suppose. Looking at it in terms of lives lost—" He shrugged again. That was Ottaviano's problem.

Lives. Ottaviano hadn't considered that. How expensive might it be to hold Ascolet against a merciless and impatient Gaston, who might have men diverted from Herne if he so desired, reinforcements provided to speed victory here and free Gaston to meet Prospero? How long could Ottaviano hold out? Golias and his mercenaries would melt away as soon as Luneté's gold was all in their hands, and that would not take long, for they were expensive to hire. There would be no military assistance from Lys, for Luneté had—after such delays as she dared use—raised the Emperor's levy of troops there for Gaston and could send no more to Ascolet without treason.

If they were facing Josquin, who (from what Otto had heard) was far and away the least competent of the Princes, or one of Gaston's subordinates in the Imperial Army, the chance of victory would be much greater. Ottaviano had not expected to face the Imperial Marshal himself—nearly in person, the other day, separated by a dozen strides on the battlefield, swinging his long sword and lopping an arm off one of Otto's men. King Panurgus had appointed the Marshal because he was the best man for the job of defending and expanding Landuc. Emperor Avril had kept him on for that reason.

King of Ascolet, Baron of Ascolet. Which was better? It was easy for Dewar to toss off witty remarks about kings and barons. It wasn't his name, his future at stake. Ottaviano had decided when he first learned of his ancestry that he would be King of Ascolet, and by the Fire in him he would do it. But what did it mean to be king of a place conquered, precariously, at the cost of the lives of so many of its able-bodied men? They had lost a tenth of their force already. Otto hadn't expected so many deaths, so much slow-killing pain and so many frozen bandages. Would the throne be secure, set on bones and blood of its own citizens?

Otto opened and closed his heavy knife: big blades, little blades, awl-punch, corkscrew . . .

Suppose, Ottaviano thought, suppose he won here now and were deposed later, by citizens or Prince Gaston. Looking at it as a problem he faced from the Emperor's side, Otto would be dead. The Emperor took a dim view of rebellion; the fates of Prince Prospero's old friends and allies showed that. Dead was a pretty permanent state to be in. There wasn't much chance of improving it. A live Baron, however, might better his position at opportune moments—later.

Ottaviano snapped shut the blades of his knife, one by one. "I'll ask you, Dewar, to act as spokesman again, tomorrow," he said. "You'll tell him I accept the offer."

"Surrender!" Golias exclaimed.

"If you don't want to be included," Ottaviano said, "I'll do what I can either to get you a safe-conduct or to cover for you while you leave. Up to you. We can try to freight that title of Prince with more material ballast."

Golias looked at Ottaviano, imperfectly covering his contempt. "Surrendering," he repeated, shaking his head slightly, and he looked at Dewar disdainfully. Dewar seemed to be dozing in his chair, but Ottaviano saw his eyes glittering under lowered lids. "I'll speak for myself," Golias said. "I cut my own deals."

The silence was charged. Dewar said nothing. Ottaviano felt his face redden. The implied insult was galling; but Golias had said nothing answerable, nothing openly offensive. Otto couldn't challenge him for it. Perhaps he could take the quarrel to other terms and win.

He forced himself to relax, to smile, to nod. "Good enough," Ottaviano said. "You're your own boss, and you know best what kind of deal you want to cut." He paused, just long enough to let the topic go, and went on, "Speaking of cutting and dealing—weren't we going to play cards tonight?"

* * *

The young guard outside Otto's tent had looked very familiar to Dewar as he went in. As he went out, he paused, taking out a pipe, letting the others go ahead of him.

"Luneté," murmured Dewar around the pipestem, glancing at her in the torchlight.

She glared at him. "Shsh," she mouthed soundlessly.

He lifted an eyebrow and looked at the other guard. "Pondy," he acknowledged the Castellan of Lys.

"Sir," Pondy said blandly, saluting.

Dewar looked again at Luneté, still glaring at him from under her earflapped, sheepskin-lined helm. "One cannot hide the moon in a rainbarrel, madame," he murmured, amused. Otto couldn't possibly know she was here. It was very funny and, Dewar thought, rather sweetly romantic. The sort of thing a girl brought up away from Court on too many troubadour's ballads would do. He smiled more widely, puffing on the pipe.

"Lovely evening," he said to the icy stars overhead. "They're off to a card game, but I care as little for it as they care to have me play; I'm too lucky, and honest too. A pleasant and quiet watch to you both."

"Sir," Pondy said again. Luneté said nothing, but Dewar could feel her watching him walk away.

When the guards changed at midnight, he put away his books and papers and sat at his narrow table with an elaborately etched five-lobed hourglass, watching the sands run slowly, measuring the long winter midnight. Before much of the hour had moved from the middle sphere to the lower, he heard a murmur of voices outside.

The tent-flap moved.

"Message from the King, sir," said one of his own tent-guards.

Dewar lifted his eyebrows, nodded once; the guard stood back and admitted Luneté.

They looked at one another over the candle's flame.

Dewar beckoned her near with one finger and pointed to the other chair, across the table from him.

"Sir," she said in a low voice, still standing, "I—"

"Come closer and sit down."

She hesitated, did so.

"No one can hear us now," Dewar said pleasantly. "Wine?"

"Howso? No, thank you."

"A spell," Dewar said.

Luneté looked around, shivering visibly.

Dewar studied her. "May one ask," he said after a moment, "what you're doing here? Or must one draw conclusions from one's perhaps excessively creative and lively imagination?"

Luneté's cheeks reddened brighter than the winter cold had left them. She took off her gloves for something to do. "I have been worried," she said. "He has not written."

"Otto is not a diligent letter-writer," said Dewar.

"Not when things aren't going well," she agreed, looking away, and then looked back. "So you are surrendering," she said.

He sighed. "He is."

"Why?" she whispered, a hot hard word.

"Because it is the prudent thing to do," Dewar said, leaning back in his chair. "Because Otto shall have what his father had, and that is enough for most men. Because Otto does not like seeing his friends bleed and die. Because Golias's services are expensive and Otto cannot keep him on hire through the winter. Because Prince Gaston has taken Erispas back. Because it is better than losing everything."

"You couldn't lose."

"Otto could lose," Dewar said. "Madame, I am not in the business of giving advice, but I submit to you that Otto has a long life ahead of him in which to plot, scheme, and fight, never mind the portions of it which he would spend with yourself, and were he executed now it would put a serious blotch on that rosy future."

Luneté opened her mouth to speak.

"Do not asperse him for it," Dewar said. "He has won some of his battles and lost others. He is getting out of it very well, all things considered. Were Prince Prospero not in the West—"

"What?"

"—and Prince Gaston at full leisure to pursue this war and lesson Ascolet thereby in loyalty, I assure you you'd be a widow before ploughing season came. And that would be a great shame." Dewar took out a pouch of sweet-smelling herbs and packed his long-stemmed pipe again slowly.

"He—" Luneté began, and did not finish.

"He has done all in his power. No one could do more. He is outclassed here. That is the simple truth. Were we facing, say, Prince Josquin—the odds would be different. But it is Prince Gaston, the Imperial Marshal, and Prince Gaston has trapped us, and he knows it, and he has other things to do, and Otto is a little more useful alive than dead. Are you familiar with the terms?"

"I heard surrender."

"But it is a confectionery surrender, sugared with clemency. Otto and Golias abandon this war. Otto holds Ascolet, Baron as Sebastiano was. Golias is granted the title Prince. In payment, so to speak, or atonement, they both go west with their men to support Prince Gaston and Prince Herne and the Empire against Prince Prospero, who attacks there with great boldness and great success."

Luneté drew her breath in, the blood fleeting from her face, ivory in the darkness. "It will kill him," she whispered.

"His chances are better there than if he continued here," Dewar said, lighting the pipe off the candle and puffing smoke around his words.

"I mean the dishonor!" cried Luneté.

Dewar gazed at her over the candle and smoke. "Otto's honor seems rugged and durable enough to withstand a compromise," he said. "He knew the odds when he started the game, Luneté."

"I want him to fight on," she said. "I want him to have Ascolet, and not as another man's lackey. I want him to be himself, independent and unchained, not bound to the Emperor."

Dewar shook his head slowly. "Perhaps later," he said. "Perhaps it might be done were there no Prince Gaston to flank and counter and anticipate as he does, with the flood of men he commands. He will still be Otto if he is a baron and not a king, Countess. He will lose nothing of his essential self."

"You don't know him—"

"Perhaps not," Dewar admitted, sucking the pipe thoughtfully.

But they both knew he did, and that she did not, and that he had lived more closely now with Ottaviano than had Luneté his wife and for longer. Luneté bit her lip and looked away, at the little wood-burning stove which barely warmed the tent.

"It is not for me to make his future, I know," she said after a moment, "but—Dewar, I do not want him to be hurt."

"It will sting, but it will not kill him."

"I mean in the West."

"He probably doesn't want to get hurt there either," Dewar said, shrugging.

"Will you do what you can to protect him?" Luneté asked, her eyes on his.

Dewar sat very still.

"I will pay you," she said in the silence.

"I have other concerns," he said, sighing a long stream of pale smoke. "Moreover I am not ashamed to say I have no more desire to face Prince Prospero than Otto has to face Prince Gaston, and for very similar reasons."

"Oh," she said, and with a flick of acid, "I was forgetting. You don't sell your sorcery."

Dewar was master enough of himself not to answer the implied insult. "No, and the Emperor doesn't buy," he reminded her. "There would be no point in me going there; they would not have me, would not trust me. Otto does not quite believe that I stay here now, and for me to go west with him to face down the most powerful sorcerer of Pheyarcet—" He snorted. "They would chain me in a madhouse, rightly too. It is beyond all reason. I have important work to do, which goes undone while I play court-wizard with these petty wars and politics."

"You could go for the same reason you came here," Luneté said.

Dewar lowered his eyes from hers and watched the hourglass run.

"Are you not his friend?" she whispered. "You said so."

"It is not so much a question of that, madame—"

"You said you would help him because you liked him," she reminded him, still whispering. "You are a gentleman as well as a sorcerer. Will you not follow this through to its conclusion? Assuredly he has needed you here. He will need you more there. Would you deny that?"

Dewar said nothing, studying the candle-flame now instead of the running sand in the hourglass.

"There are things I must do," he said to the flame, "but when I have done them, I will join him and Prince Gaston in the West again. They will not need me at once; it will take them some time to travel thither."

Luneté's breath made the flame bow to Dewar, a cloudlet of black soot rising as it kissed its well of melted wax.

"Anything in my power to give you—"

"I do not sell my sorcery," Dewar said in a voice without emotion, turning the words back on her as she had turned them on him.

She stiffened, looked down. "I—"

"Nay, Luneté," he said, and rose, leaned over the table, took her hands. "Let us not quarrel for pride. Let us be friends, as we have been."

She stood too, clasping his warm hands with hers that were cold. "Thank you," she said. "Let us be friends." His eyes rested on hers, and she felt that disconcerting swimming warmth move through her body again. "Will you accept, not payment, but a token of my friendship?" Luneté asked softly.

He began to say no, and she forestalled him.

"Something of no value, save to a friend—"

Dewar bowed his head gracefully. "Then I am honored."

Luneté let go of his hands and took off her helmet. Her hair was braided and pinned tight against her head beneath the metal and wool. She undid one of the plaits, drew her knife, and cut a long russet-glinting lock of it.

Dewar watched, unspeaking.

"This is a precious thing, and of great value; I thank you," he said low, bowing deeply as he accepted the gift, coiling it round and round into a ring. Did she know that she had just handed him full power over herself? Was she so ignorant?

Luneté, blushing, put her hair up again.

"There is a favor I would ask of you, Luneté, in friendship's name," Dewar said.

Her eyes glanced at him and away.

"Do not tell Otto we have spoken thus," he said.

The winter sun was blazing hot. Indifferent to its rays, Prince Gaston stood on the Erispas road's packhorse bridge, arms folded, waiting for Ottaviano's party to dismount and join him.

Behind him, waiting with the same patience displayed by their commander, were arrayed in a semicircle the Fireduke's four principal captains and a standard-bearer who carried the Imperial standard and Gaston's own on a single staff.

First down at the canyon's mouth was a blue-cloaked man, whom the Marshal recognized as the fellow who'd acted as messenger between his camp and Ottaviano's while they negotiated, followed immediately by Ottaviano himself and Golias. Golias was dressed in the same leather and mail he wore to fight. Ottaviano had a new-looking surcoat. Three other men and a boy carrying their standard were with them, witnesses for their side.

The lanky emissary walked beside Ottaviano, avoiding slush-puddles without looking down; they were talking about something, Ottaviano nodding. The standard-bearer was on the emissary's other side, eyeing the bridge, which had been cleared of the previous day's wet snow and ice. The river underneath was too fast-moving to freeze, and the ice that fringed it was wet and dripping today under the sun's brief appearance.

The emissary glanced up, caught Prince Gaston's eye on them, and smiled slightly and nodded once, a greeting to a peer. He fell back half a step to join the others. Gaston realized he didn't actually know the man's name. He had always identified himself as the Representative of the King of Ascolet, Count of Lys.

Ottaviano and Golias walked onto the bridge, and Gaston's attention was drawn from their follower, who had his hands behind his back and was looking off to one side at the stream now.

"Good day," Gaston said.

"We meet without steel, for a change." Ottaviano smiled, suddenly nervous. The Fireduke looked no smaller now than he had on the battlefield, bloodspattered and on horseback. He was soft-spoken, but the power simmering under the quiet courtesy was tangible in his handclasp.

"Thou art Ottaviano. I am pleased to know thee, nephew. I am Prince Gaston, Marshal of Landuc."

For a moment, Otto bristled: doddering, decrepit relics of the early days of Panurgus might call their servants *thee,* or their dogs or great-grandchildren—and then he realized that in truth, Prince Gaston was a relic, but a vital, living, dangerous one, who had survived and adapted to change after change in the world around him. Why should he not call Otto, *thee?* He was but a century or so younger than the Well, and he was Otto's eldest uncle to boot. Ottaviano backed away from the dizzying prospect of Prince Gaston's age and attended.

Golias and Gaston were bowing to one another. Gaston smiled his ambiguous smile. " 'Tis even greater pleasure to face thee so, Golias."

"I hope so," Golias said curtly.

"Let's get to business," said Ottaviano. "As soon as the sun goes behind that mountain everything's going to be under a sheet of slick ice, and I'd rather not ride back that way."

"Well-put," Prince Gaston said. "Here's the accord, drafted by my clerks. Review it as ye would, and the copies, here. I have already done so."

There were twelve copies altogether; Ottaviano handed four to Golias, took four himself, and half-turned and nodded to his emissary. "Make yourself useful."

"You demand much of your allies," said the man, smiling, and Ottaviano chuckled as he handed the sheaf of parchment to him. The emissary stood beside him at the table, reading.

Golias read skeptically, murmured three times about a word or a clause to Ottaviano, and finally nodded grudgingly. Ottaviano read it all twice and went over Golias's share as well. The emissary read quickly, nodding to himself as if making mental ticks, one eyebrow unconsciously lifted, a faint smile on his lips. Gaston thought for the dozenth time that he knew he had met the man, somewhere, and rummaged for the occasion, for a name. It was not like his memory to be so vague. He was a distinctive character, handsome, well-bred, and an excellent swordsman.

Ottaviano did not review the documents his emissary had checked, but accepted them and the man's nod with a private look of inquiry and then a nod of his own.

They were intimate, thought Gaston. Friends at the least.

"Very well," said Otto, and his smile evaporated. He set the parchments down.

"The witnesses for the Emperor of Landuc, who here is represented by myself today," Gaston said, "are Sir Vittor Cadine, Sir Blanont of Montfrechet, Sir Michael Torcarry, and Sir Piscos the White." The standard-bearer, Gaston's esquire, did not count.

"The witnesses for Ascolet, which is me, are Sir Halloy the Rider, Sir Barnet Fridolin, Sir Ustos of Champlys, and Lord Dewar."

Gaston didn't quite catch the last name, but surmised that it applied to the emissary. Lord of what and where? he wondered in the back of his mind as he bent to the business of signing.

Ottaviano's signatures were tall-capitaled and firm; only the first held a quiver in the final *o.* Gaston's was neat and compact, flourished distinctively though unfashionably; Golias's name sprawled. The witnesses inscribed names and sealed seals against them in the space provided. Lord Dewar had no seal, and he signed his name only a precise, small "Dewar."

The standard-bearer of Ascolet watched with interest.

"Now for the tough part," muttered Ottaviano, straightening and looking up at Prince Gaston, all jesting gone.

Gaston nodded once and took a single step to his left, so that there was no longer a table between them.

Ottaviano looked around as if savoring this last moment, and then, very slowly, unbuckled his sword belt and handed it to Gaston. He bent one knee and knelt before the Prince on the bridge. Gaston leaned forward slightly and enfolded his nephew's hands between his own, holding the man's eyes, knowing how vulnerable and humbled he felt.

"I, Ottaviano, do solemnly swear by the Well of Fire that nourishes me. . . ."

Low and clear, no tremor in his voice, spoken directly to Gaston or to something somewhere behind Gaston.

Gaston moistened his lips and said, "I, Gaston, Prince of Landuc, on behalf of His Radiant Majesty Avril, Emperor of Landuc, who reigns with the force of the Well, do accept thy fealty and appoint thee Baron of Ascolet and grant thee all the rights, privileges, and honors pertaining to this rank, and in return for this boon do lay upon thee the duties of rendering to the Crown the Crown's share of the revenues and of promptly and without delay providing men at the Crown's request to carry out war . . ."

The vow weighed heavily on Ottaviano, Gaston could see. But the boy had lost—lost and hardly lost at all, for he had now been granted his father's position. Admittedly one could dispute that he need not have gone to war for it in the first place, but Gaston was no starry-eyed dreamer. Justice demanded to be served with steel. He released Ottaviano's hands and the Baron of Ascolet rose.

"Shall be repeated at Court when circumstances permit," Gaston said.

"I'm so looking forward to it," Ottaviano said, and wryed his mouth, accepting the return of his sword.

Gaston looked at Golias.

There was a more bitter oath to give and one to take. They regarded one another tensely, Gaston standing over his opponent and waiting for him to make the vow which would surrender Golias to the Crown and to offer him, in return, a kind of legitimacy.

Golias rose quickly, disdainfully, having taken the oath, and Gaston caught him by the shoulders.

"Prince Golias," he said quietly.

Golias stared at him and then nodded, smiling with only one side of his mouth. "Yeah."

"Welcome," said Gaston, and released him after another half-second's clasp.

"Thanks," Golias said.

Gaston's eye fell, as he turned back to the table, on Lord Dewar, whose expression was grave and remote, sadly vacant or turned on some distant prospect.

"We will begin moving to join you in Erispas tomorrow," Ottaviano said, "weather permitting—"

"It will," said Lord Dewar absently.

Ottaviano chuckled. "Then we will. And you, Marshal?"

"I'll meet you there, and we'll take counsel together o'er the business of going West as speedily as may be done."

Ottaviano nodded and looked at Golias, who nodded also.

"Farewell, then, until the morrow," Prince Gaston said.

Lord Dewar turned and went off the bridge to the squire who held their horses, and Ottaviano frowned after him a moment, breaking off his own farewell. Lord Dewar mounted quickly and urged his horse forward toward the bridge.

"Beg pardon, gentlemen—"

"What? Where the hell are you going?" demanded Ottaviano.

"I have affairs to attend to," Dewar said. He had a long black staff in his hand now. "Farewell, Otto, and a safe journey to you."

Gaston's eyes widened fractionally. He stared. The sorcerer! Of course! Gaston had been blind as a—no, surely the man had been fogging perceptions of himself with illusions, keeping himself from being noticed closely. Gaston stepped forward to get a better, last look at the sorcerer, Lord Dewar.

"What about your promises, sorcerer?" hissed Golias. "You abandon us when we need you—"

"That is a lie, Golias," said Dewar, "in that it implies that I said I would not, and never did I so." He nudged his horse forward, and the animal began to walk.

"That's true," Ottaviano said, following him. "Look, sometime we—"

"And farewell, Prince Gaston, a pleasure to meet you." Dewar smiled a brief, brilliant smile at the Prince Marshal.

"Farewell," Gaston said, surprised and amused.

"I thank you," said the sorcerer over his shoulder, and kicked the horse so that it began galloping along the drover's road above the Parphinal. He went around a bend and was out of their sight.

"Son of a bitch!" Golias said. "Fucking unreliable fickle—"

"*Prince* Golias, you surpass yourself in slander and discourtesy," the standard-bearer said primly.

Gaston stared at the standard-bearer, startled again. A woman? Was nothing what it seemed to be, today?

"He sold us out!" Golias said to Ottaviano.

"Don't be an ass!" Ottaviano said. "They come and go."

"'Tis the nature of the breed," Gaston said. "Whence came he?"

"Madana," Ottaviano said. "Or somewhere."

Gaston nodded. Had he met the man before? Something about him was familiar, but Gaston could not put a name to it, or him, beyond that given: Dewar. He resolved to think on it later.

"He's going for the Nexus at Byrencross, there's a sunset Gate there, I remember he mentioned it once—" and Ottaviano broke off.

"At my back," Prince Gaston said. "I am impressed anew by the quality of the forces thou hast brought to thy cause, Baron."

"We could have won!" Golias said, still enraged.

"Nay," said the Fireduke, "for had you not agreed, Prince Josquin was prepared to join me with men of Madana, and you would have died." His holiday humor was gone; again he was the implacable leader of the Emperor's armies.

"Oh," said Ottaviano.

"Aye."

"That's not a sure thing," said Golias. "Betrayed!"

" 'Tis a certainty," said Gaston dispassionately, and he gathered up the copies of the treaty.

# — 15 —

OTTAVIANO TURNED SLOWLY ROUND AND ROUND, looking up, looking away in every direction. Above the peaks of the tents, above the poles of the standards, the sky hung high and empty, dawn sweeping up from the distant rim, the wide, long dawn of the frozen plains. Daylight exposed the army as a meagre thing in a way that the near-hanging stars had not. They had arrived at night, following Prince Gaston's troops into a bonfire-Way the Marshal had opened to Prince Herne; the night was spent pitching camp by torchlight, assigning perimeter patrols, and the like. Otto had crawled into his cold bed shortly before sunrise, and shortly after, his sharp-voiced squire had roused him with the name of Prince Herne, under whom the Marshal had placed Ascolet's troops and the mercenaries. It had all seemed routine, if a bit off-hours, in the dark. Now that Otto saw the place, the battlefield-plains of Chenay, he was taken aback. The dun and grey earth merged into the heavens; the scraps of color around the army—pennants, cloaks, fluttering laundry—were piteously insignificant.

"What's biting you?" Prince Herne demanded, halting and looking back at him.

"It's . . . flat," Otto explained.

"These *are* the Western Plains," Herne retorted. "Step smartly; the Marshal waits."

The Marshal emerged now from his tent, frowning a little; the frown disappeared when he saw Prince Herne, Prince Golias, and the Baron of Ascolet. They were late.

Otto glanced around himself again with a shudder. It was too flat. It was like being on a plate. Prospero had chosen his venue well; the Emperor's army was exposed in every way. Otto had been on prairies before, in deserts, on oceans, and he hated their naked sweeps of space and sky.

Prince Gaston was waiting, though. Ottaviano saluted and greeted him, then was stopped as he started into the tent by Gaston's hand on his shoulder.

"Sir?"

"Hadst thou difficulties in the journey?"

"None. No. The men, a few of them didn't like it, but they came through. We had some panicky horses. And they're all finding it strange here."

"Strange?" the Fireduke prompted him.

Otto gestured, embarrassed. "Well, it's—flat. It's like—like being on top of a mountain," he said, "all the time. Seeing so far. The air's thin, even."

" 'Tis an unwonted bitter cold strike, from Prospero's hand no doubt," Prince Gaston said. "Aye, the land's not like Ascolet."

"I don't like it, sir. We can't do anything."

"We can. We can advance."

Ottaviano nodded. "Yes, sir," he agreed, and the Prince let him go. But as Ottaviano went into the tent, he glanced back again. On the monotonous horizon, a blue-violet line of storm swept toward them from Prospero's forces, and Otto wondered how far anyone would advance against that.

He had the answer sooner than he liked. The Emperor's men could not advance. They could barely hold their own. Prospero had momentum, and Prospero had sorcery the like of which had not been since Panurgus and Proteus had divided Hendiadys into Pheyarcet and Phesaotois, and Prospero had weather. Hail hammered down, and fierce small cones of black cloud whipped over the land and through their lines, sucking men up and crushing them when they fell. The weather mocked them; a few hours of sun or stars would precede a stinging near-horizontal rain that soaked through their tents and gullied and rutted the encampment. They froze, but snow never fell, only icy, glazing rains.

Ottaviano admired the weather-working; it took fine Elemental control to do it, the sort Prospero had been rumored to have, but seeing it in action was deeply disturbing. When the very air a man breathes can turn into a hostile wind, morale suffers. Gaston's troops seemed to take it better; perhaps their proximity to the Fireduke heartened them. Golias's portion of the army had it the worst, or claimed to, and Herne's men were bogged in mud.

Yet they did progress, feet by days. Prince Gaston attacked Prospero anyway, and Prospero fell back sometimes and held sometimes. Prospero's object, Gaston said, must be to reach the River Ire, which he could use to move very swiftly past a number of obstacles to land relatively close to the capital. Landuc's Bounds barred him from using sorcery to go so near and prevented him from some of the direst workings, and he must fight his way as any invader would.

"If Panurgus were alive," Otto muttered to Golias, as they walked to Golias's tent to dine and play a game of cards with Herne and Clay, "he could strengthen the Bounds and push Prospero back. That's how the damn things are supposed to work."

"Were the old bastard alive, Prospero wouldn't be, simple as that," Golias said. "Who's there?" he added, half-drawing, turning to face a torch-bearing figure racing toward them.

"Baron! Sir! Prince," said the messenger, one of Gaston's squires. "His Highness the Prince Marshal, sir, wishes you to come to his tent now, Baron, sir."

Ottaviano could think of reasons for Gaston to send for him at this time of the night, but none seemed plausible. "Now? Well—Golias, go on without me, I guess."

Golias nodded and turned away, slogging on alone in the icy drizzle Prospero had sent them today, and Otto plodded through the encampment to Gaston's tent.

There were an unusual number of guards around the place. Ottaviano followed the squire in past four grim-faced helmed men waiting outside the door.

"Ah, there you are," said Dewar cheerfully.

The first thing Ottaviano noticed about the sorcerer was that he was bone-dry, unlike everyone else within sixty-four miles of the sodden battlefield. Dewar was clean, clean-shaven, and clothed rather better than war might dictate, the emerald pendant in his ear; he looked like a foppish landowner visiting his gamekeeper as he sat across from the Prince Marshal.

"What are you doing here?" Otto asked, before Prince Gaston could say anything. Was Dewar acting as an emissary again—this time for Prospero?

"I thought I'd see how you were getting on with this war," Dewar said. "The last one wasn't nearly as interesting." He smiled, lifting an eyebrow.

Ottaviano stared at him, shook his head, and turned to the Marshal. "Sir, I do swear by the Well's Fire that I did not know he was here, or coming here, nor did I ask him to do so."

Gaston nodded. "I do believe thee," he said, "for meseems 'tis harder to take a sorcerer unawares than this one was."

"It is not impossible to catch a sorcerer napping," Dewar put in from where he sat. "It is difficult, but not impossible. Some are careless—just as any man might be."

"What are you doing here?" Ottaviano asked again.

"He said he wished to see thee," Gaston said, sitting down and nodding to another empty camp-chair. Otto sat slowly. "No more than that."

Otto shook his head. "More fairy-tales?"

Dewar shrugged. "I was curious," he said.

"That's going to get you into a lot of trouble, one of these days," Otto said. "Curious?"

"Yes. And now I am interested."

"Interested," Gaston repeated.

"And hungry," Dewar said. He paused hopefully and

then went on, "But yes, interested. I have not seen ever so one-sided a conflict as this. Prince Prospero has considerable force in his hands."

"The Emperor," Otto said, "won't hire a sorcerer."

"I do not sell my services," Dewar replied haughtily, lifting his chin and raising an eyebrow.

"So you came to watch us get ground into compost," Ottaviano said. "That's real neighborly of you." He thought suddenly of Luneté, of the note in her voice when she spoke to the sorcerer, of the way he didn't like her smiling at Dewar, of the way the sorcerer smiled back sometimes—

Gaston interrupted the beginnings of Otto's seizure of jealousy. "Lord Dewar," he said in his usual even way, "under the circumstances, the presence of a strange sorcerer is not welcome here." He shifted in his seat. Light flashed from the long hilt of his sword at his back as the Fireduke moved a shoulder.

"But I'm not strange. Otto knows me," Dewar said, with a hint of dandified drawl, "and I have come to visit him as any gentleman might visit a friend. I assure you that I am not a partisan in this conflict. I have no interest in seeing Prospero conquer Landuc, nor in seeing Landuc defeat Prospero. I am simply here."

"Simply here, simply visiting. Civilians seldom find welcome in the midst of the battlefield," Gaston said.

"Rotten weather you're having," Dewar said.

"We've noticed," Otto replied. Gaston's straightforward hints wouldn't make a dent on Dewar, he knew; the sorcerer liked games.

"It's much better a few miles west," Dewar continued. "Snappy—cold—but none of this vile rain."

"Doesn't seem to be bothering you," Otto said.

"Ah, well, I came prepared," Dewar said. "Didn't you?"

"Prepared? With umbrellas issued to all ranks. No, not if that's what you mean," Otto said.

"There's probably not so much as a wind-rope in the whole camp, is there," Dewar said. "I'm disappointed; I had heard such glowing reports of Prince Gaston's military acumen."

Ottaviano kicked Gaston beneath the table as the Fireduke tensed and drew his breath. "Well, Dewar," Otto said, "do you have any suggestions? The Emperor hasn't allowed the Marshal to hire a sorcerer. Refuses to deal. I heard a rumor that Oriana offered, too."

"The deals Oriana offers," Dewar said, "nobody wants," and now he grinned, "not even those who rather fancy her. She's quite charming on short acquaintance, but I understand she becomes," he paused as if seeking a word, "wearing with longer exposure."

"I've heard that too," Otto said. "And the Emperor's a married man anyway."

Dewar made a dismissing gesture, his eyes on Otto's. "You shall all be dead in about twelve days," he said.

"How might you know that," Gaston wondered.

"Because in eleven days there will be a Day of Flame," Dewar said.

"Days of Flame come every year; they are not uncommon to the calendar," Gaston said.

"On Days of Flame," Dewar said, examining his fingernails and pushing the skin back from them, "the Summoning and Binding of Salamanders is easier than at any other time. There is a Firebound about six miles east of you. There is a Firebound about ten miles north and another eighteen miles south. Prospero has one at the lines. You cannot see them, but I can. He can Summon a Salamander, have it harried by his winds, and let it do his work for him, contained by the Firebounds. No guarantee that that's what he'll do," Dewar added, "but I can't think why a sorcerer would install those elaborate protections if he weren't planning exactly that. Such things take time." He licked his lips and looked pointedly at a bottle of wine breathing on a small table at the other side of the tent, Gaston's dinner wine.

Gaston didn't move, either missing the cue or unwilling to offer hospitality to an unknown sorcerer. Otto stood, got the bottle, put it in front of Dewar, and sat down again.

"Why, thank you, sir," Dewar drawled.

Gaston said nothing, but after a moment he rose also and opened a chest, from which he took a round glass. He set the glass by Dewar and poured.

"And thank *you,*" Dewar said. He sniffed and tasted the wine, then drank, saluting Gaston with the glass first.

"Thanks for the tip," Otto said. "We'll have to arrange to be elsewhere."

"How?" Dewar asked, lifting an eyebrow.

"Through a Way, I suppose," Otto said. "Or the Road. I reckon the Marshal here isn't keen on all of us getting immolated by a Salamander."

"You might find making a Way rather difficult," Dewar said.

"It is impossible to prevent," Gaston said.

Dewar raised both eyebrows in such a way as to convey that he was too well-mannered to disagree openly, but that the Fireduke was not properly informed.

"How can Prospero prevent the Marshal from opening a Way?" Otto asked with a sinking feeling.

"I don't know, but I tried to open one to leave here. It doesn't work. Prospero has not been idle; he has advanced certain aspects of the Art intriguingly."

"We can march," Otto said.

"Not fast enough. He can throw Bounds around you faster than this many men can move. Your Marshal knows that."

"Well, thank you for letting us know, then," Ottaviano said. "I'd better go write a will and put it in a fireproof chest."

Dewar poured himself another glass of wine, smiling slightly. "You really have no idea what to do," he said. "Really?"

The Fireduke frowned, catching Otto's eye. Otto shrugged.

"You have a suggestion?" Gaston said.

"Actually I have a question, or a criticism."

Gaston inclined his head, waited.

"Why don't you have Bounds on your encampment?" Dewar asked, setting the glass down, genuine wonder in his voice. "You're facing a sorcerer, and you don't have the most rudimentary of Bounds."

"I know not the Art of placing them," Gaston said, "nor does anyone who is not a sorcerer, and we have no sorcerer among us."

"Hm," Dewar said. "Panurgus's doing. I see. Pity."

"I cannot make contract with a sorcerer," Gaston said bluntly.

"I don't sell my services," Dewar said. "I just came to see Ottaviano, how he was getting on. I shall convey, sir, your respects to your widow," he added, rising to his feet.

Ottaviano kicked Gaston again, hard, and stood himself. "Don't bother," he said, and dragged his temper under control. Gaston had risen too now and appeared to be holding some hot words in his clenched teeth. It reminded Otto of the coy conversation he had had with Dewar before, when Dewar had been obliquely letting Otto know that he would help Otto with his war. "Perhaps you'd like some supper," Ottaviano said. "Let's go to my tent. It's not far."

"Very kind of you," Dewar said, that annoying smile returning. "I shall accept with all the gratitude of the famished, if the Marshal will allow me to leave his presence without sending those husky fellows after me everywhere."

Gaston looked at Ottaviano, clearly considering whether this were some treacherous game or weird plot. He nodded once. "Baron, thou shalt wait on me at midnight," he said.

And report on what this is about, Otto filled in. "Yes, sir."

"And whilst Lord Dewar is in the camp, bear him company at all times."

"Yes, sir."

Uninvited, Dewar sat down in the one real chair Otto had in his tent, a rather nice one Luneté had embroidered with a picture of the famous Ascolet castle, Malperdy, on its back and a fine big ram, representing the acknowledged fundament of the Ascolet livelihood, on the seat. She had

had some trouble with the ram's right legs, so that he appeared to be fixed to his hillside at an angle, and his gaze was a touch cross-eyed. Still, it was an excellent chair, having upholstered arms and built to be tilted onto two legs, and the Baron of Ascolet nearly suggested that Dewar might be more comfortable on one of the three-legged sling stools.

But Dewar slouched and propped his feet on a chest at the foot of Otto's bed, and Otto sat on another chest.

"I hope you meant it about the food," Dewar said after a moment, opening his eyes and looking sharply at Otto.

"Sure I did. I'll send someone. There's usually stew at least." Ottaviano went out again and found one of his squires, who was a few tents away giggling and dicing with two other boys and a predatory off-duty lieutenant from Herne's troops. Otto sent the boy off to find them a late bite of supper and considered, as he squelched back to his tent, that perhaps he should find more work for his squires, if only to keep them from losing their shirts and the Sun might see what else.

Dewar was rubbing his forehead and yawning.

"Tired?"

"The Marshal's wine in an empty gut brews instant hangover," Dewar said. He smiled thinly. "He would have been happier to see Prospero himself, I do think."

"I'm sure that if he does, he'll offer him a drink," Otto said. "Gaston doesn't seem to take this whole thing personally."

"But of course not. Is it not the Emperor whom Prince Prospero opposes? The Marshal is, hm, standing in the way. Not a good place to be, between a sorcerer like Prince Prospero and something he wants."

Otto sat on the bed again. "Not a good place at all. Even less good in a few days, if what you said is true."

"It's true."

"Did you drop by just to tell us that?" Otto asked.

"No," Dewar said, after thinking for a moment.

The wind flapped the tent's sides. Dewar got up, thumping the chair, and went to the tiny wood-stove in the center of the tent. "Coal would be better," he said, stuffing two days' ration of wood into the cast-iron belly.

"In Ascolet we use coal," Otto said; "we've got a lot of it. Out here there's nothing to burn but dung, which stinks, so we're leaving that for the foot troops and as a special concession to the officers the Marshal let Herne haul in some wood."

"Most of the heat goes right up and out," Dewar observed, standing and closing the stove, looking up the pipe.

"Why are you here?"

The sorcerer dusted bark from his hands. "Have you ever seen Prospero?"

"Yes. Well, at a distance. A great distance. I thought it was him."

"I dreamt of him," Dewar said, turning and sitting on the stove. He and Otto eyed one another by the dull light from the lamp, whose chimney needed to be cleaned.

"Did he tell you to come here?" Otto asked, trying to keep his voice level. He didn't believe in supernatural dreams, dreams of foreseeing and dreams of far-sight.

"He laid a geas on me," Dewar said, "to seek him until we met."

"Hell of a geas," Otto said. "What did you do to deserve that?"

Dewar lifted his eyebrows. The stove was becoming warm enough to penetrate his trousers. He shifted his seat. "Well," he said, "when I first had it I was in his tomb."

Ottaviano opened and closed his mouth. Trespassing in the Royal Tombs? How? Why? But Dewar wouldn't answer questions, certainly. "You get around," he said.

Dewar inclined his head, smiling. "Lately," he said, "the geas has, in a manner of speaking, been roused. I could ignore it before. Have you ever had a geas?"

"Uh, no, not that sort."

"They're a pain in the neck," Dewar said thoughtfully. "Dreadful nuisance. Particularly that sort, the very vague and wide-ranging sort that, if one isn't aware, hangs over one's every deed and either shapes or shadows it. One forever has a feeling that there's something else one ought to be doing. Not pleasant at all, particularly when one is doing something that one is quite sure is what one *wants* to be doing." Dewar nodded slowly, his eyes looking past the tent to something outside, beyond, with detached, remote interest.

"So," Otto asked, when the sorcerer had said nothing more for several minutes, staring into nothing, "Prospero put a geas on you, in a dream you had in his tomb. And you've been looking for him since. How long ago was this?"

"Oh, years. Years," Dewar said, blinking and shaking the geas's veil from him. "As I said, one can ignore a geas, for a while anyway. But all that talk in Ascolet about Prospero woke mine."

"What are you going to do, then? Walk over there and introduce yourself?"

"I hardly think so. He's patently in a fire-first, worry-later temper; he snapped a bolt at me when I prodded one of his Bounds today. If I'd known he was nearby I wouldn't have done, I assure you."

The tent-flap flipped back, and all the feeble warmth whooshed out and a cold slab of winter fell in. Otto's squire entered, carrying a covered tray. Dewar watched as the boy laid the rough table with a cloth, dishes and green glass goblets, napkins and utensils.

"We'll not need you to serve," Ottaviano said. "Stay out of Tick's tent and his games," he added. "Did you finish oiling those boots?"

"No, sir," said the boy.

"Do it," Ottaviano commanded, and the squire, with a sullen look, left with another gust of cold air. "Shall we eat?"

The food was ham, a bony stewed rabbit, and mutton; there was bread also, and Dewar concentrated his first attention on the loaf, eating with the quiet ruthlessness of sharp hunger. When they had supped as well as they might, both sat back and regarded one another.

"You could call him to a duel," Ottaviano suggested.

"No, thank you. I have no quarrel with him, nor do I desire one." Dewar wiped the loaf-end meticulously around and around the rabbit-dish, removing every trace of gravy, and ate it.

"But here you are," Otto said. "Right in the path of his possible firebath."

"Ye-e-s. . . . Do you know how the calendar really works?"

"What?"

"The calendar. Events such as Days of Flame happen regularly and for a reason."

"Well, yeah, everybody knows that. Holidays."

"Landuc observes only Days of Flame," Dewar said, "but there are others. Tomorrow will be a Day of Stone."

Otto slapped the table, exasperated. "I don't understand. We should get religion? Could you say something straightforward, Dewar? It's late, I have to go tell Gaston why you're here, and I can't figure you."

Dewar chuckled. "All right," he said. "I can't imagine what passes for education here. Tomorrow is a Day of Stone. It's the most auspicious and efficacious day for working with that Element. The most sensible thing for you, for Gaston, to do, is to use that day to put up Bounds of your own and get inside them. Stonebounds can repel a Salamander, properly made."

"Thank you for the suggestion. It is inconvenient that none of us is able to do that."

"I can," Dewar said.

"Obviously you can, but why would you?"

"Because," Dewar said condescendingly, "I have a geas gnawing at me, and I don't like it, and I intend to putter about in the area and get a better idea of Prospero, what he is and so on, before I let the geas rule me altogether. It's much stronger with proximity."

"I see," murmured Otto. "So you're—volunteering. Again."

"I suppose one could look at it thus. Or one might say that I am using Gaston and his army as a piece of distracting business while I observe a potential opponent. Whether or not Gaston wants me, I will be here. Whether or not he likes it, I shall certainly forge Bounds to protect myself. He can allow me to make myself, from his point of view, useful."

"You're insane."

"Unconventional," Dewar said, smiling. "Now it is nearly midnight. Run along and tell Gaston he has a sorcerer, for the nonce, if he wished to retain me, though I know he can't, and I don't sell my sorcery; and that if he does not want me, I shall be here anyway."

"Truth to tell," Dewar said, "I rather like this rain. It's thoroughly wet." He was soaked to the skin, his cream-white linen shirt molded to him in dark folds, water running down his face.

"Part sheep, are you?" Otto gibed.

Dewar bared his teeth at Otto in a humorless grin—from his point of view, the jest lacked taste and humor—and tossed wet hair from his face. The torch in Prince Gaston's hand sputtered and hissed at the spray of drops. "Is the horse ready, Prince Herne?"

"He doesn't like it," Herne said, "he's a warhorse, not a—"

"Yes, yes. He'll manage. If he bites me I'll geld him," Dewar added, "on the spot."

"What do we do?" Golias asked.

"You, if you're smart, will all go about three hundred feet from here—that low hill should be all right—and watch," Dewar said. "Since none of you is a virgin, or so I believe I may safely assume, none of you can possibly be of assistance. Give me that end of the rope. Marshal, your men have marked the gaps I surveyed?"

"Yes. There are two greater, east and west, and two lesser. The stakes were further apart, east and west; I assumed you meant them so."

"Very good," Dewar said. "Hm, one of you can carry this plough while I lead the horse. Thanks, Prince Herne. This way; we'll start at the west side, as that's the most important. No, put it facing—yes." The sorcerer and the Prince walked to a tall upright wand and Herne set the plough down. "Go, join the others," Dewar said, suddenly urgent. "Take my lantern. Hurry. Dawn comes."

Prince Herne bit back a retort and left, not running but not lingering. The lights he carried bobbed away among the bushes.

Dewar stood in the predawn rain with a crude plough, to which Herne's horse had been harnessed, and a long rope, which led off through the foul weather and darkness to the center of Gaston's newly-chosen campsite. Closing his eyes, he laid his hands loosely on the plough-handles and concentrated.

There it was: the first trickle of daybreak, and the Well's muted roar beneath it. Dewar's hands closed; he lifted the plough, set it down, and shouted "Gee!" to the horse, adding a kick of the Well to the word, so that the huge horse started and sprang forth, dragging the plough.

The ploughshare dug into the ground, making a shallow furrow, and Dewar strode forward, chanting in a low monotone. The earth rumbled and shivered and began to flow behind him; the wind switched around to hammer rain in his face and parted screaming in his wake. He did not look back; once he had put hand to plough and begun the Bounds, he must not look back until the circle was completed. A Well-fostered nimbus crackled on the ploughshare and gradually spread up over the handles, over Dewar, over the horse.

"Holy Well," muttered Herne, reaching the hilltop and looking back.

An ethereal, glowing figure of a ploughman as high as a mountain was striding around the perimeter of the camp, following a ghostly horse, and the furrow he made was a deep, steep ditch, and the earth he turned was a high dike inside the ditch. A thin line of fire led from the plough to a tall pole of sparks, snapping discharges of power, in the center of the plough's circular path.

Gaston and the others said nothing, watching. If one squinted, one could see in the distance the tiny Fire-limned figures of Dewar, the straining horse, and the plough.

A whirlwind, black and conical, whipped toward Dewar from the west. Prospero had taken note.

Dewar, head down, felt the Well pumping through him,

and he felt the rippling approach of Prospero's whirlwind. He was nearly to the first break; he would be vulnerable as he carried the plough over it, not digging, and so he tried to hurry the horse, so as to be past when the wind struck. The whirlwind stitched and kinked, delaying; was Prospero controlling it from wherever he was? Dewar came to the pole; the whirlwind's roar was behind him, approaching swiftly, and the sorcerer jerked the ploughshare out of the ground and walked slowly forward.

The storm hit with a pummelling wind. Dewar screwed his eyes shut. The horse stumbled and caught his footing. The plough was pushed toward the ground; Dewar held it higher and pressed on, feeling the line of the Well's Fire burning from the center of his Bounds outward (the spell now suspended between his plough and the point where it had left the ground), drawing more power from the Well than before, and chanting still as the power built up and then shot into the whirlwind.

A rushing implosion shook the plough in Dewar's hands. The whirlwind was gone; moreover, the rain had stopped. Panting, feeling hollow and light-headed, he arrived on the other side of the gap and dropped the plough to the ground again.

There came no further overt opposition. He had been tested and had passed. Prospero had learned that he was facing a sorcerer, not a fool trying to plough a Bound without knowing what he did. They would meet again, later. Dewar wrestled the plough through the half-frozen earth, feeling the ground part before the bite of the blade, and pressed on, his mouth automatically continuing the Summoning chant, his hands beginning to bleed from the chafing.

He had never forged such a large Boundary before. Protecting the city Lys from Sarsemar had been far less difficult, because of Luneté; of Lys blood, a virgin, and the mistress of the city, she had gone around the ancient, weakened Bounds with him, dragging a half-peeled green staff on the grass, and that had been all: a festive occasion, a procession with flowers and drums and afterward a picnic and dancing.

Dewar had had to do nothing strenuous, and neither had blushing Luneté, for the fortuitous combination of innocence and power in her person had made for a textbook-perfect Bounding. In this weather-blasted waste, fighting Prospero's wind, battered by bushes and stones, he seemed to be taking forever to reach the third gap, and then he must go even further to reach the end, the last pole.

The sorcerer was stumbling and the horse was barely lifting his hooves by the time he lifted the plough and set it back in the center of the first gap he had made, which now let on a causeway through the ditch-and-dike thrown up by the plough.

Dewar leaned on the plough's handles with his forearms, his knees locked, his back aching wretchedly, and hoped that someone would have the decency to bring him wine. The temperature was falling. He could feel the air drying, a different kind of weather blowing in.

"I am *knackered,*" he told Herne's horse. The horse had halted when Dewar did, his head hanging wearily downward, his back probably aching as much as the sorcerer's. Dewar began picking splinters out of his hands.

"Dewar!" someone yelled, and he nodded, not wanting to turn and look. Ottaviano shouted again; hoofbeats pounded nearer.

"Lord Dewar," said the Prince Marshal, dismounting.

"How do you like it?" Dewar asked, pushing himself up, his spine creaking.

"Well done," Gaston said. "It is nightfall, nearly."

"Of course," Dewar said. "You must bury the plough here. Here. Tonight. Midnight. Don't forget."

He and Gaston stood eye-to-eye for a minute. "The rope?" Gaston asked.

Dewar half-laughed, a sharp sound, and jerked the rope sharply. Ashes blew away on the breeze.

Ottaviano galloped up now, and Herne on Dewar's horse, and Golias. Dewar gazed at Gaston, noticing with his Well-sharpened vision that Gaston was illuminated from within, that flame streamed in his every gesture. "Forgive my lack of conversation," Dewar said. "I am imminently asleep. Good sorcery is pleasantly tiring."

"Like screwing, eh?" Herne said. Otto guffawed, throwing Dewar's cloak around his shoulders as Dewar's eyes closed.

"Sorcery's better," Dewar mumbled, and sighed, and slept, still standing balanced.

"Well," said Gaston. He had not expected such exhaustion; Panurgus had never seemed wearied by sorcery—rather, invigorated, rejuvenated—on the few occasions when Gaston had seen his father ply the Art.

"Leave him there," muttered Golias. Herne was grumbling about his heaving horse.

"Baron, do thou bide here with him," Gaston said, "and I'll send a litter. Let us move him aside until there is a tent for him. Hath done as honest a day's work as any man in the Empire today." And he took off his cloak, and they tipped Dewar into it gently to carry him slung in it, and he stirred as much as a log might.

All night, unearthly lights played up and down, earth to stars and higher, at the edge of the Bounds Dewar had made. Gaston stood and watched a long time, and he saw that the lights were made by shapeless dark things from Prospero's direction striking the Bounds and immolating themselves on Dewar's defenses.

"For the nonce are we more evenly matched," the Fireduke whispered to the faraway sparks of Prospero's campfires. "Let us see what cometh now."

# 16

PRINCE PROSPERO STOOD TO RECEIVE HIS guest.

Ariel's arrival made the flames in all the candles flatten and gutter; the door swung open and the cloak-tangled man stumbled in.

"Here he is, Master," said Ariel triumphantly.

"Well done, Ariel. 'Tis all for now."

"Shall I go and—"

"Aye, do that. I'll Summon thee later."

Ariel left with a gust and a bang of the door.

"A Sylph," said the windblown man, shaking himself out of the blue-green wool, turning to watch Ariel go.

"Aye," Prospero said.

"And powerful."

"Aye."

He ran his hands through his hair, and looked at Prospero. "I find myself fairly ba . . ." His voice trailed away, and he stared at Prospero.

Prospero regarded him steadily. Now that he saw this fellow face-to-face, in the same room by the still-trembling light of the candles, now that he traced the line of brow and nose and jaw with his own eye directly, there was something to him Prospero knew he knew.

The young man closed his eyes and shook his head as if dizzy.

He looked at Prospero again with a new expression of wonderment.

"It *was* you," he said. The dream-memory, brief and intense, ringing with the clarity of a true experience, flickered through his mind.

"Was't?" Prospero blinked, feeling the Well purl and catch at him.

"You. Your tomb. Strange custom they have here."

"Barbaric. I'd liever be composted in a mushroom farm than trapped in one of yon ego-fattening marble mausolea. What of my tomb?"

The other was surprised. "Do you not remember the geas?"

Prospero caught at the Well, which, he recognized, knit the two of them together in an ancient pattern. "A geas." He moved closer to the man, studying his face in the calmed candlelight for a clue, and found it in his remarkable eyes. But once before he'd seen such eyes, their intense color matched by their intense intelligence; he had seen them in a dream, a portentous dream on an important day, the memory now dredged from its bed beneath the sediment of intervening years. Yes, they had met after a fashion. "Aye. The geas," he repeated. "Other things too," he muttered, still studying the younger man's face. "I do remember. Indeed. Come sit down."

"Why did you lay that geas on me?"

"I desired to know why 'twas I should have seen thee in my dreaming, and I guessed that we were bound one day to meet: thus I wished to know thee. For such visions are never insignificant. Now. I trust Ariel did not drag thee through ditches nor drown thee in streams?"

"Not at all. Not at all." Slowly, Dewar sat down. The geas was strong. It rose in his throat and seized him, and before he could halt himself he stood, bowing, and said, "Dewar." He sat again, fighting down the compulsion to say more. Some of the geas-pressure was gone; the rest could be put off.

"I am pleased to know thee, Dewar. I'm Prospero. Allow me to offer thee some of this port. Art hungry?" He poured, the deep-faceted decanter sparkling in his hand; the goblets were transparent frail crystal too, made solid by the golden port they held.

Dewar shrugged noncommittally, but accepted a goblet, and Prospero laughed gently and rose. He pulled a bell-cord and returned to his chair.

"I—" began Dewar, the word exploding from him, and Prospero held up his hand with a piercing look.

"Not yet. Let us savor this moment. There is no knowing, for me or thee, what cogs thy geas's release will set a-moving. Let us enjoy a moment of peace."

Dewar nodded, self-commanded again after the surge of the geas. His thoughts wheeled away from the past; he spoke without thinking, simply to speak and distract himself. "A strange thing from a man who has taken Landuc to war."

Prospero snorted. "I suppose. I am old enough to contradict myself when't please me." He tasted his port. Dewar did the same. It was very fine stuff.

"Good," Dewar murmured, his mouth warming and the rest of him beginning to thaw.

"I daresay even Gaston would agree with thee. How fares he."

"I daresay you know, but he's well." Dewar found that he didn't mind Prospero's speaking down to him, and he thought it was for the same reasons he never minded Gaston: the men were ancient of days, wiser than Dewar, and superior to most everyone alive. And they were both courteous otherwise.

"Uninjured."

"Not lately. No—pardon, he took an arrow in the knee joint of his armor. Twelve days ago."

"Ah. I hope he's up and about." Prospero was smiling.

"Well, naturally."

"Naturally," chuckled Prospero, and his smile faded. "I would like to spend another afternoon with Gaston and his palate," he said, "one such as we had long ago, going through the wine cellars, tasting—never mind. Such mawkishness will kill me someday."

"Not if you guard against it."

"That's a young man's notion," Prospero said, eyeing him. "A man who believes he commands himself and the world around him to whatever degree he cares to do so."

Dewar flushed and set down the port.

"Thy work hath made an impression on me," Prospero went on.

"Thank you."

"I will further flatter thee by telling thee I cannot fathom how thou'rt contriving much of't."

Dewar smiled, pleased though knowing the blandishment for what it was. "That's good to hear."

Prospero looked at his guest, who had leaned back in his chair slightly now, relaxing, comfortable. "May I ask a professional question?"

"I may not answer."

"Of course. I've wondered what thy fee might be."

Dewar began to speak and stopped, appearing embarrassed—at least, he looked away, at the tapestry of the laughing girls with their garlands of flowers held high. "I'd rather not say."

"Thy pardon for asking. Avril in the past hath refused absolutely to barter with sorcerers in any way, as thou'rt doubtless aware."

Dewar nodded. "He expressed a vehement dislike of me on principle—"

Prospero snorted.

"—I'm told. Of course he might have personal reasons for that," and Dewar grinned mischievously, for although the Emperor might have personal reasons to dislike Dewar, the Emperor himself could not be aware of them. "No telling. Is he sane?"

"Avril?"

"The Emperor. Avril."

"Why, I know not. An thou hast doubts, perhaps not. I've never seen more than cold self-interested reason in his deeds: could call it sanity. On t'other hand, many of his habits could be considered symptoms of madness, the madness of the over-focused mind that seeth but one purpose. Ask Gaston. He'll answer thee or not."

"He is good that way."

"Aye. He never lies. He'll tell thee naught—sin of omission—but he'll never utter untruth. He's the last honorable man in Landuc."

"You have been away. Perhaps there are new ones."

The door opened and a shuffling, brown-robed and hooded servant entered pushing a serving-cart of covered dishes. Dewar glimpsed a long—was it furred?—nose within the cowl, and the hands that rested on the cart's handle were short-knuckled, oddly twisted, and grey. His host was demonstrably a gentleman, and a dangerous sorcerer nonetheless.

"Thank you, Ulf. 'Twill be all."

The servant bowed wordlessly and shuffled out.

Dewar shuddered, and his geas twisted again in his throat as half-drowned memories of other such creatures rose to perturb his mood. Aië . . . the geas pressed upon him; Aië oppressed him, suddenly close. He drew his breath in sharply.

"Cold?"

Dewar mastered himself. "No. The fire is very pleasant."

"Winter . . ." murmured Prospero, uncovering dishes, rising and setting them on the table between them. "Nay, thou'rt my guest, sir; permit me. The lavabo's through there," he added, "shouldst thou care to recover thyself from Ariel's attentions to thy person."

"Thank you, yes." Dewar went through the indicated door; there was a chill, dark-paneled hallway with doors in the paneling to either side and another door, ajar, at the end. The lights were yellowish candles in reflective sconces shaped sensually like flowers, the candles glowing stamens emerging from the half-wrapped cones of the petals.

Prospero laid out the meal and added wood to the fire. He stood at the flames, watching the new logs catch and burn.

Dewar joined him there a few minutes later. Prospero glanced at him sidelong, and an odd feeling gripped him: anticipation, excited dread. This young man was barely a finger's-breadth shorter than Prospero himself, and the haze of power around him was intoxicating. Prospero again felt the thrill of recognition, bone-deep, as if he had known Dewar for years and had but awaited him. Was it his death he saw here, blue-eyed and fair to behold?

Dewar looked from the flames to Prospero inquiringly. In that moment of preoccupation, the geas rose up to claim him. He swallowed, teeth clenched, seizing control of his throat again. He would not let it rule him.

"Let us dine," Prospero suggested.

They sat. Prince Prospero poured the wine. Dewar, the Prince noted, was indeed hungry; he, the host, urged him to eat well and did not demand conversation.

His guest seemed completely at ease. "This is very pleasant," said he, smiling suddenly at Prospero, pushing his pudding-plate away from him at last. "I have not had a meal like this in long and long."

"I'm grieved to hear rations are so short," Prospero twitted him.

"I mean—oh, I don't know what I mean. Never mind. I don't mean the food, the wine—not just those anyway. I should not have spoken."

Prospero smiled and topped their glasses off with the last of the third bottle of heavy red wine that had accompanied their supper of onion-tart, venison, baked mushrooms, small game-birds in a sauce of currants and cherries, ham pie, and other rustically wintry fare. The cheeses lay before them still: a thick golden hemisphere with a criss-crossed rind and a richly turquoise-veined beauty, gently reeking.

The geas whirled around Dewar as the wine ran into his glass, surprising him in mid-sigh before he could resist. "Odile the Black Countess of Aië," said Dewar suddenly, almost explosively.

Prospero's goblet was bumped from the table by his elbow as he jerked away, straightening.

The wine spread over the carpet unregarded. The crystal goblet did not break.

"What of her?"

Numb with shock at what he had said, Dewar replied, "My mother." Damn the geas, and damn Prospero for laying it! What had Dewar's ancestry to do with anything? Odile was all the ancestry he had, and he had renounced her.

How strangely her name lay upon his tongue. He had not said it in years, not since he had fled her house, not in the years with his master, nor after, not even on this side of the Limen between the Stone and the Well. People in Phesaotois knew better than to speak such a curse-freighted name lest they draw the attention of its owner to themselves. Dewar's skin prickled into cold bumps, all in the instant as he realized what he had done.

"Thy—" Prospero's throat tightened suddenly, and he had to set the bottle down very carefully to be sure it stayed upright. A cold inevitability gripped him: here was his fate, here his nemesis, here his end. "Thy mother."

"Yes." The geas lightened. Dewar could feel its ebb, as he had felt its presence for so many years. It left a curiously irksome vacancy in the underpinnings of his thought, and he wondered, afraid and then detached, how much it had influenced him.

Prospero leaned on the table, over it, supporting himself on both his hands. "Thy father?"

Dewar blinked, coming out of contemplation.

"Who was thy father, then?" demanded Prospero more sharply.

Dewar shrugged, puzzled. "I don't know. She receives few callers. Some poor fool she ensorcelled, I suppose."

"Suppose."

"I don't know which particular pig he might have been," Dewar snapped. "How is it you know her? There seems to be little commerce between Pheyarcet and Phesaotois."

"Once I knew her full well," Prospero said softly.

Dewar looked at him more warily now. "She has no love for me," he said. "Nor I for her."

Prospero stared at him still, quivering. "When wert thou born?" he asked.

"It doesn't matter."

"It does!" The Prince's blood pounded in his ears.

Dewar stared at him. The geas pulsed; his tongue held the answer; he temporized. "I suppose you're right," he said, "it's part of the geas—"

"Dost know when?"

Dewar withdrew from his intensity. "I might be able to figure it out," he said. "A moment." He closed his eyes, clearly calculating. "In the fifteen hundred and twenty-third Great Circuit, fourth dodecade, twelfth year," he decided. "Give or take one or one and a half or so."

Prospero lowered his head, displeased, and growled, " 'Tis hardly nice."

"Nothing in Aië is—almost nothing." Dewar glanced at the door involuntarily, the door through which the hooded servant had departed. The niceties of Aië were unpleasant in their elegant rigor.

Prospero resumed his seat. His foot struck the goblet, which rang faintly; he bent down and picked it up, frowning at the winestain, deeper red on crimson.

Fifteen hundred and twenty-third, twelfth of the fourth. Or thereabouts. No end, but a beginning.

He bore something of her face in his. Hard to tell with that beard, though. Her straight nose. Her brows were smoothly-curved neat lines, and his were nothing like that, angled and arched. Eyes . . . How could Odile's son have missed inheriting Odile's beautiful eyes, the dark windows on Otherness? Because he was a man, and there was no Otherness to him?

"Prince Prospero, you are far from here."

"Aye," Prospero replied curtly, and leaned back in his chair to study the man further. "I've seen thee in the battle, too," he remarked after a moment. He had held his sorcery back one day to see what Dewar would do. Dewar had spurned the opportunity; he had not attacked. Instead he had held his defenses and had ridden down to fight in a melee beside a fellow in the old Ascolet colors, using earthly weapons as effectively as his sorcery.

Dewar pushed his chair back slightly, slouched a little, put his right ankle on his left knee and steepled his fingers.

"Who taught thee swordsmanship?"

Dewar let his head tip a little to one side. "Sir, I think that is a piece of my history that does not concern you."

"It concerns me nearly, boy. Was it Gaston?"

"No."

"No. Canst handle the blade like a gentleman born to it, yet . . . thou'rt a sorcerer."

"I *am* a sorcerer."

"Damn it, I'm not challenging thee. I brought thee here with the intent of arranging such a match, but I think now 'twere unwise."

"You flatter me."

"Hardly. I dislike killing people; 'tis difficult to undo. Wasteful."

"How odd that both you and Prince Gaston have expressed similar sentiments about killing, yet both of you—"

"Don't be fatuous," Prospero snapped.

Dewar didn't finish the statement.

"With whom didst thou apprentice in the Art?" asked his

host more softly after a brief, uncomfortable silence.

The younger man said nothing, but his gaze was disdainful.

Prospero sighed and his left eyebrow quirked up. He regarded Dewar, memorizing him, noting the tautness of his jacket over his shoulders and arms and the steadiness of his hands, the length of leg and angle of rest, the brightness of his eyes, his attitude of readiness. He was a thing of deadly beauty, and like most such, wisely to be destroyed. It lay within Prospero's power to do that. He had the fellow here in his palm, and though between them they would destroy the province down to the primal fire below, Prospero would be victorious in a duel. That would be great shame, a vandal's way to deal with such a fine creature as this courtly young sorcerer. Herne killed things out-of-hand. Prospero knew better.

"Lord Dewar," he said at last, in a heavy tone, "I shall send thee away now, unchallenged."

"I am sorry to hear it."

"Why?"

"It would save a great deal of trouble if we settled it between us, but, on the other hand, if I lost, I'd die, and I cannot imagine a cause worth so much of my talent as that. Not Landuc, to be sure. Perhaps the Emperor would strike a deal: if I lost, Esclados dies—"

"The Emperor's incapable of bargaining with sorcerers." Prospero reached over the untouched cheeses to the nearest candle and closed his hand around its flame. He concentrated a moment and then opened his fingers; a brilliant spark of gold light darted out of them like a fish, zigzagging through the air.

"Follow," Prospero commanded Dewar, putting the Well into the word, catching him off-guard.

Dewar stood, his eyes fixing on the spark—an ignis fatuus.

"Farewell," said Prospero to him, standing also. "We'll meet again, and then I'll tell thee of thy ancestry."

Dewar did not seem to hear; he slung his cloak absently around him and followed the ignis fatuus out of the room.

Prospero sat and listened to his light footsteps descend the stair.

Gaston heard crashing and thrashing as he crossed the coarse wooden bridge they'd thrown up to replace the stone one destroyed in a battle. He recognized the voice cursing after half a minute's surprise and reined in. The pre-dawn sentry inspection could wait.

"Lord Dewar!"

"By Flame and Ice!" Less-intelligible expostulation followed, and suddenly a fireball erupted out of the brush-filled gully. A few twigs in its vicinity glowed briefly and fell, instant cinders, and by its bobbing light and his own lantern's glow Gaston saw Dewar, scratched and torn and wet, clambering up the steep side of the gully. The sandy, gravelly slope must be nearly impossible for him to scale, and Gaston considered offering to fetch a rope, but then reconsidered as Dewar, grim-faced and determined to rise without assistance, began going sideways.

Gaston dismounted to help the sorcerer past the overhanging, crumbling lip.

"Thanks," gasped Dewar, scrambling over, sitting on the ground.

The Fireduke bent over him. "Art injured?"

"I've pulled a muscle. Be fine. Damned ignis. Bastard! I'd swear he did it a-purpose— Ouch."

Grabbing Gaston's arm, Dewar tried to rise and wobbled.

"Here," Gaston said, and helped him up. "Where's thy staff?"

"Not with me. Else there'd have been no problem. Ouch. Maybe I broke it. Ouch."

"Lord Dewar, what's passed here?"

Dewar, leaning now on the horse, looked away and shook his head a little, then looked up at Gaston. "I'm not sure."

"Yestereve came a windstorm hath blown half the camp away—"

"I'm not surprised." Dewar snorted. Ariel the Sylph had been sent away on other business, having dragged Dewar into Prospero's hands to be entertained: the Prince was a thoughtful host and a wily enemy.

Gaston grabbed his shoulder. "Thy doing?"

"No, no, no. I was leaving Golias after going there to find out what he planned for tomorrow. A—a kind of a wind, a Sylph, grabbed me and hustled me—I don't even know just where or how far, it blew me around so—to Prospero."

"Prospero!"

"Yes. He wanted to have dinner and a chat." Dewar brushed twigs out of his hair, looking weary all at once. Gaston removed a few leaves from his cloak. "He'd sent the Sylph to bring me in. It's his. I mean he owns it. Never mind; you don't understand the implications—so we dined and talked of this and that—"

"Talked," Gaston said, his voice very low.

"Just talked. You see— It's a complicated tale. Can I beg a lift of your horse to camp? This is that perishing bridge, isn't it?"

"It is. Here, I'll give thee a leg up."

"Thanks. Ah! Ow. Hell's bells, I owe him for this."

In Gaston's tent, the Marshal saw that Dewar was considerably more battered by his fall than had been evident. His clothing was wet and his face bright with cold. A large bruise was coming up on his head and his hands were embedded with thorns and splinters; he settled stiffly into a chair and let Gaston call a bonesetter to look at the foot.

Gaston opened a small cabinet and took out a wicker-wrapped bottle of something colorless. He poured a tumbler half-full for Dewar, splashed in a few drops from a smaller brown jug, and topped the tumbler off with a thick golden Madanese wine.

"Thanks. Painkiller?"

Gaston chuckled and poured for himself in another tumbler.

Dewar tasted it, coughed, and wiped his eyes. "What is this?"

" 'Tis wholesome fruit, the essence—cherry, apricot, berries. . . ." Gaston emptied his glass.

"Whew." He sipped, coughed again, and swallowed manfully. The Madanese wine was soft, a sweet wash over the stronger brew. His stomach began to glow. "Where was I?"

"In a ditch." Gaston smiled slightly, refilling Dewar's tumbler: less wine, and more of the wicker jug's contents.

"Oh. He summoned up an ignis fatuus to guide me back, and the blasted thing waltzed me all over the countryside and guided me into the ditch. All of me but my head missed the bridge by six inches. They're rotten little fuckers, fickle and never fixed—" Dewar sampled the stuff in his glass again. It wasn't so bad, once one got used to having a numb tongue. There might even be a flavor to it. He drank a mouthful. The warmth was pleasant, and it distracted him from his pounding head.

"What did Prospero want?"

"To challenge me, he said." Dewar was suddenly hungry. The meal with Prospero had been hours ago. He drank more of Gaston's wine.

Gaston set his glass down, frowning. "Art resolved that this be wise?"

"He didn't challenge me, though. Said he'd changed his mind." Perhaps Gaston would send for breakfast . . . meanwhile, the liquor warmed him.

"Why?"

"Personal reasons," Dewar muttered, and had another swallow of his wholesome fruit-essence. He coughed, but this time he did detect a hint of apricot and cherry in the fire. An acquired taste, no doubt.

The squire came in and said that the bonesetter was not to be found. Gaston sent him for his surgeon. Dewar stared at the mica-paned lantern and sipped mechanically at the wine, fighting the coldness of his wet clothes.

"Of what did Prospero speak?" Gaston asked softly, when the squire had gone.

"Oh, all kinds of things. You. War. Her. Suchlike gossip." Dewar drank again, suddenly nervous. Thinking about Aië made him perspire at the best of times. He emptied his glass and rubbed his hands over his face. The bruise just tingled now.

"Her?"

"He knew her. Knows her. Seems like her kind of fellow. My dear, dear mother."

"Why, who's she?" Gaston tried.

"Thought I told you. Odile of Aië. Most dangerous woman in the universe, Oren used to say. Did you never hear of Aië?" Curious: this time when he said her name, there came no stabbing fear. Had he lost that with the geas?

Gaston prompted quickly, "So th'art from Aië?"

"Left as soon as I could," Dewar said, yawning, leaving his eyes closed, dozing an instant and snapping upright as he began to slump, glaring at the Fireduke. "What's in this? Is this one of your exotic soporifics?"

"Nay, nay. Pure fruit-essence, nothing more. 'Tis nigh to dawn; th'art weary. So Prospero knows Odile."

Dewar shuddered. "Yes, it seems so. He behaved very bizarrely. Said he wanted to know when I was born. Guess he wanted to cast my horoscope."

"What didst tell him?"

"I gave him a broad answer so he couldn't. I'm not stupid. Then he wanted to know where I studied and all kinds of things, and when I didn't answer he dismissed me. With his cindered little ignis." Dewar slumped in the chair, clumsily turning the tumbler in his dull fingers. "Said we'd meet again, and he'll tell me of my ancestry . . . Has he always been so eccentric?"

"Aye," Gaston said, and poured a little more into Dewar's glass. "Didst know he knew thy mother?"

"No. I dough nidea. I'd no idea. I must have walked a score of miles tonight. In the dark. Damn' bug. Prospero. Wine at dinner was good, though. Humph." He sipped, emptied the glass again in two swallows, and slouched further, eyes closing without interruption. He was so tired. Gaston wouldn't mind if he just rested for a moment.

Gaston watched Dewar's face relax, the courtier and sorcerer leaving it, weary youth remaining. Why had Prospero released him?

* * *

His hands, his hands were gone, become hooves—his tongue was thick and unlimber—a frightened bleat began in his chest, and his body jerked. Awake, Dewar stared down at his body. His body. Not the other. Bandages around his hands, mittening them. The bandages had set off the nightmare. He looked around him, unsure where he was. He couldn't recall returning to his tent. No, this wasn't his tent. Armor hung on a stand beside the tent-flap— It was— Sun above, it was Gaston's. He was in the squires' anteroom.

What had he done? he wondered, and he moved and felt his foot twinge. It brought the night's events back to him.

There was a note pinned to his jacket, which was on a stool beside the bed, his boots underneath. *See me. G.*

Prince Gaston had helped him out of the ditch and brought him back here. Yes. Dewar had fallen asleep before the surgeon had tied up his foot, though. Gaston's damned inflammable intoxicant had knocked him out and left him with a tooth-aching headache.

He should have known better than to drink anything the Fireduke swallowed without cutting it with nine parts water; Gaston's gullet seemed to volatilize the strongest distillations. Dewar made a disgusted sound and threw aside the blankets with which he'd been tucked up. His own cloak was on top of the pile, brushed, and he reached for it. The surgeon had cleaned and lightly bandaged his hands. He lifted them, staring: thumbs, fingers, wrists—all there, covered with smooth human skin and linen, not the hooves and hide of his nightmare. Dewar pushed the dream from him: it was over, gone. Another bandage was around his head. He didn't recall being that badly hurt, but when he put his feet on the floor and felt the bruises along his body wake up, he thought that he might have been very lucky not to break his neck.

Respectful of his aches, he pulled on his boots and gloves. The bandage made the left boot fit tightly, but the tightness supported him better, and Dewar was able to walk, limping slightly.

One of Prince Gaston's pages ran up to him as he lifted

the tent flap and stepped outside, a boy with glossy, evenly-cut hair and an unbroken, piping voice.

"Lord Dewar, Prince Gaston's respects, and he'd like to see you."

"Yes, he left a note," Dewar said. "Is he free?"

"I'll take you to him, sir," the page offered—Dewar shrugged and nodded.

Gaston stood at one side of the practice ground, arms folded, watching one of his sergeants put a tough-looking group of Golias's men through a formation drill. The page ran ahead to the Prince Marshal and tugged at his sleeve, speaking to him; Gaston looked down, nodded, and left the sidelines to join Dewar, who was leaning against an oak-tree up on a low rise. The page ran off on some other errand.

"How boots thy foot?"

"I think it will be all right. I don't even remember the surgeon."

"'Twas Gernan. Hast cracked a small bone belike, but 'tis not significant an thou favor it."

"Thank you for picking me up." Dewar smiled. "What did you want to see me about?"

Gaston's eyes flicked over his face. He stood on the lower side of the slope, so that the difference in their heights was eliminated, and he was eye-to-eye with Dewar. "Last night didst thou tell a curious tale, and I'd be sure I heard aright."

Dewar lifted his eyebrows expectantly, hiding a sinking feeling.

"Thou saidst Prospero was acquainted with thy mother."

Had he said *that?* To *Gaston?* Dewar supposed he must have. "That's what he told me."

"Lord Dewar, canst thou repeat his words exact?" The Prince kept his voice casual and friendly.

"I can, but I don't know if I care to do so," Dewar said.

Gaston bit his lip. "I ask not to idly pry, Lord Dewar."

Dewar gave him a closed look of veiled hostility. Gaston did nothing accidental; Dewar was certain he'd been given the strongest liquor the Marshal had, to loosen his tongue.

"I'm sure you don't. I consider the conversation a professional encounter not pertinent to anyone else. Is that all? I've work to do."

"Dewar!" The Marshal caught his arm—he did not want Dewar to be angered by his questions, yet he felt he must have the answers, or partial answers if the whole truth could not be told. "Where lieth Aië?"

Dewar began to answer and stopped; Gaston's urgency was familiar to him from other places, other times. What had he said of Aië? Nothing, he hoped; nothing, he was certain, for he loathed the place sincerely. "I'll do you the favor of never telling you, Prince Gaston," he said softly, and shook his head.

" 'Tis in Phesaotois?" guessed Gaston.

Dewar blinked.

"I'm correct."

"Yes. Prince Gaston—"

"I've no plan of faring thither."

"Gaston—"

"Dewar."

"Look, I—"

They stared at one another for a long, long minute. Dewar was hot and cold at once; he felt a turmoil of emotions, of which fear seemed to be strongest, a lonely lost fear. Could he never escape Aië?

"I'm not here to make trouble," Dewar whispered finally. "I— What do you think I am?"

"A sorcerer," Gaston said low-voiced, watching him. "A foreign sorcerer working without contract, for reasons wholly opaque to his allies."

Dewar folded his arms and watched the sergeant bawling at the men, the wind carrying the sound away. "And so you don't trust me. Golias never does either."

"I trust thee, Dewar."

"Then please—let this lie. Please. Ask nothing of Aië, think nothing of Aië; it is not a place for you." Dewar glanced at the Marshal and wished he had not; he could not look away.

"Hast let things lie, thyself," Gaston said, his eyes fixed on Dewar's.

Dewar, not understanding what he might mean, lifted his eyebrows.

"I have never asked thee," Gaston said, "why thou didst join us here after leaving Baron Ottaviano in Ascolet. I will ask thee now, and I desire an answer, a truthful answer."

Dewar looked down, rubbed his nose which itched suddenly, and shifted his weight. He leaned against the tree again. "It was something to do," he said finally. "I'd hate to see Otto get killed." He glanced up at Gaston.

"He is thy friend."

Dewar shrugged and looked down again.

"Why didst make cause with him?"

"I liked his fight," Dewar said at once. "I met them on the road, and I thought they were—his cause was a good one and I wanted him to succeed. It will always gall me that we lost. Why did you support your brother Avril when he seized the throne?" he asked.

It was a question of comparable intrusiveness, Gaston supposed, and so he answered. "I did not wish the kingdom fragmented, as might have happened. Th'art outside that; thou seest not the inner tensions. For a time, it seemed possible that Landuc would be shattered into internecine, fratricidal rivalry. 'Twere a great evil. When Avril moved to take the throne, I supported him; meseemed he'd make a fit monarch. Prince Prospero was exiled by King Panurgus, and though the throne must be said to be his by right, by politics hath it been alienated utterly. We were at war with Golias and needed a king, and—perhaps th'art not fully aware—a sorcerer monarch, Prospero, even were 'a favored, might not have been accepted so quickly as Avril was. For Panurgus disapproved sorcery, beyond his own, and the general opinion followed him in that."

"It seemed the right thing to do." Had Gaston done otherwise, had Landuc's leadership been broken, Pheyarcet might become like Phesaotois: a disorganized collection of feuding petty sorcerer-lords.

"Summed in few words, aye. And thy reasons are similar, then."

"They could be. I haven't viewed them so idealistically. —Do you think I will betray you, Herne, Golias, Otto? Is that what you fear?" Dewar said, angry.

"I think that unless thou hast understanding of why th'art here, thou'lt stumble to explain thy position to another and to justify it to thyself."

"Prospero made me no such proposal!"

"I am glad to know't, but to hear it is not why I question thee."

Dewar drew a shuddering breath. "Prince Gaston, I swear to you—to you personally, not to Landuc about which I care not a pin—by the Well and by my life, I will not betray your fight here."

Gaston shook his head regretfully. "I require no such oath of thee, Lord Dewar. Nor do I expect it, nor do I consider thy participation here as anything more than a personal favor to Baron Ottaviano."

"Good." Dewar began to turn away again, and Gaston caught his arm as he had done before.

"Dewar."

"Now what?" Dewar half-yelled, wheeling on him.

"I trust thee."

Dewar regarded him a long time, and his ire ebbed as he did, and finally he said, "Thank you."

"Let this remain in our ears only."

"Personal."

"Aye."

A blurred confusion of emotions flowed over Dewar's face, and all of them combined and cancelled one another to leave a smile, a very small, almost shy smile.

Gaston smiled also, relieved.

"I'm going to my tent to clean up," Dewar said.

"An thou hast no objection, I'll walk with thee, because there's a matter of which hast yet heard naught."

"Hm. Attack?"

"Nay, but soon."

"You keep saying that."

"Prince Josquin shall join us with reinforcements from Madana, and then we shall attack." Gaston watched the sorcerer, sidelong.

"Prince Josquin!"

"Aye."

"Herne, Otto, Golias, and I aren't enough for you? You need him too?"

"Not so much him as the men he will bring. I have fought Prospero before, Lord Dewar. Dost know of't? 'Tis the latest engagement in a battle that taketh years to move through its feints and parries. Last time we fought we parted, neither the victor, and before that 'twas the King's lingering death resulted from Prospero's defeat. My desire is a swift end."

"Victory at a stroke."

"With the least number of blows, the least of losses. Prospero's a tenacious, creative, wily fighter, and no less than crushing loss can even discourage him. Hath the weather in his hand, even. Were it not for Panurgus's Bounds—" Gaston interrupted himself. "Hast seen how he adapts himself to all thou dost, to every military move."

"He almost seems to read my mind."

"Aye. He's brilliant in more ways than one; he— He's like our father so, leading his enemies to defeat themselves, weakening them with their own weapons. With Prince Josquin's reinforcements I shall have the force I desire."

"What will happen when he is defeated?"

"I know not."

"Execution?"

" 'Twould sate the Emperor," Gaston said after a moment.

"But not you."

"Prince Prospero's my brother, Lord Dewar. Hast belike no siblings, but I'm loth to murder mine, no matter how objectionable they may be, no more my other kin."

"Thus Ottaviano lives, and is at least administratively rehabilitated. . . ."

Gaston said nothing.

"I consider that no weakness, Prince," Dewar said after a moment.

"Nor I."

"When will Prince Josquin arrive?"

" 'Twill take him at least sixteen days to come here, now he hath assembled the force, though he travel with all haste on the Road and then, the last move, through a Way. The greater numbers slow the pace."

Prince Gaston left Dewar at his tent and walked slowly to his own quarters. En route, he answered questions, gave orders, inspected automatically each soldier he saw with an unforgiving eye; yet all the while his body carried on, a part of his mind sat apart. He thought of Dewar, of his quickness and his sorcery, his hands and his thoughtful squint, his youth and his easy, unconscious superiority. And he thought of his own brother Prospero, whose least gestures spoke of command and power, cold-eyed and dark, a connoisseur of fine things who had devoted the days and nights of his long life to his search for knowledge, and he wondered what manner of woman Odile of Aië might be. A sorceress herself, Gaston suspected, if Dewar described her as dangerous; potent and deadly, known to Prospero.

How might she be known to a Prince of Landuc? Well, Gaston thought, Prospero was a sorcerer also; sorcerers all seemed to know one another, an uneasy fraternity, by name at least and often by doing business with one another. They traded amongst themselves, Prospero had once said. Traded what? someone had asked, and wintry Prospero had smiled and said. Why, intelligence that thou hast not, lugwit. Prospero might have traded with this woman of Aië. Dewar's mother.

Gaston reached his tent and sat down at a veteran wooden desk, giving his whole attention to the idea germinating in his thoughts.

Prospero was interested in Dewar, kindly so. Else he'd have challenged him. Prospero had duelled Esclados, a swift challenge that had ended swiftly with Esclados wracked and nearly dead and fleeing to his hideaway, where he'd lurked humiliated and silent ever since. Esclados had breached contract in the flight; he wasn't dead, but he might as well be, and only cowardice had spared him. Dewar would stand to his own destruction in such a duel. Prospero had not challenged him, had wined and dined his young opponent with a courtesy mostly missing from the world nowadays, had questioned him and gotten answers. About Dewar's mother. And had then released Dewar.

Gaston turned a dagger in his hands, staring at the light on its blade without seeing its flash and dance.

His heart's-feeling was that Dewar was not treacherous. He was brash, adventurous, young and admittedly inexperienced, but he had been holding his own defensively against Prospero. And no more could they ask of him than what he might choose to do, without contract.

Prospero had countered Dewar's spells, had sparred with him during skirmishing, but Gaston knew the protocol of sorcerous war was as any other: the older man had been testing and studying his adversary, waiting until the right moment to take him on full-blooded and life-staked. Dewar had said so himself when questions had been put to him in a staff meeting. Golias had asked Dewar if he would meet the challenge when it came and Dewar had pointed out that he was not under contract and had received no support from the Emperor. It was his answer to many questions. Gaston took it to mean that Dewar didn't know what he'd do; in the heated excitement of battle, he might well lock himself up with Prospero and fight to the end of either or both. Such premeditated unreliability galled Golias and Herne, unexpected common ground between them for muttering and dark glowering, but Gaston could not fault Dewar for it.

Such a battle would put Dewar beyond usefulness during the earthy, earthly fighting around it, but would also preoccupy Prospero, who was his own marshal-general.

Gaston twirled the dagger, its point on a block of blotting-paper, his eyes half-closed.

Now suppose, Gaston thought, suppose Prospero would not engage Dewar at all. It would be expensive, but if Dewar challenged Prospero, he must answer. But if Dewar would not challenge him, and Prospero would not challenge Dewar, then things would continue as they had, neither sorcerer at great risk.

But there would still be some risk. Gaston had seen Dewar after a hard bout, his third skirmish with the Prince of Air. Missing him after the battle, they'd sought and found him ash-white, trembling, blood running from his nose, so sick-exhausted he could not speak or eat, and Otto had put his cloak around him and sent for wine-laced soup, which he poured from a coffee-pot down Dewar's throat until Dewar was able to stand and stagger from the hillside. Dewar had kept Prospero from striking directly at the Emperor's forces—actually Prospero aimed most at Herne's troops and at Herne, under whose command Gaston had put Otto and his Ascolet and Lys men—but it had cost him; even a restrained duel could injure a sorcerer. Dewar had kept to himself for two days, and Otto had become the butt of soldiers' jests by his concern, sitting watching by his bed for the first half-day. Certainly there was danger to Dewar.

Prospero knew that.

He had brought Dewar to him to challenge him to a fight Prospero would certainly win and had changed his mind.

Gaston stopped twirling the dagger and forced the budding idea into full-flowered thought.

How much did Prospero want victory?

Did he want it enough to kill this Dewar, who reminded Gaston every day of Prospero before he had wrapped himself wholly in sorcery and power, before the dead King had exiled him?

Suppose Prospero, for some reason, renounced sorcery for the battle, or at least the great workings that had moved him this far so swiftly. Suppose Prospero held his spells back and relied on his steel.

Gaston would win, he was certain of it. It was the combination of sorcery and mortal warfare that had worked for Prospero thus far.

Gaston pushed the dagger slowly through the blotting-paper until it penetrated two fingers'-breadth into the wood.

He considered how well Prospero might know Dewar's mother.

# 17

BENEATH A SHIFTING BED OF CLOUDS which toss to veil and show the stars and thin-pared moon, the peaked roofs of Valgalant are a miniature mountain-range. No window's light betrays inhabitation in the dark bulk of the house; no soul stirs above the stables, where a messenger stands beside a saddled horse, tucking into a saddlebag a bundle which the cloaked man who holds the horse has just handed over. The messenger's hair shines fair in the moonlight, uncapped in the cold air, the face beneath the bowl-cut fringe set and intense. No badge or emblem decorates the messenger's leather jacket; the high riding-boots and tight-woven trousers betray nothing in their color or cut.

"Father, the ring," the youth whispers, turning from the horse.

The man holding the horse's reins bows his head. Slowly, from beneath his moon-darkened cloak, he reaches a gloved hand, and as he pulls the glove off slowly so does the messenger remove a glove as well, so that they both stand a moment with one hand bare in the bitterness of winter midnight. Slowly the cloaked man draws from one finger a heavy silver ring with a smooth oval dark-blue stone. The ring flashes in the moonlight as he hands it to the messenger.

The messenger's fist closes on the ring; it tingles with the silver of the moon, the cold of the wind, the bite of snow.

"Put it on," whispers the old man, and the messenger does, and pulls the glove on over it all in a sudden hurry, and seizes the old man's hand and kisses his cheek, and mounts the horse with wordless haste. It is done before the old man can speak; he is looking up at the pale intense face before his hand has dropped.

"Farewell," one of them whispers.

"Keep well," one replies.

"I must go!" half-cries the messenger, and the horse's heavy body is fired to move at his command, and the horse's hooves strike sparks from the cold dry cobbles on the path out of the stable-yard.

The old man stares at the homely stained face of the moon. The moon sees all; the moon still sees the mounted messenger with his weightless burden of heavy news going more slowly and cautiously along the dark-rutted road; the moon sees the whole of the journey, every road and river, before the messenger, and all the traps and snares that lie between this dark house and the journey's end. If someone were looking through the moon, as in a mirror, sweeping his gaze across the world as the moon's path swept it, would he not see the messenger too? Would he know the messenger to be bound for him?

"Oh, Miranda," whispers the old man to the moon, "may the Well send thee home again to me."

The moon turns its face toward a veil of cloud and disappears. The old man walks slowly, groping with his feet, back to the house alone.

# — 18 —

IN THE NIGHT FOLLOWING HIS DISTURBING interview with Gaston's young sorcerer, Prospero left under cover of a storm which Ariel raised. The storm had the additional benefit of battering the Landuc camp—Prospero's own forces were spared all effects—and Ariel paid particular attention to the supply tents, making sure they were flattened and thoroughly soaked.

Prospero left the war in the hands of his captains, reluctant, but fearing to postpone his errand. His black horse Hurricane carried him at a constant gallop away down the

Road; between Landuc and his destination Prospero halted only three times to rest and recover, drawing on the Well to sustain himself. Hurricane was half-made of Well-force himself now, having been fed on it so long, and never tired.

The long journey through the desolate marshes took another day. Hurricane balked at the Limen, whose thickness and color and brightness fluctuated in unrelated, irregular cycles.

"Softly, softly," Prospero murmured, stroking the horse's neck. " 'Tis painful to thee, we've been here ere this, but fear it not, we'll pass it and go on. There's naught to fear of it, good fellow, good Hurricane . . ." and so on, until Hurricane lifted a hoof, placed it fastidiously in the marsh, and walked, shivering, into a rosy haze that turned a bilious yellow-green as soon as they touched it. Pheyarcet and the Well were left behind with that touch.

The passage was brief and not overly difficult; Prospero was relieved. He had known it to seem days long, when forces from the Well on the Pheyarcet side and the Stone in Phesaotois had escaped to lap at the edges of their domains. Once across, Prospero praised Hurricane and stopped to give the horse water and a nosebag of oats.

As Hurricane ground up his oats, his master stood on a low dune-rise with his eyes closed, turning through a half-circle, seeking and sensitizing himself to the Stone that stood on faraway Morven. The thin trailing lines of its untapped power were few here; he observed their strengths and their locations relative to his and then sat down with a Map of Phesaotois and other tools to place himself in the universe he had now entered.

That took but an hour, and then he packed, mounted Hurricane, and nudged him to trot away into the monotonous dunes, following a meager Ley of the Stone. Hurricane went mortally slowly at first, until Prospero began drawing the Stone's power through the horse, and then he tossed his head and picked up his feet and cantered with something of his usual vigor.

Four rests were necessary before Prospero reached his goal, and he rested again just before crossing what he judged was a threshold of awareness of sorts—another's, not his own. He repaired his travel-stained condition in a dark stone inn whose patrons were taller than he with sinewy, dark limbs and mottled long-nosed faces. Hurricane bore him onward after a few hours' sleep. Prospero carried now a blue tortoise in a sack behind him, and he stopped at a certain wide, flat place on a road that wound up and down through eroded sandstone hills to array its carapace and certain of its internal organs in the pattern prescribed by his Phesaotois Ephemeris.

Hurricane bore him on again, but now the hills to either side, ahead, and behind were indistinct to Prospero; he had joined the Road and stayed a few hours on it before leaving at a pair of giant white stone half-man half-lions who reared up on their hind legs, facing one another, to form an arch. Prospero rode under the arch to a Ley, which brought him after a few more hours of hard riding to a brook. On this side, where he sat a moment letting Hurricane drink, there was nothing of great interest; the landscape was gently rolling, overgrown with trees and bushes, fallen into neglect. Collections of disorganized stones marked quondam dwellings here and there in the forest.

On the other side of the brook were green, neatly-kept fields and velvety lawns separated by low walls or hedges, adorned with prettily-distributed copses. Animals could be seen grazing in the fields or among the trees, and over all lay the warm light of late afternoon.

After fording the brook, Hurricane lifted his head and laid his ears back.

"Easy, my friend," Prospero whispered to him, and laid his palm on the horse's head. He drew on the Stone and the horse tossed his head again, snorting, as the Stone surged through him. Prospero nudged Hurricane, and Hurricane went forward at a walk.

Meanwhile, the beasts grazing had taken notice of the intruders, one head after another lifting from the blossom-spattered sward as the alarm spread. Cattle, swine, horses, goats, and sheep came charging from all directions and pressed around Hurricane and his rider, pushing them toward the brook again.

"Back!" Prospero cried. "I have an errand here. I am duly grateful for your efforts to deter me, but I cannot gladden you by departing."

The beasts milled about. Eyes rolled; nostrils flared. Among the bluish trees of the nearest copse slunk a low, grey shape: perhaps a dog or wolf.

"I pray ye permit me free passage; I would not harm ye, but I must go on," Prospero addressed the animals around him again.

Reluctantly they fell back and gradually dispersed again among the fields and trees.

Hurricane tossed his head again haughtily and cantered toward a narrow track which Prospero saw some distance away over the fields. Attaining it, they followed it for several miles through the lush and pleasant hills, all dotted with animals who lifted their heads to watch Prospero's passing mournfully or phlegmatically, and at last crested a long rise to see, on a high, symmetrical hill before them, a great black pillar-porched temple.

White and black birds decorated the temple's steps with hyperbolic curves of long-feathered tails. Prospero dismounted, took off Hurricane's bridle that he might graze, and stood for a moment murmuring a warding spell over the horse. Then he slung one of the saddlebags across his chest beneath his cloak. The cloak concealed the bag, but did not conceal the black hilt of a sword at Prospero's left side.

He climbed the steps slowly, deliberately. Though the sun had lain on it all day, the stone was without warmth. The birds scattered unhurriedly before him, and a few went inside the shadowed porch.

Prospero followed them. The shade was cold and very dark.

Before him was a door as tall as the temple itself, a double door with tarnished, unworn cross-shaped brass handles at chest height in the center of each half. The doors were

carved in bas-relief, but exactly what was carved on then
was not visible in the darkness of the porch.

Turning the left-hand handle and pushing gently on th
door, Prospero entered.

The door swung lightly away from him, and lightly swun
closed at his heels with a dull echoing bang.

The interior of the temple was thick with black column
as the exterior had been thick with darkness. However, i
was possible to see, because the roof extended only halfwa
over on all sides, leaving unroofed in the middle a wide
square black dais raised eight low, shallow steps above th
floor. The sun was past the central opening in the temple'
roof, but that central open square was bright; the darknes
among the interior columns was less oppressive than tha
around those outside.

On the dais were four tall black torchères, a transparen
flame shimmering in the pan of each one, and in the cente
of the dais was a seated woman. She wore black, a soft
velvety black, veils and layers of it draped around her
clouding the shape of her body, a stark setting for th
paleness of her long throat and face and arms and hands.

Three of the white birds clustered around her feet, thei
tails trailing gracefully down the stairs.

Prospero's mouth twitched a little. He walked withou
haste to the dais and stopped at the bottom step.

"Odile."

"I knew you must return sooner," said she, "or later,'
and smiled.

Prospero set one foot on the step and leaned forward
hand on his knee. "Which am I, then? Soon or late?"

Odile shrugged. Her eyes were half-closed, her expressior
distant, amused.

Prospero shrugged also. "I am here now. I will give
gratis, three guesses as to what the reason be."

"I would not demean myself by doing so," Odile said
"What is your errand, sorcerer?"

"I come to assay the risk of a certain business before me,'
Prospero said. "A green journeyman hath challenged me. I
have reason to believe you'd raise arms to avenge the chal-

lenger when I drub him and kill him. My Art so far exceedeth his that I've all confidence that I'll do so; he's a gadfly, a most peremptory nuisance, who hath hired himself out in a war."

Odile said nothing. Her eyes never moved; her face changed not a muscle.

"The challenger's name is Dewar, and he claimeth descent in the most immediate degree from you, madame."

"Interesting," she said.

"I've no desire to be at odds with you," Prospero went on. "If indeed he be your blood, I'd not kill him but confine him, a salutary lesson but not fatal."

"He is my son," Odile said. "Confine him; and if you would have my goodwill, hither return him, that I may undertake to remedy certain lacunae in his education which resulted from his premature, willful termination of his apprenticeship."

"He seemeth a rash boy," said Prospero.

"He is headstrong and treacherous. I rue his introduction to the Art, for his temperament is ill-suited to it."

" 'Tis a regrettable, but a natural, error of affection," Prospero said.

A brief silence passed, during which Prospero studied Odile, smiling slightly, and Odile studied Prospero without moving in the smallest degree.

"So you are at war," she said.

"Still."

"This is a long war you are about. Or is it a different one?"

"A battle in the same, though mine own goal hath altered."

"I am surprised to hear that. Unswerving devotion to purpose hath ever been a pillar of your character."

"You flatter me, madame," Prospero said, and bowed from the waist, not deeply but elegantly.

"You flatter me yourself, for I know you are not so easily flattered."

Prospero laughed quietly. "Alas, Countess, the courtier's arts are wasted here; sorcery discards them as a child's paper dolls, vain trash. But, madame, I have a further doubt regarding my challenge now, one which you may allay."

"What is that?"

"What will his father say to my prisoning the upstart? I am sure you understand me when I say I've no intention of avoiding one offense and committing another unwittingly."

"Bring him here, and I shall deal with the . . . ancillary issues," Odile said.

"Ah," said Prospero. "Then there shall be difficulties."

"I think not."

"I prefer certainty to best approximation, madame. Let us inform his father of his son's activities."

"No."

"No?"

"No."

"Plainly, no."

"You have heard me correctly."

"What will you, then, Odile? I have much afoot; I cannot go forth to this challenge without knowing I shall not lay myself open to a greater. I Bind the boy; I deliver him to you, his mother, for sorely-needed correction in certain grievous errors which appear to be ingrained in his thinking; and you promise me there will be no further consequences?"

"Not to you. To the boy, yes. He must learn the protocol of interaction and challenge."

"I agree. He is about to learn something of it. But you do not concern yourself over his father's reaction, so long as his father is ignorant. I think you shield the boy."

Odile said nothing.

"You are too fond, Odile," Prospero said. "I fear you will scold him roundly and box his ears and send him abashed on his way."

"That is nothing of your concern."

"Very well," Prospero said, "I shall not concern myself about it further. Thank you, madame, for this interview. I shall see you next with this Dewar in hand."

"I am looking forward to it," Odile said.

He bowed, turned to go.

"You leave at once?"

"It doth not do to let things hang too long," Prospero said, pausing.

"Allow me to offer thee some refreshment ere thou goest."

He hesitated, then nodded and turned back to face her fully. "Thy courtesy is not amiss, Countess," he said, "to offer, but I fear delay."

"The delay will be but a few hours in thy journey," said she, "but if it be so urgent—"

"Not so urgent as to offend thee by refusing, then," Prospero said, and he smiled.

Odile rose to her feet. The birds, disturbed, fled in three different directions among the pillars to the sides and behind Prospero. Her veil-like robes swirled and settled around her foggily with the movement of her standing; Odile stood as still as she had sat for the time of one heartbeat and then, slowly, descended the dais. Prospero bowed deeply and offered her his arm; she took it and they stood another beat of Prospero's heart eye-to-eye (for she was tall). Then, at a stately pace as if they were leading a procession, they walked together around the dais, to the rear of the black-pillared temple.

The three white birds waited at the edge of the pillared darkness, heads bowed. Odile touched their heads negligently with a drifting finger as she passed, not looking downward from Prospero's silvery gaze, and when she had passed, three fair white-clad serving-maids, slender and soundless, hurried away to fetch refreshments for their mistress and her guest.

Dewar opened the bottle of wine and poured four glasses. He handed the first to Prince Gaston, the second to Baron Ottaviano, the third to Prince Golias, and the fourth he raised himself.

"To Prince Josquin," he said. "A generous man." The wine was Madanese, from the new supplies.

Golias laughed and drank. Ottaviano snorted, grinned, and drank also. Gaston tasted the wine, then sipped. Dewar's smile was secret, mocking.

"So he's almost here? Or what?" Golias said, wiping his mouth.

"He is where he should be, and on the morrow shall we confer all together to plan our next attack," Gaston said. "Lord Dewar hath provided such knowledge as he may safely gather about the enemy's disposition; to wait longer would be needless delay, for what we know now is adequate."

"It's about time," Golias said. "All the time we've been waiting for his dandified highness, that bastard's been building up forces and spying on us."

"With Josquin," Ottaviano said, "the numbers are ours."

The sorceress Odile rose noiseless, naked, from her silk-draped couch and stood at its foot. Behind her, through an arched doorway, the moon hung between two pillars of the temple of Aië, and its light was but little, for it was a pared old moon. Yet the little light cast a shadow, Odile's shadow, before her, cold and black-edged, a shadow cut from the moon-stream; and another, deeper, more perilous and potent stream came in with the moon, that cast a shadow also: unfathomably deep, and darker still. Odile looked into her shadow, where her visitor lay, his eyes closed, asleep for an instant: long enough.

"Nay, Prospero, I'll not delay thee," whispered Odile, as thin as the moon's edge. "Haste from here: haste to thy wars and workings, and haste thereby to thy end." Odile's hands moved, cupping the darkness, and it grew more dark, all light seeping from it. "Seek thy own blood, and find defeat and destruction."

The darkness seeped from her hands, a silent trickle onto Prospero, who slept in her shadow.

When Odile's white hands were empty, she lay again, a soft and silent movement, beside Prospero, and touched him lightly, and his eyes opened.

"Madame," Prospero said to her, "dear though dalliance be, I may not tarry; I may not linger another minute here."

"That I wit well," said she, "for hast thou not said it afore the sunset? and in the dusk? and now as the moon doth rise and open thy Road to thee, will I believe thee. Lo, I did not hinder thee; 'twas the Stone and the moon."

"True enough, madame. If I rest another instant, sleep would claim me, nor would it be thy doing that it keep me from motion."

"Hast never been a restful man," she said, and drew dark draperies around her, veiling her body. He rose then, and clothed himself alone, for she left through the moon-limned archway, and when Prospero had dressed he followed her and took leave of her at the dais, bending over her hand in the light of the four tall torchères, turning and leaving her motionless there.

Prince Josquin was hardly recognizable in leather armor and a helm. His fine blond hair was cut short to lie fur-smooth against his skull; he was thinner and harder-looking than he had been when Dewar first met him in Landuc some years previous. But his speech had the same arrogance over the Madanese drawl and his movements the same sensual deliberation, and his pale-blue eyes had the same good-natured expression.

Dewar slipped into his chair at the table as Prince Gaston presented Golias to Prince Josquin with elaborate courtesy. Ottaviano was already there, engaged in drawing in his notebook. It didn't look like his usual subjects: arbalests and onagers, bridges and water-wheels.

"What's that?" Dewar asked in a low voice, keeping half his attention on Josquin's leather leggings.

"Just this thing I saw," Otto said evasively.

"A cannon." Dewar was familiar with them through his travels on the Road.

"Yeah. The Marshal said the Prince Heir has a few."

"Good. I'm tired of being all the ordnance. Primitive design, that."

"I'm a primitive artist." Otto's pencil broke; he took out his strange red folding pocket-knife and began whittling the pencil-point sharp.

Gaston, Josquin, and Golias had completed their introductions and were sitting down. The other two looked up.

Dewar kept his face bland and emotionless.

"Lord Dewar, I did not see thee join us," Gaston said. "Prince Josquin, here is our sorcerer."

Josquin looked from Ottaviano to the man beside him in sea-blue silk and black leather. The Prince Heir's breath paused, quickened as his face was touched with more than wind and cold's reddening. "I am pleased to meet you, Sir Sorcerer."

The sorcerer rose to his feet, holding Josquin's eyes with his own, and bowed fluidly without looking down.

"The pleasure is mine, Your Highness," he murmured.

After passing the girdling Limen which the warring brothers Panurgus and Proteus had forged to separate Fire from Stone, Prospero built a large fire and through it opened a Way to a certain place near his headquarters. Hurricane, an old hand at this, allowed himself to be led without balking into the fire and through to the other side of the Way, a flat, open place of stones among the scrub. The midday air was cold and colorless. Beneath his and Hurricane's feet, the ground thumped with the hollowness that freezing brings; a high, thin glazing of cloud hinted at snow.

Swinging himself into the saddle, Prospero nudged Hurricane, and he, who knew well the way home from here, walked between the trees, choosing his way to the narrow, rutted road. As they travelled, occasional things seen and unseen fluttered around them and then departed, sentinels of the occupied territories. Prospero was their master, and so they made no interference with his passage.

The house which he had made his occupational headquarters became visible as he left the winding low road. Prospero's eyes saw things that others could not: shimmering, insubstantial lines of warning spells and Bounds; Elementals flitting, flowing, or creeping; in the distance behind the bare black sticks of the weather-twisted winter-nude trees, a skyward veiling glow between his lines and Gaston's, coruscating up and down the spectrum as the opposing spells Dewar had set against him touched it.

Hurricane pricked his ears forward, pleased at the sights

and smells of their temporary home. He trotted to the house, ignoring the doings of the Elementals and other creatures with august indifference—he, after all, was the Master's preferred steed, his intimate in many enterprises—and to the stable-yard.

"Thank you, Hurricane. Good fellow. Odo!"

Odo was a boy who had remained behind when the rest of the manor-house's residents had fled before Prospero's advance. He had been in the stables, and in the stables he had stayed, apparently completely uninterested in whose horses he curried and fed. He came running a few minutes after Prospero had dismounted, from a far corner of the paddock where he had been clearing the stream.

"Sir," Odo said, and took Hurricane from his master. "Good 'orse, good 'orse, good 'orse," Odo chanted under his breath, leading him away.

Prospero patted Hurricane's neck and went into the house carrying his saddlebag. In the room where he had received Dewar, he summoned his captains to a meeting and reviewed with his second-in-command Utrachet the immediate business that had arisen in his absence. Strangely, there was none.

"They have not made any but small sallies," Utrachet said.

"He is waiting for something."

"He may have gotten it, my lord. Today Stachan saw activity in the turncoat Golias's camp which might signify some large movement."

"Interesting. It could be a feint. They know we watch."

"They have attempted to conceal their doings this time, but I am suspicious."

"I shall call in my watchers and see if they can add to't. In the meantime, pass the word: prepare for an attack two days hence."

"Yes, sir. We have been in readiness for days now."

"I know. I dislike this stalemating, but we have no choice. The time was not yet right."

When Utrachet had gone, Prospero unrolled maps and weighted them down flat on his table, and he stood a long time gazing down at them moving himself and Gaston through possible encounters in his mind.

Prince Gaston's page came to him where he sat writing orders in his tent and announced Prince Josquin, who was on his heels. The Marshal sent the boy out and offered Josquin a seat. He poured two tumblers of wine and offered Josquin one; Josquin accepted and drank, then set the tumbler down with a thump as if deciding something.

"I left and came back," Josquin said, "because I didn't want to be seen. No guarantee I wasn't, of course, but at least I've tried. Your sorcerer, Uncle Gaston."

"He is not mine, nor anyone's but his own. Had thy father deemed fit to contract with him we might call him ours."

"Exactly. Uncle Gaston, that is the man who stole my Map and Ephemeris."

" 'Twas years ago, well-nigh a score. Art certain?" the Fireduke asked.

"I'd know him among thousands," Josquin said, and his face was high-colored as his uncle studied him. "He's the one," said Josquin.

Gaston nodded once slowly. Dewar was a man to leave a strong impression behind him, having many fine traits to catch the eye—particularly an eye like the Prince Heir's. "Aye. I'd thought 'a must be."

"You what!"

"Thy description then was particular and he fits it surpassing well, and he hath every mark of having passed through the Well's Fire."

Josquin sat back and nodded slowly. "But he is of use to you."

"Josquin, 'tis not judged that 'a hath committed any greater misdeed than cozening thee. 'Tis not, per ensample, a crime to approach the Well, though the Crown seeketh to keep the Well for itself. Once 'tis done so, there's naught to mend it. I cannot think of a previous case of't."

"Does my lord father know he is here?"

"I have not mentioned it to the Emperor because I am not certain."

"What doubt could there be? How else could he use the Map and Ephemeris? Why steal them if he had not been to the Well?" Josquin found his uncle's cautious reasoning, as always, opaque.

" 'Tis evidence by circumstance," Gaston said. "Thou saidst at the time that he employed a spell to render these senseless."

"To put me to sleep. Yes."

"Thus he had some measure of power already competently at his command. I'm no sorcerer; I know not whether 'tis essential to command the Well in order to use the Roads and Leys and all, though I've believed so. It may not be the case. He may simply be a very clever man."

"Too clever. Gaston, how can we be sure of him?"

"I trust him," Gaston said. "Do not accuse or antagonize him, Josquin. If no other reason will still thee, then because we need his cooperation to defeat Prospero. Without him I had long since lost."

"Marshal!"

"Prospero hath a peculiar array of forces at his disposal. He is using more sorcery and more magical beings than ever hath done before. We should have been roundly defeated more than once but for Lord Dewar's help."

"Which you accept unquestioningly—"

"I have conversed with him enough to understand him. If we accept him and his assistance now without censure or remark, he will be an enduring ally."

"Hm. He is testing us."

"An thou wilt. He is no more certain whether he should trust Landuc than Landuc can be that it should trust him."

"It's to no one's advantage to make an enemy of a sorcerer. Very well, I'll say nothing if he says nothing." Josquin rose.

"An if he speak of't? Hast vengeance in mind 'gainst him?"

Josquin shrugged and twisted his mouth. "What could I

say? Give it back? Challenge him? He beat me in the one fencing-match we ever had—he's good, you know, very good! He befooled me and did me no harm at all." He chuckled. "And I helped him. Good night, Uncle Gaston."

Gaston held up his hand, halting the Prince Heir's departure. "A word, Prince," he said.

"Yes?" Josquin, startled by the title, waited.

Gaston looked at the younger man ready to dart out of the tent, bright-eyed and smiling. The Marshal's expression was impassive and his voice without emotion as he said, "I shall remind you that in my command, I allow no fraternization 'mongst mine officers."

Josquin's smile vanished. His face flickered with anger; a wash of color flooded and left his cheeks. But he said, "I remember, sir."

"Good night, nephew." Gaston rose and escorted Josquin out.

At the edge of the forest, Freia sat on a long log destined to become a bridge piling and watched the people of Argylle laughing and talking, cooking and eating, around their bonfires in a fenced, stubbled field. Her hands were clasped and pressed between her knees, and her shoulders were hunched and tight; she stared at the festivities without seeing them. She had brought them a wood-elk to cook, out of her awkward, abiding sense that she must give them something, but further involvement in their feast was outside her training. She had no children nor lovers in the crowd; she had no gossip about others' children or lovers; she did not think they needed her help to prepare the food; and she supposed, in her dissociation from them, that they felt no association with her.

Someone took up the wood-elk's rack and began prancing around the fires, holding it over his own head. A line of laughing, clapping, whooping others followed him in a moment. Freia looked up at the thin-scattered stars. Beneath the woodsmoke and roast-reek, the night air was sweet and warm; but this was the celebration of taking the last summer grains, and some of the children were waving the first yellowed boughs of autumn in the train of the horned dance leader. The season and the sky had turned; the harvest made it certain. Until the ripe grain had been cut, she could tell herself that summer still reigned.

Sparks rose in a tower from one of the fires, welcomed with delighted shrieks. Freia stared at the stars still and tried to picture the Landuc star-patterns Prospero had taught her. Winter was coming. How far away was Landuc, among the strange lands Prospero had described?

"Brr, it is cold," said a woman softly.

Freia looked down from the sky. "Cledie."

"Come to the fire and be warm, Lady. The food is ready, or most of it." Cledie wore a loosely pinned mauve tunic that left a breast bare until she, shivering, pulled the cloth tighter around her. She went to one knee beside Freia, to see her face by the fireglow.

"I'm not hungry, thank you."

"It is not possible," Cledie said firmly. "I can smell the meat cooking even here. A stone would salivate."

Freia smiled but shook her head. "It's your feast," she said.

"And yours, as the grain is yours, and the meat and the fruit and vegetables," Cledie said. "Someday you will admit it."

"None of it's mine. You did it all, yourselves."

"Here comes Scudamor to argue it with you, apple by peach by bean if you will, Lady."

"Freia."

"Freia," Cledie said, smiling, touching Freia's arm once, light and quick. "If you will be our Freia, then you must eat with us."

"Lady," said Scudamor, crunching over the stubble, a dark earthy-smelling bulk. He crouched on his heels in front of her, beside Cledie. "If you are hungry, Lady, there is food to eat now. Come and eat."

"Scudamor," Freia said, "summer is over today."

"I feel you are right, Lady." Scudamor sighed.

"No, no, there will be many more warm days," Cledie protested. "Why, summer will not end, truly end, for half a season yet."

"You exaggerate," Freia said, "and you said yourself a moment ago that it's cold."

Cledie laughed. "But in comparison to the fireside, it *is* cold here in the stubble and wood-pile." She shivered comically. "Perhaps it will snow."

"The harvest is in, and summer is over," Scudamor said. "I have always thought of it thus. The year wheels on."

"Yes. Time, more time, and no Prospero, nor any word from him. It has been too long," Freia said, pulling her hands from her knees and straightening.

"It has been a long time, Lady," Scudamor agreed, reluctantly. "Yet not so long as to be all out of memory."

"He said he would be home last winter," Freia said, "and here it is nearly autumn again. Something must have happened to him."

"What could befall Lord Prospero?" wondered Cledie.

"He might be in trouble," continued Freia, "and we cannot know, waiting here."

"He said he would return," Scudamor murmured. "That he might be delayed. That we must wait."

"I want to know where he is," Freia said, gesturing once, sharply. "It cannot be taking this long just to make a war. They meet, they fight all at once, and Prospero is King. That was all there was to do."

"I know nothing of war," said Scudamor helplessly. "I know he said we must wait."

Cledie spread her hands. "What can we do? We are here, and he is not. We must wait."

"I am going to follow him and seek him out," Freia said. "I am not waiting any longer. Soon it will be winter again, and he will have been away a year more than he said. It is too much time. I want him to come home."

"How can you follow him?" Scudamor asked. "He has taken the strange path away, he said, over the sea; he said we could not find Landuc if we sought it. I cannot pretend to understand, Lady, as you must, but Landuc is not here, not anywhere to go from here. So he said."

"I will go with Trixie," Freia said. "She knows Prospero, and she can find him anywhere. I . . . I have already tried, a little. We need him here. I must go."

Scudamor and Cledie looked at one another, dismayed, and Cledie said, "But before you go, then, come and eat with us." And her hand rested on Freia's arm, lightly.

"I'm not—" Freia stopped herself.

"Lady," said Scudamor, "you are welcome among us." He caught Freia's eye and nodded tensely, until she rose to her feet and walked with them back to the fires and the feast.

# — 19 —

DEWAR HAD CHOSEN THE HIGHEST GROUND he could find for his vantage-point for the battle, which Gaston and his gut had told him would probably decide the war. He had intended to ride in with the Prince Marshal, as he sometimes had in the past, but on studying the draft of maneuvers that the Marshal had provided him, Dewar decided he'd do the most good out of the fray, throwing what aid he could to each of the captains below. The previous night he had supped with Ottaviano, drinking two bottles of the best wine they could find with the best food the cooks could prepare. Otto had arranged for further amusement—a pair of brown-eyed Ithellin girls younger and healthier than any of the women Dewar had seen on the fringes of the Imperial encampment. Dewar had declined that portion of Otto's hospitality and left the Baron to entertain both of them (the girls a bit miffed but Otto not at all), and the sorcerer had spent the night with notes and instruments, preparing himself for the day.

Now, with a quick bread-and-cheese breakfast sitting on his stomach like lead, Dewar wrapped his cloak around himself against the wind that gusted from Prospero's camp.

It was the other's command of Elementals that had presented Dewar with the core of his challenge. Dewar, though he had worked with them, had never done so in the depth and detail that Prospero obviously had. The Prince of Winds had Elementals of every kind in his army—Salamanders, Sammeads, Sprites, Sylphs—and an array of strangely mixed creatures as well. There were things like variably-sized glowing bars which tumbled end-over-end to crush men and sweep them away. There were black-and-brown brindled four-legged creatures with agile, flexible bodies and four arms on a headless thorax-like protrusion. There were skate-shaped birds made of razor-sharp metals, with long trailing whiptails which scythed through flesh and some armor. There were things like bundles of sticks, snakelike things, tusked wolves nearly pony-sized . . .

And men.

Prospero's men were of two types: the known and the strange. The strange men fought well; Gaston, Herne, and Golias had all remarked on their strength and skill. Their battle cries were alien, though, and their shouted words to one another were incomprehensible. The known men were recruited from outlying areas of Pheyarcet, and they were good soldiers, but without the heroic stamina and ability of the strangers. They died in greater numbers than the strangers.

But all of them could die.

Dewar's materials were arrayed around him; he shivered in the cold and sought the Prince Marshal's banner. There it was, in the vanguard: the full golden sun on red beside the silver-on-red of Landuc.

Couldn't they parley? he wondered. So many deaths would happen today.

The carrion-birds knew. Every variety waited overhead.

He looked through the other lines for Prospero and could not find him, even with the aid of a spyglass.

A horn sounded: Gaston's call.

Behind Dewar, a twig snapped beneath the thorny, bare tree which shared the hilltop with him. He whirled on his heel and saw, outside his protective Bounds, Prospero. The Prince was on foot. Dull black chain mail cased his body beneath his gold-trimmed blue cloak. A huge black horse with a white off-fore sock was behind him, its nose snuffling Prospero's shoulder. Hung on the saddle were Prospero's gold-plumed helm and longsword. Though sheathed, the sword fairly smoked with sorcery: that was the weapon that had wounded Panurgus.

A challenge after all, Dewar thought.

"Nay," Prospero said, shaking his head. "A truce."

"A truce?"

Below them, the armies crashed together. Prospero inhaled, looking down on the fight from the closest point of Dewar's Bounds to Dewar.

"Looks like you're too late."

"I suggest a truce 'twixt us. No sorcery to be used in this battle."

Dewar shivered and folded his arms tightly. "I have a feeling that the Marshal will find such a truce objectionable."

"Thou'rt here to counter sorcery. An I use none, he'll need none."

"Why a truce?"

"Personal reasons."

"Hardly a compelling argument, sir. You keep me from my work." Dewar glared at him. Was Prospero attempting to ruin the small allotment of honor Dewar had been grudgingly granted here?

Prospero chewed his lip. "I've spoken with thy mother," he said.

"You interfering bastard," Dewar said, furious: that this man rummaged in his life so casually; that he was kept from his work; that Prospero assumed he, Dewar, was his inferior.

"I'd not seen her in long," said Prospero. "I told her thou hadst challenged me and claimed her as kin, and I said I wanted to know if she'd challenge me in turn an I defeat thee, as was certain I would. Odile said she would not, and asked that I bring thee Bound to her." He looked at Dewar, who was rigid, his face bloodless. "Fear not that. I know her custom."

Dewar exploded, "Thanks a shitload. Can we gossip later? I—"

"This is the answer to thy question."

"Spit it out then."

Prospero looked at him hard, sharply arching his left eyebrow, and Dewar blushed.

"Hast passed too many idle hours with Golias," Prospero said drily. "When I was last in Phesaotois," he went on after a moment, "I desired knowledge regarding transformations and transfigurations. Naturally I went to the acknowledged expert and . . . negotiated for a few scraps. I was able enough to ward me 'gainst her preferred tricks. Odile had never been thwarted thus before, and 'twas a new and annoying experience. I shall dock a long tale and say that in the end we came to be on very good terms, amiable terms. I dwelt seven years in Aië."

Dewar was half-listening, following Herne's progress through his spyglass.

" 'Twas the price Odile and I settled on," Prospero said, "a thing I was quite glad to give her: myself. But it seems that when I left after seven and a half years there, I had given her more than intended."

Something in his tone brought Dewar's attention to him again. "Intended?" he repeated.

"She was incensed when I left; of my free will I'd o'erstayed her term, but, after all, I had much to attend elsewhere. I left, and we parted in disharmony. I spoke not with her again until her name arose in our recent conversation, and then—" He paused and went on, "I looked on thee and saw traces of thy mother, and I saw also things I could not clearly interpret. Thou wert born not long after I left Aië; albeit thou madest shift to confuse me on that issue, I confirmed it otherwise."

Dewar changed his grip on his staff, in his left hand, and leaned on it more heavily.

"You think you're . . ." he began, but his throat shut and no more sounds came.

"I'm sure of't," Prospero said, and smiled quickly at him. "Therefore let us keep truce 'twixt us this day. After this, however it end, I would talk more with thee . . ."

Dewar was speechless still. He stared at Prospero, unable to organize his thoughts and emotions into anything coherent.

". . . an thou hast no objection," Prospero concluded low-voiced.

Dewar made a small sound and shook his head.

"Good. Until later, then. Truce 'tween us." He mounted the horse, turned him with his legs as his hands adjusted his cloak, sword, and helm, and trotted away over the crest of the hill and down its back.

Dewar sat suddenly down on a boulder, his face slack with shock. He swallowed and his eyes watched the battle's waves of attacks and his mind stumbled through other matters, while the cold bright sun reached noon.

He rose slowly and broke his Bounds. The tide of the battle had moved away; Prospero's western line had fallen back. Dewar walked down the hill to a temporarily lulled place on the field, took a sword and shield and helm from an arrow-throated corpse and dragged a shirt of mail from another, and donned them. He was trembling uncontrollably, and he could not understand why nor stop.

Ottaviano was with Golias to the northeast. Dewar went to join them, commandeering a dead man's horse on his way, and became Otto's shadow, protecting and moving with him. Otto shouted something at Dewar when he saw him, but Dewar ignored it and set, cold-faced, to the loathsome butcher's work at hand.

Herne brought Prospero down with a length of chain on a handle which had been a morgenstern, but which had lost its head. He wrapped the thing, flail-like, around his brother's sword arm and dragged him from the saddle.

"Yield thee, pretender!" Herne bellowed.

"Whoreson bastard!" Prospero shouted, truthfully, and he and Herne engaged on foot.

Prince Gaston saw. He was not far off; Ottaviano and Golias were pressing a disordered clump of Prospero's spike-helmeted troops down a slope, having cut them off from retreat to their camp, and they saw it too. Dewar saw, riding behind Otto, and he threw the blood-clotted sword in his hand away.

"Yaaaah!" hooted Ottaviano in pure blood-lust.

"Kill him!" screamed Golias.

"Herne, hold!" shouted the Marshal, his voice carrying over the din of battle, and Herne whacked Prospero on his helmed head with the chain he still had in his left hand. Prospero staggered; Herne went over his counterswing easily and hit him again with the flat of his sword, then whirled the chain again and disarmed him.

Gaston was charging, on his blood-spattered warhorse, over corpses and around knots where combatants were still engaged; the standard-bearer couldn't keep up with him.

"Yield!"

"Herne! *Hold!*"

Prospero lay on the trampled ground before Gaston, Herne having knocked him to his side with the disarming blow. His left arm had folded beneath him. He was not moving. Herne lifted his sword two-handed to strike again, a sure-fatal stroke, and Gaston's long blade whipped around, singing in the air, to ring against his brother's blade and prevent the blow, knocking Herne's sword to one side and Herne off-balance, so that he stumbled a step away from the fallen Prince. Gaston's sword returned and whizzed toward Herne's neck, too fast for Herne to parry, so that if Gaston had not pulled the blow, half a handsbreadth short of striking, Herne had been a dead man.

The Marshal took a deep breath, commanding himself. "I said, *hold,*" Gaston said, and his voice was soft. The sword was quite still and quite close to his brother's gorget.

Herne glared up at Gaston through the visor of his helm and then stepped back.

Ottaviano, with Dewar behind him, joined them.

"He's stunned. There's no common bond I'd trust to hold him," Gaston said, jumping down lightly, as if he were not plate-armored from head to heel. "Dewar, do thou confine him with thy sorcery."

Dewar's ears roared. He looked wildly at Gaston and

then blankly, despairingly, at Prospero, who suddenly shook his head, recovering, and rolled onto his back with an audible pained hiss.

"Confine him!" Gaston repeated, watching and knowing that Prospero was strengthening himself for another fight.

"Wake up, man!" Ottaviano reached over and shook Dewar's elbow.

Herne lifted his sword and held the chain ready.

"Dewar!" Gaston snapped, and glared at the younger man, who was breathing heavily and seemed entranced.

"Damn you, Dewar! *I'll* do it," Ottaviano said, stabbing his sword into the ground. He moved his hands, gathering power as he walked around Prospero, addressing the forces of the Well and forging them.

Gaston suppressed his startlement at this hitherto-undemonstrated ability of the new-made Baron of Ascolet and waited.

Dewar closed his eyes to close out the sight of the world shifting jerkily from side to side before him. He feared he would fall from his saddle. Before Ottaviano finished the invocation of Binding, he spurred and wheeled his horse and raced the tired animal away across the field of carnage, forcing him through the dead and dying men and animals.

"What the fuck!" Herne cried. "Treachery—"

"Let be!" Gaston shouted him down angrily.

Prospero, as the sinews of Ottaviano's spell constricted around him, had shaken his head again and sat up, pushing up his visor in time to see Dewar turning and fleeing. There was blood on his face, but no obvious wound.

"Aha," he said, in a strained voice, looking at Ottaviano. "Neyphile's boy."

Otto blinked, reddened. "I know you not, sir."

"Of course not," Prospero said, with the ghost of a chuckle, and leaned on his opalescent black-bladed sword to rise, holding his left arm close against him.

He and Gaston regarded one another for a minute, a minute and a half.

"So, Gaston."

"Prospero."

"Avril hath not the stomach to fight his own fight, and you champion him."

"I fight for Landuc."

"So did Panurgus."

Gaston reddened. "I will not argue this with you."

"Nay. Your best argument is there in your hand, Marshal."

Another tense half-minute of silence passed.

"I am your prisoner," Prospero said quietly, in a stronger voice, and after perhaps three heartbeats, he unfastened his helm and dropped it on the ground. It bounced at Gaston's feet and bounced back to Prospero's. "If yon journeyman will be so good as to break these Bounds, I'll yield my sword." He wiped the blade on his cloak.

"Do it," Gaston said without looking at Ottaviano.

"Sir—" Otto started.

"Gaston—" Herne said, and stopped at a glare from the Fireduke.

Ottaviano murmured and gestured concisely. Prospero chuckled drily again and nodded. "Very good." Ottaviano flushed and scowled at him.

Prospero offered his sword unceremoniously, hilt-first, to Gaston.

Gaston accepted it, his hand closing around Prospero's on the hilt for a moment. Prospero unbuckled the scabbard and handed that to Gaston as well, and their eyes never left each the other's.

Prince Gaston gently slid the black blade, stained forever with King Panurgus's blood, into its scabbard. "Let us go see to things," he said softly then, and, taking the reins of his horse, gestured back to the encampment with his chin.

Prospero whistled one note to Hurricane, who stood some distance away watching, calling the horse to him. Hurricane came slowly to them and Prospero mounted, not using his left arm, which he tucked into his belt. Escorted by Ottaviano, they left the battlefield, and Prince Herne, cold-faced, mounted his own horse and rode off to organize the imprisonment of Prospero's men.

* * *

Prince Prospero dismounted and stood leaning against Hurricane a moment longer. He stroked the horse's neck, grateful, and breathed in a long ear, "Go, friend. Find Dewar. Serve him as me."

The Fireduke approached. "Are you injured? Let me—"

Prospero slapped his horse mightily on the rump and Hurricane reared, whinnied, and raced away as if his tail were afire, leaping over wagons and dodging narrowly around a knot of soldiers arriving to guard Prospero, knocking two down, galloping back toward the battlefield.

"Too fine a horse to fetter here," Prospero said.

Gaston looked at him a long, weighing moment, and then nodded. "Come into my tent. We've much to discuss."

# 20

THE SORCERER SAT ON THE ROUNDED, grey-lichened stone where he had sat before. He watched the dark birds arriving to inspect the battlefield below him.

The sun was setting. Clear, cold night was coming; the sky was uncluttered with clouds and the fire-colors progressed seamlessly from the round horizon, broken by higher hills leading to the faraway mountains at his back, to the unfathomable zenith. Dewar watched as lights appeared here and there in the north where Gaston was encamped. He had discarded his battered mail shirt when he had gotten clumsily off his horse. The horse was presently tearing at the winter-dried grass down the hill.

Dewar's cloak had a deep hood. He had pulled it over his head and muffled himself up so well that in the waning light he appeared to be nothing more than a taller rock among the many which littered the hillside. His eyes were open; he had watched the sun set indifferent to the beauty of its going and now watched the coming of night with the same blankness. His thoughts were all within himself. There he revolved slowly in a circle of anger, disappointment, fear, self-hatred, disgust, and grief, going from link to link in the chain until he had returned to the beginning again.

He wanted to leave this place, and he knew he could not without dishonoring himself so thoroughly that his next goal would have to be self-destruction. Yet his allies, sometime friends to him—and his father, his unexpected father, finer than any sire Dewar had never expected to find, who had refused to use sorcery today and been defeated without it—he could not leave them without a word of explanation or excuse, and there was none. His place was somewhere below, there among the wispy lights and sparks of the armies.

But with which army? Free or captive?

His friends, his chosen companions . . . his father, his blood-kin, his own kind.

Dewar moaned softly and put his head on his knees, presenting a lower profile to the night wind.

It was thus that Ottaviano found him after the gibbous moon had risen above the eastern mountains and made Dewar's and the thorn-tree's shadows hard and bright.

Otto stopped a little distance away and looked at him for a time, noting his hunched posture, and then dismounted, threw a blanket over his horse's back, and let him go at the grass with Dewar's. Otto walked slowly to Dewar's side and squatted on his heels, looking over the night-flooded landscape.

"I'm sorry," Otto said softly.

Dewar did not acknowledge him.

Prospero had been quiet and dignified giving orders to his captains to surrender. He had unknotted a slew of sorceries, with Gaston only to witness, and loosed his bindings of the weather. Otto had felt the world twisting around him, half a mile away, and before his eyes a flat, throbbing dark bar, one of those that tumbled and swept, had dissolved. Prospero was a fool, thought Otto, or playing a deeper game than just this war. With such power, why surrender?

Golias and Herne had called Dewar a traitor that night at the staff meeting. Gaston had said only, "There was no treachery here today," and ordered them to be silent. Herne desired ardently to kill Prospero, and he was pissing angry at Gaston for interfering. Golias . . . well, Golias would have been as happy to see Gaston dead as Prospero; Otto couldn't fool himself about that. Or Otto himself, maybe. Golias hated Landuc more acidly than ever.

Golias said he would find Dewar and haul him back here for an explanation, and Ottaviano had jumped in and said he'd find him. Gaston nodded at Otto and said, "Go, then," and had Golias begin organizing patrols to hunt down the loose tags of Prospero's forces.

So Ottaviano had gotten a fresh horse and ridden up this hill.

"Mighty strange war," Otto said after Dewar had remained silent a long time, "when the best sorcerer in Pheyarcet swears off sorcery and loses."

Dewar said nothing.

"He's a good strategist," Otto went on, "but the Marshal's that much better, and Prince Josquin turned up where he wasn't expected, just like the Marshal planned." He paused. "Prince Josquin's not the twit I thought he'd be. And the Marshal is a lot smarter. I guess living as long as he has you learn to look beyond your nose or the end of next year. Maybe Prospero would've lost even if you hadn't been here. Maybe not. We'll never know." He was nattering. He stopped himself.

Otto waited, but Dewar was stone-silent.

"I was thinking," Otto said, "if you're not busy, you might want to come to Landuc with me, seeing as Luneté and I have to go take oaths and stuff. Might as well spend the winter there, getting cultured. It's a lively town. I know people you ought to meet: there was this surgeon's daughter, Zebaldina, that ran a bath-house, and she used to—anyway, think about it."

Dewar hadn't moved, hadn't indicated he was alive.

"It's been a long year," Otto said. "More'n a year of killing people. I kind of think that's enough." He paused and said, "Well, come by my tent. I've got a bottle of Ascolet mountaintop sunshine I forgot about and it's not safe to drink that stuff standing up or alone. All right?"

Dewar was still motionless and wordless. Otto nodded and stood, satisfied, and mounted his horse and rode away.

Dewar had heard him, he was sure. Otto had used the meeting to assure himself that Dewar wasn't now under a geas or spell. There was nothing detectable. Earlier, probably; it seemed the most likely explanation, that Prospero had hit him directly and hard and Dewar was ashamed and embarrassed at being invisibly but painfully defeated. Or perhaps, Otto thought, the geas Dewar had spoken of had been more limiting, more stringent, than Dewar had known. But he'd come around, Otto was sure of it.

When Otto had gone, Dewar continued to sit. The moon rose at his back. He watched the shadows move.

A scrabbling sound and a stone bouncing down the hill past him next interrupted his musings. Had Dewar lifted his head and looked, he would have seen a cloaked and helmeted squire or messenger on a wheezing horse. The newcomer gasped, "Oh!"

Dewar stared ahead, his chin on his hands still.

"I thought you to be a rock, sir."

He said nothing.

"I pray you tell me, sir," the squire continued, coming closer, "if that be Prince Gaston's army I see encamped there . . ."

There was no answer, and the squire, frowning, dismounted and stood beside Dewar, bending, thinking perhaps he was some deaf, flockless shepherd who sat here out of habit or madness.

"Sir—" and stopped. This statuelike man wept; the starlight glistened on dampness on his face and beard. "Sir," said the squire, more gently, "I beg your pardon for hectoring you, but I must know if that is the Fireduke's force below."

Dewar heard nothing, walking again through his mental circuit of fear and castigation.

"What grieves you, friend?" asked the squire softly then, going to one knee and touching his arm gently, pitying him.

Leaning around, eye met and spoke to eye, and finally Dewar blinked.

"Who are you?" he whispered hoarsely.

"A messenger, sir. I am sorry that I interrupt you. I must know if the lights I see there are the army Landuc has sent to oppose and throw back Prince Prospero."

"It is both armies, or none," Dewar said. "Gaston has taken Prospero and victory, and their forces that were divided in violence on the field today are one uneasy mass tonight."

"Oh . . ." said the messenger. "Prince Prospero—defeated? Taken, you say?"

"Captive." Dewar closed his eyes. What could he do? What could he do?

The messenger's pale eyes studied him. "These tidings sadden you, I do believe."

"It is a sad business that sets men of the same blood against one another."

"It is. Were you of Prospero's company, then?"

"No," whispered Dewar. "I've done him no harm, though, nor any great good. Whom do you seek?"

"I bore a message from Landuc which, it seems, is not needed now." The messenger's head bowed.

Something tickled the side of Dewar's arm, some little inconsistency in the world which tingled up to his neck and brain and drew his attention from the emptiness before him to the messenger kneeling at his side. He wore no livery, just plain, rough clothing, and his blown horse was no fine animal. Cloak, boots, legs were all bespattered with muds and clays from every highway between here and the capitol. From beneath the helmet pale wisps of sweat-draggled hair stuck to cheeks and neck.

"A message," Dewar said.

"It matters naught now. I am too late."

Dewar reviewed their conversation and studied the messenger more acutely. "Your message was for Prospero," he guessed.

A flash of alarm came and went in the messenger's face as he stood swiftly, and Dewar rose too.

"My destination is secret," said the messenger, and his hand was on his dagger.

"No longer. Am I correct? You bore some word for Prospero and are too late arrived for your word to benefit him. Any message to Gaston would have been relayed by means of the blood-alloyed Keys his kin employ to Summon and hold one another's attention."

The messenger grabbed the horse's bridle and began to mount. Dewar ducked around the animal and prevented him.

"What was your message and from whom? I would hear of another's shortfall today."

"My message shall never be spoken," began the other, and Dewar interrupted.

"Does Prospero have allies, friends still, in Landuc?"

They stared at one another in the milk-light of the moon. Slowly, making a decision, the messenger removed his foot from the stirrup and put it down again. "Aye," he breathed. "In truth."

"A few only. The Emperor hath long besmirched his name and mired his brother's brilliance with muck. Other things too have drawn from Prospero's camp those who would have supported him—time foremost among their reasons now. It is not long since the Emperor usurped the throne, but people have nearly made themselves forget that usurpation."

"None would dare openly support Prospero."

"One only. You have little knowledge of Landuc, friend—if you are that—"

"I know not if I can be anyone's friend, but to Prospero I owe a debt which I must discharge. Tell me your tale."

"You must first tell me yours."

Dewar studied the other's thin, white face and then said, "It is brief. I am a sorcerer, who fought with Ottaviano of Ascolet—"

"That Dewar of whom I've heard."

"I'm famous? Or perhaps there's another of the same

name. I fought for a free Ascolet, but Gaston was too much for us. When he offered Ottaviano a kind of mercy, it seemed best to take it, so Ottaviano now is Baron, Golias Prince—and the price of the Emperor's compassion was to come here to oppose Prospero. I had other affairs and went to tend them. But I returned here to keep Ottaviano alive if my sorcery could do that, for he has been like a friend to me; and for that have I fought on Landuc's side, yet without allegiance, against Prospero. We never met until he had a Sylph blow me to him some nights past, to his quarters where we dined and chatted amiably. He quizzed me then about my kin, and sent me away saying he'd no desire to challenge me as he'd intended. Then today he came to me here, as I stood preparing to do battle with him as sorcerers do and to raise forces to oppose his. He said he desired a truce between us, us two, so that we'd use no sorcery today. For his reason he gave a cause I can neither adopt nor reject: that he is my father. I bind on you silence in this matter: you will tell no one, neither that you have met me nor of what we have spoken here tonight," Dewar finished, and laid with his last words a geas on the messenger.

"Indeed you are a sorcerer," whispered the messenger, shivering as the geas fell. "On my honor I will say nothing."

"You cannot, now. Tell me of your message."

"My father, Lord Gonzalo, has long been Prospero's staunch supporter, to the extent that he has been all but exiled from Landuc to his country estates where we are watched and whispered at. Yet he still has friends in Court, and received word by one of them that Prince Josquin had been sent to Madana to raise there an army equal again to Gaston's and to lead it here, over the Roads open to those who've survived the Fire of the Well, to join with Gaston and secure victory for Landuc. My father sent me to warn Prospero of this; I know Prospero, he knows me—'twas I as his page gave him the very stirrup-cup on that Fortuna-cursed day he fled Landuc—he has never been less than a friend to me, and I knew that an I bore him this word he would penetrate my disguise and trust me. I left the day after Prince Josquin did. I have failed." The messenger's mouth twisted, then pressed together tightly. He turned away, and Dewar saw his hand go to his eyes, wiping at sudden tears. "Ah . . ." he sighed or coughed or sobbed.

"Lord Gonzalo's a name I heard once or twice in Landuc when I was there years ago," Dewar said, "but of you I have not heard at all."

The messenger laughed, a high, strained sound.

Dewar blinked.

"You're a woman!"

"Aye, so is half humanity. I'm Lady Miranda, Lord Dewar. Our fathers are friends. Let us be so."

Dewar stared at her, surprised and then admiring. Finer-boned and fairer than Luneté of Lys, Lady Miranda was clearly her superior in bottom as well.

"So you rode, overland, all this way."

"Yes. I've rested little, and now I fear to rest, for if I'm found hereabouts it will be the certain death of my father. There is none but would guess I'm here for treason of some degree. Twenty—no, more—nights and days of sleepless riding and I have lost count of the horses." She sighed. "And for naught."

"How did you find your way here?"

She smiled. "Why, I have a guide: a ring my father had of yours long ago, a sorcerer's ring which leads the bearer to the owner. It, alas, takes little reck of bridges and tracks, and so I have tacked and come about perhaps needlessly, wasting hours I fear—"

Dewar took her hand as she lowered it from her face and bowed over it deeply.

"Lady Miranda, I salute your bravery, your loyalty, and your devotion."

"All naught, Lord Dewar. Prospero is taken, and all's naught." She shook her head slowly, resigned to grief.

"Not yet. He lives."

"Not long. The other part of my embassage is that the Emperor, despite Prince Gaston's vehement dislike of fratricide, will grant Prospero no boon but a quick poison. The Emperor's men are threaded through the Marshal's command, and one at least hath wherewithal to carry out Avril's will."

Dewar's breath went in. He stared at her. "You are certain."

"It is reliable news, my father said. —Soft. Someone comes; a horse, hear—"

The horse was trotting toward them from the north, along the slope and upward.

"Who's that?" Dewar called.

A snort answered him, and the horse became visible as it left the shadow of an overhang below. Saddled, bridled, and huge, he was black as coal in the moonlight, a ghostly thing but for the sounds of his heavy hooves.

"Hurricane!" Lady Miranda exclaimed.

"What?"

"Prospero's horse, a marvelous beast."

Hurricane had veered toward them. He picked his way among the stones and nodded his head, whickering, at Dewar. Dewar stroked the animal's long neck. Prince Gaston rode a horse as big, and Prince Herne another nearly so: it seemed impossible that such a large creature could be as docile under a rider as this affable fellow.

"That is no mortal horse; Prospero hath ridden him since I was a child and years before," Lady Miranda said. "Ho, dost remember me? Out of place, out of garb, yet in heart unaltered."

Hurricane snuffled her hand and stood quietly.

"What can this mean? Has he fled the camp? Or what . . ." Dewar murmured, and checked the saddle for some note or sign. "Perhaps Prospero sent him away."

Lady Miranda nodded. "To you, Lord Dewar, I would dare say."

"Then welcome, Hurricane, and help us with whatever I fear we plot. No, there's no plotting needed—it's all as obvious as the moon."

"Which will only be obvious until the sun rises," Lady Miranda said, "and if we're to accomplish what I hope you intimate, we'd best be about it ere dawn."

"You have this ring of Prospero's."

"Yes. Here it is." She took it from beneath her gambeson, on a thong around her neck.

"Mmmm." Dewar turned it in the moonlight. A line of fire seemed to run from it in a straight line to Gaston's camp.

"But how we might get into their camp—" Lady Miranda began sadly. "Though you're a sorcerer," she added. "You might make us invisible."

"Us? No. No one need be invisible. And you mis-speak. It's not *their* camp, strictly speaking, for I am of their number."

Lady Miranda had had a panicked split-second of fear that he would betray her and then understood his meaning. "Ahhh," she whispered.

"He is confined now. Sorcerously. I have confidence that I can break that spell."

"By yourself cast—"

"No. By Ottaviano, who—"

"He studied with the petty sorceress Neyphile; this my father knows."

Dewar lifted an eyebrow; it was interesting, if true. Otto did seem to know something of the Art, remarkable here. "Perhaps. At any rate he knew enough to do what I could not, would not: Bind Prospero. He's doubtless Bound still, but a Binding may be loosed."

Lady Miranda nodded. "So you may go to him, and free him—and then what?"

Dewar looked over the camp, chewing his lip.

"Hurricane, were he with you—Prospero might use him to escape—"

"Prospero might use any number of means to escape. He could open a Way, for example, and leave no trail behind."

"For that would he not need a glass or fire? Were I holding him or any sorcerer, I'd keep those from him."

Beautiful, brave, and intelligent: Dewar's opinion of Lady Miranda rose with each word that fell from her lips. "True. Fire's easily made. Hurricane would better serve by carrying you, Lady Miranda, away from here."

"I would not flee."

"I'm sure, but on the other hand you've much to lose by staying. You said if you were seen, the penalty on your house would be severe."

Now she chewed her lip and stared at the army too.

"Sometimes," she said finally, "the cause is best served by not helping. Very well, I'll go, but not on Hurricane. He's Prospero's own."

"Your horse is useless. Take mine; he's eating his way to foundering down there. I'll ride Hurricane and use him and this ring, if I may keep it, to find Prospero again when he's fled, for we have much to—to say. And thereby are you rid of a piece of incriminating evidence should you meet anyone."

Lady Miranda nodded slowly. "A reasonable plan, and all are accommodated. I'll not ride far tonight; I must rest else kill myself falling off the saddle in my sleep."

"Well enough." Dewar bowed his head, acquiescing; he left her and caught his horse, bridled him and brought him to her again. "A half-knackered horse—this is small thanks for your labors, madame. I shall undertake to return you better, when we meet again."

"I thank you; this is all the thanks I need, or merit, for a half-done task," she said, taking the reins, then handing them back to him. The stirrups were too long; she shortened them, hurrying. "Good night, Lord Dewar, and Fortuna's favor to you." Lady Miranda mounted, quick and light, ignoring his lifted hand.

"Good night, Lady Miranda; may the Well keep you safe until we meet again."

"Perhaps we shall not," she said, smiling in spite of herself.

"Now that would be most unkind of Well and Fortuna both. No, let us undertake to meet again, at your father's house, in fairer weather and better times."

"I shall welcome you, fair weather, and better times there with all my heart," said Miranda. "Until then." She raised her hand in farewell and turned the horse's head away. Dewar watched until she was out of sight in the shifty light.

# — 21 —

HURRICANE, AS SOON AS DEWAR WAS settled on his back, started toward the encamped army. Dewar had slipped Prospero's ring on his finger, under his glove, and Hurricane walked along the line drawn by the ring. Dewar decided to let the horse pick his way as he chose, since he obviously understood, and busied himself reviewing a spell for boiling smoke from the earth, which might be useful to cover Prospero's departure, and another for invisibility. He took out his staff, which had been inside his doublet shrunken to a spiral-carved black wand, and then put it back again.

Three times he was challenged, and each time was recognized and allowed to pass without difficulty by the patrols and then the sentries. His heart's thumping was an annoying distraction, and so Dewar stopped Hurricane just at the perimeter of the first circle of tents and made himself breathe slowly and deeply for a few minutes.

Relaxed, under better control, he went in. Hurricane wanted to go directly to Prospero's tent; Dewar thought it would be best if he first sought Gaston. However, Prince Josquin, also on horseback, found him before he reached the Fireduke's quarters.

"Lord Dewar," said Josquin.

Dewar nodded from the great height of Hurricane's back. "Your Highness."

"You were not at the meeting . . ."

Dewar shrugged and looked away.

". . . and I thought perhaps you might join me for supper, very late but not, I hope, unwelcome. I have just come from seeking you at your tent."

Dewar must look at him; he had no relish for flirtation now, nor for the honor of an intimate, personal meal with the Prince Heir. "Oh. Thank you. I'm not hungry, Your

Highness. Thank you for the invitation. Later perhaps."

"Tomorrow-later, I hope," Josquin said, with a comical expression of mock-distress, "for it's already the fifth hour of the night and my belly is long emptied. Very well. I'll see you on the morrow, then, Lord Dewar."

Dewar nodded again, and watched Josquin go along the path between the tents. He wondered why he felt no resentment at the Prince Heir for being the weapon Gaston had used to finally cut Prospero down. But Josquin was Landuc's, and there was no reason for him to do other than he had done.

Prince Gaston's tent was in the center of the camp; Prospero's ring told Dewar that Prospero was somewhere east of it. He dismounted at a mounting-block (it was still a stretch) and walked Hurricane to the tent, which had two torches outside and a couple of guards. Having looped the horse's reins loosely at the post, he started toward the entry.

One of the guards held up a hand. "Hold."

"I'm Lord Dewar," Dewar said, pushing his hood back.

"A moment, sir." One guard leaned inside, just into the flap, and talked to someone; half a minute later, the flap was drawn back by one of Prince Gaston's squires, who bowed, expressionless, to Dewar.

Dewar went in, ignored the squire's quick protest and evaded the boy's hand as he brushed past him, and passed into Gaston's inner tent. For privacy, the tent was doubled: an outer area about six feet wide insulated an inner chamber about fifteen across. Thus the Marshal could make plans with his captains, and none could overhear them. And thus he could talk to his brother the Emperor via a Lesser Summoning, without eavesdroppers getting the gist of their conversation.

Dewar stopped in the doorway, the red-faced squire behind him afraid to grab at the sorcerer's arm and drag him back.

Prince Gaston looked at him over a fireball and held up a finger: Wait.

"That is all for now," he said to the flame.

Dewar shifted his perceptions and synchronized them

with the spell. The man there had his back to Dewar, or so it seemed; he wore purple and gold, a wide-collared, embroidered robe perhaps.

"You're interrupted. I'll speak to you again tomorrow."

"Surely," Gaston said. "Good night, Your Majesty."

"Good night, Gaston. I am trying to think of rewards you haven't had yet."

"Give them to Herne," said the Marshal indifferently, perhaps distastefully, and snuffed the flame. He looked up at Dewar again, who blinked, having lost for an instant his purpose in coming there. "Good evening, Lord Dewar."

"Hello."

Gaston's eyes moved over the younger man's face for a few seconds. Then he nodded to a chair beside him at the table. "Sit," he said, collecting his apparatus.

Dewar sat, a little heavily, and swallowed.

"Wine?"

"No—yes, watered."

Gaston nodded and served him from cut-glass bottles that stood on a dark wooden brass-bound cabinet to one side. He poured a tumbler for himself and sat again.

Dewar looked down at his hands. He wasn't sure where to start: he was here to get permission to see Prospero, but he could not baldly ask it. He would have liked to have talked to Gaston about something else. Wine, maybe, or mutual acquaintances—they had none—or books or music. Something neutral. Something that had nothing to do with armies or wars.

Gaston waited quietly and then said, "Tomorrow 'twill snow, our local men do say. At long last. They speak of returning home and penning their flocks and herds ere the snow lieth too deep."

Dewar's mouth twitched. "Will you let them go?"

"When I've no further need of them, though not as soon as they would like. But I'll not keep them when there's no need, when they have work elsewhere. 'Twould sour them 'gainst Landuc. As it is, they are well-disposed now. Many are dead, but the survivors are paid in coin, that's scarce here. They've tales to awe their kin and wives. They've won.

There's no profit in wasting their goodwill."

"This isn't exactly a dubious part of the realm."

"Nay, but to them the capitol's a bright fiction, the Emperor a myth. Now all's more real. The realm is strengthened by their loyalty as it would be weakened by its loss."

"There are a lot of dead men out there, Marshal," said Dewar softly. "Lost and without loyalty."

"Their families are compensated. Pensioned."

"They'll never go home," Dewar said. "They're dead."

Gaston turned and looked into his eyes. "I would that war could be conducted without Death's complicity," he said. "I've been named Death, myself."

Dewar looked down, away, at the wine. "Without Death's complicity, and that of at least two other parties," he agreed. "I don't mean to bait you, Prince Gaston. I'm sorry." There was something calming about Gaston, perhaps because of his deliberate speech, his quiet voice, his age. Dewar's agitation had ceased; his heart was slow and his breath restful. The bone-struck chill had left him and he felt warm, though the fire in the stove was as ineffectual as any against the deep cold.

Gaston nodded, still studying his face as he had since Dewar entered the tent. "I would that this war had been accomplished without my complicity at times," he said, "and at other times it hath seemed inevitable to me. Yet the death of each of the soldiers on both sides saddens me, though with their deaths they have purchased life for Landuc. Each death is a death, permanent and forever, and none of the dead will walk again. True, there are many soldiers in Pheyarcet to fight our wars; there is a finite number but it is so great as to be infinite for our purposes. That maketh not any one of them less valuable."

Dewar swallowed and nodded, then looked at the Fireduke again. "I think I will not engage myself in wars henceforward. It has proven little to my taste, the blood, and I would accomplish the ends of war in other ways if it were possible."

Gaston nodded again, once, as he always did.

"It's late," Dewar said, and finished the wine in his glass.

"Prince Gaston, I have been none too useful a tool to your hand today, but I am here to ask a favor of you."

Gaston waited.

"I wish to speak to Prince Prospero."

Gaston scrutinized Dewar minutely now, every muscle in his face, every weary line. His own expression was calm, neutral as always, betraying nothing of his thoughts.

"Tonight," Dewar added after the silence had grown too long.

"I will grant thee this," Gaston said slowly, and sighed.

"We have things to discuss," Dewar whispered, and looked down.

"Of course," Gaston said then, and rose.

He knew, Dewar thought, but he stood and followed Gaston out, standing aside as the tall Prince took a heavy red cloak from a coat-rack.

Hurricane, outside, was stamping in the cold; Dewar undid the reins and looped them around the hand, his left, that bore the ring beneath his glove.

"A fine horse," Gaston said.

"I found him wandering around—I was . . . wandering myself."

Gaston said nothing more, but led him through the torch-lit camp to a tent ringed with uneasy guards.

Could he be attempting this in truth? wondered Dewar. It was the stuff of cheap popular ballads. He dropped Hurricane's reins and left him standing outside the tent-flap when Gaston lifted it and ducked in. Going in behind him, Dewar nearly bumped into him because the Marshal had stopped.

Then he straightened and saw why. A brittle, not-quite-visible shimmer in the air marked the edge of a circular Boundary drawn to confine Prospero here.

Prospero had looked up with an expression of chill inquiry which hardened as he recognized Dewar. He was not asleep, not even resting; he wore a heavy cloak, under which his left arm could be seen to be in a sling, and he sat on his cot, reading at a low table by a sickly green light.

Foxfire, Dewar realized. An illumination so energyless as to be useless as a focus for sorcery.

"Lord Dewar hath desired of me that he speak with you privily," Gaston said. "Is this agreeable to you?"

Prospero closed his book deliberately, and Dewar was unnerved to see that he was really thinking it over. "Very well," he said. "We've professional gossip to change, and this midnight's as good an hour as any other for't."

"I knew you would not yet lie asleep," Gaston said.

"Go sleep yourself, and sweet dreams, Prince," Prospero said, a note of irony in his voice. "You've much to look forward to tomorrow."

Gaston's lips pressed together and his nostrils flared, but he said evenly, "Very well. Lord Dewar, I shall tell the guards one quarter of an hour."

"Thank you, sir." Dewar bowed his head, speaking quietly.

Gaston bowed slightly to him and left.

Dewar moved around the perimeter of the unseen-but-felt Bounds until he was closest to Prospero. Prospero looked at him, his eyebrows drawn together, with a pained, not unkind expression.

"Thou, idiot," he informed Dewar.

"I know another," Dewar said, pricked. He removed his glove and held up his hand. "Recognize this?"

Prospero leaned forward, then stood and came to the Bounds. "How didst thou come by that," he hissed.

"A gift from a lady," Dewar said softly.

"A lady."

"A friend of yours."

"I see."

"She would have liked to come and talk to you herself, but I convinced her it was not the wisest thing to do. We have another acquaintance in common."

"Have we?"

"Four legs, twenty hands—"

"Idiot!"

"He's outside." Dewar reached into his jacket and took out his wand, beginning to draw power into it, into his hands, changing it, restoring its shape.

Prospero, who had begun to turn away, spun back and

stared at Dewar. "Where is she? Thou canst not be in earnest," he whispered.

"I wouldn't be, but for something the lady said before leaving."

"That, being?" Prospero would have pounced on him if he could.

"She has it on excellent authority that the Emperor has the cold cup ready for your gullet. This despite Gaston's objections; indeed, he may not know of it as such. To be slipped past Gaston to you as soon as possible. Perhaps for breakfast, who knows."

"Avril would keep that to himself. Here." Prospero pointed at a spot on the floor across from where Dewar stood, and Dewar went around to that place. He saw that it was a knotlike focus for the spell. " 'Tis there he closed it."

"I'll try my key in his lock. I didn't know he had the Art. The Well was plain in him, but not more."

"Didst not? Aye, he was with Neyphile, yon half-tutored vixen. She'd been prowling for a Prince. She had that knave false Golias awhile, lacking better company. A sweet pair of playmates, each to wreak 'pon the other by turns, poignant, pungent games of pain and steel in th' embrace of mutual vice."

Dewar covered his surprise, snorting. "Gossip indeed."

" 'Tis the sort can keep thee alive, thou young idiot."

"It's congenital," Dewar said, nettled. "Don't interrupt me."

Prospero, who had opened his mouth to do so, chuckled, holding his head in his right hand and shaking it. "Who'd believe this in a romance?" he muttered. "Why, nobody. Certainly not I."

Dewar was moving his staff, passing it from hand to hand slowly and gracefully, eyes closed now, following the spell. It was a simple but durable construction. There were three false knots to it and a fourth true knot; the false must be loosed first, and so he did that with all the care and meticulous attention he could muster. The spell was built of Well-force, and Well-force was a white line, an additional nerve and sense in Dewar's spine.

"Haste," whispered Prospero, watching him, still disbelieving. At least it was winter, so the quarter-hour they had been granted was long. He turned and rumpled up the bedding, then half-covered the foxfire with his book, dimming the interior. "A grey-bearded ruse," Prospero muttered, shaking his head at the unconvincingly mock-tenanted bed. It might buy a few seconds' reprieve.

Perspiration ran from Dewar's forehead to sting his eyes. He finished the third and began the true knot, moving the staff more and more slowly, as the resistance of the spell increased. Otto, luckily, didn't seem to have built any traps into the thing; there were a few odd tingles and pops, but Dewar ignored them as minor flaws or flairs and concentrated on taking it apart.

He slammed the staff down. Sparks shot up its length as force was channelled out through it, through Dewar and back through the staff to dissipate, and a glowing rush poured in from the Binding as it came apart around him.

"Right peremptory-beautiful," whispered Prospero, smiling. He gestured, three quick loops, drawing the Well into his own hands and shaping a spell with economy. The air around him shimmered and thickened.

Dewar leaned on his staff, panting and soaked; he mopped his face.

"Hurry," he whispered in his turn, and started for the tent-flap.

Prospero completed his spell just as the flap was moved by a guard outside. Dewar grabbed the canvas and stepped under it, face-to-face with the guard, blocking his view of the interior.

"Time's up," said the sorcerer to the soldier, who, startled, nodded and stepped back.

Prospero, unseen, brushed past Dewar, jostling the tent as he did.

"Thanks," said Dewar to the guard, dropping the flap, "and have a quiet night."

"Good night, sir," said the guard, stepping back to his position, and Hurricane stamped and snorted.

Since the horse was right in front of the guards, Dewar supposed it was impossible for Prospero to mount now, and so he took the animal's bridle in his right hand and walked away. The ring told him Prospero was on the horse's other side.

When they were away from the guards, Prospero moved around to Dewar's left.

A whisper in his ear: "Smartly done. Give me that ring; I'll see it returned."

Dewar reluctantly tugged the ring from his hand; it was plucked out of his fingers and vanished.

Prospero's voice murmured, "I shall not leave my sword here."

"Oh, shit."

"Mend thy tongue. Who comes?"

Dewar heard the footsteps as Prospero did, and turned to see Ottaviano in shirt, pants, and boots, jogging up to the tent, speaking to the guards, ducking inside.

"Otto. Mount and get out of here!"

"And thee! Hurricane—"

Ottaviano shot out of the tent and started toward them at a run.

"Mount! Go! I can manage him!"

Prospero mounted, then bent and grabbed Dewar's arm, hauling him halfway up. Dewar cursed and stepped on Prospero's invisible foot in the stirrup, swung his leg over the horse's back behind Prospero, and Hurricane sprang forward.

"What about your sword?"

"I'll fetch it later!"

"Dewar! Get back here, you son of a bitch! Guards! Stop them!"

"Hark, the cur gives tongue," Prospero said to nobody in particular, and leaned low on Hurricane's neck. "Ah, my kingdom for a Gate, a Way, a Road!"

Ottaviano, surprisingly, was still in sight where he ran after them, and his shouts were rousing the camp. Three sentries with halberds ran to intercept Hurricane; he gathered himself as he approached them (Dewar felt the Well flow into the horse) and leapt, a wondrous flight-like jump, over them, past them, landed running, a miracle, and one he repeated a few seconds later.

One of the halberds, swung high by an angry guard, clipped Dewar's head on the second leap, grazing invisible Prospero too. Prospero grunted; Dewar gasped and clutched Prospero to stay on the horse. Warm blood grew cold with the wind of their travelling on his face. People were shouting alarms; hastily-aimed arrows passed them, though one stuck in Prospero's unseen thigh, a weird sight; they seemed to pass through Hurricane or perhaps they only missed. Dewar shook his head; blood flew and his vision darkened momentarily, then stayed dark. Or was it shadows? Hard to say. Dewar drew on the Well and felt clearer-headed. He could see Prospero now greyly in the moonlight. They were racing through the camp, pursued by shouts and somehow dodging all the attempted interceptions.

Hurricane leaped again—the dry moat, Dewar realized—and flew through the air. Was Prospero making for his own headquarters, for reunion with his captured forces? Or fleeing? If only they'd had longer to talk—Hurricane galloped now—

Herne was beside them, on his huge dull-red horse, edging closer, closer—

Prospero was shouting something, and Herne shouted back. He had a naked sword in his hand and he was pacing them as Hurricane took a low rise at an impossible speed. Prospero was pulling Hurricane away, gesturing, and a fire left his hand and sizzled in a line through the air to splash off Herne's whirled sword.

"Ariel!" Prospero bellowed.

"Master!" rang from the air around them.

"Keep our pursuers back!"

A true hurricane joined Hurricane, blowing in his wake, a screaming headwind that slowed Herne's horse no matter how he fought against it. Prospero bent Hurricane's head to the west again. Dewar could not quite focus on the Well now. Confused, he thought that might be due to Ariel's turbulence. He let the Well go from him and slumped forward against Prospero's back. Hurricane's muscles gathered and stretched beneath him, and the cold air flowed past his face. He was flying, he thought, and flew on alone into blankness.

# — 22 —

OTTAVIANO WOKE WHEN THE TINGLE RAN over his body. *Something is wrong,* it told him, and he lay, keeping his breathing soft and even, listening acutely and reaching with another sense for an explanation.

Nothing had broken the covertly-laid Bounds of his tent. Something else.

Otto tensed and sensed, eyes still closed.

The Bounds he had forged around Prospero were gone!

He shot out of bed, grabbing at his breeches and struggling into them, getting his boots wrong-footed and then getting them right. He stuffed his shirt into his breeches as he ran out into the freezing night, racing past sentries through the moonlit camp toward the guarded tent where Prospero had been confined.

"Has anyone been here?" he demanded of the one who moved to intercept him.

"The sorcerer, sir, with Prince Gaston—"

Otto half-screamed an obscenity and tore the tent flap aside, seeing what he knew he'd see.

The guard gasped.

Otto held up his hand and said "Stay out!" as he ducked inside. Once in, he closed his eyes and swept a hand, extended by a strand of Well-force, through the interior: Prospero was gone indeed, not just invisible.

But not long gone. The disturbance of the spell's breaking still quivered in the world; they could not be far off. Otto ducked back out. Prince Gaston would have a lot to answer for at Court, he thought, and the Emperor might just lose his temper—

"Prospero's gone! Which way did they go?" he demanded of the guard, but then he saw the movement of someone mounting a horse a few hundred paces away in the shadows, and he sprinted toward them, away from the shocked guards.

"Dewar!" he shouted.

Dewar leaned forward and the horse leapt and started away, accelerating quickly to a gallop.

"Get back here, you son of a bitch! Guards! Stop them!" bellowed Otto, seeing the horse race past three who simply stared at it. In the cloud-patched moonlight, he saw that there was only one man visible on the horse's back, Dewar from his cloak, but that he was seated far back and thus Otto was sure Prospero sat before him, invisible.

He kept them in sight as they raced through the camp. Dewar looked back once to see him. The sentries at the perimeter, alerted by Ottaviano's shouts now, tried to intercept them; Otto saw a halberd-swing that must have connected, but Dewar lurched and grabbed unseen Prospero for support. Otto shouted "Arrows! Use your bows!" at the men. At the ditch, he lost them. Prospero's supernatural horse jumped the damned thing.

Herne thundered past Ottaviano as he jogged to a halt, unable to follow them over the ditch, but Herne's roan horse, as fast as Prospero's black, swerved, tore over the bridge, and galloped after the fleeing sorcerers into the night.

"Ottaviano!" shouted someone; was it Josquin?

"Baron!" another said. "The Marshal wants you." He stood beside Otto and waited, the Fireduke's right-hand man, Captain Jolly.

"I bet he does. Shit. Oh, shit. He's going to be sorry for this," Otto said, looking around, walking slowly, breathing hard from his sprint. Prince Gaston, wearing a chain-mail shirt (maybe he really did sleep in his armor, Otto thought) and leather pants, bareheaded and highbooted and holding

Chanteuse du Mort naked in his hand, was coming, giving orders to men who hovered at his side long enough to listen and say, "Yes, sir," and rushed away into the camp.

Otto and Captain Jolly went to him.

Prince Gaston looked at Otto, lifted his eyebrows.

"Prospero's escaped," Otto said.

The Marshal's face smoothed and then tightened. He slipped the sword into its scabbard. His lips thinned; he turned and stared in the direction in which Prospero's horse was last seen travelling. "Ah," he said.

"Why did you let Dewar near him?" Otto yelled. "What in freezing hell were you thinking of?"

Jolly inhaled sharply beside Otto.

Prince Gaston flicked his eyes at his captain, who bowed and began to move away. "Get a horse," Gaston said. "Follow Prince Herne. Thou understand'st my will."

"Do my best, sir." Captain Jolly, like the others, ran off to carry out his Prince's orders.

"No better can we," Gaston said, a little bitterly.

"What were you thinking of?" Otto demanded. "You knew, I knew, what—"

"Quiet." The Fireduke's hand gripped his shoulder, warm through the thin shirt, and the Fireduke's eyes finally drilled through Otto's outrage and held his attention.

"Sir," Otto said, through clenched teeth, "if I may—"

"Nephew," said Prince Gaston, "come with me."

Otto blinked. The Marshal had never referred to him that way.

"Come." Prince Gaston took his elbow and led him away. "Jolly will run them down," he said to a man who approached him—Captain Addis.

"The Duke of Winds has escaped!" said the Captain.

"Prince Herne rides after him," said Prince Gaston. "We shall bide here, rather than panic." He said *panic* contemptuously; Captain Addis reddened, saluted, muttered an acknowledgement, and backed away.

Otto and Gaston walked through the buzzing camp. As they went, the Prince Marshal spoke to a few men, here and there, just a word or two, and the place settled in the wake of his passing. Ottaviano admired his command of the men; they had absolute faith in the Fireduke, and he apparently had equal faith in them.

Prince Gaston's squires were awake, waiting in the outer part of his tent with an oil lamp and the Fireduke's plate armor, talking as they cleaned it. It was clean, but Gaston frowned on idle squires. Their labor and chatter halted as he entered with Otto behind him, jumping to their feet and looking expectantly at their master.

"Go back to bed," Prince Gaston said to them gently. "There's naught ye may do."

"Yes, sir," they said in muted, chiming adolescent voices, and one left the tent as the other returned to his bedroll on the ground.

The Prince took the lit lamp and ushered Otto into the inner tent.

"Sit," he said.

Otto took a camp chair. His host poured wine for them both and sat down on the other side of the table. "Thou think'st I was lax," Prince Gaston said.

"I'm not too clear on what happened," Otto admitted, looking down. "I, uh, shot my mouth off perhaps prematurely—"

"Dewar came to me," Prince Gaston looked at a small traveller's hourglass in a polished brass case, "three-quarters of an hour past. He desired to speak briefly with Prince Prospero. I consented and escorted him there. Prince Prospero received him; I gave them a quarter of an hour and returned here." He paused, studying Otto, and continued in a lower voice. "I take it thy Bounds were not impervious to attack."

"If I'd thought they were going to be tested from the outside, as well as from within, I'd have made them differently," Otto said, biting his lip. He realized that he did not look very good now, himself. "I didn't expect Dewar to turn coat. After all his claims of loyalty—"

"Meseems a man who hath daily stated that he is here on whim, cannot be considered to have turned coat," the Marshal said.

"But you trusted him alone with Prince Prospero—"

"I'd no cause to deny him privy speech with the Prince. But a few hours past Prince Herne visited; they quarrelled, as ever."

"You're blind, Your Highness," Ottaviano said, thumping his hand lightly on the table. "You saw the way Dewar hung back today! Prospero might have bought him off against just such an event." He said this, but he didn't believe it. Dewar's notions of honor and ethics were too nice, too otherworldly-idealistic, to allow him to play the double agent. Otto's own notional ethics held him back from speaking of Dewar's geas: it was the sort of confidence a gentleman would not betray, and telling Gaston of it now—too late to use the knowledge—would be useless.

" 'Tis possible," Prince Gaston said slowly. "In that case I would expect Dewar to have confined him, however, thereby to leave a flaw in the binding."

Otto nodded and tasted his wine, then put it aside. His good work, undone; his sorcery, exposed—the stuff might have been water. He said wearily, "Prince Gaston, why did you let him in there?"

Gaston scrutinized his nephew's sharp, stubbled face for a full minute and then said, "To spare Prospero's life, nephew."

"To what?" whispered Otto.

Prince Gaston continued studying him.

"Save his life? After what he's done—"

"What hath he done?"

"Made war on the Emperor—"

"His war hath been judged just by many," Gaston said.

"Your Emperor!"

"My Landuc," Prince Gaston corrected him. "Baron, th'art an intelligent man, and I think thee not without perception. Suppose Prospero, in a few days' time, be delivered up to th' Emperor, and th' Emperor then execute him; hath said 'a would. What followeth?"

Ottaviano frowned a little. "Peace."

"Think beyond this war."

Ottaviano thought further. "Anyone the Emperor

doesn't like, dies," he whispered. "You, Prince Herne, me, any of us. Princes or not, Well-born or Well-user or not, anyone who cramps the Emperor's style goes without negotiation or mercy. By this precedent." And he thought further: King Panurgus had not executed people. Exiled, yes, but not executed; why, he had exiled Prospero. The King had taken subtler vengeances than murder.

"Dost think peace would prevail under those circumstances?"

"People would get worried," Otto decided slowly, thinking hard. "Maybe—a split, a coup . . . no, I guess it wouldn't be too peaceful. But, Marshal—Prospero has caused a lot of war already. It has not been peaceful. Is his life worth so much death?"

"I know not," Prince Gaston said, "but I know how many Princes there are, and what we are, and who we are, and I think 'twere ill to lose one to fraternal malice."

"You are a traitor."

"Nay. The realm is safe. His forces are bested."

"He'll be back. The Emperor won't let you off the hook for this. What are you going to say, Prince Gaston? Are you going to blame me for not Binding him strongly enough?"

"The Emperor and I will discuss this privily," said the Marshal.

"You're not indispensable, Your Highness."

"I have never pretended to be so."

Otto swallowed, drank some wine. It mellowed in his mouth. "I don't think he's worth it," he said softly. "One Prince, even if he is the Prince of Air, the Duke of Winds, is not worth so many lives, so much bloodshed, so much war."

"Art certain?" the Prince asked him, without inflection.

"No," he admitted even more softly. "I guess I'm not. You've thought about this a long time, haven't you."

Prince Gaston had been thinking about it since before Ottaviano's father was born. The corner of his mouth twitched, and he said, "Aye."

"You're conservative. You prefer the status quo."

"I'd liever another status quo, one in which Prospero

keepeth peace, one in which he's reconciled. 'Tis ill for us to be at one another's throats."

Ottaviano shook his head. "He's not going to give up," he said. "Not unless—" He stopped, an idea stirring through his words.

Prince Gaston watched the lamp's flame and then looked at Otto expectantly. He was a bright fellow, quick and deep-striking, and his wits were nimble; the boy was a better thinker than Sebastiano had ever been.

"Unless," Otto said slowly, "you can get some kind of oath or vow from him . . . Hm. And for that . . . Does the Emperor really want him dead?"

"There hast thou the very kernel-question," said Prince Gaston. "It is one only the Emperor can answer."

Ottaviano's horse, Lightfoot, was as groggy as he, but the exercise of trotting along in Prospero's wake woke them both up. He had left a note for Prince Gaston, saying that he was attempting to follow Prospero, and had departed the camp with Lightfoot and a lantern.

He stopped at Prospero's tent and prowled the place, looking for some trace which might be used in finding him. The sorcerer had been careful, though, and after searching everywhere Otto had to make do with a pillow on which he had lain a little while. It was not going to get him far, but he hoped it might put him in the right direction.

The sky had clouded over and the air had taken on the sharpness of snow. Ottaviano wondered, as he rode, if Prospero had somehow—being the Prince of Winds—kept the weather favorable for war, and now, without his influence, the postponed winter would descend with added weight. The conjecture seemed plausible. The man commanded his element the way Prince Gaston commanded his men. The storms which had raged over them had left Prospero's lines unscathed.

Otto thought that if he were Prospero, he'd slip into Landuc and nail the Emperor with a lightning bolt. It would save time and blood.

Once outside the camp, Otto stopped and wove around the pillow a low-powered spell of affinity. Riding onward, the spell guided him over some of the roughest and worst ground in the region; the action of water on and in the limestone here meant the terrain was irregular, cut with gullies and chasms. Many times he had to detour around places which were impassable in the dark, over which Prospero's horse had to all appearances flown.

By morning, he was miles from the camp, and the chasms and gullies had given way to the long, level highlands. Heavy snow was falling. Ottaviano began to draw on the Well's currents for his sustenance, but they were thin here, comparatively, the area never having been much favored though it lay so near the Well, and he derived less good from them than he hoped. He stopped to rest Lightfoot often, but dared not stop too long.

As he rode, he took out his Landuc Well-Map and studied it, and at once his path became clearer. Prospero had headed for a Ley. At a Nexus at the end of the Ley, there was sometimes a Gate.

Even as Otto realized this and smiled, the affinity-spell jerked the pillow from his hand. Otto snatched at it, surprised, and missed. The pillow plumped onto the snowy ground.

"Hm," Otto said, and reined in Lightfoot to stop for a look.

The snow was thin and dry. He brushed the pillow; the spell had snapped apart under the excessive stress of proximity and it was only a pillow now. Then, under a dusting of snow, he saw what it was that had brought the spell to an end.

An arrow.

Rather, a broken arrow. Ottaviano lifted it, beginning to smile broadly, and then he laughed. The head was stained with dried and frozen blood: Prospero's own.

"Thank you, thank you!" he shouted up at the snow clouds, and remounted with fresh vigor, chortling. He ripped up the pillow and wrapped the arrow in the fabric.

"Lightfoot, we'll find some water, take a rest, and burn ourselves a trail," he told the horse, and gave him a nudge to start him walking again.

Down the Ley, through the Gate at dawn, and along the Road went Otto, led by the bloodstained arrow in his pocket. It was as bright and clear a beacon as the full moon; it felt like a string reeling him in toward the Prince, and the feeling grew stronger as he travelled. The arrow led him away from Landuc, a roundabout route. He checked the Ephemeris and found that indeed, Prospero had been able to take a more direct path. At a Gate where Otto had had to leave the Road and travel for more than a day on a Ley, Prospero had been able to go straight through.

The arrow guided him through a scrubby forest where he rested a few hours, having left the Road. He was no longer on a Ley, either; this might mean he was close to his quarry. Ottaviano ate the last of his food, but found no water. The place was cold and arid; the leaves leathery, and the wood tough and unburnable.

He rode out of the forest late at night and followed the arrow onward. It led him through low-walled pastures to a rocky shore, down a steep slope to a cliff-edge where a small house stood, as grey as the thick clouds overhead. The house was nearly indistinguishable from the stony ground around it; the sea roared below its ill-repaired walls and sent spray up to its roof.

Otto reined in and looked the place over.

This was it. Likely Prospero was still here. Otto's heart skipped and began to race in battle-rhythm.

He sent Lightfoot scrambling up the bank. Otto was perishing with thirst, so he led the horse back toward a muck-edged waterhole he had circumnavigated earlier. Three-toed footprints stippled the mud, and over them moon-shaped hoofprints. He let Lightfoot drink after filling his waterskin; no knowing what kind of animals they kept here, and the water was slightly funky, but it was better than nothing.

That done, he led Lightfoot back among the stones and picketed him.

On foot now, in the dim cloud-strained light that had not changed, Ottaviano made his way quietly back to the cottage. The arrow he had buttoned under his jacket twitched and throbbed. Ottaviano crouched behind an array of stones and discarded clever and elaborate plans.

The place was Well-poor, making sorcery difficult for him, and anyway he knew he couldn't expect to challenge Prospero to a sorcerers' duel and live.

Otto closed his eyes and let the part of his mind or body—he was never sure whether it was one or both—that fed on the Well dominate his senses. He sensed no sorcery in the area; the stone hut was without reinforcement from the fire of the Well, and the dull glow of life within was unmoving and quiescent. Another living thing was on the other side of the building, most likely Prospero's horse.

Could Prospero have been so arrogantly confident as to have not bothered with protective spells? Otto looked again. A cautious man himself, he could not believe that anyone in Prospero's position might stop without warding himself nine ways or a dozen.

But there was no sign of the weblike knitting of Bounds nor of a protective spell.

Otto studied the place again through his Well-sense, and found nothing, no sorceries. Perhaps it was not Prospero—but the arrow strained to get to the place, Prospero's own blood.

He stood and picked his way to the hut, avoiding loose stones and making as little disturbance in the world as he could. Out of sight, a horse stamped and chewed.

Ottaviano stood beside the uncovered low doorway, listening. Light snoring. The arrow thrummed.

Great and glorious Well, was the sorcerer Prince simply stretched there asleep? Was he so smug as to think no one could follow him in his flight? Was it to be as easy as this?

Otto took a dagger in one hand, drew his sword quietly with the other, and stepped swiftly into the hut. He froze, tense and ready; the breathing of the occupant went on. His eyes grew accustomed to the dim interior; he saw a long shape on the ground, dark-muffled, and in the light of the doorway a bandaged hand, blood-stained. Otto took two quick steps and lifted the dagger, bringing the pommel down hard.

Prince Herne saw the Baron of Ascolet first on his return to Gaston's camp. Prince Herne was still furious about Prospero's escape, and the Baron's empty-handed arrival set him off again.

"He ran fast and far," Ottaviano said again and again. "I lost him. I tried to find him, but I lost him again." His grimy state and his horse's exhaustion—he had ridden hard to return from Malperdy, abused Lightfoot to make two Gates and the Road—attested to his story, and finally Herne, with a last snarl about useless jack-sprats, left him alone. Otto breathed a sigh of relief. He would tell them the truth, he fully intended to do so, but in his own time, when he'd rested and decided what the price of Prospero would be.

"Pay him no mind," Prince Josquin said, coming up beside Otto as he passed a tent.

"Your Highness. You heard—"

"Herne and Fulgens share a temper, thus either has but half."

"I didn't take it personally, sir. I've seen him blow up before."

"Ah. He and Golias were at blows this morning, and not on the training ground."

"Setting a good example, my lord?"

The Prince chuckled. "Cock-fighting," he said. "I won two royals on it."

"I want a bath, my lord," Otto said, "and a lot of food, and about twelve hours of peace and quiet. Think I'll get any of 'em?"

"Just pop round and say hello to the Marshal," Prince Josquin advised him. "We were going to have a briefing tonight, but he'll postpone it till tomorrow since you've returned. Good news?"

"No news."

"Bad news."

"Right. Good news for Prospero, though."

Prince Josquin's eyebrows went up. "True. And bad news for somebody, certainly. —He's an amazing fellow. We can't work out where in the Well's bright worlds his army came from. Can't understand a word they say, and it's mutual."

"I thought the Well granted the gift of tongues, my lord."

"So did we, but this lot speak pure jabberish. Damned frustrating. Their commander, Prospero's second, speaks a bit of Lannach, and he's getting testy. The Marshal hasn't admitted that we no longer have Prospero, you know. I'll lead your horse to the grooms with me; I'm going there myself. Tito! Take the Baron's horse."

"Thank you, Your Highness. You're very kind."

"Do enjoy your luncheon, Baron. Toodle-oo," said the Prince Heir, and his squire led Lightfoot away behind him.

Ottaviano gazed after him. It was hard to figure Josquin. When was he acting? There was something serious to him; he was good in the field, good enough for the Marshal to trust him as much as Herne, but the flippant, foppish veneer was difficult to penetrate. Dewar liked him—in fact, they were panting after one another as discreetly as possible—but Ottaviano couldn't see what the sorcerer might find so intoxicating in the Prince Heir. Perhaps Dewar, who had refused Otto's laboriously-located wenches, wasn't interested in girls, despite his continual flirting with Luneté in Lys. More likely, Dewar was uninterested in men or women, which would be usual for a sorcerer, and simply enjoyed playing eye-games with the future ruler of the Empire.

The Baron of Ascolet made his way to the Marshal's headquarters. He was kept waiting a few minutes and then beckoned in by one of the squires, who was repairing a mail-coat when he wasn't minding the door.

"Good day, sir," Otto said.

Prince Gaston nodded to him and nodded to a chair, the same Otto had occupied before. "Hast been away," he said.

"I went hunting. A good run, as they say in the chase, but no kill."

"I did not think thou wouldst succeed, and I'd have ordered thee forgo it," the Marshal said.

"I went without leave. I know. I thought it was worth the risk." Ottaviano summarized the route he had followed after Prospero—truths and fictions. "I lost him at Fiargate. How long was I gone?"

"One day. 'Twas quickly ridden. —There's a matter of weight I'd bring to light with thee."

"Uh, Lys—"

"Thy sorcery."

Ottaviano nodded, as if he'd expected it. "I know a few tricks," he said. "Book-learning."

They studied one another. Prince Gaston was obviously waiting for more. Ottaviano tried to tough it out and found the Fireduke's unwavering regard too harsh.

"That's about it," he said. "I'm not Dewar."

"Clearly not," Prince Gaston said, which felt vaguely like an insult. "Yet hearsay claims 'twere needful thou attend initiation at the Well, ere thou couldst perform a Binding such as thou hast done."

Otto felt his face redden against his will. He hadn't expected this; he had forgotten in the excitement of the hunt and capture. Prince Gaston wasn't one to let anything pass without at least letting it be known he had noticed.

"Um," he said.

"That's all," the Prince said impassively. "Go thou, eat and rest. We'll confer at the first hour o' morning. Tomorrow we're breaking camp."

Ottaviano got up and got out of there, grateful for the Fireduke's mercy, and hastened to his tent without seeing anyone else of consequence. Soon he lay in bed, unable to rest despite being dead tired and stuffed with greasy cold mutton. He thought hard about Gaston.

He had just been warned, Ottaviano decided. The Marshal thought he was up to something. Gaston needed his cooperation for now, but any crap from Ottaviano, and Gaston was going to come down hard on him. Ottaviano had high-tailed it out of camp after Prospero and Dewar. That looked bad. He had done it without informing his commanding officer. That was bad. He had failed in his cockeyed mission, ostensibly. That meant he'd wasted time, which was bad too.

The Prince Marshal had let the Baron know, obliquely, that he did not trust Otto, that he knew there was something fishy going on, and that he did not want his war mucked up by another sorcerer.

Ah, shit, thought Otto, and rolled onto his stomach.

He thought of Malperdy, a severely-made fortress in Ascolet, and smiled. The Marshal might think he'd wasted his time, but this time the Marshal was wrong. When the Baron of Ascolet showed what he had accomplished, Gaston would be surprised.

# — 23 —

"DULL COMPANY THIS MORNING," PRINCE JOSQUIN murmured to Otto, passing him the mulled wine. The Marshal allowed no servants in the briefings.

"Send for a clown, Your Highness," suggested Otto.

"Alas, the Marshal's agenda has no item for tumblers and jesters." The Prince Heir smiled and sipped. "But where's Prince Golias?"

Otto's wine was too hot. He set it down. "He said he'd be a few minutes behind, said he had something—"

Prince Herne came in, followed by Prince Gaston. Outside the sounds of the camp's disassembly were coming in through the wind-shuddering canvas. It was still snowing.

Actually, thought Ottaviano, maybe it was just the aftermath of the battle. Maybe the wounded and dead were dragging the spirit of the camp down. The dead had been buried in the day Otto was gone, in a long ditch which Dewar had blasted in the earth to halt Prospero's advance; there was insufficient fuel for so many pyres, so only one token purifying, transubstantiating fire had been lit. The crowd of dead men would have to make do with that. Thrifty Gaston.

"Where's Golias?" Prince Gaston asked him.

"He said he'd be a little late. I had breakfast with him," Otto said.

Prince Herne sat down heavily, dropped his leather pouch of papers and maps before him, and folded his arms. The Prince Marshal poured himself wine and sat at the head of the table, taking out his own notes.

Golias lifted the tent flap and entered, a blur of snowflakes accompanying him, and took his seat on Otto's side of the table. Dewar would have been between them, across from Josquin; that place was empty now.

They sat a few seconds in silence, glancing at one another, and then Prince Gaston nodded.

"Several items," he said laconically. "Item, Baron Ottaviano, plain to see, hath returned, and took no prisoners in his hunt of Prince Prospero and Lord Dewar."

"How far did you get?" Prince Herne asked him.

"I lost them at Fiargate, sir," lied Ottaviano, wondering at their easy acceptance of his newly-revealed ability. He suspected that gossip had been busy in Otto's absence.

"Ah," said Prince Josquin. "I know it. Complicated junction."

"Yes, sir. I don't know where they went then, but they did go through there. But from there, there are a lot of places they could go."

"We'll not pursue it, or them, further," the Marshal said.

Herne glowered at Gaston. "You should have let me kill him."

"Herne."

A taut silence. Josquin studied his immaculate fingerends. Golias watched Herne and Gaston eyeing one another until Herne looked down.

"Item, the dead were fired and interred 'fore sundown yesterday. Let the crews be praised and rewarded," Prince Gaston said. "Item. Have you met delays in breaking camp?"

"None. My men are nearly finished," Herne said.

"The Madanese cannot wait to leave." Prince Josquin grinned. "I believe we're setting a record for camp-striking speed."

"My company's ready," Golias said.

"We haven't got much to break down, sir, and it's going smoothly," Otto said. Much of his and Herne's encampment had been destroyed by Prospero's forces in the last battle; they'd doubled-up since with Golias's and Josquin's men.

"Good," the Marshal said. "All must be ready to go at noon." He glanced around the table; they all nodded. "Item, the prisoners. His Majesty hath desired they be conveyed under strong guard to Perendlac, overland. Prince Herne, take thou the Sixth, and under thee shall go Baron Ottaviano with his men, to escort them and guard them once there. That shall be but a holding-place; we've no means to repatriate 'em, and 'twere unwise to allow them to remain long together."

Execution, thought Otto. Would Emperor Avril order the death of, what was it, six thousand? Sure. They were Prospero's. As long as they were alive, they'd be dangerous. The sorcerously-bound allies had disappeared when Prospero acknowledged his defeat in Prince Gaston's tent, taking the vanquished's oath. The Pheyarcet men Prospero had recruited would be returned to their native lands, their rulers penalized.

"Prince Herne, do thou further question his second and discover what thou mayst about their origin," Gaston said, "and how they came hither."

Herne nodded, smiling slightly.

The door-flap stirred. Gaston frowned and turned, standing as he did; it was one of the squires.

"Captain Gallitan is here, sir, and he begs audience at once, sir, 'tis most urgent."

"Let him come."

The flap went up and down; out went the squire, in came Captain Gallitan, agitated, his eyes black sparks under his shaggy brows.

"Sir, your pardon, sir," he said, and saluted the Prince Marshal.

"What is it?" Prince Gaston asked.

Gallitan's gaze slipped to one side to meet Otto's for a fraction of a second and then back to Prince Gaston's. "An incident, sir."

The Marshal frowned.

"A prisoner, sir, attempted to escape and has been killed," Gallitan said slowly.

Prince Gaston nodded, waiting.

"Prisoner is a woman, sir," Gallitan went on, stiffening up and glancing at—no, Otto realized, at Golias, not at Otto. "The woman was being held by Prince Golias's men, sir," Gallitan went on. "She is not of Prince Prospero's force." He inhaled again.

Prince Gaston nodded, a single down-up, and Ottaviano swallowed a little wine.

"I recognize her, sir," Captain Gallitan went on. "Lady Miranda of Valgalant."

"Indeed?" said Prince Gaston, his brows drawing together.

"The treasonous cockatrice!" Prince Herne shouted, leaping to his feet.

"Thy prisoner?" Prince Gaston rounded on Golias.

Captain Gallitan stood rigid, staring straight ahead.

"My men picked her up," Golias said calmly, "in a sweep for prisoners, deserters, and so on. They brought her in and I questioned her—"

"Thou didst not report this to me," the Marshal said. "Hast questioned her?"

"Of course. She could not give account of herself, no explanation of why she was riding away from here as fast as Lord Dewar's horse could carry her. I recognized the horse as the one he'd used during the battle, when he was swinging a sword instead of using his sorcery for us. She admitted this morning that she was here to warn Prospero of certain movements of Prince Josquin; apparently she got here too late for it to do him any good, and so she was sneaking homeward when we caught her."

"Killed," the Marshal said, to Gallitan.

"Dead, sir," Gallitan said. "I have the men who appear to be involved under guard, sir."

"My men—" began Golias, his eyes flashing with anger.

"Didst not inform me of this," the Marshal said, in that very quiet voice, cutting him off. "Thou knewest who she was."

"I was going to bring it up," Golias said. "You're holding my men prisoner?"

Prince Josquin was staring at him, his brows drawn together slightly. He turned his gaze on Ottaviano, coldly assessing him.

"Lady Miranda? You did not see fit to inform the Marshal that you found Lady Miranda here?" Prince Herne demanded.

"Captain Gallitan," said the Marshal, "what passed?"

"It's still not clear, sir," Gallitan said. "I gather that the woman, with hands bound behind her, managed to escape the tent where she was held and started away, but was intercepted. The men claim there was a scuffle. She died of a stabbing."

"Hold the men apart from one another, and let the body be treated with all due honor," Prince Gaston said. "Dismissed."

Gallitan saluted and left as quickly as he'd entered.

Prince Gaston turned and fixed Golias with a brilliant stare, downward from his height to seated Golias, a burning glare. "Art aware," the Fireduke said slowly, "of what furor this shall incite?"

"She was a spy," Golias said.

"She was Gonzalo of Valgalant's daughter," Prince Gaston said. "Regardless of her identity, thou didst not inform me thou hadst privily such a prisoner."

The snow hissed on the sides of the tent.

"I meant to tell you at this meeting," Golias said sullenly.

Prince Gaston looked from him to Ottaviano, but said nothing. He sat again, and Prince Herne slowly sat down beside him.

"All prisoners henceforward shall be under Prince

Herne's authority," said the Marshal. "To return to our agenda," he said, "Prince Herne shall take the Sixth and Seventh to guard the convoy of prisoners to Perendlac. Prince Golias, shalt accompany them with thy men." He glanced at his notes for the first time. "Item, the locals are being paid and dismissed. Any difficulties?"

"None reported, sir," Prince Josquin said. He had brought the Emperor's gold and silver and the paymasters with him.

The meeting went on. Ottaviano, Josquin, Herne, and Golias reported on their total count of casualties; they discussed, in subdued voices, supplies and transportation of the wounded in a special convoy, and at the end, Prince Gaston said, "The death of Lady Miranda hath placed a particular burthen on me. I shall carry her body to Landuc myself, through a Way, today. Ere I go I'll obtain a full account of the matter for the Emperor."

"Don't be a fool," Golias said. "She was here as a spy, committing treason. Let her vanish—"

"Dost know," Prince Gaston said, "who Lady Miranda of Valgalant is? Was?"

Golias blinked.

"Nay, thy ignorance is clear," said the Fireduke coldly. "I'll speak with thee anon."

"Uh, Your Highness, a word," Ottaviano said, catching his cousin the Prince Heir outside the tent.

Prince Josquin, still with that remote, chill look in his face, looked at him expectantly.

"Who's Miranda of Valagant?"

"Valgalant. Gonzalo of Valgalant's daughter."

"And who's he?"

"A prominent, noble, but exiled, partisan of Prospero whose daughter and sole child is widely speculated to have entered a private engagement, perhaps even a marriage, with her father's patron against the time when he would rule," said the Prince Heir. "Prince Prospero has the highest regard for her; he was her name-sponsor when she was born. Valgalant still holds much land around Landuc, directly and indirectly. Of the nobles who supported Prospero, Gonzalo was the only one whom the Emperor did not execute after the last war."

"Oh."

"Oh," Prince Josquin agreed. "An ancient, illustrious family, favored by Panurgus and still of consequence despite diminished numbers and unfashionable politics."

"Do you—did you know her?"

"Oh yes," said the Prince, and he bowed slightly, turned, and walked away.

"Prince Gaston—"

"Baron." The Marshal nodded, preoccupied, sparing but a word for the Baron of Ascolet. His tent had been taken down; he was just finished speaking with Gernan the surgeon, Captain Gallitan, and Prince Herne, all of whom cast cold glances at Ottaviano as they all three left.

"Sir, I have a request."

Gaston waited.

"I, um," Otto looked down. "I haven't been— It seems to me, sir, that my presence isn't needed to lead my troops; my second, Lieutenant Clay, is capable of doing that. I request permission for a leave."

Gaston frowned slightly. "To what purpose?"

"I'd like to see my wife, sir," Otto said.

"Thy wife, the Countess of Lys," Gaston said. "The journey would take some time, Baron. More time than I prefer to have thee absent. I must deny thy request, but I shall endeavor to grant it when 'tis possible to have leaves of absence. Prince Prospero is at large; the war is by no means over, simply in hiatus."

"Sir, we—it's been very hard on her, I can tell from her letters—"

Gaston lifted his eyebrows. "The request is denied," he repeated.

Otto gave it up, seeing that no argument would be accepted. "Yes, sir."

"Absent thee again without my leave, and the consequences will be severe, Baron."

Otto dared not hold his gaze; he looked down. "Yes, sir."

"I overlook the first instance as inexperienced enthusiasm. There will be no second."

Otto was on probation, was what the Marshal was saying, Ottaviano thought. "Yes, sir," he said.

"A further word, Baron."

"Sir."

"Lady Miranda was dead ere she left Prince Golias's tent: the men taken with her were disposing of the body. Know'st thou aught of this?"

"No, sir," whispered Otto, looking up swiftly to meet Gaston's eyes. His hands went damp with sweat at what he saw there: for an instant, the Well burned in those eyes. Ottaviano was very pleased to have been able to answer truthfully. He hoped the truth would suffice.

"She was badly used before her death. Know'st thou aught of this?"

"No, sir."

"Thou wert with him that morning, in his tent: what didst thou see of her?"

"Nothing, sir. Nothing. I had never heard of her."

"Dismissed," said the Fireduke curtly, and he looked over to his squire, who approached, ending the interview.

Dry-mouthed, Otto bowed and went through the camp to his quarters, near Golias's, where the men of Lys and Ascolet were getting into marching order. He wished he had not stopped at Golias's tent that morning; Golias had been in a rare high mood and had made some coarse remarks about Luneté (about whom he could know nothing), and Otto had left quickly. But not quickly enough, it seemed, for he'd been seen and now he was associated with Golias even more strongly.

Visiting Luneté had been the best reason he could think of for taking leave. That Gaston had denied it rankled, but he also had to admit that the Prince Marshal's reasons were uncontestable and that the request had been, under the circumstances, not only a long shot but a foolish one.

He would just have to wait.

*Dear Luneté,*

began Otto that evening, and stopped, pen in midair. There were so many things he did not dare convey to her thus. . . .

*Dear Luneté,*

*Much has happened since my last letter. We have won this lap of the war. Prospero was taken in battle a couple of days ago and escaped the same night, but his army remains prisoner and so for the moment he is toothless—until he gets another army. That could take a few days or a few years; we don't know where most of this lot came from. The Fireduke is holding all in readiness for another assault any moment, and he has denied my request for a leave. I will not be home this winter, I fear; the war will not be over until Prospero is taken and brought before the Emperor and put to death or imprisoned.*

*Dewar aided Prospero in his escape, but it is unclear to me whether or not his help was compelled in some way. It's certainly possible, for Prospero had talked to him before the battle and could have laid a geas on him then or subverted his will, but I do not know, for Dewar is gone with him and none knows where. Sorcerers cannot be fathomed. Yet Dewar was of great help to us in Lys and Ascolet and has been useful here, and on his side it must be admitted that since the Emperor refused to make a formal agreement securing his aid he was free to do as he wished when he wished, and he never promised more than he has delivered. Still it is infuriating to have had the real end of the war postponed by his actions.*

*I cannot write more, the courier is ready to leave and so I fill the rest of the letter with love and thoughts of you.*

*Ottaviano.*

He sealed and addressed the letter and gave it to the courier riding to the Palace with accounts and other mail. Luneté might get it in half a month, likely longer. Ottaviano wished he had taken the opportunity of his recent unauthorized leave to visit her, but he had not thought of it and now he could not go.

But Luneté had been prepared for a long separation. She had spoken of it as a disagreeable inevitability when they had talked of it first, planning the war in Ascolet, and when that had come to a quick end, she had accepted his going away with Gaston with stoic grace. He knew she didn't like it, but there was nothing to be done about it. She would wait for him; she was firmly in love with him and her future lay entirely with Ottaviano.

# — 24 —

DEWAR WOKE MOANING.

There were so many pains in his body that he could not tell one from another in the dazing ache of cold.

His eyes were stuck shut. He wiped at them clumsily with a numb hand and brushed grit and ice from the lids. Blearily he blinked at whiteness. It was snow, tiny unmelting stars on his hand where it had fallen in front of his blurred eyes. He held his breath, studying perfect hexagons, and then exhaled. The snow melted reluctantly on his wax-white skin.

He tried lifting himself on the hand that had rubbed his eyes clear, and the arm would not hold him. Broken bone grated and he fell back, grunting.

Where was he? He couldn't remember.

Dewar swallowed, thirsty, and moved his head to lick at the snow. It had not yet begun snowing when he had . . . when he had fled with Prospero. What was he doing here? He remembered riding pillion behind the Prince on his horse Hurricane. What had happened?

He supposed Prospero must have dumped him, trying to distract Prince Herne from the pursuit.

Herne evidently hadn't taken the bait, though he had never hidden his dislike of Dewar.

"Snumabish," he mumbled, or tried to mumble.

A high-pitched *kee-aaaaa* cry rang off the snow. The world dimmed and brightened, a flickering. The snow blew about in an eddy of wind. Dewar tried lifting himself on his other arm, but it didn't obey his commands—at least, it didn't seem to be, but he felt himself tumble over onto his back, and he cried wordlessly as fresh pain surged through arms, legs, back, and body.

His mouth wouldn't work properly. Turning his head, he licked at the snow again. His face hurt.

"Hey!" shouted someone above him.

Rescue! They must have been out all night looking for him. He'd have a hard time explaining this to Gaston. At least they'd feed and bandage him.

"Hey!" came the shout again, high and thin, and thudding and scrambling accompanied the cautious descent of a young man in brown leather clothes, muffled and gloved, fleece showing at his cuffs and collar. Unfamiliar uniform. Not one of the Emperor's men.

"Ungh," Dewar said, smiling weakly, and then recalled the local custom of killing and robbing the wounded. The man brushed at the snow on Dewar.

"You *are* alive. I thought not," the leather man said, a lilting accent marring the words. He turned and floundered back up in the snow, which was much deeper than Dewar had assumed.

The leather man returned with an assortment of things hung off him. He had a wineskin, and he raised Dewar's head and poured heavy, cold red wine into his mouth until Dewar coughed.

"More?"

"More," Dewar whispered, swallowing the first deluge.

"Here." He managed the flow better this time, and Dewar swallowed. "What's wrong with you?"

"Broke arm," Dewar wheezed.

"I can see that. There now. You lie back. So. I have to figure out how to get you out of here. Did you fall?"

"Don't know." Dewar tried to grab the other's shoulder, to rise.

"Don't do that! You've broken your right leg, I think. It's

bent wrong. I wouldn't be surprised if you cracked a few ribs too. One of the, the Emperor's men, aren't you?"

Dewar wasn't sure what to answer.

"If it matters," said the leather man to himself, ignoring the non-response, and went on, "I'll make a stretcher. Don't move!"

He went away in the snow, which fell with tiny pats on Dewar's closed eyes and cold cheeks. Dewar listened to the snow and his own breathing, delicate whispering sounds. He was too cold, he thought, and in a minute or two he'd get up and make a fire. Plenty of brush around him. He'd glimpsed it adorned with snow just now. It was resinous; it would burn easily. Warm him up. Yes. He'd just rest another few minutes and then make a fire. Easily done. Elementary Elemental Summoning, that was all. He framed the words in his mind, jumbling them up, but he'd get them right when he spoke the Summoning . . .

"Hey! Stay awake."

Dewar made a small sound of protest.

"Maybe the wine wasn't a good idea. Here, suck on this. It's honey."

His mouth was opened and a grainy, coarse lump stuffed into it.

"Gah!" He choked.

"I made a stretcher. I'm going to get you on it, tie you to it, and then pull you out of this ditch. You're too big for me to carry."

Dewar's mouthful of runny sugar didn't permit a reply. He gritted his teeth as the leather man began lifting his shoulders. When he hauled Dewar's legs over to the left, Dewar couldn't keep from shouting at the agony, fire and ice in his bones.

"Sorry!" cried the leather man. "One more."

He did it again, shoulders and then legs, and by then Dewar was moaning and panting. The first jolt as his head was lifted and the foot end of the stretcher bumped over a rock made him scream, and then he fell over into darkness.

* * *

He woke feeling water on his face.

"Bleh."

"Do keep your mouth closed. I've got soap," said the leather man.

Dewar closed mouth and eyes, which had glimpsed light and something white-and-dark. Hot wet cloth patted his face and throat, interspersed with splashing sounds, and moved down to his left arm and his chest. Another cloth was laid over him.

"Just to keep you warm."

"Better," Dewar tried to say, and managed, "Beher."

"I dare say. I straightened out your arm and leg while you were fainting. Why did they leave you there? Did they think you dead?"

"Dunno. Think I fell."

"At least that," the leather man said, bathing him. Dewar yelped as a hot pain flared in his side. "Ah. I thought so. There's a cracked rib or two here. I'll tie that up too."

"Good of you," Dewar mumbled.

The leather man didn't reply, rubbing something on Dewar's sore side. An herbal smell rose in the air.

Dewar hissed a few times as his body was wrapped up in a long wide bandage. He kept his eyes closed and his teeth clenched. When the strapping was finished, the bath resumed with gentle strokes on his hips and thighs and cautious swabs at his groin. Startled, Dewar looked at his benefactor.

"Hey!" he said. He'd been mistaken as to his rescuer's sex.

"What's wrong?"

Dewar blushed crimson. "I—um . . . I can—"

"You can't, either. Not with your leg splinted. Never mind the broken arm and ribs. Save your blushes for real embarrassments," said the young woman who was giving him a sponge-bath, keeping him down with her hand flat on his chest. "And please stop trying to move. You'll hurt for it." She wasn't smiling, but her voice was amused and her eyes crinkled over her wind-pinked cheeks. Her dark hair was pulled back untidily in a fraying braid.

"Who're you?" Dewar said, forcing himself to relax.

"I found you, remember?" She pulled the blanket back onto him.

"Oh," Dewar said. "Uh." She still wore the leather trousers and jacket that had deceived him, just as he'd been fooled by Lady Miranda. She was certainly not Lady Miranda—had Lady Miranda had an ally, a confidante similarly disguised? No—she would have mentioned it.

"When I'm finished washing the muck and blood off you, we'll eat."

"Hungry."

"I should think so. You're in fine health for a fellow who slept in a blizzard. Lucky." She was rubbing more salve into his left leg, the same pungent unguent. The touch hurt.

"What are you doing there?"

"This is very good for bruises. It will feel tingly and warm."

"Unh." Indeed it tingled and warmed already, blending with the nearly-painful tingling from his hands and feet: the touch of the cold, withdrawing. He turned his head, trying to forget the shock of finding himself stretched naked in front of a strange woman, and looked at the fire. The furnishings were good-quality; on the floor lay a fine crimson carpet, and a high-backed blue-upholstered chair at the hearth had things draped over it to warm. In the coals stood a three-legged covered kettle, and there was wood stacked to one side leaving a mess of bark and mould on the carpet.

The warm water felt good on his skin. She towelled him dry as she bathed him and added another dab of salve here and there. Her hands were gentle; when she dressed his bruises, he could feel that she was trying not to cause pain. Dewar watched the flames until she said, "There now," and drew bedclothes up over him.

"Thank you," he said, looking at her at last.

"You are welcome." She smiled a small, brief smile.

He glimpsed the water in her basin—he had been filthy. Since the great battle he'd not bathed, he realized, nor eaten; agreeing, his stomach growled.

"I'll empty this and we will eat." She left the room through its high, dark old door, eight panels of some antique carving grimed with time and wax-fixed dirt.

Dewar exhaled and relaxed. The clean sheet next to his skin was soft and silky, fine-woven expensive stuff, and the blankets over it were lofty, wispy, costly Ascolet highland goat's-wool dyed brilliant blue. The featherbed cradled him. The bed hangings were pulled back, bits of red and blue patterning visible in their dark-grey folds. The sorcerer closed his eyes and thought of the flames of the fire, and he reached through them to the Fire, to the Well. Its heat washed over him; tired and weakened as he was, he had but poor control over it. But his command was sufficient to direct it to those parts of himself that ached and throbbed: ribs, arm, legs. The ribs would be easiest and soonest mended. He concentrated on them, hurrying his healing, strengthening and warming himself.

The woman returned with a tray on which bowls, spoons, cups, and a loaf of bread were dwarfed by a bottle of wine. Dewar, with plump tasselled pillows behind him, was able to sit up and eat slowly: dark, rich stew full of chunks of onion and venison, bread soaked in the broth, and red wine. He devoured four bowlfuls and all the bread save a heel the young woman ate, and then she tucked the blankets up around him and left him to sleep.

Dewar found it humiliating to require assistance to use a chamber pot, though his rescuer was blasé about it. They glared at one another in grudging grey morning light from the wide-paned windows.

"You cannot stand up yet," she told him, arms akimbo.

"Get me crutches. A cane will do." He clenched his teeth against the pain that shot from his leg. His ribs ached and burned; his arm had felt well until he moved it, so now it too throbbed.

"You have a broken arm and ribs and a broken leg. Your precious dignity is going to have to suffer. If you make any more fuss about it I'll leave and you can welter on your snapped bones alone." Briskly spoken, without malice: a doctor's threat to an immobilized client.

He glared at her. The hot-poker pain in his leg assured him that she was right, but he didn't have to like it. "May you come to the same one day," he muttered.

"I'd be ill-paid for helping you if I did," she replied, turning away—but not before he saw her hurt expression.

Dewar bit his lip, regretting his hasty ill-wish, and drew on the Well, dulling his pain to discomfort. "And I hope there's someone as kind as you've been to me, to help you then," he added.

Startled, she glanced at him from the fireside, where she had begun taking clothes up and shaking them. Dewar smiled apologetically. "I'm not used to being laid up like this," he said. "I never have been before. I'm no warrior." He wondered how he had ever taken her for a man; her shape was obviously female, her rose-cheeked face young and wary. She wore a dress today, long full-skirted high-breasted brown wool, an apron too.

"Oh," she said, not smiling back. "You're much better today." She lifted a dressing-gown and displayed it wordlessly, lifting her eyebrows.

To further smooth her temper, he said, "All your doing. The soup last night was restorative as well as delicious. Thank you." Dewar, with her help in managing his splinted arm, shrugged into the dressing-gown, wool and silk.

"There are hen's eggs for breakfast if you like them. The geese won't let me near."

"I am at your mercy insofar as cooking goes." He smiled again, warmly, trying to elicit a smile in return. "And all else. Where are we?"

"A big house. There's nobody else here."

"Your house?" She might be a maid, or some servant of the folk who'd fled the battles and disorder.

She looked at him sidelong while she folded linen.

"You're of Prospero's army," Dewar realized, and regretted saying that. "Let us not speak of the war," he went on, to cover it. "It is done."

"Done," she repeated, staring down at the white fabric, stopping. "Is he dead?"

"No, not dead as far as I know. He escaped them after being taken. You did not know?"

"I was—away from here."

"Oh. Yes. There was a great and mortal battle; he was captured and he surrendered, but made his escape that very night. I daresay the Fireduke was sparked by it."

"You did not see it?"

"The battle? I saw. I was in it. Some of it."

"And they left you in the ditch like that! They are—" She stopped herself. "I'll fetch breakfast," she said, and left the folded clothes to hurry out.

"Eat with me," Dewar called after her.

She did, subdued. Dewar wished he had not mentioned Prospero. What could have been her role in the army? Perhaps a surgeon. She must have been at Ithellin, he thought, or perhaps caught out between one post and another. It would be more comfortable for both of them if they did not speak of the war and its ancillary issues. He would not bring it forward again.

As he ate an omelet, soft pungent cheese, and flat griddle-bread, he realized that she had given him no name, nor asked one, and he understood that she might not wish to know too much about him. Let there be a vacant space around them for a few days until he could maneuver on his own, and then they would go their ways separately. That was wisest.

"Are there books in this house?" he asked her.

"I saw some. I'll bring them to you. Is your arm paining you?"

"A bit." It throbbed and felt hot beneath the veil of the Well.

"You're moving around too much," she said. "I shall strap it so that you'll keep it still and allow it to set."

Meekly, Dewar submitted.

Another great snowstorm battered the house. Dewar's chapped-faced surgeon sat sewing at the end of his featherbed, a blanket around her shoulders, and Dewar, bundled in blankets too, read to her. The house was cold; the chamber was drafty. She thought it was because only the single room was heated. "And the kitchen," she had said that morning when she shivered in with his breakfast of salt-fish hash, stewed fruits, and griddle-bread, "even with the fire there, yet that's colder. The pump's frozen," she had said.

Dewar had said, "We can melt snow."

"Plenty of that. I'm glad I tied a rope to the barn yesterday when it clouded over. I'd have been blown away." She had a mount in the barn, she had said.

"You could put him in the kitchen," Dewar had suggested.

"I think not," she had demurred; and, "Anyway, we're housebound."

"You're not. I am definitely housebound for another ten days."

"True." She had not promised, but all indications were that she'd stay till he could get around on his own. Besides, the weather was prohibitive.

"Would you consider selling me your horse then?"

She had shaken her head. "I've no horse to sell you."

"Oh, well. Would you consider finding one for me?"

"They left nothing behind. I wonder when the people who live in this house will come back."

"Spring I suspect," Dewar had said, twisting his mouth.

"That's true." She'd brightened.

"Do you like chess?" he'd asked hopefully.

"I'm told I'm an execrably bad player. —I think I shall bring up food so we can hole up here."

"And wood."

"I filled the hall with that already," she had said. After she had provisioned them, putting food in the hall with the wood, she sat down in front of the low fire with sewing in her cold hands. Dewar read a book that he had found beside his bed.

"What's that book about?" she asked when they ate lunch.

It was a Madanese account of the Flange Wars, written in Madanese by one of the admirals. "History," he said.

"Oh."

After a moment, she said, "I saw it had maps."

Dewar nodded, and then he understood. "Would you like me to read aloud to you while you sew?" he suggested.

A smile, the first he had gotten from her, was his reward, and a warm body cozily tucked at the other end of the bed who listened with wide-eyed flattering attention as he read and who fetched him other books, a tall stack of them, epics and histories and chronicles. All were written in Chenaran, the old local tongue, instead of the King's tongue of Lannach, which Dewar found curious; and their perspectives and subjects were Chenaran as well. The house and its library were antiques. Finding history dry, he abandoned it for a lush romance with beauteous princesses, noble and base knights, improbably powerful magicians, and unlikely coincidences. The cadence of his voice gave measure to the storm outside, and the time and the storm passed in chapters and verses.

Dewar had had nothing to do but observe the young woman for several days now, and he thought he knew her better than she meant. He also supposed she was hoarding notes on him. It wasn't worth being worried about; it was a game, to see how many sound conclusions he could draw on accidental evidence.

She was not of the upper classes; she had said, "Oh, no lady I," once and had amused him enormously with a couple of straight-faced indelicate remarks, one on a plump juicy sausage which had spurted heroically when pierced in the pan. She cooked very well, and that and her medicinal knowledge made him think her some camp follower of Prospero's army, left behind accidentally. She was practical and efficient, neat and quick with her needle, and accustomed to being self-reliant. She was sober of mind and not quick to laugh; often his jests passed her utterly. And she was generous and humane, having dragged him half-alive out of the ditch and succored him here.

He did not know how she felt about being here nor why she had come with the army nor what her plans were.

She was not worn and frayed as the camp followers of Landuc had been. Providing the services of laundresses, nurses, cooks, general heavy labor, and sexual accessories for the armies, these lackluster women had been pathetic, anything but exciting to Dewar. He supposed that if a passive vessel for release were all that was required, one would do, but he preferred more engaging encounters and had ignored the pack of them. Prince Josquin was under his uncles' eyes and had been a model of princely decorum and restraint, by Josquin's standards, anyway. Neither of them had acknowledged their brief prior acquaintance, though Dewar was certain the Prince Heir had recognized him. Their friendship in the army camp had included fencing together in practice-sessions, there exchanging a few unguarded heated glances, but nothing more intimate than that.

His companion in the hollow manor-house was sexually neuter. She treated his body without noticing it, and she dressed and undressed in the bedroom's dressing-room, out of sight. Her skin was fair, though wind-chapped, her hands lightly callused, her arms stronger than most women's. Dewar thought she was pretty enough when she smiled, but that otherwise she was unremarkable: an innkeeper's wife, perhaps, or a craftsman's, or a seacaptain's pragmatic and durable helpmeet.

She wore plain gowns scavenged out of the cupboards of the house; they showed little of her uncorseted form save that it was female. Sometimes a soft breast would press his arm as she helped him move, but there was no spice of flirtation in it.

She slept on the floor in front of the fire, bundled in blankets, and did not snore.

But all in all, Dewar thought, he knew very little about her, and he admired her caution. Her speech was accented, which was queer; having passed the Well's fire, he should not have heard an accent on her tongue. He knew nothing of her family, her home, her estate; he did not know what she had been doing in Prospero's army; he did not know her origin, and he did not know her wishes in anything but that the snow might stop. She slogged out to the barn where her mount was stabled (whose name he also did not know) daily, and reported the height of the snow on her return.

"Waist-deep," she said, holding her hand at her ribs.

"I wonder if there is a tunnel to the barn. Places that get such heavy snow often include that as a routine convenience."

"I thought these storms were unusual."

"Why?"

"You said something about how they had been delayed," she said.

He had? Yes, he had. "They were late, for the region," he said. "I suppose they may be unusually severe as a result of that. Pent-up." With a sorcerer who commanded his Element as Prospero did, Binding the winds, it was as close to a sure thing as one could come, but Dewar thought he would not get into a discussion of the defeated Prince's strategies and abilities with his partisan.

The storm abated after five days, leaving snow shoulder-deep at its shallowest.

"I won't need a horse," Dewar said dolorously, when she reported this.

"The drifts are at the windowsills on this floor! The first floor's covered right up, except on the lee side and the windows are half-covered there."

Dewar wanted to see. She allowed him to hop, leaning on her, to the window, to peer out at the white glittering featureless plain that covered the landscape, and then made him return to his bed.

"I can get up—" he protested, despite the pains moving had started.

"Please, not yet. You must give that leg a little more time to set. Three days. And where will you go in such a hurry?" she asked him. "Sliding on boards like the hairy mountain-men you told me about?"

"I suppose," he conceded.

Dewar had thought about this, as her reports of the weather came in day by day. He was in no condition to ride, nor even to mount; though his ribs felt nearly healed, the leg and arm must take longer, even aided by his drawing on the

Well. He would leave by other means, after her. Which meant he must encourage her to abandon him here after he could get about reliably by himself—

His thoughts on promoting her departure pulled up abruptly. If the snow lay so deep, then she could hardly ride out and away herself, no more than he could.

She herself seemed to reach a similar conclusion after ploughing out to the barn again and back after breakfast.

"How's your faithful friend?" he inquired.

"Wanting to stretch her—legs," the woman replied, gnawing her lip abstractedly.

"Something wrong?"

"I cannot open the big barn doors," she said. "The snow's too high; it has covered them, and the winds blow more on every hour."

The wind had been moaning disagreeably at the chimney, plaintive without the rattle of ice, all day.

"Ah," said Dewar. "And it's rather deep for riding anyway."

She nodded, morose, and went to stare out the window, around the curtain. "Trapped," she said, shoulders down. "Useless."

Neither of them had mentioned the war.

"Come sit down," Dewar said, "make us some tea, and let's think about it. Certainly there's more than one barn door."

"None's big enough, and most are blocked. Do you want tea?"

Dewar nodded.

"We're going to get fat as pigeons, eating out the winter here," she said crossly, and went to fill the kettle from a barrel of melted snow-water.

"Make less for us to eat."

"If you like."

Surly and silent, she made tea and poured it, scalding, and ignored hers, glaring at the fire. Dewar read to himself, not aloud. The wind keened. The woman jumped up abruptly and left the room with a bang of the door.

Oh, no, thought Dewar. She'd been a pleasantly bland

companion thus far. If she were going to become snarling and unsociable on realizing her snowbound predicament, he'd take the first opportunity to leave her. In a few days when she went out to the barn, he could build up the fire, open his Way, and be through it ere she returned.

A simple solution to an otherwise uncomfortable and tedious situation. He tucked it away in his thoughts and read about the Lucin War, fifteen centuries past, in which Prince Marshal Gaston had distinguished himself for his great mercy toward the defeated.

She left him alone all day and returned long after the brief sunset. No luncheon. Dinner was a plain dried-vegetable stew and bread. Dewar supposed he was being penalized for suggesting they eat less and made no comment nor complaint. His companion said not a word and, soon after the meal was ended and the dishes cleaned, she unrolled her bedroll and curled up in it with her back to him.

Dewar hoped she'd be in better temper in the morning.

She was not. The temperature had dropped again, and the cold drove her in to huddle by the fire and work distractedly at something that involved many needles sticking out in different directions—an apt analogy, thought Dewar, for her spiky mood.

The screaming of the wind in the chimney was maddening, and it batted and fanned the flames and blew ashes and cinders into the room gustily from time to time.

Her crossness made him fidgety, and he could not keep his mind on his book.

That day went slowly and dumbly to its grim close.

On returning from her visit to the barn the next day, Dewar's companion presented him diffidently with a pair of crutches.

"Here. Try one under your left arm. You can't use the right yet."

He blinked. They were new-made; they smelled of fresh-cut, cold wood.

"I'm sorry I've been so snappy," she added, looking down. "I don't like winter."

Dewar nodded and accepted a crutch. With her help, he got up and hopped awkwardly, then less so, across the room and back.

"A great improvement. I can make it to the jakes alone," he joked.

She left him to practice shifting and moving his weight without hurting his broken arm and leg or still-sore ribs. Dewar limped to the door as she closed it and followed her into the hall. It was long and narrow, panelled with dark wood and unlit.

"Wait, wait," she called, unseen, "there's lumber all over, I'll make you a light—" and a moment later a light flared and settled halfway up the wall, some distance down the hall ahead of him, and showed him that the hall was an obstacle course of boxes, barrels, piled wood, and cans of water. She had laid all this up here, he guessed, to wait out the siege of the storms.

"There. Be careful."

"I will."

"Mind the stairs, around there. Three down, and then a big flight, but you'll see the window. I must go back to the barn." She lit another wall-sconce from the first and thumped off around the corner and down.

Dewar, hissing when he jarred his leg, made slow progress down the hall to the light and paused there, staring at it.

It was shaped like a flower, the candle rising from the half-open petals at its base, polished silver leaves behind forming a reflector.

Dewar looked up and down the hall swiftly. Yes, the lights were the same, the panelling patterned at the top with a chequering of light and dark wood, the carpet soiled now but the same. Disregarding the flaring pain in his leg, he hastened to a door, opened it, tried another beyond it, thumped back past the chamber where he had been confined, and at the other end found a T-intersection beyond a door.

"Ah," he muttered, and at one end, indeed, was the lavatory and jakes and at the other was the room where he had dined with Prospero.

Dewar summoned an ignis-spark and kindled a five-light candelabrum. The place had been ransacked since his dinner there. A draped brocade curtain had been pulled right down off its rail at one window; the window itself gaped through a shard-edged opening at the top. The desk was overturned, its drawers emptied; a sideboard had been tipped over, and there was broken glass in the fireplace. Dewar pegged slowly forward. Snow and rain had come in through the window, staining the lovely carpet; the table where he'd sat was still there, though the chair had been hurled at a mirror to break both.

Of course they—Herne from the look of it—would have searched the place for Prospero's effects. Dewar scowled anyway, disgusted at the desecration of a place where he had passed a pleasant evening with an uncanny host. A few half-burned books were in the fireplace with the glass; was this where the woman had scavenged the books he'd been reading? Dewar riffled pages; these were estate account-books. He tossed them down. Glass jingled.

There was nothing left of the contents of the desk. All confiscated; Gaston or Herne had probably gone through it all. Dewar snorted. Were they any kind of sorcerers, they'd have passed on the desk and searched for Prospero's bed and his clothes. Those things, attuned to him by his daily use of them, would have led them straight to him as surely as the ring Lady Miranda had had, if they knew how to exploit the link. He paused in his rummaging through the rubble by the desk. Very likely he had been lying in Prospero's bed himself.

Dewar poked with his crutch among the broken bits of wood and glass that had been chair and mirror. No, this hadn't been a sorcerous mirror, though Prospero had been using it as such. His rage at the vandalism was replaced by melancholy. He turned from the ruin and limped out, his leg aching and burning.

In the hall he yelped when he bumped into a barrel, and he cursed the pack-rat behavior of his companion. She was as bad as the plundering soldiers who'd fouled Prospero's study, a mess-leaving animal with no appreciation for a fine house or a fine carpet. In fresh fury he made his way to the stairs, where he practiced going up and down.

"How are you getting on?" she asked, coming into the hall at the bottom.

Dewar shot her a quick glare, softened it when she stared startled back. "The house is very cold," he said. "The exercise heats me."

She said it was colder outside.

"I'll not attempt that today, I think," he said.

"Not for many days. Spring maybe," she nodded, and walked step-by-step up and down three times with him.

When he grew tired, she took the crutch and added padding to the handgrip and armrest, velvet-covered wool wadding, and Dewar bit his tongue to keep from asking her what the hell was in all the barrels and boxes and whatever did she think to do with them.

Instead, he went back to bed and rested there, feeling pleased beneath his irritation. The leg hurt, but not agonizingly. Dewar drew on the Well, attending to it. He was certain he could get around his tower without assistance. Tomorrow he would leave this place of war and woe, making his Way to the agreeable surroundings of his own library and workroom.

She had put his satchel by the bed when she had first brought him in. Dewar knew she hadn't rummaged in it, for it was tied just as he'd left it. He lay abed in the darkness after she had gone out, as she did every morning, and counted deliberately to one hundred, then rose and dressed rapidly. The satchel he hung on his neck after taking from it a square cube of stone, his token for returning to his tower in its cul-de-sac of Pheyarcet, and then he threw wood on the fire until, despite the battling wind, flames roared perilously high up the chimney.

Dewar, holding the stone before him in his right hand, lifted his voice above the fire and began to chant, invoking the Well of Landuc through the fire and his thorn-girdled tower through the affinity of his stone for its origin.

The fire whirled and whorled, became a bright tunnel leading into darkness.

The door opened and Dewar did not allow himself to be distracted by a gasping scream of shock from the young woman; he stepped forward into the tunnel and was swept through it to its conclusion: just on his own doorstep, surrounded by flowering, bristling vines which drew away from him. The red and white blossoms bobbed with the breeze of his arrival and then stopped. It was summer here; the heat was welcome on his head as he opened the tower door and hobbled in happily.

There was no place like home, he thought, and smiled.

# 25

THE ROADS OF LYS WERE FROZEN and buckled with the freezing. The fields of Lys were greenless and cold, and the trees bore no leaf nor bud. Dewar hastened past scenes which would have caught his eye in fairer seasons and delayed him. There was no snow, only ice; durable black ice on the ponds, brittle white fringes of ice in the road-ruts, and the earth around wore mourning colors. He met few travellers, and they laconic or silent. The wind grieved unceasing, Prospero's curse on the realm.

He stopped at a kingstone he recalled passing before with Otto and Luneté, and there under the ice-bearded head of Panurgus he composed and uttered a glamour-spell which put an outer likeness of an unremarkable and unmemorable stranger on him. This accomplished, he mounted again and continued toward the city of Champlys. His intention was only to get word of Otto's and the army's whereabouts and fortune, and he believed the most reliable source would be Otto's wife, Luneté, who had shown clearly that she trusted Dewar in their earlier acquaintance. He had recuperated a quarter of a year in his tower, and that time here had been but days owing to the rapidity of the Eddy which housed the Tower of Thorns' pocket-world.

Dewar's summer in his tower had been shadowed by a cloudy, swelling desire to find Prospero again and come to a clearer understanding of their relation, though Dewar was ambiguous as to what that understanding was to be. Were Prospero his father—and there were ways to be certain—then what importance were they to place upon that? Blood-kinship created only disagreeable complications in the social interactions of sorcerers. Dewar's past was criss-crossed with such limits. In Phesaotois, he had seen Lord Oren chafing under blood-restrictions in his sorcery, his territory surrounded by descendants of Primas, his power limited by their prior claims and his ability to challenge them limited by their blood. Oren, with Dewar's help and careful scheming, had managed to get a senior brother killed in a duel and increase his standing. Dewar could live only under Oren's protection, for Odile's vendetta against Dewar prevented him from claiming any territory of his own. In the end he had left for Pheyarcet, seeking a foothold there—and he had easily found one, a stable, strong Eddy, among the Well's disintegrating strands. Would he have to defend that now against a competitor? None of the other sorcerers and sorceresses of Pheyarcet had deigned to notice him. Would Prospero claim the Tower of Thorns, seek to steal and use Dewar's spells, sap him and oppress him? Dewar was determined that he should not. Dewar might leave Pheyarcet when he had solved his Third-Force problem, but in his own chosen time, not hounded by another parent.

In a Champlys ale-house he learned that the Countess was in the city and that her husband was still at the wars with many men of Lys, and he heard Otto's name spoken less kindly than it had been before. Ottaviano was named an adventurer who had taken advantage of the Countess's favor, and the men of Lys muttered that no Lys blood would have been spilled had Ottaviano not wed the Countess and dragged them into his quarrels. They seemed to be forgetting that the Emperor would have levied troops from

Lys anyway, as was his right. The Countess, curiously, took no blame; rather her late guardian Sarsemar and the Emperor were held responsible for not marrying her off to a better man.

Dewar nodded sagely and said empty things. He left the ale-house to find another near Luneté's small castle.

At this better ale-house he bespoke himself a room, and that night when the curfew had rung he closed himself in and worked more sorcery.

Unseen, he opened his small chamber's casement and climbed agilely down the rough stone wall. Unseeable, he passed through the streets and, close on the heels of some guards, he slipped into the castle of Lys itself. Once inside his way was easily made to the Countess's bedchamber, which was reached through a solar.

The heavy-panelled solar was empty; linens hung before a fire there, and candles burned, but no one sewed or sang. The chamber door was ajar, and it too was empty, though ready; the fire warmed the room and made it drafty and the bedclothes were turned back. There were candles burning here, too. Dewar snuffed three of them and waited in the corner so made dim.

Laudine, Luneté's maid, entered and put wood on the fire, fetched something from a cabinet, then went out again.

Dewar waited. Women's voices murmured in the outer room, heralding the Countess of Lys herself preceded by light-bearing Laudine and followed by two maids. The maids began undressing the lady, and Dewar grinned invisibly and then turned his back as a gentleman ought. Luneté's women were clumsy, and she chided them often; they were slow to undo laces, careless with the gown, too rough with her hair while brushing it.

"That will be all, Laudine," Luneté said presently.

Dewar turned. Luneté was seated on the edge of the bed now, dressed in finely pleated saffron linen, her rich-colored hair gold-glinting.

Laudine was kneeling at the fire with a long-handled brass bedwarming pan; she looked round at the Countess. "My lady, shall I not warm the bed?"

"That's my husband's duty, Laudine," snapped Luneté. "I said that will be all. Leave me."

"Yes, my lady." The maid set the warming-pan aside quietly, rose, and curtseyed. "Good night, my lady," Laudine said, bland-faced, and went out, after extinguishing all of the candles but the one at the bedside, which was sweet beeswax as thick and as long as Dewar's arm.

Luneté lifted her voice irritably. "*Do* close the door! There is a draft."

The door clicked.

The Countess of Lys opened a casket on the bedside table and took out a small object.

"Luneté," called Dewar softly.

She jumped and stared around the room, at the door.

Dewar whispered the words to dispel the spell around him.

"Don't call out," he held up his hand to caution her as her shocked gaze fixed on him.

"Dewar!"

He came forward into the candle's light and bowed.

"How came you here?" whispered Luneté, and she put the thing—a locket—into the casket again and closed it quickly.

"Sorcerers have ways," whispered Dewar back, smiling.

Luneté stood. "This is my bedchamber, sir, and an untimely hour for an audience," she replied, but she did not sound annoyed.

"I knew not what manner of reception I might find in your house, Countess," he said. "I am here only to glean gossip-grains, and for no baser purpose."

She stared at him. Her breast rose and fell. She moistened her lips. "Gossip?" she repeated.

Dewar nodded. "What have you heard from Otto of late?" he asked.

Luneté's eyes blazed. "You'd know better than I," she snapped, and repented when he lifted his eyebrows. "Why do you ask that?" she added.

"Madame, I have given offense in the intrusion, but I assure you—"

Luneté's eyes moved over his face, his body, and she clenched her hands to stop them shaking. "Did he send you?"

"Otto? No. Nobody sends me, my lady. I am a free agent," Dewar said, and he wryed his mouth. "So you have no news," he said, "no fresh news, at least."

"Nor any stale news, to cram a goose and cook it," said Luneté, walking to the fire. Dewar followed her. She stood holding her hands to the flames, trying to warm them.

"No news at all?" Dewar said, frowning. "Well, I do not mean daily reports, Countess—"

"Luneté," she corrected him in an undertone.

"Luneté," he said softly, looking at her high firelit cheekbones, her straight mouth. "I only ask in general."

"I cannot marshal you even a general report, Dewar. I have not heard from Otto in—I will show you his letters—"

He caught her arm, detained her at the fireside. "No need. He doesn't write." Dewar released her arm, but somehow kept her hand.

Luneté shook her head, looking at him with a certain hauteur. "He is a mean correspondent, a miser with his words as with his hours," she said. "I have had no word, and no sight, nor message, since you all left Ascolet. Nothing to speak of. Quick lines—nothing telling, nothing speaking, nothing such as a husband might write his wife in time of war."

Dewar felt constrained to put some small defense forward. "He was very busy in Chenay," he said, "with the fighting."

"Has no courier gone to or from the army?" She lifted her eyebrows in disbelief.

Dewar looked down and shook his head. "I . . . certainly they have, Luneté. The Marshal's lines of communication are superb."

"The Baron's are not."

He sought for something to say and found it. "I am sorry, m'lady. I am sorry to have flicked a wound, and I am sorry to have no better report of him for you."

"He sends no message by you."

"He doesn't know where I am," Dewar said, smiling. "I left the army under something of a cloud—a snow cloud of a sort—and I have not and shall not rejoin them."

Her other hand joined his, ten fingers cradling five. "We have had rumors of a victory. They say Prospero is taken."

"Taken and escaped, Luneté. It is but a piece of victory."

Luneté lifted her chin, defiant. "I cheer for him, then, and I curse the Emperor's fortune and Landuc's. May Prospero win and rule, and may he throw down all those who oppose him."

"Including Ottaviano," Dewar half-inquired.

"Indeed," said Luneté, and her eyes burned at him.

"I confess," Dewar said, "that I myself was the agent of the Prince's escape, for he had—he has conducted himself better than many others would, and generously, and as a gentleman, and I loathed to think of the Emperor taking his head."

"Good," said Luneté, and pressed his hand. "Good. When you return—"

"I shall not be returning to Gaston, Otto, and their armies," Dewar said. "I have no interest in benefiting either side in the quarrel, and there are better ways by far for a sorcerer to spend his time. I intend to engage in some of them."

Luneté's eyes on his were dark. Her lips were slightly parted; her fingers, still clasping his warmly. Barely above a whisper, she said, "Indeed, the time may be better spent on many things."

The fire's heat lay on Dewar's thigh and leg. He looked into Luneté's wide eyes, surprised and then comprehending: she was sincere. A shiver, not of cold, went over him. In a voice softer than hers, he agreed, "Indeed," and put his mouth on hers, and as he did she released his hand and embraced him. They swayed together, twining arms around one another, and stood close-locked on the hearth. Luneté's kiss was uncertain at first, and Dewar ran his hands down her back, pressing her body against his as he kissed her more and more deeply, inflamed by her unexpected heat.

"Bed," he breathed against her temple, kissing her eyes, her cheeks, her forehead, and thus they did.

Heated, they pushed the wool and linen bedclothes back and lay cooling in the candlelight. Dewar stirred first, moving to one side, kissing Luneté's body up and down, shoulder, chin, throat, breast, belly, knees, thighs. She sighed and started, trembled with surprise, and he went on kissing, moving his tongue and mouth on her and stroking with his hands, rolling in sensation as he loved to do in the sea's waves.

When the tide that carried her had receded, he lay beside her again and held her, drawing up the sheet. Luneté kissed his mouth cautiously, then warmly.

"Mmmm," Dewar murmured, thinking what a fool Ottaviano was, a journeyman half-educated in other things than sorcery. "Are you pleased, Luneté," he whispered.

"Oh yes. Was I supposed to do—"

"Whatever you like, as long as you enjoy it," he assured her, smiling, embracing her. "I would please you," he added, his mouth behind her ear.

"You did. Oh, Dewar . . . That was so— It wasn't at all like when—"

He put two fingers on her lips and stopped her. "It's always different," he said. And, he thought, a lady never makes comparisons; her inexperience was sweet, appealing of itself.

"Is it?" Luneté asked, and smiled, brilliant-eyed.

Dewar smiled slowly and said, "Yes," and they set out to establish that as true.

"Different?" he asked, a husky whisper in her ear. He kissed her neck, nibbled the tender lobe.

"Ohhh." Luneté arched her back.

"I shall take that as a yes."

"Yes, do."

The fire was nearly out. Luneté turned onto her stomach and lay flat, smiling, her chin pillowed on her hands. Dewar stretched beside her and held her, and soon she fell asleep as he knew she would, smiling still.

He considered how he would depart. The hour was late; doors and windows would be locked. He had not planned to be in the castle so long, nor to make love to her. Carefully, he sat up and reached down to the floor for his shirt. As he pulled it over his head, it brushed Luneté and she woke with a start.

"You're leaving."

"I must."

She nodded and turned over, pulling the bedclothes to her chin as she sat up. Dewar pulled them down and kissed her.

Luneté pressed her lips to his cheek. "Don't go," she whispered.

"I shall go, for your countrymen speak against women who please themselves," Dewar said. He trailed his fingers up her spine and moved a lock of her hair from her cheek. "I cannot stay; it would be held to your blame, Luneté, and I will not contribute to your harm."

She smiled reluctantly. "I beg you pardon a woman's weakness. There's reason in what you say, reason and good sense."

He lifted her hand and kissed the back of it lightly, then bent and found more of his garments. Luneté put out a hand and took her golden smock from the foot of the bed. She pulled it on to cover her small breasts, her pale smooth shoulders.

When he was dressed save for his boots, she said, "Dewar," and he looked again at her dark eyes in the candlelight. "When might I see you again?" she asked softly.

Dewar thought of one answer, then another, and then a third which pleased him well, and he said, "Tomorrow night, if you will it so. I cannot tarry after that, but tomorrow . . ." He let his voice fade.

"Yes," she said. "Shall I send for you? Where do you stay?"

"I will not tell you, nor shall you send for me. I'll come to you as I did this night."

"Very well. At the same hour?"

"As tonight. Do not look for me; I will be here." He smiled.

Dewar watched Luneté's maids disrobe her, watched Laudine brush out her hair and plait it. The Countess was in a mild humor, or her women more adroit; no reprimands were uttered. There was a tray with a bottle and a goblet on it on top of a chest near the fire tonight, Lys wine. Lys did not grow much wine, but some of the southern river-valleys had produced locally-salable stuff.

After her women left Luneté alone, Dewar stood silent and still, looking at her. She had risen from the bed and gone to stand at the fire. He watched the light play on her face from four paces' distance, and when she glanced away he stepped quietly over to stand behind her, slipping his arms around her waist.

"Luneté," he murmured, stilling her startled gasp with his hand. He kissed the back of her neck, whispering; his body shimmered into visibility again.

"Dewar," she said, turning in his arms and embracing him ardently, and they said hardly a word more for several hours.

Then they lay cheek-to-cheek on the pillow, agreeably exercised, and watched the flame of the thick honey-scented candle consume wick and wax.

"Are you real?" Luneté said lazily, lifting her head.

"Yes," Dewar answered, lifting his eyebrows. He moved a strand of her hair out of his eyes.

"You appear and disappear like one of the wood-spirits my nurse used to warn me about," she said, smiling as she reached down and stroked his thigh, "out of the darkness, into the darkness, perhaps changing into a stag or a bull. . . ."

"I promise I am no incubus, but a sorcerer."

"It's the same thing."

"It certainly is not," he retorted, "although," he continued thoughtfully, "some of the superficial characteristics may be similar." And he moved her hand and lifted her hips, shifted his body under her. "There?" he suggested, and began to rock.

"Oh," she said, and bent to kiss him, and they swayed together as her "Oh" became a low, throaty moan.

Later, beside a shorter candle than before, they rested again, wordlessly kissing and touching. Luneté stretched, her body tingling and tired, and then sat bolt upright.

"Someone's in the solar!" she whispered.

Dewar threw her nightdress at her and rolled out of the bed, snatching at his own clothing strewn here and there. Luneté pulled the shift over her head. Footsteps and a murmur of voices were audible on the other side of the door.

"Under the bed!" she whispered. "Quick!"

Dewar didn't argue; the door handle moved. He hit the floor and rolled.

Luneté flopped down, bedclothes over her, and feigned sleep. Dewar saw that one of his boots was visible still, reached out to snatch it under the bed with him. The floor was cold and gritty. He'd slid to the side farthest from the candle's light, with no time to don a stitch.

A light glimmered on the floor. Footsteps. A male sigh. Rustle.

"Luneté," said Ottaviano softly.

Dewar stuffed his shirt in his mouth, stifling his snort of laughter. The cloth smelled of Luneté. He stifled another reaction, and then more laughter at himself.

"Otto? Ottaviano! What are you doing here?"

"Missed you," said Otto. The mattress moved. "Move over, sweetheart."

The bed bounced.

"Get out of here!" said Luneté angrily.

Oh, no, Dewar thought. Luneté would ruin it—

"What?" replied Otto. "I'm taking a hell of a chance being here at all—"

The bed bounced again and dust sifted down onto Dewar lying naked on his back beneath it. Luneté continued, "You certainly are! Who do you think you are? What do you mean by sauntering in here? You shall lie elsewhere, sir!"

"I'm your husband, remember?"

"It seems to have slipped your mind not long after the wedding! Where have you been?"

"At the war! You know that! What—"

"Why haven't you written to me? You've sent three brief letters and two one-line notes. I've read more engaging tax bills! What do you think you are, that you can go off to Landuc or wherever you were and take half my able-bodied men with you—"

Dewar grinned. The Countess of Lys was a shrewd tactician.

"—to fight your damned war, not mine, and then show up expecting me to greet you with open arms! You're a fine one to talk about being a husband. What kind of husband never writes his wife? I'd just about decided you were dead!"

"I couldn't—" Otto began, and changed his line, "I've been so busy, so tired—"

"Busy! Tired! Then get out of here until you're at leisure and rested. I'm busy too, and I'm tired, tired of waiting for you to write or send a message or come back and resume the marriage we put off so that you could take my people into Ascolet and get them killed and tramp off with that rotten Prince to get involved with things that are none of our business! What's kept you so busy, Otto? Tell me! And to what do I owe the remarkable favor of this audience with Your Highness?"

"Luneté! Be reasonable! We've been in Chenay, way the hell out West, and Gaston's given us the filthiest duties, and by the Well don't get sarcastic with me, Countess! I've had a bad time of it while you've been sitting snug and secure here in Lys!"

Luneté's bare feet hit the floor and walked away from the bed. "Oh, how sad. You left home and went to war and didn't like it! Could that be because you were not victorious?"

Ottaviano's scarlet-stockinged feet thumped down and followed her. "What's got into you? You thought this was a fine idea. You sure didn't mind. You thought the risk was worth taking, Countess of Lys! I never concealed the possibility of a loss from you! Never!" he said, his voice lowering on the last word.

"You certainly didn't tell me it would mean I wouldn't see hide nor hair nor word from you in three-quarters of a year and more," she hissed. "I have misgivings, Baron. Our marriage could still be annulled, you know. The Emperor hasn't acknowledged it yet."

"What? Annulled! Luneté, this is a temporary war, not permanent. It's going to be over in a few days—"

"Days! I don't believe you. I've heard nothing good from any quarter about the fortunes of your army and your great Marshal against Prince Prospero."

"He's captured."

"And escaped," Luneté retorted. "Fine bunch of soldiers you are."

"Where did you hear that? Bad news really does travel— Yes, captured, escaped, and captured again! He was careless. I took him myself and I've prisoned him in my own Malperdy in Ascolet. And believe me, madame, I swear by the Well that he shall not leave there save on my word. Gaston was stupid, an honorable idiot, and he trusted that turncoat renegade Dewar alone with Prospero, and of course Dewar was in his pocket."

"I don't believe that either. Dewar never said he was anybody's. He said he was with you because he liked you and he liked your cause. Remember? He wouldn't sell his services. Unlike some of your friends."

"Flames of Eternity! Leave him out of this—"

"You brought it up. If he did release the Prince, good for him! It's an evil day for the world when the Emperor and Princes kill each other out of spite."

"He's a rebel."

"Avril usurped his place. He has a legitimate quarrel. His quarrel! And the Emperor's! Not ours. Not Lys's! I want my people home again before any more of them are killed in this stupid fight of yours and the Emperor's and the Marshal's."

"You are bound by fealty-vow to provide the Emperor with troops whether you like it or not—"

"I have taken no vow yet to anyone but you, and I'm sorry I took that one. Leave my chamber! I married a husband, not a mercenary."

"You married me," Otto said.

"Touch me not, sir!" Luneté cried, and there was a quick step, a muffled sound, and then the thud of a blow followed by a wooden clunk as Otto yelped. "Lu!" he gasped.

"And get out of here until you've learned to behave like a gentleman."

Otto was swearing in a whisper. Below the belt, Dewar guessed, and muffled another snort of laughter in his shirt.

Luneté stood still for a moment and then walked to the door. "Laudine!" she called, distantly.

"Lu, get back here," Otto demanded, his voice still tight, and Dewar heard him get to his feet and follow her out of the room.

The sorcerer under the bed took the opportunity to squirm agilely into his breeches. Voices continued in the solar; he pulled his shirt over his head and succeeded in donning most of his clothing except his boots, which he would not put on until he was nearly outside. Luneté and Otto left the solar and went elsewhere, still arguing.

Dewar rolled from under the bed and rose cautiously. He ducked behind it in the shadow of the hangings and closed his eyes, drawing on the Well and murmuring the spell of concealment which would wrap light and shadow around him. He was not interrupted; the candle burned steadily, and the fire's coals lay passive on the hearth.

Unseeable, Dewar began to leave, but paused at the fireside. The wine stood untasted. He lifted it, studied the label, and removed the loosened cork.

With a ceremonial air, he filled the goblet, turned and toasted the bed silently with a bow, and drained it. Goblet and bottle he replaced on their tray. Good, he noted to himself; a solid domestic white with no pretension to greater than local interest, but with a pleasantly acid afterbite. Refreshing.

Grinning, boots in hand, he padded out of the room and away.

# — 26 —

CLOAKED IN AIR AND DARKNESS AND good double-woven wool, shod in soft boots, Dewar noiselessly climbed the thousand stairs of Malperdy Keep behind the walls of the castle also called Malperdy. The Keep was the heart of Ascolet, one of the oldest fortresses in all Pheyarcet, reputedly built by Panurgus himself in the early days, and it looked its age; several times Dewar stumbled on the unevenly-worn steps, each time halting and listening for alerted guards. Curious that there was no guard at the bottom of the topmost flight, where a wall intersected the keep. He hoped that Prospero had not been moved. The dungeons would have been a likelier holding-pen for a Prince of Air: likelier, but less easy to control mayhap. Well, thought Dewar, it was not his decision, but he would have put guards at the bottom. Otto's men were slacking, perhaps.

He came around the last turning of the stair and stopped.

Someone was crouched low in front of Prospero's door, a dark bent back in the light of the torch which guttered with Dewar's stirring of the air. There was a pile of junk on the floor beside this furtive-looking person, which Dewar's eyes sorted out after a moment as discarded armor: a breastplate and helm, other pieces.

Looking round, the footpad's face was shown in the light too: Dewar held himself very still. He recognized the face; he had spent ten days getting to know it in the snowbound manor-house in Chenay, more than a quarter of a year ago by his clock but not half a month by hers. It was the young woman who had dragged Dewar out of the ditch and doctored him. She was dressed in the sheepskin jacket and trousers and boots she had worn when he'd first met her, now somewhat the worse for wear.

For a long, breath-holding moment she stared through

him at the empty stairs, and then, biting her lip, she turned back to the door. Dewar smiled. Lockpicking.

A loyal partisan indeed, she had tracked her leader here and—how, the Sun and Moon could never know, probably—slipped in. He suspected she was the reason there were no guards at the bottom of the stair.

"Please work," he heard her breathe. She took something from a bag at her feet.

Dewar smiled still, and weighed his next move. He could help her. He could not help her. On the whole it would be more amusing to help her. Her industry and determination in making her way here were admirable; it was the sort of thing that his acquaintance Lady Miranda of Valgalant would do. Dewar whispered the sibilant words which put aside the air and darkness around him; the woman turned and lifted a cocked crossbow, pointing anxiously at nothing, resigned fear in her face.

"Don't shoot!" Dewar hissed as he became visible and the bow swung to aim at him.

Her finger tightened on, but did not close, the trigger. "You," she said, not moving the bow.

"I think we have a common goal, to open that door. Am I right?"

"You're the Emperor's man."

"I certainly am not. I'm freelancing. I have personal business with the fellow in there."

She swallowed, nodded, lowered the bow. "You have a key?"

He sprang lightly up the stairs. "No. I work other ways. Let me see the lock."

She moved aside. "Hurry. The sentries go round and they'll raise an alarm as soon as they find the guard missing," she whispered.

Dewar made no answer to this, but knelt at the door as she had. She had been trying to force the lock with a small knife. As he lifted his hand to the lock, something cold touched his throat: a line of steel.

"I know you're one of *them.* Any tricks, you're, you're dead," she whispered.

The crossbow was butting against his back.

It was best not to argue. "Understood."

"Open it."

He did. He took the broken-bladed knife from the lock and put a square iron nail from his bag into it. Lighting a match at the nail's flat head, which protruded from the lock, he chanted the low, singsong rhyme for copying the key which had last been in the lock: the lock was utterly unprotected from sorcery. These people were fools, he thought, and felt the iron move and flow in his gloved fingers. It was hot, but he turned it in the lock and the lock gripped it and tumbled.

"Ohhh," she breathed at his neck.

"May I stand."

"Yes. Slowly."

"Your servant," Dewar whispered.

Her knife left his throat; the crossbow stayed in the small of his back. He pushed the door open and got up in one movement. The woman had picked up her saddlebag and was on his heels as the first shout came up the stairs.

"Hell's bells!" she said, and the crossbow left his spine.

"Get in!" Dewar grabbed her and pulled her in, turning; he closed the door, taking his magical key from the lock and letting it latch again. The room was not-lit by a faint greenish line of light in a circle on the floor. The place was freezing cold.

"Prospero!" she called softly.

No answer.

"Make a light!" she hissed.

"Should have grabbed the torch."

"Prospero! It's me!"

No answer.

Dewar felt nothing alive in the room. He said, "No, stay here, don't move, it might be a trap," and the woman, who had been stepping forward, stopped and returned to his side. Murmuring the Summoning under the shouts and clangor outside ("Send for the Captain! Get Captain Vandel!"), he invoked an ignis fatuus, which popped rosily into sight and hovered in midair.

The circular room it showed was empty. A bizarrely boiled-looking opening was seethed through the meter-thick stone wall, melted as if the stone had become taffy and run.

Dewar tsked softly. Elemental work.

The circle of foxfire on the floor was broken by similarly boiled stone. Inside was nothing but a wooden plate and a bucket.

"He's gone!" the woman cried. "Prospero!" She ran to the opening in the wall; Dewar followed her. It let on the sheer side of the tower which rose over the less-regular but equally straight cliff. "Prospero!" she shouted out.

"It appears he has rescued himself," Dewar said.

The guards were battering at the door. Dewar crossed to it, to close it more permanently.

"We're caught!" she said, turning and staring at the door, and added, "At least, you are." Leaning from the opening, she put her fingers in her mouth and whistled.

Dewar was fusing the door to the wall, sealing it with an affinity-spell only axework or fire could defeat. It would do for now. Someone was trying a key in the lock.

He looked round at the woman, who was still whistling. "What are you about? Calling a wind?"

The lock rattled and stopped. The door bounced, held; a crack appeared at its top. Dewar glanced at it. It wouldn't endure long. He'd have to make a Way, fast—but there was nothing to burn.

Something vast and dark occluded the stars beyond the hole in the wall, then passed again, then returned and blocked it completely. Dewar saw a huge hooked beak, feathers, claws; there were scrabbling noises from the stone outside. The young woman climbed into the opening and looked back at him. "Good luck, sorcerer," she said, and put a leg out.

"Don't jump!" he cried.

"I'm flying." She slipped out, sideways, and the opening was cleared. He heard shouting from the battlements below.

An axe-blow split the door from top to bottom; Dewar glanced around and realized he was in a bad spot. It was a single-panel door, not cross-grained; the next strike took out a plank of wood, sending it bouncing into the room. He ran to the hole over the cliff to see if he could scale it, as Prospero must have done, and the dark shape returned, hovering in the tower's shadow.

"Stuck?" she called.

"Yes!" he screamed.

"Are you sorry?"

"For anything! Yes!"

"Jump, and we'll catch you!"

He stared at her. The door lost another plank, behind him. Someone shouted, "There he is!"

"Catch me?"

It was a long way, straight down. Half a mile? Far enough, in the faintly silvered darkness. He felt, rather than saw, the dead stone below.

"Jump, fool! Now!" she cried.

The third plank on the door gave, and Dewar, by his ignis, saw a guard duck in, waving a glaive.

He had no time to do anything; he hopped up to the hole in the wall, put his legs out, and dropped. He closed his eyes. Ice-thin air rushed past him, filling his cloak and tossing him around. It was an undignified and untidy way to evade capture, a desperado's end rather than a gentleman's.

If he died, he thought, it would be fast. If he died, it would hurt, for only a moment, and then all's done. Damn, he *did* want to solve the Third-Force problem, and he was so close now; he supposed he'd know, when he died. If he didn't die, he'd rather—

Something slammed into him from the side and clutched him.

"Gotcha!" shrieked the woman.

Dewar opened his eyes, swinging head-down under a gigantic bird, and vomited.

The ignis, faithfully stupid, had plummeted harmlessly from the window with him (though not so swiftly) and now hovered a few feet away, pacing them through the air. The bird's talons were tight on Dewar's legs and midriff, and he was short of breath. It plunged downward still, downward and sideward, and he was buffeted and battered by wind, his cloak, and gravity. Wrenched and sick, Dewar considered what he could have done, had he not let the woman divert him from thinking: Summoned a Salamander to keep the guards back while he made his Way out of there, for example, or collapsed part of the tower.

He vomited again.

"Landing!" shouted the woman.

The bird drew him up, toward its musty body, and with a turbulent backflutter of immense wings came down. Dewar was dropped inelegantly and the dark body of the bird went over him with a bound and a stinking draft. He lay unmoving, face-down, wondering if he had lost his wits or died after all, or was dying: hallucinating rescue.

"Are you all right?" came a soft voice a minute later.

"No."

"Drink some water. It will settle your stomach." She hauled him onto his back. The ignis showed him her solicitous expression and the round leather-covered canteen she held. "I'm sorry it was rough. It's difficult when she's carrying things." She uncorked the canteen and put it to his lips.

"Ech," Dewar agreed. He sipped the cool water. "I think I'll just lie here a moment."

"All right. Here's the water." She got up and walked away. He heard her talking to the bird.

Dewar closed his eyes and breathed deeply and regularly, holding each breath and releasing it slowly. He might be bruised, but he wasn't gravely hurt, and his stomach settled as he swallowed more water and drew on the Well to stabilize himself.

Feeling better, he sat up and looked around. The ignis illuminated the stony slope.

The bird was about ten paces away; its head snapped round as he stood slowly. He saw that it wore a kind of harness and that its wings were set farther back on its shoulders than—

Dewar blinked again. Four legs not two; and a tufted tail swung from its oddly-made hindquarters. The woman walked around the big, hook-beaked head and smiled slightly at him under her leather-and-metal helmet.

"Interesting animal you have," he said.

She lifted her eyebrows and nodded, the smile gone.

"Does it have a name?"

"She's Trixie. A gryphon."

"Hello, Trixie." The big head's black eyes watched him intently.

"Don't get too close."

"I won't."

There were dark stains on the bird's feathers.

"Is she hurt?"

"No, she killed something, I think."

They regarded one another. Their prior acquaintance made this more like a meeting of friends than enemies, though they had little basis to be either.

"So . . ." Dewar looked around them, paused as he recognized the moon-gleamed bulk of Malperdy five or more miles away from them, silhouetted against the sky. ". . . ah, what's a nice lady like you doing in a place like that?" He looked back at her in time to see her head tip skeptically to one side, to see the smile struggle onto her mouth, and to see that he had judged aright: she laughed, light and delight in the sound. Dewar had only made her laugh once before, in Chenay; he felt a curious sense of pleased accomplishment at doing it now.

"I'm *not* a lady," she replied, shaking her head.

"I mean, you were there to help Prince Prospero, correct?"

"Yes. Unfortunately he has helped himself, or so it looked to me. He is very bad at letting people know what he's about."

"Yes, he could have left a note. 'Stepped out.' "

She laughed again, and Dewar laughed with her.

"And you?" she asked.

"Obviously, much the same."

"Obviously? Hardly." Her smile and amusement vanished and she was quite serious. "You say you're not the Emperor's—"

"I'm not. In fact I am wholly uninterested in that tedious

war between them. My business with Prospero is personal."

"Oh?"

"Yes. I wonder where he's got to."

She shrugged, shook her head. Absently, she stroked the throat of her gryphon. Dewar watched Trixie extend her neck; she hadn't taken her eyes from him.

The conversation had taken on an awkward feel.

"I'll track him down," the woman said, "eventually."

"That was my plan also."

"Mmhm. And what sort of business do you have to do?"

Dewar had not noticed: while her left hand stroked the feathers, the right had brought the cocked crossbow to bear on him. "We met recently, under flurried circumstances, and parted inconclusively: not on good terms or ill, just suddenly. I wish to finish the conversation we had begun, and to understand what our future relationship will be."

"Mmhm," she said again, her eyes on his. "You're not exactly lying," she said after a moment, "but you're so full of deceit it's hard to be sure."

"I mean him no harm, no injury. I may even be able to speed you to him, if you ally with me for the search."

"You're one of these sorcerers," she said, "of whom I've heard that everything is for sale. Your help wouldn't be free."

"We'd help one another," Dewar said. "I do not engage in commerce."

"Mmhm. I suspect I'd come off short, as I did last time I helped you. You'd be taking care of yourself first."

"So would you, certainly. It's only natural."

"Had I placed myself first the first time we met," she said, slowly cradling the crossbow (glittering starlit steel) in both hands, "I'd have left you with a big pile of food, a barrel of water, and good-luck wishes—before the storm trapped me there."

Dewar looked away, chewing his lip. If she had truly placed herself first when they had first met, he would lie now stiff and cold under a slowly-compacting cover of snow, dreaming unknowing of darkness.

"I'm too soft-hearted," she said, and turned away.

"That's what I've been told, anyway, and I guess it's true," she added, and walked back around the gryphon. The animal crouched.

"Don't go!" he said, as her head and body appeared between the wings.

"I don't think I want you to help me," she said, "but I'll tell him you're looking for him when I find him."

"Do that, then," said Dewar.

She did not reply; the gryphon turned quickly, light on great taloned and clawed feet—how could anything so big fly?—and trotted awkwardly, then leapt upward, wings seizing the air and mounting it. Dewar tipped his head back, watching; the gryphon went forward, down, caught a draft, and he lost it in the night.

Dewar noticed that she had left him her canteen. The mountains were nearly waterless, besides being of barren stone and thin on Leys and firewood. He'd need the canteen to get out of here, which he'd have to do the hard way: on foot.

# — 27 —

DEWAR, LEANING OVER THE EDGE OF the well, pulled the mossy bucket up. The frayed rope was iced, and it tried to freeze onto his gloves every time he touched it. But the water was wet and refreshing and he filled the canteen and drank slowly, relieving his thirst with reverent animal pleasure. It had been most of a night and a day since he'd drunk; he'd found no open water on his route to the village, nor even ice to thaw. Where was the snow? There'd been plenty of it in the South all autumn.

The village was deserted. Doorways gaped doorless; shutters banged unevenly in the whistling wind. There was no sign of recent inhabitation; as Dewar looked around at the weathered and crumbling houses, he knew no one could have lived here for some years. Grass grew on thresholds and birds' nests were visible in unlikely places. Why abandon a place with a good well in these parts? Ascolet was an odd country. He shrugged and filled the canteen again.

A sound more regular than the flapping of a shutter came to his ears as he drank. Dewar recognized it as hoofbeats, approaching at a fast, purposeful clip. He tightened his belt, capped the canteen, and readied himself for an encounter which could hardly be pleasant in these wild places. Some of Golias's loose mercenaries, most likely.

But only one horseman rode into the square, and he pulled up five or six paces from the well and stared at Dewar. The horse was tired, wheezing and frothing; its sides were blooded from the spurs of the mailed rider, who wore Ascolet livery and a closed helm.

Messenger? wondered Dewar, and waited, ready.

"I challenge you," said the other. "You are a cowardly, sneaking intriguer, and the world will be lighter without your soul."

Dewar looked at the well. "Is this some local custom?" he inquired. There'd been nothing in the Ephemeris about meeting a mortal challenge at this well.

"Eliminating vermin is a universal practice," said the knight.

The voice was familiar, though altered by the helm.

"Who challenges me, then?" Dewar asked, humoring him.

"Ottaviano," said the knight.

Dewar blinked. "Otto? What's your problem?" Perhaps Luneté had told him of Dewar's visit after all.

"Choose your weapon."

"I don't think you're quite—"

"Choose your weapon or be ridden down!" screamed Otto, who had fired himself to a blazing rage during his ride and meant to be rid of Dewar, who had twice now released Prospero, Otto's prisoner and the lynch-pin of Otto's future.

"I have no reason to fight you," Dewar said, bemused, "so—"

Otto spurred his horse, which screamed and leapt forward, exhausted though it was. In less than a second he was on Dewar, and Dewar, astonished, threw himself down, rolled out of the way, and rose and drew. The horse swung around and came back, and Dewar deflected a wide decapitating swing from Otto and then grabbed his wrist and yanked him sideways. Overbalanced, Otto fell, but he drew a dagger as he did and gashed Dewar's arm.

The horse staggered away a few steps. Although being mounted gave him great advantage, Otto did not pursue it and instead went for Dewar again, dagger in one hand and his wide-bladed gold-damascened sword in the other.

Dewar abandoned argument and defended himself, using his cloak to confuse and screen his movements and to foul Otto's dagger blade, which had bitten deep. His forearm ran with blood; he hadn't time to bind it nor to draw on the Well for strength.

A high scream came from overhead. The horse whinnied in rolling-eyed panic and stampeded out of the square down a side street. A shadow passed over them, and as it did Otto fell back under a determined attack from Dewar. Dewar wanted to disarm his challenger or wound him enough to stop the fight; he had no intention of dying over jealousy sparked by a woman, which he suspected was the germ of the quarrel here. Lunetė, surely, would not have told Otto of their dalliance, and Dewar considered it irrelevant—she had started it, after all—but Otto was edgy and hot-tempered and might have leapt to his own conclusions without evidence.

The shadow had left a musty-smelling draft behind it. With a scrabbling *whump* the gryphon which had carried Dewar from the castle tower and left him on the hillside landed on the other side of the fountain.

"Stop!" cried the young woman who owned the beast, running toward them. She dove at Otto, dodged his dagger hand, and ducked away as he whirled on her; Dewar, using the opening, struck Otto's sword down. Otto spun back and swung at Dewar again, a wild but strong blow, and yelled in protest as the woman from the gryphon grabbed his cloak and pulled him off-balance.

Dewar laughed at the incongruous sight, a mouse pulling

a cat's tail. But Otto rounded on her and she cried out as he punched her, his left fist glancing across her face and staggering her, and then the gryphon pounced into the disorderly melée too and knocked him down, taking a nick or two as Otto flailed and fell.

"Trixie! Stop!" The woman stomped on Otto's left arm and knelt on it, keeping him from stabbing the gryphon.

"Yield, fool!" yelled Dewar to Otto.

Otto cursed the woman up and down her ancestry and then lay still as Dewar lifted his visor so that he gazed straight up at the gryphon's beak. Blood ran from the young woman's nose and spatted on his helm and face.

"What the fuck is that?" Otto shouted after a moment.

"Trixie," said the woman, breathing hard. "Gryphons don't like people who hurt their riders." She cautiously massaged her face where he had hit her and wiped tears from her cheeks. "Ouch."

"You get the hell out of this fight, and your gryphon can mind its own business," Otto bellowed, red-faced. He scrabbled for his sword, which had fallen from his hand.

"What are you doing here?" Dewar asked her in a low voice, closing Otto's visor again and stepping on his right wrist.

"I ch-changed my m-mind." Her voice quivered. She blotted her nose with a tattered handkerchief.

"So perhaps we may be of use to one another?" Dewar suggested. He took out his own handkerchief and began wrapping up his gashed arm.

"Maybe." She nodded and wiped a few more tears and her nose again.

"Then perhaps we don't need an audience for our negotiations," he said. "This hot fellow," he rapped the helm, "is Ottaviano of Ascolet, who has much to gain from working against what you want. I personally, as I've said, have decided I'm neutral to the whole mess, but—"

Otto yelled something indistinct in his helm.

Dewar hit the helm again. "Shut up, Otto. As I was saying, but I think your concerns are partisan." He smiled pleasantly, holding her gaze with his.

"Y-yes," said the woman, staring at him, her brows drawn a little together. Her nose had stopped bleeding; she put the handkerchief away.

"Therefore, we must dispose of Otto."

"I don't like killing people," she said, "or even . . . unless there's a very good reason to do it. Why are you fighting with him?"

"I don't know. I just got here—and I would not have made it this far without your canteen, by the way, for which my thanks—I arrived, drew water, drank, and was set upon without explanation by Otto, who seems to have been on my trail."

She nodded. "Let's tie him up then."

"Hm. He's a journeyman sorcerer. It may take more than that."

She mimed to Dewar: you turn him over, I'll knock him out.

Dewar nodded. "Perhaps he'll listen to reason if we give him a chance," he said.

She picked up a rock from the dilapidated well enclosure. "Trixie, back."

Reluctantly, the gryphon took her foot from Otto's breastplate and torn surcoat and backed away, still watching him fixedly. Otto lunged toward Dewar, and the young woman hit him hard on the back of the head with the rock.

He swayed and fell.

"That was easy," said she, surprised.

"I think he's not used to women putting up a fight." Dewar smiled. "It seems not to be the custom hereabouts." He picked up the dagger Otto had gashed him with and cleaned it on his cloak.

"Swine," she said, standing, nudging Otto with a toe and making a *hwoinch-hwoinch* noise. "No, not a piggy, not to eat," she added hastily to Trixie, who had lurched forward again. "We'll find you a piggy somewhere else."

"Let's go before he rouses."

She nodded gravely. "Hop up behind me. This is a bad place to fly out of, but we'll manage. Right, Trixie?" She was on the gryphon's back already, buckling herself into a saddle of sorts.

"By the way," Dewar said, scrambling onto the surprisingly slippery rust- and gold-colored feathers behind her, "I'm Dewar."

"Hullo. I'm Freia."

"An honor to make your acquaintance, m'lady."

"I'm not your lady or anybody's," she said sharply. "You have to get closer. Right against my back."

Trixie was walking uneasily around the fountain; Dewar pressed hard against Freia's back and felt the gryphon's gait become lighter.

"That's right," Freia said. "Pull in your cloak and get closer."

Dewar pushed his legs against hers, drew his cloak tight around him, and embraced her, cheek at her neck under the steel-and-leather helmet. "Close enough?" Any closer, he thought, and they'd have to get married.

"You puke down my neck and you'll fly by yourself," she warned him. "It's where the weight is on her back that matters, you see?" Freia tugged at one of the leather-covered chains which made up the gryphon's tack.

"I see. I've not eaten in a while. Li—uuuups!"

Trixie had gathered herself and bounded up to a rooftop, claws scrabbling, then bounded again, spreading her wings and catching the air. They hung a sickening instant, dropped in an even more sickening one, and then began to rise steadily under power of great swoops of the broad wings. Freia held her in a spiral.

Dewar had closed his eyes, finding the lurching more distressing than he'd expected, despite his empty stomach. They went dizzyingly around and around. He swallowed, breathed slowly; his nose was tickled by a whiff of warm perfume from the shirt collar beside his cheek. Hm. He turned his head and pressed it closer to the sweet scent, distracted from his discomfort.

The air was cold, thin, and dry. The mountains whirled past; he peeked and closed his eyes again. It was, however, better than the wild night ride he'd gotten from the tower, and after a few swallows his stomach thought his eyes could look about. He did, carefully, peeking down past her breast and shoulder to see the ground below. It was spinning, but more slowly, in wider loops; he began to pick out the wrinkles of the mountains, a seam of a watercourse, tousled bushes and bristling trees.

"Are you all right?" Freia asked him, turning her head a little.

His lips were near her ear. "This is *delightful.* Oh my word yes."

"This is—" Freia began, but stopped. "Well. I guess we can talk now."

"Yes." Dewar realized that he was gripping his wrists so tightly his hands hurt. He relaxed slightly.

"Hold on *tight.* There can be lumpy air, places where it goes up and down. I'm in the saddle, but you might bounce," Freia warned him. "Tuck your hands here," she added, and pushed them under her belt.

"What a way to travel," Dewar said, still staring at the mountains, dry-sided and bare-topped. It had been a droughty winter in the East; he wondered if Prospero's cloud-herding Sylph had something to do with that. "Anyway," he said, "yes, let's talk, or if you'd rather land—"

"Two is the load limit, no luggage; Trixie's fine. I've carried someone as big as you before." Freia was guiding the gryphon through a pass and along a valley. "Keep your head down!"

"Aerodynamics," he said, tucking his chin on her shoulder again.

"Yes. You'll be dynamicked right off her back. I want to find Prospero, and I'm having difficulty doing that. You're a sorcerer and I know you can find things. You found him before."

"He's as slippery as a wind himself. There are a number of ways to find someone. One is to have something of his—a lock of hair, a rag stained with blood—anything intimate will do, you can use a button if the person has worn it a while before losing it."

"Oh. I don't have anything. Not with me."

Mistress? Lover? wondered Dewar. He continued to speak in her ear. "Second way will not work with him. He's certainly proofed against sorcerous Summonings."

"Summonings," she repeated.

"It is a usual practice. Unfortunately he is probably also proofed against the class of lesser spells which afford vision of a person without actually intruding into his sphere of experience. And that leaves the classical method."

"What's that?" Freia asked.

"If you were Prospero, where would you go next?"

"You're joking."

"No. Where would you go?"

"That's all you can do? Guess?" Her voice rose with disbelief.

"Are you going to throw me off here?" He was sure she wouldn't.

"No . . . . I thought—I'm sorry. I *don't* know where he'd go," she said unhappily. "Where would you go if you were him?"

"I'd probably run to earth for a while. Hide, lick my wounds, plan another attack."

"He hasn't."

"You're sure?"

She nodded. "I wouldn't have come looking for you if I were."

"I see. Let me think about it then."

"How did you find him in the tower?"

"Ah, actually Ottaviano, whom you just met, told his wife where he was, and I happened to be listening. No sorcery, just luck."

Freia sighed. Trixie's muscles moved rhythmically. Dewar's legs were cramping with the effort of clinging to the animal's slippery, silken back; the furry feathers, or feathery fur, were dense, soft, and hard to grasp. His face was cold; he ducked down more, using Freia as a windscreen.

"It would help me to guess," Freia said after a minute or so of silent scenic flight, "if I knew more about how that last battle went."

"He was defeated and he surrendered."

"More than that. Where are—where are his men? His allies? Dead?"

"Not last I saw. The survivors of his army were taken captive. I suspect Gaston would move them as rapidly as he could to some safe holding area."

"How do you know so much, may I ask, about how and who and what?"

"I was working with Ottaviano," Dewar said, "but not under contract, and I decided to free Prospero after he was taken. And I did."

"You betrayed your side?"

"They aren't, and weren't, my side. There was nothing to bind me to them but friendship, and I saw no harm in helping Prospero escape from certain execution."

"Execution," she repeated.

He felt her pulse jump.

"Yes. The Emperor hates him."

"He never said—" she stopped herself. "Execution!"

"What would you expect? He's attacked Landuc before."

She shook her head. "Why did you help him escape?"

"It seemed a great waste to me. Personal reasons. Whimsy. Mischief. I'm not sure. Perhaps he laid a geas on me to do it, when I wasn't looking."

"Hm," Freia said.

The mountains were flattening out. The valley bottoms held bluish evergreens and brooks, and Dewar had spotted white specklings of sheep on the hills. Or cattle, perhaps. Out grazing in winter—it was odd weather, indeed.

"Usually the snow here is shoulder-deep by now."

"Is it?"

"Yes. I was here last winter and there's no getting around after the solstice. Sun turns and sky churns, they say."

"Maybe it all fell where we were. I never saw so much snow. —I'm looking for a place to set down," Freia said. "Trixie's tired, and so am I, and you're slipping a bit."

"It was a long walk out, let us say. However, I am glad you changed your mind and came back for me."

"He would have killed you."

"Oh, I think I'd have taken him."

"He wanted to kill you. I never saw anyone so angry. He was berserk."

"Hm. He might have a streak of that in him. They say old Panurgus had terrible rages."

"You've fallen back. You must move closer while we go down."

"Sorry. You're right, I'm tired." He hunched close to Freia again, feeling her body moving inside the leather suit she wore. Practical for flying: warm, windproof. Trixie was swooping in long, slow spirals. Freia was aiming for a pile of stones which resolved itself into a tumbled hut or fold. The descent took far longer than the landing, which was a brief, bone-jarring impact.

"It's difficult with two," Freia said, and clucked to the gryphon, petting and praising her.

Dewar disentangled himself from her and slid awkwardly to the ground. His legs were sore, pressed and strained in strange places by gryphon anatomy. He walked in stiff circles while Freia took saddlebags and a bedroll from the animal's neck and talked to her fondly. Trixie bounded into the air then and rose quickly.

"Where's she going?" Dewar asked.

"Hunting."

"Ah. Let's see what the lodgings have to offer here."

"I need to sleep for a few days," Freia said, yawning and looking over his shoulder into the half-fallen shelter. "Hay."

"Someone else camps here," Dewar said, indicating the fire-ring on the dirt floor. "Hunters or shepherds."

Freia pushed past him and began pulling at the hay, levelling it into a bedding pile. Dewar found a stack of wood behind the hut and made a fire with it; by then, Freia was stretched in the hay rolled up in blankets from her saddle.

"Food in the bag," she said. "Pots. You clean up." Her attitude made it clear that he was on his own for the meal.

He boiled water, cooked a handful of grain and some dried fruit in it, and ate thoughtfully. The hot food warmed his wind-chilled and chapped body; she had a packet of leaves too, possibly some kind of tea, but he didn't want to experiment with unfamiliar herbs. Instead he cleaned the pot with his fingers, fed up the fire, and shook out his cloak in the hay beside Freia. The sun was setting, and the air was getting colder. Dewar closed his eyes, curled against the warm body of his companion, and fell asleep at once.

# ⌒ 28 ⌒

DEWAR WOKE UP COLD AND BURROWED further into the blankets, then slept again. When the frosty dawn brightened the air, he roused to hear Freia talking to the gryphon, but she came back in and flopped in the hay beside him, taking half the blankets away.

"Cold," he mumbled, tugging the blankets back.

"Hate it," she said, and huddled next to him, shivering. Together they were warmer than if they stayed apart, and so they slept in a nest of hay and wool until midafternoon sun sloped round to warm and light the hut.

"Hm," said Freia then, waking up.

"Hm yourself," Dewar said. "Damn, it's cold. Wish we'd found a decent inn. Featherbed."

"Featherbed yourself. It'd have bugs."

"Trust a woman to spoil a beautiful dream," he said, and he was kicked in the shins. "Ow!"

"Time for you to start earning your keep," she said tartly.

Dewar sat up and glared at her. "What did you have in mind? It *is* cold."

She threw hay at him, a big handful, and he laughed at her and threw some back. Then he lay down beside her again. She had unbent now that they were allied. He already liked her more than he had after their first enforced intimacy.

"Earning my keep," Dewar repeated, and pulled his cloak back around him. "You want me to conjure up smoked pheasant and champagne, perhaps? It doesn't work that way."

"No, I want you to figure out where Prospero is."

She had pretty eyes, actually, thought Dewar, distracted. Long lashes, lovely shape. Some part of his imagination, whetted by proximity, undressed her and decided that the rest of her person was probably not unattractive. He hadn't noticed her body in the manor-house. The baggy borrowed dresses, perhaps, or his own pain, or maybe it was riding hard against her back on her gryphon yesterday. . . . "I'll try."

"You're not looking for him to challenge him to a fight, are you?"

"No."

Freia studied him still, and Dewar felt goose-flesh rise on his back. She wasn't using sorcery, but he was being plumbed, his sincerity assayed.

"What do you think he'd do," he asked her.

"Was he hurt?"

"Yes, but not gravely. Minor to such as he." He decided that if she were willing, so would he be. Even in freezing cold in a haystack.

"Hm."

"He didn't go where you thought he would."

"No."

"He went somewhere else, then." Dewar pictured the two of them, swaddled in wool in the spiky old hay, clumsily coupling, and smiled. "That's obvious," he added, to account for his accidental smile. Leave dalliance for featherbeds and better weather. "You know, nobody else seems to be following him as you do."

"What do you mean?" she temporized.

"None of the rest of his army nor staff are trailing him as you have. How can you do that? What makes you special?"

"Nothing. I'm nobody special. I was just worried. He's in trouble."

"Where are the rest of his army and staff?" Dewar asked. No point pushing the subject until she refused outright to tell him how she was following Prospero, as she certainly would. She was cautious, but not adept at concealment, and he was sure he could get much from her with subtlety.

"You said imprisoned somewhere—" Freia blinked. "Of course! I'm thick as clay. He'll go to them, to bring them home! He won't leave them here!"

"Exactly," Dewar said. "Find them, and he's near or among them."

"Easier said than done, surely." Freia's shoulders slumped. "I've no idea where—I've just been blundering around."

Dewar hmm'd thoughtfully. "Have you some token of any of the men in captivity?"

"No," she said apologetically.

"Then we're reduced to indirect approaches," he said, sighing. "Well, that's life."

"What are indirect approaches?"

"Sorcery. —You must be hungry."

"Yes, I am. Trixie brought us meat, if she didn't eat it all herself already. We can cook it and eat, but we'd better leave at sunset."

"Afraid not. We'll be here until moonrise and after, in order to find out where we're going."

The fire gave light, but little heat. Freia had coaxed Trixie around to lie blocking the dry northwest wind, and that had helped warm the two travellers more than the fire. The musty, glossy gryphon's body was an implied monstrosity in the shadows and moving light from the flames. Her great eyes were golden with reflected firelight, watching Dewar.

Freia's eyes were wide, too, dark-pupilled and wondering. Wrapped up in one of her blankets, she sat in the hay an arm's-length away from Dewar as he worked over a small hemispherical silver bowl filled with water. Dewar, for his part, embroidered the spell and added meaningless difficulties to it, standard practice: she wouldn't be able to describe it accurately later, for example to Prospero.

He had rummaged through his bag and found several useful items. He had a pack of playing-cards once Josquin's, which Dewar had pocketed after a last game with the Prince Heir, Otto, and Golias on the day before the battle. At that game Golias had lent Dewar a wooden pipe, kept with more benign absentmindedness than Josquin's cards. Herne distrusted Dewar, but had lent him a whetstone three days before the battle, and Dewar had dropped it into his essential supply kit and forgotten it, until now.

A stone, a pipe, a pack of cards. They lay on the ground before him.

"What are you going to do?" Freia whispered.

"Shh," he said, and picked up the pack of cards and put it in the water.

The water was bright with trapped moonlight, so that the cards simply vanished under the light. Freia leaned closer, interested more than afraid.

Dewar sing-songed the last binding of this Summoning under his breath, but clearly, and the shining water gradually took on an image.

Josquin, with a faint look of perplexity, was looking around himself. He sensed the one-sided Summoning of Seeming and Sound, but couldn't identify it.

Dewar muttered a modification to the spell, expanding the sphere of its vision and shrinking Josquin. The Prince Heir was in a tent, eating his dinner; a triple candelabrum on the table gave light and focus for the spell. A liveried young man stood to one side, serving him.

Freia had crept up, the better to see, and was leaning half-around Dewar's shoulder.

"Who's that?" she breathed.

"Prince Josquin. All we can do is watch and listen. He cannot hear us, but he sensed the Summoning—however, since he's sorcerously ignorant, not only did he not recognize it but he also could do nothing about it." Dewar smiled unpleasantly. "I feel like a wolf among lambs. We shall see if we can discover something of his location from this, and whether he is near the prisoners of war."

"Oh," Freia said. She shifted her weight and sat down, preparing for a long siege. "People don't usually say things like, 'Here I am at Castle Cathouse,' do they?"

"I know. It's cues and clues I want. It may take a while, but the connection is strong." She was sitting very close to his shoulder. "It's cold," he said. "Mind if we share the blankets and the heat?"

"It *is* cold," she agreed, and they rearranged themselves. Dewar, under the baleful, unblinking gaze of the gryphon, put a folded blanket over some of the hay, and they sat on that and pulled his cloak and her other blanket around them, shivering. Freia put a pot of water next to the fire to heat for tea, and they sat watching Prince Josquin, who was dining slowly. Dewar's arm slid around Freia's waist a few minutes later. After a moment's shy stiffness, she relaxed against him. Indeed it was warmer to sit this way.

The Prince finished his dinner and put on a heavy green cloak. "He's not in Madana, anyway," Dewar said, half to himself, as Josquin left his tent and crunched over snow. Two guards with a lantern followed him, and the spell now focused on the lantern's flame. The Prince walked among tents, met a man when he was well past them. The man saluted briskly.

"Sir!"

"As you were, Corporal. All quiet?"

"Yes, sir!"

"Keep it so."

"Yes, sir!"

Josquin was inspecting his sentries. He went slowly around the perimeter of the camp, and the exchanges were all similar.

The water boiled. Freia shook leaves into it.

At the last post Josquin turned back to the camp, trailed by his guards. He stopped at a tent and asked the guard who stood there if Lord Grumond were within, and the guard answered yes and bent down, lifting the flap and announcing His Majesty the Prince of Madana.

"Ah!" said Grumond, standing and smiling. He had been feeding a stove; the spell fed on the light of his oil-lantern. Dewar recognized Grumond: Josquin's Madanese second and sometime lover. Hm. Should it become too intimate he'd break this off.

"Damn! It's as cold in here as outside. Carry on, by the Sun!"

"Wood's all damp with snow," Grumond said, "and it's not taking." He knelt again and began fussing with the fire. "Any news, m'lord?"

"No. I'm going to ask the Marshal if he means to kill his own allies sitting out this accursed winter. Apparently Prospero escaped from the Baron of Ascolet again, while the Baron was out for a day or two visiting his wife."

"The Countess of Lys . . ."

"Yes. Heh-heh. The unlucky bridegroom. As soon as there's a front, he'll be the first sent to it, and good riddance. Sneaking around and trying to pull the wool over Gaston's eyes, which can't be done."

"The upstart bastard. He and that damned sorcerer of his— How did the devil get out of the castle? Malperdy's never been breached from within or without."

"I don't know the details, but he had help and there was sorcery involved. I rather strongly suspect our boy Dewar went after him again."

"Treachery," Grumond growled at the stove.

"You've got too much fuel in there," Josquin said, "that's why it isn't taking. Pull half of it out or two-thirds."

Grumond did that and added more tinder and a lit twig.

"If he's escaped," Grumond said, "our troubles shall soon begin again."

"Yes. The Prince Marshal commands us to be ready to move in an hour."

"You had us hold ready anyway. Good thinking, m'lord."

"It shan't be over until Prospero's head bounces twice. So the Emperor has said. I shall be glad of it; this has become rather a bore, and I never liked him terribly anyway."

Freia moved a little, agitated; Dewar squeezed her against him.

Grumond's fire was catching. He held his hands to its bright light eagerly.

"Now close the stove," Josquin said, "and it'll be hotter."

"Lall's a wonder with this thing. Catches right off for him. Damned inconvenient climate, m'lord."

Josquin laughed. "For any number of things."

"Golias is going to be itchy now," chuckled Grumond, standing and closing the door of the stove.

"Where is Lall?"

"Chasing some wench. I gave him the dinner hour free. Believe he went off with Panzo, you know Panzo."

Josquin chuckled too. "Call on me later, when he's back to keep your stove going."

"Thank you, m'lord. I shall. Cards?"

"Naturally," Josquin said, and went out.

"We may not do much better than this," Dewar murmured. "I can look in on Golias next." Freia sipped tea and passed the cup to him. It was hot; welcome in his cold throat.

Freia asked, "He's the mercenary . . . ?"

"Yes. Later, if Golias is unhelpful, we can watch Josquin play cards. He's always been an obliging gossipy fellow." He broke the spell that bound Josquin and cast another for Golias, using the pipe. Since Dewar was the last to handle the pipe, it was more difficult to fix on Golias, but finally Dewar wrested the line of the spell's seeking away from himself and found the mercenary.

Freia gasped. "No!" she cried.

Dewar held her down. "Calm down and listen!"

A lean blond man stood in front of Golias, held by two of Golias's mercenaries. Around each of his eyes was a line of fresh-welling blood, seeping like tears on his cheeks. Blood ran down his neck, too, from his right ear. Golias was sitting down.

"Stake him out again," he said.

Freia's hands were cutting off the circulation in Dewar's forearm.

"So you know him," Dewar said, as the man was hauled out of Golias's presence.

Golias, scowling, filled a pipe and opened a bottle of wine.

"He's my fa—he's second to Prospero here. Utrachet."

"Then we've likely found the troops," Dewar said, "and doubtless Golias, in his own subtle way, was trying to find out what we want to know, or something similar."

Freia began to say something, and stopped. Dewar politely pried her fingers loose.

She quavered, "Sorry. I—"

"A shock," he said, and stroked her cold hands. "Now let's see if we can find out more from the captain here."

"He must be an—an ogre. To hurt him . . ."

"He is." Dewar drew the spell in closer.

Golias looked around suspiciously and paused in mid-drink. He set down the glass and waited, still tense, and then opened a brown book in front of him. A journal. Dewar recklessly narrowed the spell's focus so that Golias's pen-work was visible and leaned forward to read it.

> *Perendlac. Day VI here. Questioned P's captain again, no answers. XII more hanged, of the strongest.*

"What does it say?" Freia demanded, unable to see around Dewar.

"Uh, he's writing his journal," Dewar said, thinking quickly, "about how Utrachet isn't talking. He doesn't seem to know his name."

"Utrachet would say nothing," Freia said, "not even that, and the men speak none of the language here—" She stopped and blinked.

> *Word comes that Otto let P slip away again. Dewar did the groundwork for the escape, getting in, killing two guards, disrupting the Bounds, and knocking a hole in the damn tower wall. Told Otto to put the prisoner in the dungeons, he insisted on the tower. The fool, to have cast all away. An ill day. The Marshal and Herne wait in Landuc for word of Prospero's whereabouts. On full alert.*

Dewar translated this.

"But where are they?"

"Perendlac. Perendlac. Hm. I'll need a map. It's somewhere in the river-plains. Perendlac's a famous fortress."

Golias sanded the page, dried it, and closed the book. He looked around him, scowling again, and got up and took his cloak, leaving the tent quickly without a light. The connection faded and failed. Dewar broke the spell.

"Perendlac," he said again.

"We have to get them out," Freia said.

"Prospero is probably planning to get them out himself," Dewar said. "We have to be there when he does it."

"He's hurting Utrachet! How far away is it?"

"It's a good distance," Dewar admitted. The Road or a Ley might pass nearby. He gave the cup back to her and she refilled it.

"Trixie is fast," Freia said.

Dewar's arm was still around her. She turned, kneeling and looking into his eyes.

"We have to go there, to Perendlac," she insisted. "We can't leave them there! Prospero might be too late."

"I'm trying to think how, madame."

"You don't know where it is?" she asked.

"I do, but not in such particulars as would enable us to navigate there from here. I am thinking that, since Trixie can fly there, I can cast a spell to lead us to Golias and that may do as well as or better than a map."

"But—"

"Of course we do not go to Golias. We stop before then, having seen with our eyes the evidence of his and his army's presence before us."

"Ohhh. I see. Like following a scent."

He nodded and smiled.

"How long will it take to cast this spell? How far away is it?"

"It is hundreds of miles," he said. "This is no over-the-hills jaunt. Moreover we must avoid being seen."

Freia, agitated, began, "If you had a map—"

He put two fingers on her mouth, silencing her. "Let me think. It might be best to travel by night. Trixie is not inconspicuous. I must do some preparatory sorcery."

"How long?"

"A couple of hours. You can sleep while I do what I must."

After a long, searching look in his firelit face, Freia nodded. "All right," she said.

"I warn you I'm going to be very hungry when I finish, so I'll have to eat a big meal."

"There are apples in my saddlebag. Have some now."

He bowed his head politely. "Thank you. I'll still need to eat afterward. It's a drain."

"I know." Freia nodded, sighing, and sat back on her heels.

"You're worried about your friends," Dewar said, leaning forward and squeezing her shoulder. "We'll go as quickly as we can. I am as interested in seeing Prospero as you are. He may be there by the time we are."

"Trixie flies very fast," Freia said.

"For how long?"

She bit her lip. "I've only ridden her a long time alone. Nearly a whole day once, with a lot of soaring. This will be more work. We might push her for half the night, or a bit less."

"That might do it, if the winds are favorable. Now sleep. You'll have to be awake to fly."

"You don't want me to watch."

"Well, no."

"Say so then."

"I don't want you watching me work."

Freia nodded. "Trixie, guard," she said to the gryphon, putting her hand on Dewar's head.

The gryphon's eyes, which had been closed, opened and fixed her lambent look on the sorcerer.

He said, "You don't trust me."

"No," Freia stated.

They studied one another. Dewar's mouth quirked. "Sweet dreams, lady," he said. "I'll wake you."

Freia retreated to the hay with her two blankets and watched him for a quarter of an hour or so. Gradually, she relaxed, and when Dewar heard her breathing deepen and slow, he began arranging his spell.

Trixie wouldn't let him leave the hut. She rose and blocked him, the wicked beak half-open, ready to snap. This he found irritating, and he woke Freia before he had intended to in order to gain his freedom.

"Hm?" she said, blinking at the golden light of his ignis fatuus, conjured to eke out the firewood.

"Mind calling off your watcher so I can step outside for a few minutes?"

"What?"

"I need to piss and the gryphon is keeping me in," Dewar repeated.

"Oh. Trix, easy."

"Thank you, madame."

Freia lay back down and was asleep when he returned after a cold and starry-skied sortie around the back of the lean-to. The gryphon, which had not moved her eyes from him while he had built the spell to draw them to Golias through his pipe, had tucked her head under a wing. He hoped the animal was rested enough.

"Freia, wake up."

"Mm."

He shook her shoulder. "Come now. Wake up."

"Ah-hah," she said, but didn't move.

"If you don't get up, I'll rouse you, like it or not," he threatened.

"Just try," Freia grumbled, blinking at him. "What's that?"

"An ignis. Here, drink this, it's hot." He pushed tea at her. A slow starter, clearly; Dewar was rarely sluggish on waking and was growing impatient to be gone. "We're in a hurry, remember?"

"Oh. Yes. I forgot."

"Wonderful," he said, and began packing her pot away.

Freia rubbed her eyes, drank the acidic tea, sat picking hay out of her clothes for a minute or so, and then, with a quick "Excuse me," bolted outside.

Dewar grinned and picked up the cup and her blankets. He'd been sure the tea would get her out of the hay.

"Sweet stars, it's cold," she said presently from the other side of the gryphon. "Come along, Trixie. Oh, thanks for rolling that up."

"Let's go."

Freia, nodding, was tying the blankets and her saddlebags on. "Stretch first," she advised Dewar, doing so, joints snapping and creaking. "Ready?"

"For half an hour now, madame."

She glared at him in the ignis's mellow light. "Now what? What about this spell business?"

"We mount and fly. The heading is that way." He pointed west-northwest.

Freia looked in that direction, picking out stars, he realized. "Good," she said, and climbed onto the gryphon. Dewar got up behind her, dismissing the ignis with a fingersnap. Trixie protested with a muffled squawk and Freia had to talk to her, encouraging her. Finally the gryphon trotted in her uneven way to an outcrop of stone.

"Ready," Freia said to Dewar.

"Ready." He tightened his arms around her waist. He was pressed against her back, his cloak tucked in tightly around him, knees drawn up under hers in the advised position.

Freia reached down and pulled at his left knee. "You can put your legs around—right, like that; it might work better. Go, Trixie!"

Trixie went, a jump, a plunge; wings catching thin air and making it solid.

Dewar watched this time as the ground fell from them under the gryphon's straining body.

"This is fabulous," he murmured. He wanted a gryphon. He'd have to butter her up, find out how and where to get one.

They left the mountains in less than an hour.

"The Plain of Linors, this is," Dewar told his pilot.

"Linors?"

"Yes. Lys is here, and Sarsemar and Yln in the south."

He thought of warm, long-limbed Luneté and smiled, his cheek pressed to Freia's neck. Ah, that had been fun. Luneté was clumsy still, a virgin until marrying Otto and no time to practice since, but her shyness had made its own kind of excitement. And here he was, far above her lands, flying in the starry night.

"Good that the weather's clear," Freia said. "Can't fly in snow and rain."

Dewar nodded. The gryphon's wings stroked the air. The stars and the night rushed past.

"Dewar—"

"Right here."

"Sauce."

Impudently, he kissed her cheek. "Fresh too," he said. "I'm numb, madame, with wind and cramp: as cold as a butcher's slab."

Freia laughed. "Me too," she said, "and Trixie is tired, I can feel it. We'll have to set down."

"And dawn comes soon. Hm."

He looked down at the ground, a patchwork of fields and pastures.

"I want your opinion on safe stopping-spots," Freia said. "You know more than I do about the way people set up their farms hereabouts."

Dewar didn't think he did, but he nodded and began paying attention to the ground, which he had ignored for the stars and for occasional murmured course corrections to Freia. The pipe, buttoned inside his doublet in a pouch, tugged gently toward Golias: west-northwest.

After a few minutes, he said, "There's a wooded area coming up."

"Trees. Can't land in trees."

"Is she able to get across it?"

"Yes. There's a river up beyond—"

"Ah. We're closer than I thought. It may be the Rendlac. Look, they have haystacks here too; they're civilized. And snow. Aim for one of those big boxy structures."

"You're sure. Once we're down, we're down."

"I'm sure."

"Hold on." She leaned forward, commanding Trixie to descend; the plummet began, paused, began, paused—

Dewar closed his eyes as the ground lurched and rushed erratically.

The landing was easier than before. Trixie fell on something that squalled.

"Hell!"

"Shsh! It's a goat or something. She's hungry. Get down."

It was some consolation to him to see that Freia was as stiff and uncomfortable as he. They wobbled around getting circulation back while Trixie began ripping up the animal she had killed. Others were running away over the snow in a bleating panic.

"I didn't see that road," Freia said, squinting. "Is it a road?"

"We should be safe enough here," Dewar assured her. "Let's go look at the barn."

Followed by Trixie, who carried her kill in her beak, they stomped through the snow to the barn. It was no more than a roof thrown over a huge haystack, with hurdles around the bottom to keep the herd out.

"It'll do," Freia said, and took the gryphon's saddlebags down. Dewar got the bedroll. "That was a long one," she added. "Good work, Trixie. You've earned a rest."

"We're close to Perendlac, too," Dewar said. "Can you make her get out of sight?"

Freia guided the gryphon around to the side of the haystack away from the road.

"She'll be fine here." Trixie began eating entrails with gusto. Freia wrinkled her nose and looked at Dewar. "No table manners. She'll sleep afterward."

"Days are short. We can go again at dark."

"How close are we?"

"I'm not sure, but I know Perendlac controls the junction of the Rendlac and Parry rivers. That river looked too wide to be anything but the Rendlac after the Parry joins it."

Freia nodded and set her bags and blankets down. Dewar

walked aimlessly, swinging his arms and loosening up his body, and ignored her as she discreetly wandered off around the corner. There was a hedgerow nearby and the forest was a quarter-mile or so beyond that.

When Freia returned, Dewar said he would get them wood from the hedgerow for a fire. The field was trampled muddy. He picked his way carefully, without an ignis—no point taking the risk of being noticed. In the hedgerow he collected a large armload of wood, not difficult by the starlight, and returned with it. Trixie had gorged and now was curled up with head under wing.

The wood was damp and recalcitrant. He finally summoned an ignis to spark it.

Freia was quiet, watching the snow get whiter with the coming day. She cooked a mixture of grain, dried fruit, nuts, and dried meat for them to eat. They emptied her canteen, thirsty from the arid air.

"There is a brook over that way," Dewar said.

"It'll be mucked. Those dirty animals."

"Hm, true. Further in the wood it will be cleaner. We'll get more water tonight."

Freia nodded. "And for now?"

"We lie low." He looked around. "Up there's probably best. Trixie will surely let us know if anyone comes investigating."

With difficulty, they climbed the haystack and settled down on it. The sun was risen, red and swollen, a baleful cyclopean glare on their hiding-place.

The tension and strain of the flight had wearied them both. They slept before the sun had changed from red to gold.

# 29

DEWAR WOKE WITH A START, UNSURE where he was, and remembered: he was on Prospero's trail with a gryphon and her rider. At the moment he was on a haystack with the latter, around whose back he was curled. She was holding his hand loosely. Her rump was tucked against his crotch, a pleasant feeling to which he was not insensitive. The air was cold, but he was surprisingly cozy due to the doubling of their body heat.

He smiled. She liked him, he was sure. She wasn't unlikable herself. This could get better, even without a featherbed. They were warm here under blankets in the hay. It wasn't windy, as in Ascolet. Wonderful animal, the gryphon—they had travelled more than three hundred miles.

Freia sighed heavily. Her fingers pressed his and relaxed. Dewar moved his hand flat against her body—she'd removed her jacket to use it for a pillow. Her shirt was silky. She smelled of hay and female musk, complicated odors that pleased his nose.

"Good morning," he murmured.

"Mmhm." She squirmed a little and then rested against him again.

Dewar spoke low in her ear. "Sleep well?"

"Woke up a lot." She sighed, eyes still closed. "Worrying."

He took his hand away from her sternum and began rubbing her neck beneath the thick fuzzy braid of hair which had been hidden under the jacket. Freia sighed again. Dewar smiled to himself.

"Thank you," she murmured when he had gently kneaded the muscles in her shoulders.

He lay against her back as he had when they slept, but his hand was on her hip now. "You're welcome."

Freia's breathing was quicker than resting pace.

"Dewar," she said with another deep sigh, and turned; he kept his arm around her as she did. The sun was low, the loft dim.

"Mm." Under his hand, smooth shirt and firm waist; some resilient and warm part of her was just touching his chest, and her hip and thighs were tangled with his, softness against hardness. He pressed against her, a wordless but unmistakable suggestion.

Freia swallowed nervously. "You . . . um . . . are you . . . are you trying to . . . um . . ."

He kissed the corner of her mouth, a pleasant giddiness in his head. "Yes."

"Ohhh." Freia touched his face, and he took her hand and began kissing her fingers: salty, warm. Her palm: small, a few calluses, a dimpled hollow.

"Am I succeeding?" A small lick on her wrist. He undid the cuff button.

"Ah. I'm not sure it's a good idea. Oh. Please. Let me think. Just now."

"Thought kills action," murmured Dewar, and kissed her wrist where the quick pulse trembled. "Mm?"

"Oh. Please. Stop. *Please.*"

"Surely. There." He held her hand, breathing into her cupped palm.

"Oh," Freia sighed, biting her lip, and shivered. She tensed. He waited. "I think we should do what we're supposed to be doing," she said at last. "And I'm not sure about you. And you're so . . . so nice, so handsome, but I'm not sure. I don't know you."

"You like me, though?"

"Yes."

"You have good judgement in other things. Trust it now."

"Flatterer," she said, warmly. "No. I shouldn't."

"We may never know one another better than we do now," Dewar said regretfully. "Ah well. I like you, more than I thought I did. You're sweet as a nut, Freia: prickly and rough, but smooth and warm inside." He was surprised at how disappointed he felt, and he realized that he wanted her urgently. He hadn't expected a No. She was preoccupied by Prospero; if he pressed now, likely he would spoil his chances later. He kissed her palm softly and closed her fingers over it. "There."

"Not easy to crack, either," Freia said, and touched his cheek. His beard was rough; she smoothed it down with two fingers. "Later? Couldn't we— Afterward?"

"Madame, though I am a sorcerer, I do not engage in trade."

She was stiff. "I'm not bargaining," she said coldly.

"Sorry. Freia. I didn't mean you were. No." Dewar took her hand in his. "I didn't mean that." He wasn't sure what he'd meant; it had come out, a memory of Luneté prompting it, perhaps.

"Did you think I'd be an easy tumble?" she demanded, a sharp note marring the peace.

"No," he whispered.

"My father would—" but she stopped herself, took a deep breath. "It's none of his business," she added. "Maybe."

Dewar caught the word, correlated it. Utrachet, she had cried. Her father? Possibly. He might be wise to stay away from a girl with such a father as Prospero's second. "Freia, no insult intended. Accept my apology for the unintentional slur, ill-chosen words from a thoughtless mind. I did not and do not think of you as an easy tumble. I thought of pleasure to both of us." Anger crept into his voice: frustration and rejection gripped his heart.

"Dewar," she said, more gently, leaning near him, trying to see his face in the poor light. "I don't mean to insult you either."

He shook off the irritation. "This," he said, and took her hand again, smiling, "is what comes of lying too much together, madame." He folded his hands around hers.

"You're right."

"For too-cold winters engender heat."

She was smiling too; he heard it in her voice and saw her face move, a hand's-breadth away. "Pretty. Poetic."

"Hackneyed, Freia."

The smile still warmed her words: "But fitting. Can't a cliché be new, once in a while?"

"The frequency is what makes it cliché. I shall invoke another cliché by mentioning cold water, namely that brook and our own thirst for its contents."

"Dewar. Later? Afterward?" she urged him gently, hope in her voice.

He wryed his mouth for lost opportunity, and perhaps for a narrow escape. Women invariably wanted more than simple pleasure out of these things; Luneté transparently had. "I may have to leave suddenly after meeting Prospero."

"You said you weren't—"

"He may not like what I say to him, madame."

"If I can make him like it I will." Her hand pressed his.

The stars forfend she should fall in love with him, Dewar thought, drawing away a little. "Would that be in your power?" The intimacy of darkness, of proximity: it still held them.

"I could try it and see. I don't know. He is a difficult man to approach, but he can be very kind, very generous, for no reason at all. Princes, faugh." Freia's voice was disdainful.

Dewar chuckled. "Indeed."

They sat poised an instant.

"I'd like— It's just— I'm sorry," she said softly, and dropped his hand and turned away.

Dewar realized she was: that she regretted that her duty interfered with dalliance, and that she had heard his own second thoughts in his voice. Freia was shaking her blankets awkwardly, and before he could say anything more she had gone, slipping and sliding down the hay.

Dewar floundered through the hay and dusted himself off at the bottom. He felt as if he'd rejected her, rather than the other way around, and wondered if he should have kissed her rather than accept her refusal. The gryphon was crunching up bones; she had killed again. Freia shook out the blankets and rolled them up, took an apple from her bag and ate it in a few bites, quickly, hardly chewing, her movements quick and tense.

"Have some cheese," she said, and shared the last of her lump of hard stuff with him, giving him the larger piece. "That's it," she added, "a few more apples, nothing else." Her voice rang falsely cheerful.

He bit a winy bruised apple. "Next time Trixie hunts, take

a cut." Somehow, he had to smooth things over. She was too valuable to alienate, and besides he did like her. Kind and generous for no reason at all: herself. Dewar ate the apple core. He had devoured most of her provisions since they'd met, more generosity he could not repay. She had placed him under gossamer obligations, delicate strands made of unpriced gifts. They constrained him as much as an overt agreement, or more, with their subtle charge of duty owed.

Freia put the slack saddlebags on the gryphon, which was sanguine in the dying light, tightening straps with brusque tugs.

Dewar stood behind her and put his hands on her arms as she turned around. "Freia," he said, and kissed her mouth.

She was startled, and then she sighed and closed her eyes as he closed his, accepting and returning the gesture. The sky was full dark when he opened his eyes and straightened again.

"Thank you," Dewar said huskily. It had been as intense as making love to Luneté—slow and deep, vertiginously falling into her. They were both half-panting. He wanted to pull her down and finish it at once. He could not remember having wanted anyone so much, so quickly, so deeply.

"Welcome," Freia whispered, dazed, half-leaning on him still.

He stroked her face with both hands and repeated, "Thank you." Perhaps now was the right time after all—

The gryphon churrupped, an odd sound Dewar had not heard her make before.

Freia lowered her hands from Dewar slowly, turning away. "Trix?"

The gryphon was staring into the wood.

"Let's go," Freia decided. "Something's up."

"Up?"

She stared, like the gryphon, at the woods. "Happening. I have a feeling—" Freia bounded to the gryphon and jumped on; Dewar, with practiced ease now, mounted behind her. Trixie trotted into the field, then hurled herself into the air, spiralling up. On high, the sunset still stained the west; the stars were coming out.

Cold air dried Dewar's throat. He embraced Freia, who was taut and attentive as they climbed, and looked at the dark mass of the forest.

"No, it's—" he began, as they veered from the course indicated by the spelled pipe.

"Trix wants to go this way!" Freia said over her shoulder.

There was a light in that direction, on the other side of the bristling forest, up the river.

"Perendlac!" cried Dewar, as they came nearer, miles later.

"Prospero!" Freia replied.

The line of force between Golias and the pipe was moving: it was ahead of them, at Perendlac. Golias had been elsewhere, but was there now.

Trixie was pouring it on, her wings thundering.

"Higher!" Dewar advised Freia, and she pulled the gryphon upward. They soared over the fortress, which was on a bluff overlooking the confluence of the two rivers. Inside was tumult; Freia allowed the gryphon to descend slightly and they saw fires burning in several places, stone-shattering moving white-hot fires Dewar identified at once as Elemental in origin. Salamanders. Prospero was there, somewhere; potent sorcery whorled about the place in a vortex. The central tower rose, irregularly red-lit by fire within and without.

Freia was peering into the smoke and disorder, muttering to herself or Trixie.

Dewar didn't realize what she meant to do until she was doing it. There was a flowing movement of men, running toward one of the fires where there was fighting, a knot of men trying to surround another, attacking—

"What are you doing!" he screamed as Trixie folded her wings with a screech and plummeted.

Freia didn't answer; she had her crossbow in one hand, hanging on to Trixie's harness with the other.

Dewar tried to relax to take the shock of a rough landing and put one hand on his sword. She was going to land right on—

—the knot of uniformed men collapsed; the gryphon began ripping and rending anything in reach, and Freia was doing the same herself, one-handed with a long knife, using the crossbow as a shield and a club.

"Argylle!" roared a voice Dewar knew at once.

Freia shouted something and the gryphon reared back. Dewar slid down its rump and found himself facing three soldiers in Landuc livery. He drew.

Damn the woman—

The three men were dead; now he was carried around the tower in a press of men who had obviously been prisoners, surging toward the fire which Dewar recognized to be a huge Way.

Trixie was ripping, biting, and disembowelling still, with Freia impeding a fresh attack from the garrison, swinging the crossbow. They were surrounded by Landuc's men.

"Argylle!" Prospero bellowed again. "To me!"

"Papa!" Dewar heard Freia shout, a thin, breathless cry lost in tumult.

The soldiers had fallen back, leaving a barricade of dead and dying in front of the gryphon. Dewar fell back, jostled and shoved by the crowd of prisoners, who were running into Prospero's fire, most supporting one or two weaker others.

"I *will* kill you!" screamed someone nearby, and two of Prospero's men were knocked down by Otto, leaping forward toward Dewar as he retreated toward Freia and Trixie. Freia wasn't visible to him, but he was sure she was there.

Otto swung at him, a two-handed skull-crushing swing with a mace, and Dewar ducked and heard it sing in the air. He cut at Otto's arm and nicked him as he brought the mace around again; a crossbow bolt sprouted from Otto's mailed shoulder, though, and he lost control of the mace swing.

"Hurry!" Prospero shouted. "To me! Argylle!"

Prisoners echoed his shout. "Argylle!" came back from

the quarters of the courtyard. The melee increased in speed and desperation.

Dewar tripped on a body and rolled frantically away as Otto brought the iron mace down at his head, thumping the stone pavement instead. More prisoners were fighting hand-to-hand with the garrison soldiers, but all were falling back toward the fire.

"Hey!" Freia yelled, and tripped Otto, who punched her in the ribs and sent her sprawling over the gore and dead.

Trixie screamed and pecked at him. Otto swung the mace, smashing the gryphon in the beak and twisting the back-swing toward Dewar, who dodged it again.

Never again, Dewar vowed, would he venture within sixty-four miles of a battlefield without a comprehensive and impermeable collection of protective spells.

"Argylle!" shouted Prospero.

Freia got up, stumbling and holding her side, and staggered over the disordered corpses toward the fire where Prospero stood fighting two guardsmen. An uncoordinated mob of Imperial soldiers at one side were being held off by prisoners with scavenged weapons while their fellows ran with closed eyes and clenched teeth into Prospero's fiery Way. Dewar caught a glimpse of this as he dove away from Otto's mace, rolling behind Trixie, who raked Otto's mail shirt with her hind claws and lurched after Freia but was distracted by an arrow striking beside her left eye. With another scream, the gryphon set into a retreating group of royal soldiers, wildly stabbing and biting, pursuing them around the tower, away from Prospero, into a dark corner.

The Way in the fire was closing; the vortex of sorcery was drawing in on itself. All the prisoners in the yard were through save the group with Prospero, holding the Way secure and backing toward it. Dewar ran forward, not wanting to lose this chance. Otto pursued Dewar, then passed him, lunging toward Prospero with a knife. Freia tripped Otto again; he grabbed her ankle and brought her down with him.

"Argylle! Away!" Prospero cried hoarsely, killing a man

with a swift in-and-out thrust; his gory blade was black in the unnaturally white Way-fire light. He kicked the corpse away, into another soldier's feet so that he stumbled onto Prospero's ready sword.

Prospero's men backed toward the whirling, narrowing Way in the fire. He gestured them through, shouting, "Go! Go!" and stepped back into it himself. The Way was shrinking as it closed. Otto was nearly there; Dewar caught up to him and yanked him back, punching him ineffectively in his mailed stomach. Otto turned and struck him along the head, but Dewar twisted and caught himself and fell, tumbling into the Way with Prospero's dark cloak whirling above him.

As he fell, he heard Freia shriek "Paaaapaaaaa!" in a long keening wail.

The Way closed with a thunderous, sky-breaking bang and sent sparks and ashes flying in an acrid cloud.

Dewar landed on sand and fire, thrashed out of the fire, and brushed singeing coals off himself.

He was on a beach, near a crowd of men, Prospero's men. There were long boats in the low surf, ferrying the freed prisoners-of-war to furled-sailed ships waiting out in the bay, black silhouettes. It was cool, but not cold. No one paid attention to Dewar as he stood, shaking white sand and black cinders out of his clothes. The sky was overcast, the air mild, circulated by a velvety offshore breeze. A glow at the horizon might be dawn or sunset, brightening the purply twilight.

The men, rejoicing, shouted and called in their own language, which he could not understand, and he tried to find Prospero, who had vanished among them.

"You!" cried someone suddenly, and seized Dewar's arm.

They stared at one another.

"You're Utrachet," Dewar said to the rangy, yellow-bearded man who faced him.

"You're none of ours," Utrachet replied with a lilting accent Dewar had heard recently on Freia's tongue, and

Dewar found himself being hustled over to a collection of long torches driven into the sand where an argument proceeded hotly.

It was suspended. Prospero and four other men looked expectantly at Dewar.

Utrachet addressed them in that incomprehensible speech.

"Nay, 'tis not possible; 'twas but some illusion of his stressed mind's desire: I say 'tis so," Prospero said. "Leave this one to me a moment. Carry on the evacuation."

The men muttered and left them staring at one another.

"What wouldst thou here?" Prospero asked finally.

"We have unfinished business. I didn't appreciate being chucked in a ditch in a blizzard," Dewar said. It came out less elegantly than he had intended.

"Go to. 'Twas not I cast thee to Herne," Prospero said. "Thy hands loosed and thou didst take rude leave of me."

"I passed out from being hit on the head," Dewar replied. "I didn't want to go with you; you insisted and then dumped me. I'll not forget it."

Prospero stared at him, incensed. "That's thy message? Wilt challenge me, spratling? I warrant thee, thou'lt not find it healthful exercise."

"I'm not continuing in this farce. I've been trailing you all over the Well-be-scorched countryside to settle—"

Utrachet ran up. Dewar saw now that he was limping and hiding it badly. He spoke to Prospero quickly, agitatedly.

Prospero exploded with an obscenity. A whirlwind sprang up and whipped away down the beach, throwing stinging sand.

Utrachet spoke again, and Prospero shook his head and said, "Let us begone from here. The men come first."

Utrachet nodded and left.

"As for thee, I have no time now to give audience to thy grievances," Prospero went on to Dewar. "Canst leave o' thyself, or I'll remove thee, for I'll have none about the place not wholly of my party. I'd not be so abrupt, but I've much in hand."

Dewar's hot anger drained out of him and left an icier, more enduring fury. "I shall leave, sir," he said, bowing, "and it shall be an ill day we meet again." He pulled his cloak around him as he turned his back deliberately and walked away, into the dunes to find something flammable, to return to the Tower of Thorns and consider whether he'd been insulted sufficiently for a challenge. He halted a half-step. He should mention to Utrachet, or perhaps to Prospero, that that overly-chaste young woman Freia had aided him—but no. Let her tell them so herself, if she so chose; why, to be associated with Dewar now in Prospero's mind might bend the Prince's ill-will toward her. She'd done him no wrong to earn that. He had nothing more to say to Prospero.

Prospero shouted after him, "Look—" but was interrupted by a messenger from the flagship lying in the warm water offshore, and he stared angrily at Dewar's disappearing back in the darkness as he answered the messenger's question. Running off like Freia, he thought: damned disrespectful children. Dared they value him so lightly, selfish young creatures?

## — 30 —

OTTAVIANO TACKLED FREIA AND BROUGHT HER down, knocking the breath from her as she doubled over a dead man's breastplate.

"No you don't!" the Baron of Ascolet screamed.

The Way was dark, gone. The uproar of flame and battle had stopped. Wounded survivors were moaning and calling for help. There seemed none unwounded.

Freia gasped for air spasmodically, immobilized with Otto's weight on her. He stood, cursing, and released her for a moment; she was still breathless and lay panting.

"Shit," finished Otto, after a pause, summing up the evening.

Trixie cried out questioningly, looking for Freia on the other side of the central keep. She bounded around the corner, dark in darkness.

Freia got to her knees. Otto hauled her to her feet, putting a knife to her throat.

"Tell your animal to back off."

Freia still gulped at the air. She whispered indistinctly, hoarsely, then swallowed as the gryphon screeched and started toward them.

"Trix—go—home—" she forced out, past the cold steel too close to her windpipe. "Trix—home! Now!"

The gryphon stopped, confused. "Rrrrrrawwwwkkkh," she croaked. The arrow by her eye bobbed as she moved her head from side to side.

Four men carrying swords came from a door in the keep.

"Home—now!" Freia ordered her weakly. "Now! To Prospero! Go home!"

Otto twisted her arm as the gryphon jumped. But Trixie went up, not forward, with a long resentful screech, and she ascended around the keep before flapping away into the night.

"Get these corpses out of here!" yelled Otto to the soldiers. "Tonight!"

"Aye, sir," one of them called.

He turned his attention back to his captive, pushing the knife flat on her neck. "You son of a bitch, I'd like to disembowel you organ by organ."

Freia tried to turn her head away from the knife, not grabbing for it as it was too close to grapple.

"So I will," Otto went on, "but you're going to tell me all about yourself while I'm doing it." The uncontrollable, messy rage had left him cold and clear-minded.

Freia closed her eyes and breathed in and out deliberately.

"Starting now," Otto decided, and he frog-marched his prisoner into the charred fortress of Perendlac, where Golias had failed to hold his prisoners.

Otto forced her up a flight of stairs and down a hallway; he pushed her into a lamplit room and shoved her against the wall while he tied her hands behind her. He spun her around then and slammed her against the window-frame. With another thong, he tied her hands to one of the grates behind the iron shutters, which were closed and locked. It was too high; she had to stand on tiptoe.

Lighting another lamp, Otto turned to look at his prisoner and plan the extraction of information.

The prisoner stared back at him gravely, blood seeping from a dirty scrape on one cheek, a bruise where his fist had connected at their first meeting.

Otto looked again.

"A woman?" he said, his voice rising in disbelief.

Freia tensed and her impassivity tightened.

"Some friend of Dewar's," he mused.

He studied her. Just before he'd brought her down, kept her from following her mates into the fire, she'd been screaming to someone. Father. Dewar's daughter? Was he old enough to have a grown child? Hard to tell, with sorcerers. They changed as slowly as the Well. Otto had thought of Dewar as a young man, but he had also thought of him as a friend.

Sorcerers. Had she been yelling at Prospero?

"Or Prospero's," Otto murmured, folding his arms and leaning against the table, looking at her. Prospero's. Yes. Her accent was like Utrachet's. Dewar didn't have an accent. She'd sent her weird animal to Prospero, *home* to Prospero. But she had arrived with Dewar—who was probably working with Prospero now, if he hadn't been before. Tonight's appearance clinched that. The animal had been seen around Malperdy, the castle where Prospero had been imprisoned.

Otto decided to eliminate guessing. Furthermore, Dewar or Prospero might try to retrieve this lost baggage any minute. He closed his eyes and focused his attention inward, on the Well; Perendlac was near a Node, and the feeling of power ran tingling along his arms. Mentally he reviewed the necessary preventive Binding, a modification of a concealment. Simple and effective enough for now. He put his hand on her head, although she moved away as much as her limited freedom allowed, and put the Binding on her. *Closed, hidden, wrapped, concealed, lie beneath the bright Well's field . . .*

The Binding sat uneasily. Though she was not warded, it felt looser than it ought, but Otto supposed his own haste was the reason. Now the second spell, a Truth-Binding.

She shook his hand from her head as the slight fogging caused by the spell touched her thoughts; Otto grabbed her chin and finished it quickly.

She glared at him.

"The first spell keeps you here, and the second makes it easy for you to answer questions," he said, smiling. "What's your name?"

She put her teeth together and clenched her jaw, not allowing herself to speak.

"Uh-hunh," he said. She would speak truth when she spoke, but she could still resist speaking. "Am I going to have to invoke less pleasant compulsions?"

Her look was an eloquent answer. Nonetheless, Otto disliked the idea of using violence on her. Golias had no qualms, but Otto thought of himself as a civilized, educated man.

"You were looking for your father, hm? Prospero didn't help you, did he."

"He will," Freia whispered.

"Oh, I'm sure you'll be missed when he comes to counting noses," Otto said, pleased. "A very important thing to leave behind, a daughter. Careless. What do you think he'll do now? When he notices you're not where you ought to be?"

"He'll look for me," she whispered. "If you hurt me, he will kill you when he finds me."

"I don't think so. Interesting accent you have. Odd," he mused. She shouldn't have an accent. He, having stood the test of the Well's fire, should understand her perfectly without hearing an accent. Yet when she spoke, a lilt and trill colored the words he heard. If he concentrated, he could hear the incomprehensible language she actually used, but the unusual thing was that an accent was transmitted.

Prospero's troops had had some utterly foreign language

which not even Otto, integrated with the Well and its worlds, could understand. Their commander Utrachet had spoken some Lannach. Otto had not had leisure to study the troops, which had struck him as strange in other ways, and now he regretted that.

"Where did you come from?" he asked.

She would not answer.

He tapped his fingers. Dewar or Prospero would come looking for her. Then they could bargain. Simple and workable, if he took care of his own defenses. Dewar, he had decided, was manageable, and Prospero could be subdued with threats to the girl here. He would demand Prospero's surrender in return for her liberty. He'd be able to get a lot of mileage out of that in Landuc. That meant he must put her someplace difficult to reach, guarded by better men than the fools at Malperdy.

Otto's mind pulled up short. If Herne or Gaston knew he had such a prisoner, she'd not be his for long. The business with this Miranda of Valgalant was still hot and he'd made an ass of himself losing Prospero from Malperdy. They'd take her out of his hands and he'd lose any credit, any esteem he might have recovered.

And then two things connected in his mind, and Otto smiled in such a way that his prisoner began to sweat anxiously in her leather clothing.

He put to himself: Was not a hold on Prospero also a hold on Landuc?

Was it not so that something valued by Prospero would be valuable to the Emperor?

What would the Emperor give for something guaranteed to bring Prospero humming after it?

If she were Prospero's, she could be a more powerful weapon than the entire Army, its Marshal, and the rest of the Empire combined. Even if she were Dewar's, she could be used to bring him to heel and ensure his cooperation, or at least his noninterference. Blood called to blood.

Otto opened the door and leaned out to shout, "Guard!" He kept one eye on the girl.

A few seconds later, a soldier appeared, stopped at the

bottom of the stairs and saluted, and started up. "Yessir."

"Get Prince Golias," Otto told him. "I don't care what he's doing, he should leave it."

"Yessir."

Otto closed the door again. He would have to make it clear to Golias that the girl was to be questioned but not damaged. Where to hold her? Here? The fortress was filled with his men from Ascolet and Lys and Golias's mercenaries; a lot of the Crown's troops had died tonight when Prospero's men had made their break because Prince Herne had had them guarding the prisoners closely, not trusting the levies. Prince Herne was a fool, and he wasn't here; he was guarding the capitol. Otto thought it was an ill wind indeed that blew nobody any good. He folded his arms and leaned again on the table.

"You will be confined and questioned," he told his prisoner. "The more cooperative you are, the more comfortable you will be."

"Let me go," she whispered.

Otto laughed. "You are the key to my future happiness," he said sarcastically. "I shall take excellent care that you not be mislaid."

"My father will be very angry if you do not release me now."

"Your father is on the run at the moment," Otto reminded her, "and when he comes looking for you he'll find all the opposition he can handle. He can have you, too. But he'll have to bargain."

"He will not," she said. "He'll kill you."

"Then he won't get you back, lady." Otto smiled. With any luck, she'd be out of his hands by the time Prospero showed up anyway, and then the Emperor would have to cope with him—and the Emperor probably couldn't, not having a sorcerer on call. But by then Otto would have signed and sealed articles from the Emperor yielding Ascolet and maybe Lys and a bit of Sarsemar. Ascolet could use a port on the Sovereign Sea. The more he asked for, the more he was likely to get.

"You will regret this all your days," she whispered.

"I wasn't careless like Prospero," said Otto. "I think he's the one who'll be doing a lot of regretting."

Golias opened the door without knocking and entered. He scowled at the girl and then at Otto. "What the fuck do you want?"

"Someone very important is going to come looking for this dropped penny, and we must be sure that he doesn't find her easily."

Golias looked the prisoner up and down. "So? Who?"

"Prospero."

"The great man himself? What makes her special? His mattress-warmer?"

"Better than that."

Golias looked at the girl again, narrowing his eyes. He nodded slowly. "Kid?"

Otto saw her swallow. "Yes," he said, "it does seem that the Prince of Air has been foolish. We'll keep her here for now, below. Heavy guards: everywhere. I don't want a repeat of the Malperdy farce."

Golias smiled unpleasantly. "And then?"

"What do you think the Emperor would give for her?"

Golias laughed, grinning, and slapped Otto on the back, laughing still, and left the room, slamming the door.

"The arrogant pup," said Prince Herne, dropping the rolled paper on the table.

Prince Gaston picked it up again and unrolled it, weighting the corners with map-weights.

"We should have hanged Golias after he murdered Lady Miranda," Herne said.

"You're jealous," Emperor Avril said, smirking.

"What?" Herne stared at him.

"That they, and not you, had the good fortune and good sense to be where Prospero was," the Emperor said, losing the smirk and glaring at both of them.

Gaston looked back at him coldly. "Your orders," he reminded the Emperor in a tone that indicated he might not have agreed. In fact he had not. He had doubted that Prospero would try a strike at the capitol, but the Emperor had been convinced of it, had insisted on Gaston remaining in Landuc after Lady Miranda's funeral, had recalled Herne from Perendlac. And Prospero had struck there, not here.

The Emperor retorted, "Your consent was ready enough; but here we are. The offer is tempting."

"He is probably bargaining with Prospero also," Herne said.

"Hm," Gaston said. He read the letter again. Herne and the Emperor conversed in a circular vein of blame and speculation, and Gaston followed them with a small part of his attention while he read again the missive brought to them by one of the soldiers who had survived the uprising at Perendlac.

> *Unto His Radiant Majesty Avril Emperor of Landuc, Greetings from Ottaviano Baron of Ascolet and Golias Prince of Landuc. Our earlier report of the Raid by the Duke of Winds to free his Cohorts has doubtless reached your Hands. Yet it is an ill Wind indeed that leaves no Good behind. For on this Raid it was the Duke's Misfortune to lose and leave behind his own Daughter. This Person is presently in our Custody closely warded and confined. And it seems to us by this great Stroke of Fortuna's Hand that we have been given the Means for rectifying certain Inequities which the Crown in bargaining with us separately and jointly hath imposed on us. By way of opening Discussion between us then we propose that we shall yield up the Person of this Daughter of the Duke of Winds Prospero to the Crown in return for the Crown's Concession under Seal of certain Items below listed:*
>
> *1. That the Barony of Ascolet shall be returned to its former Status as an independent and untrammeled Kingdom;*
>
> *2. That the Crown shall recognize Ottaviano presently Baron of Ascolet as King of Ascolet;*
>
> *3. That the Lands of Preszhëanea, Lys, and Sarse-*

*mar shall appertain thereto and owe Fealty to the Kingdom of Ascolet henceforward;*

*4. That the Borders of this Kingdom of Ascolet shall revert with these Additions to their Locations on the Accession of the late King Laudunet of Lys;*

*5. That the Crown shall grant to Prince Golias the revived Duchy of Sillick, the Borders of which shall be those which held on the Absorption of that Duchy by the Crown . . .*

There was more, less audacious. The Fireduke concentrated on the major points, noting wording and order. Otto's tenacity was admirable, Gaston thought. And his nerve. But was this true? Gaston could not quite believe that Prospero might have been so careless with a daughter as to let her be taken hostage. It was believable that he could have a child. It was not believable that he would put her at risk. Surely he was smarter than that.

And Gaston thought of lithe, dark-haired, bright-eyed Dewar, his smile, his brilliance, his dexterity. There was more in him than had yet been shown, though Gaston had glimpsed something. Prospero knew Dewar's mother. Prospero, calling a truce of sorcery at the last minute before that final battle, had crippled himself and lost the war. He would not do that for any ordinary reason.

But Gaston had no proofs for his theories, only inferences and leaps of intuition.

In his present high-strung frame of mind, hearing unsubstantiated suspicions would make the Emperor accuse everyone who had been there of treason. Gaston kept his thoughts to himself.

"We've no ground for faith," he said in the silence that had followed Herne's and the Emperor's winding down, "that their hostage is Prospero's daughter. I counsel that we not parley until we have confirmation."

"Our idea exactly," the Emperor said.

"What would confirm it to you?"

"Prospero himself," the Emperor said after a moment's

thought. "Yes. The girl would say whatever she was told to say. If Prospero comes around looking for her, then it might perhaps be true. We proceed from there."

"And their terms?" Gaston said.

"The Crown shall take those under consideration," the Emperor said.

Prospero's frown was deeply graven into his face. Above his aquiline nose his brow was crevassed by profound displeasure.

"And thou didst allow her to fare hence," he said. "Scudamor, I am disappointed in thy warding."

"My Lord, I could hardly stop her," Scudamor said, inclining his head to accept the blame despite his denial. "You know her. She would not stay."

Prospero sighed and sat back in the high-backed black stone chair, looking through his Seneschal. The man stood, hands behind his back, at ease a few steps below him. Prospero gazed at the tall candles around the painted and bas-relief carven pillars, the high double door. The vast, vault-roofed room was empty save for the two men, one seated, one standing.

"Tell me what she said to thee, her words as thou heard them." He looked again at Scudamor.

"That she would seek you out. We feared the worst had befallen, my Lord. There had been no word for so long after you had said you would return."

"So thou didst not hold her."

Scudamor glanced away. "We were anxious, Lord," he said softly. "There was no word."

Prospero had to acknowledge his own fault in this. "Wounded sore I was, and weak, and must be hidden while I mended, and I could not travel hither," he admitted. "Nor did I think 'twould be so long."

"She has Trixie," Scudamor said. "What harm could befall her with a gryphon?"

They both automatically looked at a gryphon (much smaller than life) sculpted at the top of a pillar. Wings half-spread, made of finely black-veined stone the color of dried blood, it glowered down in the direction of the door.

"Plenty," Prospero said tersely.

Scudamor looked at him, not believing it. Nobody in his right mind would go near one of the largest female gryphons in the land with intent to harm her or Freia.

"I shall have to go haring after her," Prospero said, "and 'tis not as if I've not enough to contrive and more otherwise. Irresponsible chit," he muttered. "I'll ground her. Take her gryphon away for a year. Is't not what one's supposed to do?"

"My Lord, I wouldn't know," childless and bachelor Scudamor said humbly. "She went on the best of motives, and maybe she will return ere you set out."

"True," Prospero said. "She'll arrive, find all fled, and follow home; she's not such a dullard as not to understand an army's retreat. I suppose I can rely on that. And Trixie will keep her from the worst of trouble." And out of the towns, he thought, though she loathed towns. And away from people, though she disliked people too. He'd been overly indulgent with Freia, and she was become an impertinent and disobedient baggage; now need was to bear down upon her hard. He drummed his fingers. One of the men at Perendlac had claimed to see a gryphon—but it was surely delusion; Freia had no way of knowing Perendlac and he'd not tarried long himself, moreover she'd have been at his side in a trice had she been there. Indeed, if Freia's gryphon tracked him to Landuc, now she would wheel about and track him home again, will-she, nil-she. "Perhaps simply to wait is best," he concluded.

"The Wheel will turn," Scudamor agreed, relaxing.

"Thou'rt not to blame; 'tis no one's fault, her own," Prospero said. "She's obstinate and willful."

"Her reasons were the best," Scudamor modified the statement gently. "She worried about you."

"I ward myself," Prospero said, standing. " 'Tis not her concern— Well, 'tis neither here nor there. For I am here, she's there or between, and when she cometh here we'll make an end of't. Meanwhile there's the City."

"If my Lord would like to review the work on the walls . . ."

"Aye. On horseback. Let us go around the circuit and I'll see how't succeeds."

Dewar had, uncharacteristically, picked a bunch of floppy-petalled, wantonly lush scarlet flowers and put them in a tall silver ewer of water on his bedside table. The odor of them was richly spicy-sweet. The day was warm, warmer than usual for the mountains where his thorn-girdled tower stood with its views of eternal snow and a faraway waterfall that spilled liquid silver down a shattered cliff. High-piled clouds massed and re-formed, vaporous fortresses in silvered whites and greys. There would be a thunderstorm later. That would be pleasant to watch as he lounged naked in the sheets surrounded by papers, reviewing his own old notes. It was good to be at work again. The war had wasted his time and gained him nothing—less than nothing.

He had removed his moustache and beard, deciding he didn't care for them anymore, and his chin tingled still with the touch of the razor. The scent of astringent blended not unpleasantly with the flowers.

It was regrettable, Dewar mused, setting aside a sheet of three-sided diagrams and spiky plots, that he hadn't bedded hot Josquin or skittish Freia when he'd had the opportunity. That would have been time well spent. Luneté had provided satisfaction such as he'd not allowed himself for too long. As for the third interesting woman he had met, bold Lady Miranda—there was no wench to be tumbled but a friend to be cultivated; she burned with nobility and bridled power, more like the folk of Noroison than any other creatures of Landuc had been, a strong woman of thoughts and deeds. Still, there'd be time later for such diversions. Freia had been eager to take it up and Josquin would be as easily taken up himself. He had looked up Valgalant in his Ephemeris and could call on Lady Miranda formally some few months hence. Given Otto's behavior at Perendlac and before that at the fountain, it was delightful to lie here and think about the man's wife. Dewar chuckled. Another thing that might be taken up again later, he suspected, and he doubted that he'd need to draw upon the power latent in the lock of hair she'd given him, which now reposed in a sorcerously-sealed jar.

Freia, he thought, and picked up a sheet of equations. Pretty eyes she had. Brown. Blue? No, they were an odd slatey grey. Bit of green maybe. Unusual color. Brownish-grey-green, like fallen leaves in water. Anyway, pretty. He frowned a small frown.

How could she have gotten out of Perendlac?

The gryphon, of course.

Nasty fighter. He'd seen it gut a mail-armored man with one foreclaw, a messy death. Where Freia would go next—into hiding if she had sense. Of course she'd been seeking Prospero, and she'd missed the Way.

He lowered the sheet of paper, scratched his crotch, and frowned a little more. Prospero was clearly en route elsewhere, a wise general who had kept moving with his battered army and the allies waiting there with ships to carry them off. That army was in no condition for an attack on Landuc. No. Prospero would rebuild and return.

How would the girl find him, then?

A mote of guilt entered the warm, bright bedroom and darkened it.

The gryphon, Dewar thought, had some way of tracking Prospero. That was how she'd gotten to Malperdy. Yes, and that was what she'd been doing on the last leg of the trip: Trixie had sensed Prospero and headed straight for him. Yes. Strange but not unheard-of. Perhaps the animal was actually Prospero's own, so Freia would use the gryphon's finding-sense to track and follow him. Perhaps even along the Road; there were precedents for such behavior from familiars.

When she found Prospero, he considered, she would certainly tell him of her encounter with another sorcerer. She liked him. She might be an ally later. In which case it was as well he had not pressed his advantage and his attentions on her; for she could only give good report of him to Prospero, had only favorable, courteous memories of Dewar. It would soften Prospero toward him; Prospero was inclined to softness, holding back his sorcery in the war to spare Dewar for the wrong reason. He had told Dewar he was his son, foolishly confiding in him, and Dewar could have attacked him, blood to blood.

Prospero had been trafficking with Odile. Despite the Prince's distrustful words about her, Dewar knew Odile was subtle, pernicious, and poisonous. If she could strike at her son through Prospero, she would. Dewar must protect himself from Odile, and if he could use Prospero to gain an advantage, he would. Yet he must guard himself at the same time.

Not a duel, no: rather, Dewar could make of Prospero a shield and sounding-board that would at once shield him from Odile and let him know what she had afoot—but that could wait, all could wait. He was tired of people for now, and he had better work to do. The Third-Force problem had become more than interesting; it was urgent that he solve it soon. For, given a Third Force, someone must ineluctably claim it, making it the center of his sorcery and power, as Primas had found and possessed Hendiadys, as his son Panurgus had found and possessed Pheyarcet. Dewar would find the source of the Third Force and it would be his, and then he would be able to deal with Prospero and Odile both.

He picked up another sheaf of notes and equations in which he had attempted to describe the Third-Force problem and concentrated.

## — 31 —

PROSPERO RAN THROUGH THE MUD-CHURNED streets past scaffolding and piles of stone, his Castellan on his heels.

"Trixie!" he shouted to the gryphon in the meadow at the downstream end of the island.

Trixie was grooming, balefully eyeing the watchers, half

a pig visible beneath her. She stopped and tensed, staring at Prospero.

He stopped twenty feet from her. She didn't move.

"Trixie," he crooned, "pretty Trix, where'st thou been pretty thing, I've worried . . . my, I've been fashed . . . pretty Trix, wilt let me see thy bags? Good Trix, good Trix . . ."

A quarter-hour later, the gryphon was allowing him to stroke her throat and he was unbuckling the gear she still carried. It was weatherbeaten, as was Trixie; Trixie had also bitten at the leather-covered chains and tried to get them off. Prospero loosed her harness, then opened the bags and hunted through them, spilling them on the bloody grass.

Empty. No food. A few small pieces of clothing. Freia's cooking equipment. The canteen was dry.

"Where's Freia, Trix?" he said, standing again. "Freia. Where's thy Freia?"

Trixie crooned unhappily.

"Damnable dumbness," Prospero said. "If I'd known what I was about, I'd've given you all speech. Freia."

The gryphon's croon became a scream, drawn-out and deafening. She reared back and beat her wings, then dropped again.

Prospero scowled. "There's nothing for't but to find her myself," he said, covering concern with ill-humor.

Trixie squalled again and stamped all four feet impatiently. Prospero nodded. "Eat thou and rest," he said. "We'll go later."

He left the animal there, telling two soldiers to see that the gryphon was not disturbed. "And do you shoo another pig to her, if she hungers still."

Freia was in trouble after all, and Prospero felt a sinking misgiving. He hoped it was something as painless to repair as a broken leg.

Ottaviano had come to respect his stubbornly silent hostage. He questioned her diligently under all the compulsions he knew which would not damage her permanently, and she resisted him with all her will. Shaking under the strain of holding silence, she would bite her lips bloody or grind her teeth, her face contorted, muscles locked, keeping herself from answering any questions. Golias favored breaking her, forcing her further than she would be able to resist, and Otto opposed him saying that their primary concern was to turn her over to the Emperor in good condition, else he might well dispute any concessions they wrung from him. Golias conceded grudgingly.

They had heard from the Emperor only that he weighed their offer, and Golias was impatient for results.

"He's had it for ten days," he said.

"That's not very long to consider a major rearrangement of the real estate in the contiguous realm," Otto replied.

"He's dragging his feet," Golias said. "Probably planning an attack: that's what I'd do."

"We're ready for it."

"It's been long enough for him to say something," Golias insisted. "We have to put the pressure on him." He sat on the edge of the table where Otto was eating lunch, playing with a dagger, throwing it and catching it.

Otto ignored the dagger flying up and down beside his head. "What did you have in mind?"

"You have a fast tongue. Go to Landuc and start dickering. Take some of the Lys and Ascolet guys with you. A so-called honor guard. Let him know you're serious."

Otto shook his head. "If Prospero shows up here, you'll be defenseless."

"Neyphile can handle him."

Ottaviano set down his knife and spoon and stared at Golias. "I don't want her in on this."

"She's reliable, unlike your last sorcerer. And she's easy to deal with. Don't worry, it'd be on my tab," Golias said. He pared his left thumbnail with the knife. "If he shows up, anyway, and she takes him on, there may not be a tab to pay."

"Probably not. Prospero's got a lot of power at his fingertips." Otto thought. The girl was a hot property, unquestionably. Getting her out of their hands quickly was only to their advantage. Going to Landuc to negotiate the business in person would force the Emperor to step one way or another, move things along.

He had to admit that Golias had the right of it: putting a little pressure on the Emperor now would work for them.

"If you're confident that you won't have any trouble you can't handle, I'll go," Otto said.

Golias grinned. "Don't sell me out."

"Of course not. Let's go through the list of fallbacks tonight."

"How many men will you take?"

"One company of Ascolet. No need for more: that's enough to show I mean business and to deal with any . . . difficulty there may be."

"I'm going to rearrange security a little," Golias said, tossing the knife and catching it by the point. He swung it back and forth, pendulum-like. "Just in case."

"Ariel!"

"Yes, Master!"

"My daughter's gone astray. Find her."

Ariel thought about it. "Where is she missing, Lord?"

"From here, my wisp-witted friend," Prospero said.

"My Lord, I mean—know you in which of the spheres she was last to be found?"

"Ah. That I know not. 'Tis likely to be the Fire's realm of Pheyarcet."

"Oh," said Ariel, and hesitated further.

"Begone, Ariel. This is no light matter. She may be wounded, ill, or lost."

Ariel rustled through the leaves of a book on the table. "I go, Master, but it will take some time . . ."

"I understand," Prospero said. "As thou understandest it had best not take too much." He gestured.

Ariel made a popping noise. "Yes, Master," he squeaked, "I fly, I fly . . ."

"Good Ariel. When hast found her, return here at once with such tidings of her state and place as canst assemble."

"Yes, Master," sighed Ariel, and swished through the open casement.

Prospero tapped at the open pages of his book with his wand.

It was the fastest way he knew of to find anything: send a Sylph. Ariel was thorough and trustworthy, if a little distractable. There was nothing more to be done, now. He couldn't Summon her back, which was the simplest way of dealing with it; he could not Summon beyond the area dominated by the cool, liquid flow of the Spring—even as he could not Summon from Landuc's Pheyarcet to Phesaotois—and he had performed a Summoning within his Spring's realm. There had been nothing. She did not know how to shield herself, so therefore she was dead or not in range.

He preferred to think her not in range. Moreover, were she dead, Trixie would not have returned alive. The gryphon would have done anything to kill Freia's killer.

Prospero paced. Light-minded wench, he thought. He'd settle her somehow. Flouting his most plainly patent command! He muttered, "Damnation, Freia, I'll pack thee off to—nay, in sooth I'd not do that; I'd liever keep thee here where I can ward thee. Nay, no idle threat for thee. Should marry thee off. Give thee fitting matter to engage thee, hah. Scudamor's fond of thee; so's Utrachet, but I cannot quite see wedding thee, apple-daughter, to a man I know full well was a long-clawed burrowing eskor or a wildcat."

He snorted at the joke.

"Nay, 'twouldn't do," he tutted to himself, and stopped pacing to stare out the unglazed window at the stars. He must ground her, but not basely. For Freia, the mate must be a peer, and strong-minded. Had Avril found out about Ottaviano yet, or vice-versa? 'Twould be a handsome touch. Foolish Cecilie. Pull a bag over Avril's head and tie it at his neck. 'Twas ill wind that blew no good, though. Prospero would have to track Ottaviano down. See what sort of fellow he was, what use might be made of him: friendly with Dewar, could be a recommendation—apprenticed with Neyphile, though he seemed not to have surpassed her teaching or ability, nor to have learned anything from Dewar. A procedural, not an original, sorcerer.

Prospero stopped pacing and stood over his golden scrying-bowl. Dewar, he thought, and shivered. Odile's son crackled with power and anger. Yes, he had better settle Freia ere he settled with the boy.

Freia slept as much as she could, curled in a ball on the wooden bench which was her bed. There were beetles in one end of the bench, which was crumbling slowly, and she kept her feet away from them. The cell was relatively free of vermin, and relatively warm, and all she had to do, she thought, was wait until Prospero realized he'd left her behind.

The time she had fallen in the canyon and broken her leg, Prospero had brought her home hours later, with his sorcery. Where was he now?

Surely, she thought, somebody had seen her and Trixie.

Surely, she thought, Dewar would tell Prospero she had been left behind.

But it seemed to be taking a long time.

Ottaviano rode into Landuc thinking of Luneté, his wife of a year and a half's standing with whom he'd had but few days of postmarital pleasure. He wanted to see her again. Their last meeting but one—well, that had been Otto's fault, really, he'd been angry at her furious reception, had said some stupid things, had behaved like a pantomime caricature of jealousy, and he knew she'd never take a lover, she was too straitly made for philandering. Of course she was antsy, closed up in that claustrophobic castle, and she was right when she said he hadn't spent much time with her. He thought he'd made up a great deal when she'd let him come to her on his return a half-month later. He smiled, thinking of it.

He made plans to buy some peace-offerings here in the city and send them to Lys. Rubies. A tiara. Something fashionable like that. Summer silk and pictures of the newest styles.

Behind him, beside him, his men checked their weapons. They had been permitted through the Gate of Winds, inside the city walls; it remained to be seen how things would go at the Palace.

At the Palace, things were progressing rapidly. The Emperor had been informed of Otto's approach by a fast runner from the city gate. The Emperor had Summoned Prince Herne and the Prince Marshal and ordered them to tighten up Palace security. The troop of men might enter the first courtyard, under the arrows of Herne's archers. Gaston was to meet and disarm Otto and escort him to the Emperor.

"He is not come to yield, Avril," Gaston pointed out. "See the green branch."

"Parley, hah. He's come to bargain. We knew he would. He is an impatient young fool," and the Emperor grinned ferociously. "We shall have him now."

Gaston bowed slightly and went out. He had not ceased to express doubts of the truth of Otto's and Golias's claim that they had Prospero's very daughter in custody. And he misliked the idea more when he thought of Lady Miranda of Valgalant. Gaston rarely followed his hunches, preferring his reason, but in this case his reason and his hunches both indicated that some evil must come of bartering a niece (if niece she were) for victory. It was no clear conquest.

So Otto and his troop were permitted into the first courtyard, which they saw perfectly well might be an ambush, and Otto alone was escorted by the courteous and close-mouthed Prince Gaston to Emperor Avril's smallest receiving-room, which had one chair, the Emperor's.

The Emperor looked him over, meeting him for the first time.

"Sebastiano's boy," the Emperor remarked.

Otto straightened from his bow with a certain chill in his glance. He was becoming irked at being called somebody's boy—first by Prospero, now the Emperor.

"You take after your distinguished grandfather," the Emperor observed, scrutinizing him. "Let us hope you have his wits. You realize, Baron, that if you do indeed have hostage Prospero's daughter, we can refuse to treat with you and point him to you when he arrives. And we daresay he will. We can let him kill you, or you kill him, and remove the victor at our leisure."

"You realize, Your Majesty, that if Prince Prospero approached me and demanded his daughter restored to him, I would instantly comply," Otto said, "and then we would, since we both have much to gain thereby, perhaps discuss matters of common interest."

The Emperor smiled slightly. "Your last sorcerous ally did not serve well," he said.

"Prospero is a known quantity, and an honorable man," Otto said, unwittingly pricking the Emperor.

"We are all honorable men, when our honor is worth it," the Emperor retorted. "What proof have you got that the woman is indeed his daughter?"

"Her own word, under Binding of truth."

"So at least she believes this to be true."

"There is a familial resemblance," Otto added, "which buoys the idea, and moreover she was certainly aiding him in his attack. I have no doubt whatsoever. If Your Majesty's doubts are so great, then of course we have no further need to speak." He smiled.

"You are young and your haste is unwise," the Emperor said. "We have much to discuss." He rose. "Prince Marshal, Count Pallgrave, Cremmin. Accompany us and our visitor to the White Conference Room."

Otto's visits had ceased. Freia found this disruption of routine worrying, and worry occupied her too-long waking hours. In their last encounter, she had asked him what he'd do if someone took his wife and imprisoned her like this, and he had been startled that she knew he had a wife. Dewar had mentioned it, but she didn't explain that to Otto.

That had been days ago.

When a rattle which was not that of the food-slot at the bottom of the door sounded, she sat up. It wasn't, as far as she could tell, the usual time for question-and-silence sessions.

Four armed men were outside, carrying lanterns. Freia's

heart bounded and then sank. One was Golias, who had sat in on several of the sessions—the only ones when Otto had actually gotten any answers—and Freia feared him. His barely-restrained viciousness was clear to her; she smelled the reek of danger and hatred on him. She had seen him hurt Utrachet. Otto had not allowed Golias to interrogate her alone.

Golias grinned as two of the guards came in, and Freia didn't bother resisting them as they bound her hands too tightly behind her. Her wrists burned.

A veiled woman waited in the narrow, low stone corridor behind Golias. "So," she drawled, "this is the keystone of your plan."

"A hard stone."

The woman laughed softly. "We shall hammer it into shape," she said.

Golias took a dirty grey rag from his belt and shook it out—it was a sack. He put it over his prisoner's head and grabbed her elbow, dragging her along the corridor and up a flight of stairs. Freia stumbled and was shaken and hauled upright.

As they climbed, she heard sounds above the noise they made in the confined space: shouts and the bang and thud of fighting. It grew louder.

Where was Otto? Freia wondered, beginning to feel more than fear.

They skirted the sounds of the fight; Freia tripped on thresholds and then on uneven cobblestones as she was taken outside. It was cold, but bright; the light leaked through the sack and made her squint. A breeze pushed the coarse cloth against her face. It was dusty and smelled of dirt.

Golias lifted her up; someone grabbed her and dragged her bruisingly, then dropped her on wood which thumped hollow.

Wagon, Freia guessed.

More ropes were put around her, tying her legs and arms more tightly.

"The horses should be blindfolded," said the woman's voice.

The breeze brushed at her arms, her body, her legs, chilling her to the bone.

The wagon started to move. There was shouting; the woman cried something and there came a windrushing implosion, a grinding crash of stones like an avalanche. Freia's ears popped; as the air pressure returned, everything sounded dull and underwater. The fight seemed to have stopped.

"Good," Golias said, above her somewhere.

Someone screamed, a horrible pain sound. Freia whimpered in sympathy, inaudible in her sack.

"Let us begone," the woman said. "The forces are disrupted here; someone may come to investigate."

"Master!"

"Ariel?" Prospero sat bolt upright in bed and lunged over to the nightstand to light a candle. It guttered. Ariel was fidgeting about the bed hangings, fluttering the fringes. "Report!"

"I've found her, Master, I've found Freia, she is a prisoner!"

"Hell's ice! Where? Of whom?"

"In Landuc, Master. I had great difficulty searching because of the prevalence of sorceries there, and moreover I was caught up by a wind-Summoning. The Summoner of winds was a sorceress, and she used them to destroy a fortress. But in the same place as the sorceress was the Lady Freia. She was bound and hooded, and I tried to communicate with her but could not."

Ariel, excited by his own tale, had become a dusty little whirlwind carrying scraps of paper and feather and lightweight debris in his spinning form, balanced at the end of the bed. Prospero stared at him.

"Tell on."

"The place was that where the men of Argylle were held, Master. Perendlac. They left that place, however, having destroyed it, and moved up one of the rivers—I believe the Rendlac, is that not the one from the North?—to a fortress which commands a great long view being on a small mountain. They took her within. There she lies still if they have not moved her again."

"She was alive, well."

"Alive, and I detected no wound, although, Master, I am not expert at these things. She is flesh, and I cannot penetrate it."

"Of course. But she had no material hurt."

"No, Master. A prisoner, bound and hooded, held by a sorceress."

Prospero threw back the heavy coverlet and got out of bed, lighting three more candles. The whirlwind hopped into the fireplace and made circular patterns in the powdery old ashes there.

"Shall we rescue her?" asked Ariel excitedly.

"What think'st thou?" snapped Prospero. "The fool, to be taken— What did she at Perendlac, I'd like to know." Freia, taken by a sorceress: she could not have done worse had she set out with intent to do so. He threw clothing onto the bed, took his sword from the wall and half-drew it, looking at the blade, tarnished to blackness that could never be polished away: the stain of Panurgus's blood.

Ariel, who did not engage in conjecture unless ordered to do so, waited. Ashes plumed up the chimney.

"Shalt travel thither with me," Prospero said. "We leave tonight." He slammed the sword back into its scabbard and dropped it on the bed with the clothing.

# — 32 —

THE SORCERESS NEYPHILE, WHOSE SIMPLY-DRESSED hair was the color of dark honey, wore a low-cut gown of pale yellow satin with white lace. She half-reclined on a blue velvet divan, which was entirely out of place in the dank stone dungeon. In the corners of the room, things moved in the decaying straw. She considered the subject of her investigations with a remote, indifferent expression.

The subject was chained to the opposite wall, leaning back, eyes closed, panting.

Neyphile was not a major sorceress. Her bargain with Panurgus for a taste of the Fire of Landuc had been accomplished with difficulty, and only Panurgus's death had freed her of some of its more onerous clauses. Panurgus had trained her just enough that, had she been more clever, she would have been killed by her own ignorance; instead, she had made other bargains, in other places, and advanced her knowledge thus and by the dint of her own plodding labors. Competent, but never brilliant, she could not be like Prospero, a self-made adept capable of holding her own beyond the Limen, in Phesaotois; nor was she sufficiently skilled at negotiation to be like Oriana, who had used trade and blackmail to leave the limits of Phesaotois and improve her standing in Pheyarcet. Neyphile's particular interest was Bounds, and, like many other diligent but dull scholars, she had acquired a sound and extensive knowledge of this specialty, with scant comprehension of the universal.

Still, she was a sorceress.

Today she had met something beyond her reach in Golias's recalcitrant prisoner. A peculiar barrier sheltered the girl from the deepest sorcerous workings, and although she suffered greatly under them she was still mistress of herself enough not to speak.

Neyphile's curiosity was piqued, and her professional pride was insulted. After the removal of Ottaviano's spells and Neyphile's replacement of them with her own, the girl should have been stripped open, her thoughts available at the asking. This was not the case.

Press though Neyphile did, distract the girl's concentration with other things as she might, the girl held her thoughts within.

Neyphile lifted a small silver bell on a turquoise cushion beside the divan and rang.

The door opened and a guard entered, saluting.

"Prince Golias must join me," Neyphile said.

The man saluted again and left.

Neyphile continued to study her subject in various lights until Golias scraped open the door and entered.

"What is the provenance of this?" Neyphile demanded of him, gesturing at the prisoner.

Golias frowned. "Prospero's," he said. She knew that.

"From what circle of the world? Where on the Road was she engendered?"

"No idea. Why?"

"Strange," Neyphile said. "I shall have to think about it."

"Where is Prospero's headquarters?" Golias demanded.

Neyphile ran her bone wand through her fingers. "Ask her yourself," she said. "I must retire and consider another matter at present." She stood and left the dungeon. Golias scowled after her.

The prisoner was fastened to the wall by chains at her waist, wrists, and ankles. Golias went to her and lifted her head, blew in her face. She blinked involuntarily.

"Don't feel like talking?" he said mockingly.

She swallowed.

Golias smiled. "Let's see what kind of noise you can make," he said, and took out his knife. Her leather trousers were fastened with buttons. He cut them off, one by one.

Dewar's etched black tabletop was overlaid with a softly glowing webwork of light, barely visible in the midday sunshine from the high windows. He leaned over, staring at one pulsating point near the far edge of the table, in an area devoid of engraved and inlaid lines.

After a moment, he picked up a tiny lens on a golden tripod and carefully inserted it in the webwork. A line brightened. He nodded and chose a prism on a similar stand and another and placed them at junctions.

The bright spot grew brighter.

Dewar extended a finger and put it in the bright spot. Coldness spread up his arm; it was like dipping into near-freezing water. Pain followed the cold. Dewar hissed, then gasped and yanked his hand away. His arm felt flayed. He shook it vigorously, then unbuttoned the lace-trimmed cuff and looked at the skin to assure himself that all was as it should be.

The cold feeling was gone. It had stopped as soon as he had withdrawn his hand.

In its place was a not unpleasant rippling, which was fading with the pain. He buttoned his cuff again.

Dewar pulled a stool over to his table and sat down, looking at the lines of light.

"Contradictory. Cancellation," he said. "Clash of Elements."

He drummed his fingers on the edge of the table.

"On the other hand," he added.

The last time he had felt anything like that was when he had passed the shimmering, unreal Fire of Landuc's Well. That had burned through and through him—it burned yet, when he paid attention to it. That was the point.

"Theory," he reminded himself, and went over to a chalkboard.

Stone of Morven, in Phesaotois. The Bright Well in Landuc.

*Me,* he wrote between them. Water, active.

The Stone: Earth, active. The Well, Fire, active.

"Well, but the Fire didn't kill me," he remarked. "Buffered by Stone?"

He wrote this down, erased the word *Me,* and scrawled it on the other side of the Stone, out of place. No, he decided, and erased *Me* altogether.

"Can't have much to do with it at this level, or I'd be dead," he decided.

He went back to the table, his miniature recreation of the grandest plan of things. A trickle of the Third Force, channelled and amplified, and behold, he could map it if he chose. Indeed he had done so, on all the usual scales. The piecemeal maps were on large table-sized sheets, copied on smaller ones; they formed the beginnings of a new Map for his travels, implying a new world—*if* he could find their origin, if he could follow them without being able to perceive them.

Thus far he could not, not without lugging his table and

fragile, beautiful devices around, or without being able to detect it himself.

Which he could not do, since he did not know where the Third Force's source was. Now he hypothesized that it manifested as water in some way, but its location was unclear. He knew only its stray currents as they surfaced in the Well's sparser, weaker areas. This newest, strongest upwelling, far from the rest of the traces of the Third Force, only muddied the problem further. The Spheres moved continually, he knew, but rarely so quickly.

Dewar decided to consider the problem from another angle. Was there anything which could be construed as telling him where the Stone lay, when he was in Landuc? What betrayed it?

The vanes on some of the instruments spun slowly. The clocks whirled. Sunk in thought, Dewar gazed at the table without seeing it and delicately picked through threads of force with the special inward sense attuned to them.

Ottaviano sat on his horse staring at Perendlac for several minutes, unable to believe he saw truly. The tower was gone. He could see broken masonry—a wall?—still standing, but the great keep was gone.

He rode quickly toward the walls and the gate, which was closed but opened as they approached. The small troop of Ascolet men who had gone with him to Landuc followed.

"Sir!" yelled Clay, standing in the gap between the thick iron-studded wooden slabs. The lieutenant had a sling on his left arm.

"What the hell is this?"

"Treachery, sir!" Clay replied, holding Otto's bridle as he dismounted.

"Golias," Otto said, turning and staring at him.

"Yes."

They looked into one another's eyes.

Otto set his teeth, covering his sinking feeling. "Tell me about it."

"Simply said, sir, we were ensorcelled. A curse fell over all the Ascolet and Lys troops on the fifth day after you left.

We set on one another. For—I don't know how long—a quarter-hour, a bit more—we were berserk to a man, a melee, sir, and then there was a stunning loud thunder that knocked down those that hadn't fallen to their friends." Clay turned and looked at the collapsed fortress. "When we woke, sir, it was thus and Cap—Prince Golias and his men were gone. He had had a woman here—"

"In gold? Brown hair, bone-thin, heart-shaped face?"

"Yes."

"Bitch! Neyphile! Go on."

"We tried to recover bodies from the ruin, but—" Clay shook his head. "As you see. It wants better tackle than we have tools to build."

"How many killed?"

"One hundred twenty-two outright, sir. A large number of injuries too. The men are dispirited."

Otto drew his breath in and looked at the stones which had been Perendlac. It could be rebuilt.

"It would have been worse, but the roof did not come all the way down on one side, as you see," Clay said. "But it has been bad, sir."

"The prisoner? They took her?"

"No way to tell but I assume yes," Clay said. "I suspect that was the point."

"I suspect you're right." Otto closed his eyes. Things were not going according to plan.

"They went to Chasoulis," Clay told him.

"Not far."

"I've had scouts watching the place. No one's joined him."

"Chasoulis."

"I have plans of it, sir, and maps—"

"Good," Otto said, biting the word off. "He'll regret this." And in his mind echoed the words of his lost hostage: "You will regret this all your days." As stupid and careless as Prospero, now, he looked on the ruin of his plan in the ruin of Perendlac and felt the regret begin, a hollowness under his rage at Golias.

* * *

Prince Gaston on horseback was higher than anyone else in the regiment behind him. Otto picked him out easily without a spyglass and Clay confirmed his guess.

"It's the Fireduke."

Otto nodded. He had not sent word of Golias's change of allegiance to the Emperor. He had tried to negotiate with Golias, pointing out the advantages of going along with Otto, but Golias was convinced he could do better for himself. Rather as he had cut Bors of Lys out, years ago. Bors had died for that. Sebastiano of Ascolet had died after taking a mortal wound in defeating Golias. Ottaviano pushed these thoughts aside. Soon he would be as broody and half-cracked as Prospero from chewing over the injustices of history.

Prince Gaston had made no effort to conceal the force he had brought with him. Mounted and foot, with wagons carrying dismantled siege equipment, he appeared well-equipped to take on Golias.

Actually, Otto reminded himself, the Fireduke had come to take on Otto and Golias. Well, something could still be salvaged by repenting, begging forgiveness, and becoming a party man. The thought of Ascolet lost forever was unpalatable.

Perhaps, he thought, Dewar was right: they were much alike, being a baron of a large and powerful barony owing fealty to an Emperor and being king of a relatively small and poor kingdom next door to the same. Yet Otto couldn't think that without hateful gall in his throat: to owe fealty to anyone was contrary to his nature, which admitted the superiority of very few others.

Prince Gaston was drawing nearer. Through his spyglass Otto saw him examining the wreckage of Perendlac, frowning.

"Open the gates for him," Otto said, and swallowed.

The discipline in the Prince Marshal's army was superb. No chatter; alert readiness for action at Gaston's command or gesture; even the mules seemed to step in time. Otto went to the creaking gate and waited there.

"Welcome to Perendlac," he said. "Sir."

Prince Gaston reined in, looked at him, looked at the fortress, and lifted his eyebrows, dismounting. The columns of men and animals halted and waited for orders.

"Prospero?"

"I wish it had been," Otto said, realizing he did. He couldn't look like anything but a milk-mouthed naïf to Gaston when he explained what had happened. "It's not a long story," he said, and he told it—Prince Golias, hostage, sorceress, and all.

Prince Gaston stood, one hand on his horse's bridle, listening, watching Ottaviano as he spoke, seeing his acute humiliation. The boy had overreached himself. He would pay a penalty now, a severe one, but not as severe as it would have been if he'd not had the good sense to wed the Countess of Lys.

"Chasoulis," he said when Otto had done. "A relic, but a strong-walled one."

"There's a Node there," Ottaviano said, "and someone is working a hell of a lot of sorcery."

The Marshal nodded. "Neyphile," he said distastefully.

"It sounded like her from the description. I've not yet seen her in person there."

"Thou knowest her," Prince Gaston said.

Otto said blandly, "Yes."

"Hast scouted."

"Yes. Nothing has come or gone. He's waiting. For you, for me, for Prospero . . ." Otto shrugged. "I don't know what for."

"Naught of Prospero yet. Art certain of the girl's lineage?"

"Yes."

"How?"

"What I said before—she's in sound mind, and she knows she's his daughter. Looks a little like him, but prettier. Also—she has the same kind of—charge he does. Not the same affinity, but there's something of him in her, in the same way that you are infused with a similarity to your brothers. I'm sure she is his."

Prince Gaston nodded after a moment, digesting this.

"Thou canst not Summon her," he said.

"I tried. Neyphile has her Bound. I can't."

Gaston nodded again and turned to his second, Captain Jolly. "At ease whilst I review the Baron's scouting reports. We'll move again in two hours. Maintain readiness."

Jolly saluted and left them to pass the order on.

The Prince Marshal had his own scouts already on the scene, and he compared their reports with Ottaviano's. They had brought most of the news to him already; his siege and attack plans were made. Now he assigned Otto's men positions subordinate to his own force. They would bear the brunt of any attack from the castle, but not the responsibility for anything done. Cannon fodder. Otto estimated casualties and felt an inner lurch. Luneté's words rang again in his memory, demanding he return her Lys men before there were more deaths.

"Sir," Otto said, looking at the map, "do you seriously think you can break Chasoulis?"

Prince Gaston looked at him. " 'Tis not beyond possible."

"There's a big gap between the possible and the probable. We've had mild weather. One good blizzard and—"

"Timing's all," the Marshal said. "Chasoulis is not unbreakable. Hath great advantages; Golias is well-entrenched. However, I've no doubt that we'll succeed."

Otto noted the *we* and appreciated it. So he was not utterly in disgrace.

"At present," said Prince Gaston, "I concern me for the girl. An she be injured or abused, when cometh time to restore her to her father, 'twill give him more reason than ever for retaliation."

"She was well and unharmed—" Otto said, and stopped.

"When thou didst leave her," Prince Gaston said.

Lady Miranda, thought Otto. His mouth was dry. "She's too valuable to kill." You'll regret this all your days. How would you feel if someone did this to your wife?

* * *

Eighteen days later Otto's estimated casualty total was beginning to look low. Golias parleyed with Prince Gaston, who left Otto behind when he went, and the Fireduke told him that either he could have his head and turn the girl over or he could lose his head and turn the girl over. An immediate volley of arrows from the castle's crenelated walls followed Golias's re-entry, killing six Ascolet and Lys men.

Prince Gaston was methodically sapping. The frozen ground slowed the work, but he had chosen his points well, having plans of the fortress in his hands, and the tunnels progressed steadily toward a state in which the eastern wall could be brought down.

Golias made forays to disrupt the sappers, and Ottaviano's men met those attacks and repelled them with difficulty.

Otto felt like a lackey, which he supposed was the point. His task was to undo Neyphile's sorcerous bindings and protections on the fortress, on which front he had made no considerable progress, uncontracted sorcery for which his guerdon would be his head and a subservient role in Landuc for the rest of his days. It made his belly burn; he watched his men fall and die, watched the pyre-smoke rise, and he swore he would not let this happen again. He had moved too soon; he had been overconfident.

He didn't write to Luneté. He picked up the pen and put it away nightly.

After his evening meal and meeting with Prince Gaston on the eighteenth day of the siege, he left his tent and, in the white light of an exceptionally bright half-moon, ascended a small knoll near the fortress to study Neyphile's Bounds again. The air was static and pure, like thin black ice. His breath froze in his moustache and beard, on the furred hood of his cloak, and stung his nostrils dry.

The Bounds were perceptible as a thickening in the substance of the walls. He shifted his attention to them and began tracing them for the dozenth time, looking for the closure. Neyphile had gotten better at Bounds. She had a knack for work like that, for Bounding and Opening. What he had learned from her had been more superficial in nature.

A breeze clattered the brittle leaves behind him, then dwindled. Cold seeped through his cloak and faded, raising his hackles.

Otto took his mind from the Bounds and looked around him. There was no movement in the air now. Nothing happening. All still and silent. Sentries passed to and fro. A ruddy light glowed dimly around the corner of the castle where the sapworks was.

Wind. Prospero, he thought. Prospero was active in the neighborhood. That was no common wind.

A shadow moved just at the corner of his eye, near the wood's edge. Otto spun and stared full at it, but there was nothing there, no telltale shimmer of a sorcerer's invisibility spell. Otto stood stock-still, sharpening his ears for any other sound of movement the winds might let slip.

A pennant stirred, high on Chasoulis's central keep; it flapped out once and fell again.

Otto drew his breath in.

Nothing happened for the next hour. His muscles cramped; he flexed them without moving. He wasn't cold—like Prince Gaston, he ignored it—but the tension was painful and, he sensed, unrewarding. The breeze had noticed Otto. He would see nothing now.

He couldn't concentrate on the Bounds. Instead he went down to report the news to the Marshal.

Halfway to the Marshal's tent, Otto's mind revolved to turn up again the girl's voice and her still, controlled face. He admired her stoicism, her courage: she'd known her father would come looking for her. It had been a holdout game.

And Ottaviano changed his route and returned to his own tent. Damn it, he was thinking like a drone now, not just acting like one. Why should he tell the Marshal that Prince Prospero was scouting Chasoulis in his own way? Why not keep his mouth shut?

Prospero's chances of getting in and getting out with his daughter were, it seemed to Otto, better than Gaston's. When Gaston entered Chasoulis, Golias would kill the girl out of spite, to screw Ottaviano and the Emperor, obeying the pure venom in his antisocial veins. Prospero would be subtler than Gaston. If Otto said nothing to alert the Marshal, and Prospero succeeded—

In a small way, he would have compensated for the losses to Ascolet, for his own humiliation. If the Emperor lost this one, Otto would have the pleasure of remembering that for years to come. Otto's status was the same, win or lose. In that case, the Emperor might as well lose. Let the girl go with her father. Yes.

Then Prospero would owe Otto a favor of some sort.

There were a number of small things a potent sorcerer like Prospero might do for Otto.

The Baron of Ascolet went into his tent, and the moon shone down brightly.

On the nineteenth day of the siege, the sun's first reluctant rays on Chasoulis's keep were heralded by a pair of dull booms, one after the other.

Prince Gaston, up before the late winter dawn, stared in amazement as the wall his men had sapped began collapsing ahead of schedule. Another boom, this one much louder, blew out part of the wall beside it.

Fatigue! thought Gaston, and: The men, the men below.

They were dead men. The stone was crumbling and tumbling, and rather than wonder at the abrupt failure of the masonry, the Prince Marshal shouted orders for an attack.

A screaming sledgehammer wind tore the words away. It bent mature trees in the wood, snapping many, and banged into the wall, knocking more of it down than Gaston would have believed possible.

Never underestimate the capabilities of a pissed-off sorcerer, Otto thought, watching the stones fall. They seemed to go very slowly.

"Baron!" Gaston screamed at him over the wind, his voice raw.

"Sir!"

"Formation three for attack!"

"Yes, sir!" Otto shouted back, nodding, and he ran to

collect the remnants of his army in order to lead the entry into Chasoulis. It might be suicide; Golias would be ready and waiting for them. Otto's men were eager to get blood back for their comrades crushed at Perendlac. Golias's men were trapped like rats. There could be no quarter asked or given.

Otto and his men pushed in swiftly. Another section of wall collapsed; Otto wondered if Prince Gaston had figured out that Prospero was responsible. The Marshal and his soldiers from Landuc and Montgard were spreading through the yard, harrying and killing, forcing Golias's men into one another so that they interfered with their own fighting. Having studied and memorized the Marshal's maps of the place, Otto had told his men their goal was to get into the castle proper. The Bounds on the walls and buildings had disappeared with the first onslaught of winds, Prospero's work.

Golias himself was nowhere to be seen. His mercenaries were withdrawing into the castle, fighting grimly defensive fights to prolong their breaths; Otto saw faces whose names he knew, whose bearers he had drunk with, whose blood spurted red when he wounded them. He pursued them with Clay and his men, staying on the outskirts of the fighting. From the corner of his eye he saw a side door which led to a corridor which gave access to the cellars of the castle.

"Clay!"

"Sir!"

"You're in command!"

Clay didn't acknowledge, though he had certainly heard. Otto broke from the fight and, sword and shield ready, sprinted to the door and the corridor.

Winds were running through the place now, Prince Prospero's hunting winds. They whistled in keyholes and rattled the arras and windows. Otto felt them push and pull his shield and himself, some cold and some warm, one hot and dry, a desert wind.

The door to the stair was open. Ottaviano hurried down. It was dark and narrow, the air still and dank. The stone steps were unevenly worn, low and treacherous in the middle but still high and square on the sides. He heard nothing of the battle here; it was dank, cold, and quiet.

Humming tension was building in the darkness. Otto left his shield and took the last torch at the bottom of the stair, following the sorcery. Wardings, Bindings—and an Opening now, shaping the subtexture of the world nearby.

Light, and an open door. Otto ran in, feeling the tension build, and hurled his torch with a single word at Neyphile, who, with a man-at-arms carrying Prospero's daughter like a sack of meal, was preparing to step through a Way-fire.

In the moment of their surprise, Otto had time to notice that the room contained a blue velvet divan, rotting straw, a rack, a wheel, and a mixed lot of miscellaneous, unpleasant accessories. Neyphile's tastes had always been a butcher-bird's, her nesting-places never pleasant.

The torch and his shouted Unbinding word disrupted the spell. Neyphile whirled on him, her eyes yellow in the torchlight, and the man with her—not Golias—dropped the girl and began to draw his short sword. He had no shield, and Neyphile wasn't helping him. Otto half-severed the man's right hand and then shoved his sword in his belly. He fell, dying in gore.

Neyphile was attempting to reopen the Way. She and Otto stared at one another. Otto's skin chilled over; he could not look away.

"Come with me, and I'll make you powerful," Neyphile said in her light, trickling voice. "There is power you cannot have dreamed of in the world. Come with me."

The girl, whose feet were not tied, suddenly jerked herself around, jumped, and ran staggering for the door.

The Baron of Ascolet shook his head, Neyphile's hold on his attention broken. It had worked, once; never again. "Fuck yourself, bitch," Otto said, pleasantly nasty. "Prospero is going to toast you." He darted out after Prospero's daughter.

She had stumbled and fallen just a few steps away. "I'm getting you out of here," Ottaviano told her, stooping, helping her stand. She swayed against the wall, trying to pull away from him.

The light in the cell flared and died: Neyphile was gone, saving her skin rather than confront a Prince who would kill her. Otto ducked back in, grabbed the torch where it sputtered in blood, and returned to the prisoner.

Her hands were chained behind her. Her clothing was stained and ragged. She was bruise-eyed, fist-marked, sick-looking.

"You," she whispered.

"Come on, honey, we're getting out of here."

"You—"

"Me. Come on. Wait, I can undo these chains." He tried a simple Unbinding spell, and it worked; the chain fell into links, leaving the shackle-rings on her wrists though her arms were now freed. "Come on," he said to her, and gripped her arm, leading her at the fastest pace possible.

She could barely walk, certainly couldn't run. Otto put his free arm around her and half-lifted her along; he couldn't drop the torch to carry her. They loped unevenly to the stair, and he lifted her and carried her up, leaving the torch at the bottom again. The winds had stilled.

At the top, he realized that he had left his sword in Neyphile's guard's gut, and that this was unwise with a minor war raging in the area. If he could rob a corpse of one, he'd be far more likely to survive. There was a body twenty feet away—

"Golias!" someone bellowed in the main hall, whence came a sound of clattering and a sudden silence.

The girl tensed and thrashed in his arms. Otto set her down.

"I've got to get a sword. Wait here," he hissed at her. "Stay out of sight."

She staggered against the wall, looking worse in daylight than by flame. Her eyes were wide and wildly blank.

Otto hurried to the corpse. A Lys man and not yet dead.

"Erkel, friend, I need your blade."

"Sir," mouthed Erkel, eyes glazed, and Ottaviano took the blade from his blood-slick hand, his rage at perfidious Golias boiling up again.

*"Golias!"* came the shout again, and the girl cried out in

answer and ran, truly ran, down the corridor past Otto as he stood.

"Hey! Stop!"

"GOLIAS!" reverberated through the very stones of the building.

Prince Prospero had arrived, realized Otto, starting after the girl.

Prince Gaston glanced at the body on the mosaic-tiled floor, which lay in a smear of fresh blood on the worn stones. Still moving, knees curling to chest to meet the end as the beginning. He took a step away, then stopped again and looked a second time. A couple of blood-marked footprints led away in the direction in which he'd been going himself.

The light from the tall, narrow windows was wan and grey, the fading sun too weak to pierce the cloud cover which was rolling over the sky. He bent, a dagger ready in his right hand in case it was a ruse, and turned the near-corpse over slowly.

More blood, welling from fresh scrapes on the face, crimson on white-indigo-black-violeted skin, and red blood on the broken mouth. She looked at him with purpled, puffed eyes.

"Finish it . . ." she whispered, slurred but distinct.

Too dark for Neyphile, too ragged, too grimed, the Fireduke thought. This must be the hostage. Someone had sought to silence her: Golias? But she was his bargaining-piece. Ottaviano had run past Gaston, bloodspattered and pale, an instant before Gaston had rounded the corner, and Gaston frowned to himself at the coincidence. But he would get the truth of it from her later, if she lived.

"Nay," he said, and used his dagger to tear a piece of cloth from his scarlet cloak, ripping a wider gash in her grimy shirt and pressing it hard against a freely-bleeding wound in her chest. A blooded knife lay under her.

Her eyes closed. Her breath slipped out slowly: she fainted, close to death. Prince Gaston pushed aside her hair, matted with blood, and saw no obvious head injuries.

"Sir?" called one of his men, Gallitan, and then ran forward up the hall, leading a squad of a dozen others.

"Captain Gallitan. Bring Gernan the surgeon. This woman's to be kept alive. Guard and tend her till Gernan's here. Keep a guard of two on her lest they try again."

"Yes, sir."

He left Gallitan there and went on with six of the men. Scuffling sounds came from both sides when he passed the doors between this corridor and the main hall; there was fighting in the main hall around which the corridor ran, and Gaston disregarded it, confident that Captain Jolly would have it under control. The Fireduke had better prey than mercenaries in mind: Golias would be hereabouts.

A light exploded with a dull boom into the hall from a dark space to the left, and it raced up the stairs which were thereby illuminated, a tall midnight-blue-cloaked figure running behind it. Gaston hissed with recognition and sprinted, following. The other was ahead, ahead by a length of stone, by a few turns. The soldiers fell behind, taken by surprise and unable to keep up. The Marshal raced up the stairs, afraid he had seen clearly what he saw by the fireball's light.

With a banging, smashing sound, a draft of cold air flooded the stairway, fresh air from outside tainted with smoke. Prince Gaston took half a flight at a step in his rush to the last landing.

A door was no longer there. Burning splinters of wood were sprinkled around the guardroom which occupied the top of this ponderous square tower of the antique castle. There was another door open on the other side of the room, which led outside to the walk around the top. The wind wailed and mourned wordlessly through the opening.

He went out slowly, sword in hand. The wind had its shoulder to the tower and was pushing him too, but Prince Gaston paid it no heed; he put his head beside the wall and frowned, listening. Straightening, he stalked to the corner, listened again, and then sprang around it, sword ready. Nothing there, not even the wind; this side was screened by the stone tower. He repeated the stalk and spring. Nothing—no, a cry, from around the next corner, and blood on the stone here. The Fireduke took one breath and this time went slowly around the corner.

The wind which had ignored him on the one side and shoved him on the two others slammed into him here on the fourth, pressing him against the wall with its force. Gaston found breathing difficult in its powerful sucking drag and turned his head slightly, keeping an eye on the other two men on the tower.

They were fighting, not speaking, and Golias's face was to Gaston.

"Look behind you!" he cried to his opponent mockingly. "Death himself has come for you, Your Royal Highness!"

The man in the blue-black cloak gestured with his free hand, the one which did not hold the long slender pretty dark-red blade, and moved it as if to throw, and the wind gathered and punched Golias. He staggered.

Prospero, thought Gaston, and did but watch, crouching slightly.

Prospero growled something, forcing Golias into the corner with the aid of that blow from the wind, and Golias sneered.

"Where is she?" shouted Prospero.

"Dead," Golias said, and laughed, and he kicked out at Prospero, feinted, and threw a dagger with his left hand at Prospero's right eye. Prospero parried with the grace and economy Gaston had always loved to watch.

The dagger clattered into the wall and fell.

Golias used Prospero's evasion to evade Prospero and twisted and stepped—as quickly as the knife flew—to one side, along the crenelated wall, and he was no longer trapped.

But now Prospero's wind buffeted him to and fro as Prospero fought with him, making him slip and sending his blows awry, and Gaston watched, holding his breath, as Prospero started what Gaston could feel was a leadup to a killing strike.

Golias could feel it too, and he jumped back suddenly and threw his blade like a spear at Prospero, who beat it aside as he lunged forward. It spun out, over the wall, seized by the wind to tumble end-over-end away and down, brightly flashing in the thin sunlight.

Again Golias's quick heels saved him.

Gaston leapt forward to follow them around the corner in time to see the door dragged shut behind Golias and to see Prospero lose his grip on its edge and slam his fist into the door. Incipient death can give a man great strength against all the Elements, else Golias could never have closed it in Prospero's very face.

"Prospero!" cried Gaston, starting forward.

Prospero swung and glared once, a brilliant wild look, at Gaston and then stepped back. He swept his hand down, then up, clenching it, and a great blast of wind flattened the Fireduke against the wall as the door blew inward. Prospero ran in. Gaston was nearly suffocated in the screaming, howling wind that pinned him, and he tore himself free of it step by step, dragging himself along the stone, scraping his cheek bloody.

The room he entered, minutes after Prospero, was empty and quiet. As Gaston came to the door, the wind ceased as unnaturally as it had started. The splintered bar for the door lay in two pieces on the floor.

He looked slowly around, turning on his heel, and saw it: the remains of a table, blasted, fires flickering around it now and going out. Someone had left through a Way.

"Prospero," said Gaston, and sheathed his sword.

He went down the stairs then, briskly, back to the business of subduing the more mundane forces left behind and of securing the object of the battle, now a piece of its jetsam.

# — 33 —

THE DUKE OF WINDS SAT FEEDING sticks to a feeble fire in a sheltered desert canyon. Wind tossed the stunted, contorted trees on the canyon's rim, but never reached him; the resinous little smoke-trail of the fire rose without smarting his eyes. On the other side of the flames, Hurricane filled out his supper of oats with mouthfuls of grass, methodically reaped and chewed.

"All's not lost," the sorcerer-Prince said to the fire, or to Hurricane. " 'Tis no defeat: I live."

The horse looked, chewing still, at his master.

"I live. I have the Spring. I have still men, some five and a half thousand," the sorcerer said softly. "Aye, and time spins quickly from the Spring. That handful of thousands may be tripled or better in a score of years; I'll shape more—they'll make more themselves—'tis but a work for time, that, a natural work."

Hurricane took more grass, almost apologetically, and his gut rumbled loudly.

The sorcerer dropped a handful of twigs in the flames.

"I must—" he began, and halted himself. "Damned smoke," he murmured then, and rubbed his eyes. "I must recover her body. Aye. Now what Gaston did there I care not; Golias in mutiny, no doubt. He'll know naught of her; she'll be another corpse—boy-clad amongst the men, poor fool. Will he fire them all? I' this season . . . fuel's not lacking thereabouts . . . 'tis hard to know. I'd best go quickly, seek her blood with mine: and my curse upon her murderer, his life shall pay for hers." He growled the words to the flames, and they danced up, a greater Fire manifest, and fell back again. "I'll send Ariel again," he concluded. "Then homeward wend: entomb her in mine earth-womb cave; 'tis time I better housed my books, and there was she made, so there let her sleep."

Hurricane walked into the darkness. The gurgles of his drinking at the stream came to his master's ears.

The Prince poured wine from a skin into a battered wooden cup and drank it quickly. He had finished the whisky already. There hadn't been enough.

"And then the boy," he said to the fire thoughtfully. "The boy, and Odile."

He rested his head against the stone behind him and refilled the wine-cup.

" 'Tis a sorry setback," he decided then, "but the boy,

aye, and Odile: with them to my aid, or even one, there'd be no question. I was o'ertasked, sorcerer and commander-general. They're both inclined to aid me, and she can be warmed to him again; she's a woman and a mother, her heart cannot be so hard against her own." He drank, sipping, his eyes thoughtful now and cool. " 'Tis mine by right," he said. "I've lost the field, but naught else do they hold but a brief victory. Avril, thou thief of thrones, why, thou knowest not even whence I came. Hast no clew to guide thee, no line to bind me. 'Tis more than marriage to Madana nor Palace politicking maketh a ruler o' the Well." He chuckled softly. "This Dewar's the nearest thing thou hadst, and wouldst not covenant with him—mine own blood against me, most potent indeed. Time have I, time's mine ally: in time the King's Bounds weaken; in time I'll bring young Dewar to my side; in time, Avril, thy dumb-show monarchy shall lose all support, insupportable. Landuc is mine by right, and shall be mine by deed, in time."

# — 34 —

PRINCE PROSPERO LAY NUMB-HEADED AND sour-stomached beside the ashes of the night's fire, his eyes closed. All night he had dreamt of his daughter, pursuing her through Landuc's streets, through the Tombs, from room to room of the Palace. He was ill and ill-rested, and the prospect of that day's work made him feel still more ill. He must hurry, though, back to Chasoulis, before her corpse was fired. He must haste to the funeral.

Suppose Gaston were still there, as was most likely. Prospero sat up slowly, swilled his mouth with water and spat into the ashes. Well enough. He could negotiate with Gaston, who was an honorable man above all. Gaston would not make difficulties about the girl's body going home, poor foolish maid, to have ended so after such a little life.

Prospero hefted the wineskin and found it empty. He took another mouthful of water, swallowed, and stood (leaning against the rock), then further wetted the ashes. Hurricane was at the stream, eating the local cress.

"Leave that lest it colic thee! I'll not physick thee for't, I'll leave thee in the knacker's yard, thou cur's-meat. Come!" and Prospero split his own ears with a whistle.

Horse fed, brushed hastily, and saddled, Prospero turned back to Landuc, Ley to Road to Ley, until the Rendlac hurried along beside the road to Chasoulis, reaching it at midday.

The fortress was still occupied, and a pall of pyre-smelling smoke lay along the river. Prospero and Hurricane halted in a grove of trees and Prospero concealed them, air and light curved round to guide eyes away. Riding on, down a slope to the road, the smoke and its unmistakable stink grew thicker. Patrols in Imperial uniform rode past Prospero; he kept to the shoulder and they saw nothing of him.

Following the rising road, leaving the trees, Prospero saw that the open area around and below Chasoulis was still covered with the Imperial Army's encampment. The Landuc standard flew over the fortress, and Gaston's, and three piles of logs laden with the dead blazed below the castle walls, beside the river.

"Too late, too late," Prospero whispered to Hurricane, and guided him away from the camp, to an empty, trampled area. There he sat and watched the flames and smoke and cursed himself, his haste and his slowness. He should not have fled the keep. He should have held his ground the previous day, faced Gaston, demanded her body. Gaston might have tried to take him prisoner again, but might not, too. He knew Gaston well enough, he thought, to escape a free man with his daughter's corpse.

"Poor fool, my poor pretty fool." Prospero lowered his head and closed his eyes. All his plans for her, her fetching silly ways, her sweetness, her quiet happiness—annihilated by false Golias. He should kill Golias; he would, but he must return to Argylle now. There was no present leisure for a vendetta. Later he would have time, and he would take time; a slow death for Golias. Yes.

Prospero turned Hurricane from Chasoulis and set off homeward.

The Tower of Thorns was caked with wet white snow along one side. The snow had changed to rain, and the rain was washing the snow down the wall in sheets and sodden lumps. From time to time, within his cozy study, the sorcerer would see a heavy mess of snow pelt past a window while the rain rattled the panes on the other side of the round room. He sprawled in, or across, an armchair today, a proto-Map unrolled on his knees while he paged through sheets of equations and checked the Map against them.

There seemed to be an error in his measurements again. A once-strong streak of the Third Force arced in toward Landuc, beginning from far out in the Eddies. But the streak had grown steadily weaker with each subsequent regular measurement, and now it seemed to have moved and grown somewhat stronger again. There must be a mistake, but he was loth to think he had been so ridiculously inaccurate either in all the previous measurements or in the three he had made today and yesterday.

The rain and snow were punctuated by the low sound of Dewar grinding his teeth from time to time.

The afternoon wore on. The conclusion was inescapable: he'd erred. Either he had missed that second arc in the earlier measurements, or he hadn't put the earlier ones in the right place and there was only one.

"Damn!"

Dewar shoved his papers onto the floor and stomped off to have a glass of wine.

The incapability of the Emperor to maintain the Roads and Gates of Landuc meant that Prospero could not leave the place from the Gate he'd intended to use. Instead he must ride a day out of his way, find a Gate that would lead him onto the Road in entirely the wrong direction, travel another two days along three Leys, and then cut cross-country through a burned-out Eddy to another Gate to put him on his proper Road home. It was a prodigious, malicious waste of time. He cursed Avril with each fresh detour and cursed him afresh when he arrived at his Gate an hour past sunset, doomed thereby to loiter in the blasted Eddy for a day.

Foul-tempered, Prospero led Hurricane away from the Gate to a sheltered area of tipped rocks and piled boulders. The place was arid; he had seen no water at all here, and Prospero had rationed what he carried for himself and Hurricane. The Well being sparse here also, Hurricane was growing weary and dispirited. Prospero called up a greenish ignis and by its light consulted his Ephemeris and Map.

"Water tomorrow," he told the horse.

Hurricane nodded and looked mournfully at his master over his feed-bag.

" 'Twill be good to be home," Prospero said. "A futile journey, this." He put the Map and Ephemeris away slowly. At home, there would be explanations, mourning. Then they must get on with life. Perhaps he would give that wench Dazhur an hour or three to cheer himself up. Freia hadn't liked Dazhur, he recalled. She'd said her friend Cledie was prettier. Had Freia not been a woman grown, Prospero might have suspected his daughter of inventing Cledie, whom Freia accounted perfect in all things. He'd never seen her; she kept to the forests, running wild with the people and half-people there.

A breeze whirled down and around Prospero.

"Ariel. I bade thee go—"

"Master, Master, I've found her!" Ariel became a shower of sand. "I found the Lady!"

"So have I; she lieth in Chasoulis's charnel-yard, mingled with her native Element. Dost mind my command ever so poorly?"

"Master, nay, she lives! She lives, Master! They have her yet, Master, I saw her sleeping."

Prospero, disbelieving, sat statuesque and frozen, then shook his head. "They keep her carcase unfired?"

"Nay, Master, no corpse she! I did see them take her up gently, and bear her from there, and I felt her breathing lightly."

"And was this my command to thee?" Prospero demanded, suddenly enraged. Again he had been deceived, and he would open Golias's guts and see what rotted offal the man carried there.

"Nay, Master," admitted Ariel. The sand fell to the ground; the breeze became but a zephyr. " 'Twas on my way to do your bidding, Master, that I did see the Lady—you said she was dead—I thought you must wish to know otherwise—I sought you there, and found you not. Master. I go as you bade me."

The zephyr blew off westward. Hurricane turned his head and watched the wind go.

Prospero sat, staring at a point some great distance before him.

"Ariel!" he bellowed, Summoning with the word.

Some minutes passed, and "Yes, Master," whispered the Sylph amongst the rocks.

" 'Twas well done of thee to find the Lady and tell me of't. Well done."

"Master," replied Ariel, more strongly.

"Now do thou tell me: in whose company was she? What men had charge of her?"

"One in whom the Well burns strong stood over her, Master. She did not move nor wake, and she was not whole."

Golias did not have her captive, then. "Injured?"

"So thought I, Master; meseemed there was a gap in her, like the gaps in those dead in battle."

"And unconscious. She breathed, but did not wake."

"Yes, Master."

Prospero considered. He might use Ariel to locate Freia, but he had set the Sylph a weather-task and it could not be much longer delayed. He could find her himself with a little trouble and some sorcery, if she were simply held without Golias's sweet friend meddling Neyphile involved. "Good Ariel, do thou whisk along now to thy work, and take with thee my thanks for good tidings. Dost serve me well."

"Yes, Master!" The Sylph whistled with the words, cheery again, and bustled away, stirring dust-devils.

"By my Road-weary soul, Hurricane," said Prospero after a moment, "it shall not be as simple as Home again, home again, after all." Why could not Ariel have told him this news at Chasoulis? Now he must backtrack tediously into Landuc, and if Freia were hurt—though she would have had time to mend—he must travel away again more slowly than he wished. 'Twas all a mortal waste of time.

Hurricane snorted into his oats.

Prospero took out his loose-rolled Map and Ephemeris and began calculating the shortest path back to the neighborhood of Chasoulis in Landuc.

Dewar threw his hands up and cried, "I concede!"

A fresh spray of the Third Force, fine but there, rippled through Pheyarcet, and what he had taken for a rogue single-point reading had become a fixed feature among all the scattered transient lines.

The sorcerer paced up and down next to his table, glaring at the clocks hard enough to stop them, then whirled on the table and, furious, measured again.

The point; the new line.

"All right, all right, all right," he muttered, shaking with anger. "I'm not that stupid. I am going to travel to Landuc and I am going to nail this down. No bloody wars, no screwing around, no distractions. I am going to locate it and put my hands on it and study it until I know what it is and why it's doing this. And then I shall know what cursed kind of system this is, anyway, that bounces around and never settles. By Fire and Stone, by the very Spheres, I shall."

He swept the papers into a pile, swept the pile into a folio, and knotted it shut with an air of determined finality.

After breakfast the next morning, he packed a leather bag with things he had found useful on previous investigative journeys. He brought mineral samples in a flat compartmented wooden case, feathers rolled up in silk and tied with a wisp of the same, assorted dice of different sizes and probabilities, five bells in the tones of the pentatonic scale, a compass whose bezel was blank, a package of dried apricots, four pencils, a set of sorcerous lenses and gold lens-holders in an ivory case lined with velvet, a cloisonné enamelled traveller's pen-and-ink case he had bought twenty years ago in Landuc and loved dearly, one new blank notebook and his current working notebook, a collection of scraps of hides and skins, a dozen usually-useful dried herbs in glass bottles rolled up in a special leather many-pouched carrier, one large ball of string and one small, a penknife and the whetstone he had had of Herne, a lump of something aromatic like wax or ambergris which he hadn't yet identified, three clean handkerchiefs, a little bag of gold and silver money of various denominations and cultures, a level as long as his middle finger, a ring of assorted keys and some nails, a lump of chalk which left white marks on everything else as it worked its way to the bottom, empty phials with corks and wax for containing things, a slender book of sonnets, a dog-eared treatise on classification of plants which he was rereading, his Third-Force notes and the latest problematic diagrams, and a water-bottle filled at the brook that gurgled past his tower down to the far-off sunlit sea.

In another bag he put a clean shirt, two pair of clean socks, a dark hat and a muffler, and a pair of plain gloves. On top of these he put his Map and Ephemeris. He could have made shift with a cloak and a sword, but the other things had often come in handy in the past and it was less trouble to carry them than to want them.

And then, taking up his staff, he opened a Way to a certain spot in Landuc which he had chosen for its simultaneous, fortuitous, isolation and convenience, and he set off on the trail of the Third Force once again.

"Where is my daughter," Prince Prospero said, in a dry, distant voice, to Ottaviano, Baron of Ascolet.

Otto kept his eyes straight ahead. He spoke moving his mouth and jaw as little as possible. Prospero had his very sharp sword resting against Otto's throat, and he had pricked two neat ruby-beaded lines from side to side, guides for cutting. The blade of the sword was blotched as though blackened by fire: stained, Otto knew, by the late King's blood.

The stillness of the nightstruck forest around them was so deep Otto could hear his pulse echo from the trees around. He thought the cold rough-barked trunk at his back must be throbbing to his heartbeat.

"Gaston has her," he whispered.

"Gaston. Where?" Prospero let his voice reveal none of his emotion. Ariel had seen her indeed. She lived: Golias had lied. She lived: he dared not leave her in their hands.

"Couldn't guess. Landuc best. Probably still has Neyphile's spells on her."

"Thou think'st Gaston hath her in Landuc."

"Yes," sighed Otto almost noiselessly.

The sword moved fractionally to Prospero's left. The chill of the tip returned to Otto's windpipe.

"Thou hadst her prisoner," Prospero said, guessing.

"Hostage," whispered Otto. "To bargain."

"For the Emperor," spat the Prince of Air.

"Against the Emperor."

"Thou didst seek to use her to thy advantage with Avril, who'd then use her 'gainst me."

"For Ascolet."

"Ascolet?"

"Barony now. Want it a Kingdom. As it was."

A boy's own fancy! "Fool. Wouldst hold it an hour. Till Gaston or Herne lopped thy lofty head."

"Not with Lys."

"Lys?"

"My wife."

"How sweet. A love-match, I'm sure. So thou, Neyphile's former apprentice, journeyman troublemaker, claimest Ascolet."

"Sebastiano was my father."

The Prince laughed unpleasantly. "Cecilie was thy mother, at least," Prospero said. "No man can be sure of more than that. Didst prison my daughter and tell Avril she would be his as ransom for the Kingdom of Untrammelled Ascolet."

"Yes."

"And didst think thou wouldst live after."

Otto said nothing.

"Fool."

"I tried to get her away," he whispered. "Golias took her from Perendlac. He and Neyphile did. To Chasoulis. Tried to get her from there."

"Am I to believe thee?"

"Ask her."

"So shall I, when I find her, be assured. And what moved thee to do thus? Greed again? Folly on folly? Love of treason? Meseems thou hast a taste for't."

"Wanted to get her back to you. Away from Golias."

"What didst think to gain from me for the restoration of mine own flesh and blood's freedom, first stolen by thyself?"

Otto licked his lips.

"Tell me," Prospero suggested.

The sword moved a fraction more. A red bead welled up under its tip.

"Favor," Otto whispered drily.

"Favor? From me? Such flattery! What sort?"

"Indeterminate. Later."

Prospero moved the sword again. "Having kidnapped my daughter, thou didst hope to win some favor from me in return by returning her. Belike I be not the most diligent of fathers, Ottaviano of Ascolet, but I am a passionate one. My daughter's welfare is of perfervid import to me. I assure thee I'd have no favor for thee but a curse, and that hast thou assiduously earned."

Otto remained still. He had little choice. He was tightly tied to a tree.

"Now," Prospero said, "hast given me great heartache and balmed it little with the tidings that my daughter languishes still in Landuc somewhere. I shall find her anon. I shall reward thee for thy help when I do."

The sword was wiped on Otto's shoulders, a parody of knighthood, then flashed back and away. Otto did not allow himself to relax.

"Farewell, fool," said Prospero.

His black, silent horse stepped up to him. He sheathed the

stained sword and mounted in a swirl of deep blue silk-and-wool. A gust of wind followed his passing.

The girl would not talk.

Prince Gaston had questions for her, but he deemed it wiser to respect her silence than to break it forcibly, and while she was conveyed to the Palace of Landuc in soft-bedded litters and carriages he took no offense at her dumbness. Distrustful, he kept Golias far from her after the former's gracelessly-tendered swordpoint surrender. The Emperor, counselled by Prince Herne and Count Pallgrave, directed him to accept the surrender and Golias's lame excuses and repentance, and the Marshal did so without confidence in Golias's good faith—so little that he removed him from command and paid off and discharged his mercenaries. Herne hired most of them, replacing men dead in Prospero's war.

The Fireduke took charge of the girl, nursemaiding her, bringing her meals, talking to her quietly. He bathed her after she was first carried, insensible, from Chasoulis, and held her immobile while his chief army surgeon Gernan treated her. Gernan took the tiniest possible stitches to close the deep wound in her breast, saying that men's scars were maids' mars. The catalogue of her injuries was long. Gaston the man shuddered over it; Gaston the Prince Marshal observed it as evidence of what Baron Ottaviano and Prince Golias were capable of; and Gaston the Fireduke knew that such insults would not go unanswered.

When she had been installed in heavily guarded and Bounded rooms in Landuc, the Emperor had many questions for the prisoner. She ignored him, at first lying in bed, then sitting up, then in a chair, staring at her hands, or at nothing, or turning her head away with eyes closed.

Gaston slept in a room adjoining hers, broke fast with her, looked in on her during the day, bade her good-night each evening. When she moaned and cried out wordlessly with night terrors, waking him, he carried light to her, soothed her with soft-spoken reassurances, and sat beside the bed until she slept again. With his own hands he collected and poached eggs to strengthen her starved weakness, and he prepared and fed her bread in warm creamy milk, caudles, possets, and broths. As she improved, he brought her stronger fare—pigeons from the Empress's dovecote braised in wine, hothouse grapes, baked apples with cream, and capons cooked in bouillon. Her food disagreed with her as often as not, and she would be sick not long after eating; Gaston would empty the basin and fetch her another meal.

On successive consultative visits, Doctor Hem, whom the Empress had sent as a courtesy, recommended mud-plasters, then frog's-leg soup, then bleeding and purges, and finally a decoction of snails, until Gaston forbade him to darken the doorway again. The Bounds laid by Oriana, a favor she had offered gratis to the Emperor as, she had indicated, payment to Prospero for some trespass, permitted entry to Prince Gaston and the Emperor and no other, and they prevented the girl from leaving the room, yet Gaston still had misgivings about her safety—hence his dedication to her comfort and his attendance on her person. Daily the Fireduke thought of Prospero, ripping apart Chasoulis to find her—where was he now? Why had he made his Way and left? Did he think her dead, or did he abandon her?

It was unclear who had stabbed her, an injury clearly intended to be fatal. Prince Gaston questioned Golias, who denied it, and Ottaviano, who denied it red-faced, and since no witness came forward and the sorceress Neyphile had fled the place, the deed was laid to Neyphile's hand by the Emperor, who did not deeply concern himself over the matter. The Baron of Ascolet had a confused story of seeking the girl in the dungeons and seeing Neyphile leaving through a Way, and they had found the place as he described it; Golias had been here, there, everywhere in the place; and the girl herself made no accusation. Yet Prince Gaston could not help but form an opinion: he had seen Ottaviano close by her; the boy had behaved guiltily when queried; he would gain from her assured silence.

She had as much to say to Gaston as to the Emperor. It struck him as remarkable that no one knew her name. She would not tell it. Not a word had passed her lips since she had asked him to kill her, and Ottaviano had admitted she would say nothing to him when he'd questioned her in Perendlac. Gaston admired her stoicism: she would not weep, no more than she would speak; no tears slid down her pale cheeks when he cleaned and bandaged her wounds, when he sat with her at night, when the Emperor berated her. The Fireduke understood her need for self-command and defended it against the Emperor's displeasure.

"Sullen brat. She ought to be whipped or starved," the Emperor growled, glaring at the girl after an interview with silence.

"So hath she been," Gaston said, "by Golias," and he looked at the Emperor coldly.

"Prince Gaston, we find you are tending to thwart our wishes," the Emperor said softly.

"Avril," said Gaston, "our niece is weakened and ill. Would you be a greater Golias, a jackal that savages the helpless, or be a king? For myself, I am a Prince, and thus I comport myself; and my niece is a Prince's daughter, and thus shall she be hosted."

The Emperor whitened, furious at the disrespect in the presence of an intransigent chit. But he left at once, and Gaston heard no more of the idea.

That evening, before bidding her good-night in the tapestried chamber with its crimson-curtained bed and black-barred windows, Gaston knelt by her chair. He had just mended the fire and pale young flames shimmered in the mouth of the sooted red-tiled fireplace.

"Child," he said, "an thou have need of aught, mayst ask me for't."

She did not look at him.

"An there be questions thou wouldst have answered, put them to me . . ."

Her eyes were on the fire.

". . . in confidence," Gaston finished softly. "I'll answer what I can."

She said nothing, arms folded tightly.

"If not now, then later. When thou wilt." He looked at

her—purple-yellow-green shadows still lay on her skin, bruises fading—and said, "Hast suffered sore, and I swear to thee, lass, an it lie in my power to turn harm from thee, thou shalt take no more hurt from any man. Th'art under my protection, and that shall I cause to be known."

Her lower lip moved; she bit it, but her expression did not change and she did not speak.

"Good night, then. Rest thee well."

The whole business, he thought, closing and locking her door, was enough to make a man gag on his own breath. Prospero would find some way to make Avril pay Hell for it. And Otto and Golias? Death for them, at best.

Dewar, hard on the Third Force's trail in western Ascolet, looked at the deepening blue of the heavens and wondered where he could stop for the night. He had no map of the area, but any fool knew that inns were few and far between in the bush—through which he had been riding on a weak Ley on which path the Third Force appeared to travel in an overlay—and more common on the Emperor's highways. He had crossed such a highway at midday.

His dilemma was complicated slightly by the knowledge that if he was seen in an inn and recognized by one of Ottaviano's people, there would more than likely be an incident of the sort both a sorcerer and a gentleman of quiet habits would prefer to avoid. Dewar's horse, who had been drinking at a stream while his master thought about beds and mulled wine, blew and shook his head, jingling harness.

The area was not uninhabited. If he continued along this Ley by the stars' light, he was likely to come on another road, or a cot and a barn, or something more sheltered than the frozen earth and dry snow.

He nudged the horse and they climbed a ridge slantwise, dark trunks and the pallid snow monochromatic around them. At the ridgetop, the Ley ran on, and two streams seized by ice lay to either side below; Dewar could sense them without seeing. The horse went more quickly, but cautiously on account of the dark. Dewar pulled him up and took out his staff, and a few minutes later they had the company of an indignant little ignis bound to the end of it.

". . . ay . . ." came a bleating sound from the dark gully below the ridge.

Dewar's horse pricked his ears and looked toward it.

"Some dumb sheep," Dewar said. "I'm sick of mutton. Gee."

The horse began walking forward. Between his steps, the sound rose again, louder.

"Hey!"

Dewar frowned.

"Hey! Help!" shouted the man's voice, weak but carrying.

"Oh, hell," Dewar said.

The horse waited again, uncertain.

"I suppose it would be bad luck to leave him there," Dewar said. "He'd curse us or something. Though they're pretty ignorant of that hereabouts. Come on, Cinders. Humph, and he can give us hospitality for the night in return. Yes." He raised his voice. "Hey yourself!"

"Help! I . . ." the voice faded.

"You hurt?"

"Can't . . . move," the voice replied.

It was a rustic who'd fallen and hurt himself, Dewar supposed, probably chasing a dumb sheep. He turned the horse and began descending the ridge aslant as before, listening. At the bottom, he called, "So where are you?"

"Here . . . here . . . near the brook . . ."

He was east of Dewar. Cinders had harder going here; it was stonier and icier than the other side. Dewar dismounted and they proceeded carefully, by ignis-light, together.

"That's not a—" began the voice, much nearer, and Dewar recognized it as the light showed him Ottaviano, Baron of Ascolet, tied to a tree. A trio of huge black birds, screaming disappointment in rasping voices, flapped up into the branches above the stubble-bearded Baron and sneered down at him. There were large-pawed, long-clawed footprints in a circle around the tree, close to Otto.

"Well, well," Dewar said, and stopped.

A bow and a quiver of arrows hung from another tree.

"The deer fighting back nowadays?" Dewar asked.

"Dewar. For love of life, untie me. I've been here two days. I'm frozen. And I'm perishing of thirst." Hoarse and white-faced, Otto still looked healthier than he ought. Dewar suspected he had drawn on the Well to preserve himself.

"Why?"

"Why?" repeated Otto. "It snowed yesterday, I can't feel my hands—"

"Why should I untie you—hm. Interesting tattoo you've got." Otto's throat and collar were stained with blood. Dewar leaned closer, looking at the marks, holding the light near so that the tree-limbs' writhing fretwork above was illuminated from below. The birds sat just beyond the sphere of light, watching, striking their bills on the ringing wood.

"I'll tell you, but untie me! What have I done to you?"

"Shall I make a list?"

"Dewar! Please!" Otto whispered. "Please. Oaths, rewards in my power to give, deeds—name it—it's yours—"

Dewar studied him by the light of the ignis. "I imagine being bound to a tree in a wilderness for a couple of days gives a man a degree of perspective on life," he said.

"It does." Otto's lips were cracked and parched. The brook gurgled under thin ice like white porcelain two paces from him. Apparently his sorcery didn't extend that far.

"What have you concluded, then, from your new contemplative and detached—sorry—viewpoint?"

"Life is better than the alternative."

"You thought differently before?"

"Dewar—" he moaned.

Dewar shrugged and half-turned to go.

"Don't go!" rasped Otto. "No! I thought no differently."

"So it has confirmed you in views and habits you already had."

Otto stared at him.

"I think I'll leave you there, then, Otto, because your views on life seem to involve parting me from mine. I cannot support you in that." Dewar smiled, bowed, and turned to go again.

"No! No! I'll swear—Dewar, no!"

"What would you swear, Otto? And would it be worth the breath you blow past your teeth to say it?" Dewar folded his arms, his staff in the crook of his elbow.

"Nonaggression—I won't attack you again, that was stupid and—and I won't—won't—"

"You'll not interfere with me, either."

"I won't interfere. Whatever that means."

"You'll not speak of me to anyone else, on pain of suffocation in your next breath."

"I won't squeal, lest the air leave me."

Dewar drummed his fingers on his forearm. "You'll not—let's see. Oh, I don't know, that seems to address all the major annoyances. You won't plot against my life, nor collude with anyone else—"

"No! I won't! I swear it!"

"And you'll buy me a bed and whatever passes for a decent meal in this wasteland tonight."

"It's a bargain."

"Very well," Dewar said, and drew his sword to cut the ropes. "This is sorcerer's work," he observed, meeting opposition stronger than hemp. "Who put you here?"

It was the custom for Emperor Avril to take breakfast with his Privy Council each morning. Little was actually eaten, so little that most of the members broke their fast beforehand or after and tasted only token samples at the Emperor's table. The meetings were held in a long, many-windowed room, which was furnished with a table, sideboards, chafing-dishes, and a dumbwaiter to the kitchen. It would have been pleasant room for breakfast had the Emperor not been using it for Privy Council meetings, as it looked out on a long vista at the end of which a little white summerhouse and a corner of one of the ponds could just be seen.

The day after Gaston spoke to the hostage, the Emperor

entered at his usual time and paused. In his place, reading the agenda and deliberately making a mess of crumbs and butter on it, sat his brother Prince Prospero. His high black riding-boots were propped on a brocade-seated chair; his cloak dripped melting snow on the figured carpet; and he had opened a window, so that the room was uncommonly drafty.

"Well, well," the Emperor said softly.

"Well, in sooth," Prospero replied. "Why hast thou got my strayed-lamb daughter?" He crumpled the agenda disdainfully, a single crushing gesture, and tossed it to one side; it landed in the fire. The sorcerer stood and dusted crumbs from his fingers daintily.

"Daughter," the Emperor said. "Our family is a strange one, isn't it. That would be our niece of whom you speak."

"I know Ottaviano had her; I know Golias took her; and I know Gaston, thy trained duck-dog, fetched her hither. I even know well-nigh where she is."

"Then spirit her away, sorcerer."

"Someone hath been busy there," Prospero said.

The Emperor smiled.

"Oriana," Prospero said, "of her vanity, cannot resist a certain visiting-card mark on all her handiwork. Using blood in the binding was mortally clever of her."

"She thought so. There was no lack of it to use."

Prospero whitened. "What did she charge thee?"

"She was delighted to oblige us gratis, having been crossed by you in some matter quite recently. —So you'd like to see our little treasure, would you?"

Prospero left the crumb-littered high seat and was in front of the Emperor in three rapid steps. A cold wind came with him and settled around the Emperor as Prospero grabbed his lacy shirt-front.

As Prospero's hand closed on the fabric, the Emperor kicked the door to his left, shouting, "Guards!"

Three entered, weapons drawn; something touched the small of Prospero's back. He was not unprotected, but he was in the enemy's camp, and the enemy had something he wanted.

"Would you prefer to see her dead," the Emperor asked somewhat breathlessly, "or alive?"

Prospero put his brother down slowly. The Emperor straightened his garments and the guards held ready in a long, exquisite moment of tension. The Emperor smiled.

"Accompany Prince Prospero to Prince Gaston, with our compliments. He desires to view his daughter."

"Papa!" screamed the girl, and hurled herself against the doorway, which flashed and repulsed her.

Prospero cursed a blue streak, commending Oriana to the attention of a number of ills. Gaston, who was in the room with her, helped his prisoner up. She was wild-eyed, the first emotion beyond immobilizing fear he had seen in her.

"Prospero . . ." she quavered.

"Touch't not!" Prospero ordered her, waving her back from Oriana's Bounds.

"Where've you been?" the girl wailed in accented Lannach, shrugging Gaston away and coming as close as she could to Prospero without hitting the Bounds.

"Seeking thee—"

"I looked for you! I looked and looked! I looked everywhere—"

Prospero looked grey, ill. "Puss, Puss, calm thee, calm thee. Shshsh. Now I'm here, thou'rt found."

His daughter nodded, holding the doorjamb. "Can I go home?" she whispered.

"Not yet. I—I must know—" Prospero stopped and went on, "what the price of thy going shall be."

She was perfectly still.

"Art well, Freia?" Prospero said, his voice shaking.

Gaston marked it: she had a name.

"No. I want to go home."

"Not yet," Prospero said. "Soon."

"Papa, I was good. I didn't tell them anything. I didn't tell anyone. Anything. Papa. Please, I want to go home," Freia said, her voice rising.

"I know. I know. I must contrive it, Freia. I wished first to see that all's right with thee."

"I'm not all right! I want to go home!" She punched the Bounds, leaving her fist there in the painful flare until Gaston grabbed her away.

The Fireduke held her arms, not meeting his brother's eyes. "Don't hurt thyself, child." He had never seen Prospero show such concern and pain before; it startled him.

"Let me go! I want to go home!" she shrieked at him.

"Freia!" yelled Prospero. "Command thyself!"

"Papa! I want to go home, Papa!" Freia squirmed free of Gaston again and hugged the doorjamb. "Please," she said in a tiny voice. "Oh, please . . ."

"Puss, thou'rt hostage. They'll ask much for thee. I must treat with the Emperor. Dost understand?" Prospero said to her.

She nodded.

"They'll not let thee go yet," he said. "Thy Uncle Avril hath little good in him, Freia."

"He—" Freia began, and stopped.

If Freia told her father, Gaston mused, that the Emperor had threatened using force on her, then probably this room by virtue of the Bounds on it would be the only thing left standing of the Palace. He touched her shoulder; she flinched. "Thou'lt go home," he told her, "but not yet, not now." Would Prospero indeed bargain for her, surrender something for her? A wonder: that she could be so precious to him. It could not be so, thought Gaston; Prospero was a sorcerer.

Yet Prospero had given up something precious not long ago. He was not mad; he could not have handicapped himself in the war for no reason. Gaston looked at Prospero with sudden, sharp uncertainty: he was not behaving as expected.

"Thrash not so. Trust me, Puss," Prospero said, his voice rough to cover emotion. "I'll see thee home safe ere long. I did but come to be sure thou'rt well ere I began."

"I'm not well," she said in a keening voice, turning away. "I want to go home. I've got to get home."

"Thou'rt looking hale enow," Prospero said. "Now, Freia—"

"Interview's over," the Emperor announced, arriving at the other side of the door. Behind him, Count Pallgrave and Cremmin waited, holding books and ledgers. "Come, Prospero, we have much to say."

"Avril—"

"We have a little time free now," the Emperor said, "or you can wait two days."

"Father—"

"Freia, patience." Prospero turned from the door and followed the Emperor.

"Papa, *no!* Don't leave me here! *Don't leave me! Don't go!*"

Gaston caught her before she hit the Bounds and held her back, then held her against him. She struggled, trying to kick him.

"Such noise the creature makes," the Emperor's voice floated back.

A door slammed.

Freia moaned and slumped.

"I'm sorry, lass," Gaston told her. "Trust in thy father. He loves thee well, I see't, and he—he'd give much for thy welfare."

# — 35 —

THE BARS OUTSIDE THE WINDOW WERE an obstacle, but not a formidable one.

Dewar tapped. His gloved hands didn't tap well. He used the pommel of a dagger.

The bedding he could see through the gap between the drapes moved seismically, erupted. A rumpled, white-gowned lady blinked owlishly around the room.

Dewar tapped again.

Freia stared at the window and was at it seconds later, yanking the drapes aside, fumbling at the casement. It was locked—in fact, welded; Dewar saw her scowl. He gestured to the hinges. She looked at them, then at the lock, and shook her head, either not understanding or not able to do anything about it. Dewar meant for her to break the hinges; he had no doubt it would be possible, but he couldn't easily mime it to her hanging onto the grating with one hand.

Snow blew against his back. It had been raining earlier. He'd rather have rain.

He held up one finger and pointed to her with a questioning expression.

She nodded, then pointed at the next room to the left, holding a finger of the other hand to her lips.

He nodded. Gaston was there; Dewar's surveying had discovered him already. Dewar plinked the glass again with the dagger: then break it.

Freia went to the bed and got a blanket. She muffled it over the window and drew the drapes again. Dewar lowered himself a few feet on the knotted rope, crouched against the brown-ivied wall, and waited.

Chink—chink—crash! Musically, the glass panes shattered. A shard hit his thick-hooded head and bounced off. Hand over hand, Dewar climbed back up. Freia had just cautiously lowered the blanket, staring anxiously toward Gaston's room. Dewar saw why: a connecting door.

"Why doesn't it flash?" Freia whispered. "The doorway does."

"Bindings are tricky," he whispered back. "The iron grating is Bound, but more weakly than the walls. The wood frame and glass aren't Bound at all. They're not integral, you see. Makes for a weak link. And you didn't cross the Boundary by breaking the glass. I see it's a blood Boundary. Cut your finger on a piece of that glass, Freia, and smear the blood around the window opening in an unbroken line."

She hesitated, distrustful. "Why?"

"If you do that, I'll break the Bounds; or rather breach them."

Freia, flinching, cut her left middle finger on the jagged glass and began drawing the line. Dewar put his hand opposite hers on the outside of the window and drew on the force of her blood, altering the Binding without destroying it. The blood burned through the Boundary, but since the maker had worked Freia's blood into them as well as his or her own, the Emperor's, and Gaston's, the Binding-spell accepted and accommodated the change in forces and direction.

They finished. Dewar's arm was cramped from clutching the grating and rope. He shifted. Inside, Freia pressed her hand to stop the bleeding.

"Are you here for me?" she whispered.

"I thought I'd drop in for supper. What do you think? Get the poker."

"I haven't one."

"Oh. Lest you trepan somebody with it."

"I'd love to," she said, and her voice and her face trembled.

Dewar patted her hand through the grating with two fingers and smiled. "Luckily a burglar, I mean a sorcerer, comes prepared." Indeed, his sorcerous career of late seemed to be half a housebreaker's. He pushed that aside for later consideration.

"How did you get up?"

"Rope. We'll go down same way. Shshsh. Draw the drapes. Pretend to sleep. Just in case." He began breaking and picking more glass from the casement, reaching through the grating.

She obeyed, disappearing behind the folds of heavy cloth. Warm air poured thickly past him into the night. Dewar, one-handed still, rootched in the bag slung at his hip and found the jemmy bar. He began working at the bolts holding the grating.

They were newly set in the red sandstone wall for the occasion, not at all in keeping with the Neo-Ornamented architecture, and not terribly well set either. The mortar crumbled, badly packed, as he worked. He pried bolts off, picked more glass from the casement, and pried again. It seemed to take hours and to make a horrendous noise. No light came on in Gaston's room, though, and no one stirred within. Snow pattered on his shoulders.

Dewar's rope was still fastened to the grating, and he prayed heartily that the bolts he left wouldn't give up. He tugged. The three remaining bolts at the top seemed safe enough. He bent the grating back, clambered over the frame, and stepped through the billowing draperies to the floor. Glass crunched under his boots.

Freia sat up in the dark-hung bed. She looked like hell, haggard and drawn.

"You're a sight for sore eyes," he lied, smiling, and bowed.

"Did my father send you?"

Straightening, he still smiled. "No. Care to go anyway?"

"Yes!"

"Get warm clothes. Damn cold out."

She dressed. Dewar stood by Gaston's door, just in case. Gaston slumbered on. Dewar pitied him in the morning. Out of favor. He'd probably better leave town.

"Get a cloak."

"I don't—"

"Blanket."

She pulled two off the bed and stood by the window, clutching them to her chest. Her whole body was tense, expectant.

Dewar winked at her, decided to say nothing about the grating and the rope and the paved terrace three storeys below, and opened the curtains with a flourish.

"You first."

"I . . ." Freia looked out the window, at the rope disappearing into wet darkness, and quailed. "I can't—I can't. I can't."

Dewar drew in his breath to argue about it and thought better of it. "Very well. I will carry you down."

He pulled on his gloves again to protect his hands from the coarse rope, then climbed over the sill. She put a chair under the window and stood on it, crouched on the sill, and transferred herself gingerly, stiff-bodied, to his care.

"Don't look down," he commanded her in an undertone.

"Trying," she replied.

"Surely a woman who can drop off a cliff on a gryphon can manage this," he muttered.

"I can't do heights," she whispered back, and squeezed her eyes shut. "I can't look."

Dewar, exasperated, abandoned the topic. He had not expected her to be so damsellish. Fiery Lady Miranda wouldn't, he thought, and he said to Freia, "Then don't look."

She nodded.

With one arm hugging Freia's body against him, he descended without haste but without delay. She, trembling distractingly, clutched him around the neck, gripped him with her legs, and kept her eyes closed tightly. Dewar accustomed himself to the extra weight and odd balance, and then he inched them down, drawing on the Well to fortify his arms, bracing his feet on the rough wall. They rustled in the ivy and dislodged globs of slush. Once his boots slipped, and he and she dangled crookedly until he found footing again. Freia was inflexible as iron.

The window-grating gripped its sloppy masonry until they were just above the first storey. Dewar felt it go and dropped, landing solidly on his feet and putting Freia down lightly, even gracefully.

The grating hit the terrace with a thunderous clang a half-step away from them. Dewar swore softly in the shocked silence that followed.

Light blazed up in Gaston's room. Dewar grabbed her hand and, as the curtain opened, they scurried off the terrace. Gaston was shouting above them, and Dewar couldn't resist looking up and waving cockily as they crossed the pale patch of light from his window.

The Marshal stared at him, yelled "Dewar!" and was gone.

"Oh no!" Freia wailed.

"Think I'm stupid? The horse is this way."

"No . . . magic . . ." she puffed beside him.

He thought she meant, Why not leave through a Way? "Bounds in your room prevented it. Good job, who did it?"

"A lady—"

"Neyphile?"

"No!"

"Oriana. Ah well. Here he is. Good fellow, Cinders! Hup I go—hup you come—and away."

Back at the Palace rose alarums and shouts, burned lights in the rain.

Freia began "Guards—"

"Forget them."

The horse pounded into the Palace Gardens, leaving a clear trail for anyone to follow.

"Where—"

"Shh. Trust me."

Freia clutched him hard around the waist, bouncing on the horse's rump behind him. Trust him, she thought. Trust him.

Later she could never remember exactly how they had gotten out of the Palace Gardens, though hanging by the ivied wall in the rain-flecked dark stayed in her nightmares for years. Dewar sent the horse on without them, Cinders galloping away wildly in the freezing rain and digging up the turf so that the guards would follow the animal awhile longer. Beyond that she wasn't sure. She remembered a fire in a temple-like place, and being sodden, wet through, and very cold so that her body ached.

Dewar liked the rain; he lifted his face to it and pushed his hood back. Freia absorbed it, growing heavier and slower, its coldness penetrating her skin and its wetness smothering her.

The night was a kaleidoscope of darkness, water, and uncertainty. The fire was leaping and alive, defiant against the weather, and Dewar crouched by it trying to talk to her.

"Where, Freia?"

"Home," she said, and began to cry, his questions like all the others she could not answer.

"But where? Just a name, Freia! Tell me a name of a place. It would help."

"I c-c-can't," she sobbed, shivering. "Where's P-P-Papa? W-why isn't he h-here?"

He gave it up. "Come along then," he told her, not unkindly, and began talking to the fire. She huddled in a ball of misery out of the rain; her body stiffened, so that when he told her to stand she couldn't. Dewar picked her up and jumped into the fire.

Gaston's bellow of rage was still ringing from the wet walls of the Palace as he ran in his shirt and a half-laced pair of breeches out the terrace door after the fleeing sorcerer and hostage. Guards followed him. He barked orders at them in the wet dark, took a torch from one, and raced on after the two. His fury at the girl's escape—she must have been shamming, shamming weakness and illness—overpowered thinking until his boot came down on a fresh pile of horse manure and he skidded and fell, vainly trying to keep his balance on the wet grass.

Cursing, picking up his failing torch and puffing on it once so that it flared, Gaston started off again, seeing now hoofprints in the thin slush. If he listened, he could hear the horse pounding ahead of him into the groomed and dormant garden. The marks on the lawn were easy to follow. He ran, pursuing the horse through the wild wet night by the streaming torchlight, farther into the garden. Dewar, he thought, must be making for the Emperor's Ride, the forest area beyond the gardens; there were two Gates along the Ride, both guarded, but Dewar's sorcery could foil the guards' opposition.

But the horse wove and wandered, and Gaston chased it back through the gardens and, strangely, toward the Palace again. A feint?

No. He came upon the horse suddenly. He had cantered to a halt and was drinking at a fountain's rain-filled basin; the light made the animal shy, but Gaston clucked and spoke gently and the horse let him take the bridle; ruefully, Gaston stroked his neck.

"Oldest bloody trick in the book," Gaston said to him.

The horse snuffed at Gaston's chest. He was a handsome black-dappled grey; fine, but small compensation for the futile course Gaston had just run. The Fireduke led him to the Palace and met three guards, who were diligently searching, but not sure what for.

"Prince Prospero, sir," one answered promptly.

"Nay! 'Twas the sorcerer Dewar. And the girl. Look for footprints. She's not strong; they cannot be far." Gaston began directing the men. He sent the horse to the stables with one.

An hour later he called off the search. Dogs had led them to the Royal Tombs, to Prospero's own tomb where a fire smoldered outside the pillared portico. A sopping blanket from Freia's bed lay in a corner of the porch; the dogs pawed it eagerly.

"Damn," Gaston said, not loudly.

He returned to the Palace and went to his apartment to repair his clothing, but his valet told him that the Emperor wanted to see him at once, and Gaston went accordingly at once to the private royal quarters. Wet, smeared with grass, dirt, and dung, he was an unwelcome bearer of an unwelcome report.

"Where's the girl?" the Emperor demanded.

"Gone," Gaston said. "It was Dewar. I saw him fleeing. 'Tis clear how 'twas done; he scaled a rope to the window and prised the grating, broke the panes, and went down again with the girl. The grating fell. I heard it and looked out to see them running."

"You heard nothing of his prying and breaking?"

"I slept," Prince Gaston pointed out, "in another room, and the storm was loud, the window shuttered. I heard naught." He looked coldly, levelly at Avril, daring him to fault Gaston's vigilance.

The Emperor considered: should he blame Gaston for this breach, convict him and put him down for good? There were so few weaknesses in Gaston's character and conduct, it might be folly not to use this. The Fireduke served without deference, which bothered his brother. The Emperor did not trust the prevailing wisdom that Panurgus's eldest son cherished no ambitions for the throne. Gaston had made no move toward it when Panurgus died, although he had had wide support and was the obvious first choice; despite his bastardy, Panurgus had always favored him. The Emperor had never gotten more than "It does not suit me" from

Gaston by way of explanation. Yet he served, and served ably, quietly leading the Empire's armies, his support unwavering through the first uncertain decades of the Emperor's rule. Without him Landuc would have splintered in factions, for his support kept Herne and Fulgens far from the throne.

"We suppose it's possible," the Emperor said, gracelessly yielding the point with a glare. "How the hell did he get in without being seen or heard? Where were the guards? And that damned lying Oriana—she said her Bounds couldn't be broken."

"Dewar is a sorcerer," Gaston said.

"There's a guard on that terrace. Are they blind? Dead?"

"True," Gaston said, and frowned. "I did not see the guards there. I'll inquire, or rather ask Herne; the Palace guards, as you know, are his men, and I would not intrude in his domain."

"You chased them, you said—where did they go?"

"I pursued as soon as I saw them, but they were fresh and e'en horsed; they rode some small distance, but dismounted. I saw't not, following the horse's prints at a distance, and followed the horse still. They passed a Way-fire. The dogs trailed them to Prospero's tomb and we found the coals there."

The Emperor hissed an obscenity. "It shall be razed," he snarled.

Gaston shrugged. It would be wise, he thought, to distract the Emperor before he made some dangerous vow of destruction. "She is gone from our hands," he said, "and now 'twere best consider what we'll do next."

"True," the Emperor said. He sat in a high-backed red brocaded chair, but did not offer a seat to Gaston, who leaned on the flame-carved gold-leafed mantelpiece, drying the backs of his shins at the fire. "He'll be back," the Emperor said, "ready to concede for her."

"Do you think so?"

"Do you think not?" the Emperor said. "You saw them."

"Prospero does set his plans with care," the Fireduke said. "He may refuse, plan to rescue her later. We discussed this ere now, and you said 'twas what you expected; I agree still, for 'tis very like his craftiness. We did not meet o'er what the best counter would be." The Emperor had favored executing the hostage. Prince Gaston had opposed it.

"She's his. As long as we have her we have him. He'll be back to get her, in order to get the noose off his neck. Even if it means crippling himself, he'll free her, because she's his heir, she knows a lot about him, and sooner or later she'll be broken and talk." The Emperor smiled, thin-lipped and hard-eyed. "He can't afford to leave her." He stared at the flames a moment. "Of course it's possible that that Fire-blasted loose cannon of Ascolet's was doing it for Prospero. That Prospero hired him."

Gaston frowned. "Why might Prospero hire another to do something within his ability?"

"Maybe he's not as good as we think he is," the Emperor said. "He said he couldn't break the Bounds. Certainly he would have if he could."

The Fireduke was still unconvinced. "How was it done? I have not seen the room."

"Some sorcery; there's blood all over the place. We'll speak with Oriana about this—she swore it was unbreakable. Why would that little rat want the girl? To use her against him? Sorcerers feuding? It's more believable than sorcerers leaguing. Maybe he'll finish Prospero off for us."

" 'Tis dark, whether they be allied or no," Gaston said after considering the reasons. "Prospero and Dewar. They were opponents in our war, and Dewar made sorties against him—"

"And broke faith at the final battle. He was in with him, and still is. Yes. And for some reason Prospero couldn't come himself, sent the other— Shit and sorcerers. We must quadruple the price on his head."

"I knew not he was made outlaw."

"Of course. As soon as he turned coat. We'll make the award such that one of his own will turn him in: Oriana, or that witch Neyphile, or maybe Ascolet, who seems to have an axe to grind with him himself. Yes." The Emperor smiled again. "And for now, Prospero is still defeated. Be thinking, Marshal, of ways to keep him thus."

Prince Gaston, taking this as dismissal, bowed slightly and squelched, flaking dried manure, toward his apartment. The Emperor's fearful hatred of Prospero marred his insight. Gaston thought Dewar might not be in league with Prospero; he might have abducted the girl for a hostage himself. Or for other reasons. Ottaviano had described their arrival and the way she had fought at Perendlac, his tune a mix of admiration and fury at the slaughter she'd accomplished aided by a huge bird. The young sorcerer and the old sorcerer's daughter might know one another well; they might even be allies, friends, lovers. Prospero might strengthen himself by wedding her to another in the Art, binding their fates together. Or maybe they were bound already, by blood—there were only Gaston's guesses for that. Yet he knew Dewar's heart was not yet crystallized in sorcery, as sorcerers' did, as Panurgus's had.

Changing his mind, Gaston turned from his own apartment and went instead to the rooms beside Freia's which he had used while he warded her. The connecting door was closed. He opened it and looked again at the dishevelled chamber. Hastily dressed, bundled in a blanket from the bed, out a broken window (a board over it now to keep the rain out) and down the wall on an insecure rope. Shamming, the Fireduke thought again, and a spark of rage flared.

The spark faded as quickly as it came. No. She could not have been feigning. He had touched the wounds himself, had fed her for the first few days, had seen the weakness and sickness that gripped her body and soul. She hadn't been dissembling illness, no more than she had dissembled when she saw Prospero.

Gaston closed the door quietly. Perhaps it was just as well she was gone, he thought. Her situation could not be worse than it was here. With a tremor of surprise, Gaston recognized that he was more than a little pleased at her escape. He had not liked having the girl prisoner. She ought to have been received into the family, comforted, consoled; she was one of them by blood. Even if she were a prisoner elsewhere, if Dewar had captured her for some purpose of his own, it was in some way better for her to be prisoned by strangers than her own kin.

And, somehow, he was certain that she was no prisoner of Dewar's.

There was thunder outside. Freia, waking to it, pulled the pillow from under her head to over it. She hated thunder.

It rolled on and on, never stopping. She floated into an uneasy dream of storms, of Prospero raging at her for a misbegotten creature of coarse and amoral appetite, and then Prospero's wrath invoked monsters from the heaving earth at her feet and when she fell, they leapt upon her, bouncing on her face and head, thick scaled limbs choking her, mouths gaping foul-breathed in her face, and a tearing of claws in her belly—

"Freia?" woke her.

The pillow was lifted tentatively from her face. The thunder rolled up and down. Strangely, the room was brilliant with light, dazzling her. She was panting, damp with sweat.

"Good morning," Dewar said.

The dream of storm and terror clung to her senses. "Isn't it raining?"

"No, that was in Landuc," he said, amused.

"What's that noise?"

"What noise?" He listened, then laughed. "The sea, Freia. The sea. Come see," he said, and he went to the window and opened the outer casement. The white curtains filled with wind and swelled into the room, bellying around him. The room was white: white walls, white furniture, white bedding. Even the long loose nightshirt she wore was white. "See?" he said, though she didn't get up.

Now the crash of the waves was audible, the hiss of sand, the roll of stone. Salt and moisture seasoned the air. "Oh." The sweat chilled her as it dried in the breeze.

He closed the window, smiling still, and returned to the bed.

"Where's this?" she asked, pulling the coverlet to her chin.

"A place I have for stopping," Dewar said. "Nowhere very travelled. I like the sea."

"I don't," Freia said.

"Why not?"

"It's too big."

Dewar shrugged misdoubtfully. "How are you?"

How was she? Sick—she was sick. Her body was churned and disoriented, unwillingly changing around her. She was afraid. She was alone. The only cure for all must be found in Prospero. "I need to get home," she said.

"I can help you with that. Gladly." Dewar sat on the very edge of the bed, looking intently at her. He wore snug bottle-green trousers and a voluminous blue-green shirt that flowed and fell from his arms and shoulders in liquid ripples. In the white room, he glowed with vitality.

Uneasy, Freia edged away. The claws of her dream became sickness curdling in her stomach.

"Where's your home?"

"Why do you want to help me now?" Freia asked him.

He shrugged.

"You just left me there," she said in a low, haunted voice.

Her eyes held no mirth, no trust, no opening for him to build a conversation, and her words were blunt, forestalling badinage. "I didn't know you were in trouble," he said honestly.

Freia swallowed hard.

"I'm sorry," Dewar said. He looked at the cold white floor. "I'm sorry you—you got hurt. I didn't know you were in trouble. The gryphon was there." He wasn't to blame for her injuries, he told himself; yet he knew they two had gone into that fight companions, and he had saved himself and left her behind. A sorcerer should feel no qualms, but the sorcerer was losing the argument—had lost it when Ottaviano had told Dewar of Prospero's daughter.

"How can I—" Freia began, and stopped. How could she trust him? What reason was there? He did nothing without self-interest. He wanted something now. Sex? Her body hurt all over and she felt as if she might vomit at any moment. Freia shuddered. No. "What do you want?" she asked. "Why do you want to help me?"

"I want to take you home," he said. "That's all I want."

"But why?"

Dewar met her eyes again. Fear, distrust, pain: written in lines and taut shadows on her face. "I'd like to tell you that when we get there," he said, "because it's an odd and personal thing. I don't want to tell you now because—well, honestly, I don't think you'd believe me. But you will when I tell you there."

"I don't have anything," she said. "I can't give you anything."

"I don't want anything from you but for you to let me escort you home."

The sea boomed and crashed. It sounded as though it were battering down walls. Freia's head ached. Her stomach was knotted, nauseated. Her body burned around her.

"You wanted me to take you to Prospero," she said.

"Yes—"

"You left me there," Freia said. "You went away in the fire and left me."

Dewar couldn't look at the deep, dark smudges of her eyes, the chalky pallor of her face. Something unpleasant quivered in the air around her.

"You won't help me," Freia whispered, drawing her knees up and hugging them, watching him, on her guard. "You'll leave me somewhere again."

The burn of her gaze on him was too much, the emotion under her hoarse voice too naked. Dewar stood. "I'll get you something to eat," he said, and he fled out of the room.

There were two people whose intelligence and discretion Prospero trusted so highly as to take counsel with them. He considered it particularly necessary now, given the terms which had been presented to him by Avril. The net was that for his daughter's liberty he would pay with his own.

He was aware that his thinking on this could not be unbiased, and he was also aware that the agreement beween himself and Landuc must affect his fledgling world orever, coercing its tender new growth into some forced nd artificial old form. The Emperor had acted greatly mazed when Prospero said he must take counsel on the roposal. Prospero had insisted, though, and had left the alace and Landuc without seeing Freia again—sparing hem both, he thought.

On tireless Hurricane, untiring himself for most of the ourney, he made his way through the Gates and Road of heyarcet, leaving the settled, fertile areas for the barren ones. Panurgus had controlled and directed his fiery Well; he center flourished at the expense of these, devouring them n a sense. The barriers the King had set up, the Gates and thers, kept most of the flow of life-feeding energy from the Well from the outer worlds, and thus the inner regions urgeoned with the vitality of an area four times their size. Life of a sort persisted outside the favored area, but the laces it had to dwell in were harsh and hostile.

Prospero, since becoming aware of this, had ever been of wo minds as to its wisdom. Certainly there were areas aturally sparse in life. To create such intentionally, though, equired a ruthlessness Prospero knew he could muster yet nisliked to exercise. Such a decision, in a way, faced him now.

As Hurricane cantered fluidly into a grey desert unbroken by movement other than his own, Prospero on his back sounded his future. He must preserve what he had found; it must be his, must remain his. Freia had been a folly of weakness. He regretted her now. She endangered something unique and irreplaceable. Of course she was unique herself; but he had a son, he could sire more children, and where there had been one there might be another. The great good fortune of finding and claiming, without competition or objection, the Spring, a Source different in nature from either other power in the world, would never come again. In Pheyarcet, the fiery Well was in the control of the ruler of Landuc—presently the Emperor was not competent to do much with it, yet even without consciously exercising himself he manipulated it. In Phesaotois, the power of the Stone was divided by sorcerous adepts among themselves into territories and domains, and woe be to he who trespassed.

The Spring was Prospero's, only Prospero's.

The Prince gnashed his teeth. The correct choice was to disown Freia and protect his world. That was the act rational thought indicated to be most useful. Nothing could supersede the Spring's interest. It was a measure of his own deterioration as a sorcerer that the rational and right decision made him uneasy. She had brought herself into her difficulties through disobeying his direct command. She must find a way out alone.

Besides, she had long made him uncomfortable in a number of ways: little unspoken hopes and expectations, the demand for reciprocation her fondness placed on him, and his own mixed feelings toward her with his knowledge of her mixed feelings toward him. Nay, he thought, 'twere wiser to shuck her off now and let her hate him: far preferable to her insinuation into his plans and his life. The boy Dewar was a sorcerer, and a good one; Prospero knew he would be able to deal with him when the time came. They spoke the same language. But Freia was determinedly different and taxed his endurance. He would be better off without her. And she had gotten along right well without him in the past, ranging her forests and wastes.

Yet the uneasy feeling sat on the back of his neck. Prospero gnashed his teeth again and spurred Hurricane to gallop, and Hurricane did, his hooves barely touching the ground, the wind of his passing raising the grey dust and whipping it into spinning devils.

# — 36 —

THE SELF-POSSESSED, VIGOROUS WOMAN WHO HAD sent her gryphon straight down into a battle was gone. The stiff changeling whose body was laced with lurid lines of fresh scars was neither self-possessed nor vigorous.

Dewar wooed her. The strenuous escape from Landuc had sent her into a relapse, and her weakness and mild fever were worsened by nausea and vomiting. He encouraged her to rest and brought bland, nourishing food for her uncertain stomach, even (though he knew it not) as Gaston had. Freia said that she must get home soon—she mentioned it every time they spoke—and Dewar agreed, but pointed out that exceeding her strength would hurt her again. He tried to divert her with found treasures: wave-worn streaked or spark-holding stones, roseate and mottled wave-shells stranded by the tides, a bowl of giant black-stamened purple flowers which grew on seaweed mats offshore.

But Freia would not be diverted, and she winced when he touched her; she would not smile at his smiles, nor swim with him, nor walk along the surf-sculpted beaches. Disconcerted, Dewar doubled his efforts to be amiable and considerate. On the third day, he brought her pale fish, which he had speared diving in the waves, poached in broth for her lunch and sat in a chair by the bed with a thick square book whilst she ate little tentative mouthfuls.

"Now, about getting you home," Dewar said.

Freia stopped eating. She waited, wariness in her face.

"I can take you there along the Road," Dewar said, "but you're still sick and you're not getting better. I think it would be better to take you through a Way. Do you know what a Way is?"

She shook her head, a tiny movement.

"A Way is how we got here," Dewar explained. "It's a temporary connection between two foci of the Well."

Freia's expression glazed with incomprehension as he said this, and when he said "You see?" she shook her head.

"It's very simple—" Dewar began.

"I don't care about that," Freia said. "I just want to go home. Does—does my father know where I am?"

"He does not," said Dewar, "which is why I want to take you home myself. Of course, if you just want to go there alone, I'll not keep you."

"I don't know how," Freia said.

He nodded, his friendly expression still in place. "Then I'll take you there, you see. But I need to know where your home is to take you."

"I don't know," Freia said.

"How did you get here? Not here, to Landuc?"

"Trixie," she said. "She's gone. He made me send her away. I told her go home."

"Who?" Dewar asked, distracted.

"Trixie," Freia said. "She went away."

He opened and closed his mouth, swallowed a sharp retort. "Who made you send Trixie away?"

"Otto," Freia whispered. She pushed the luncheon-tray aside.

"So the gryphon was how you got to Landuc," Dewar said, "and you don't know how she got you there, and you don't know where you started." Prospero must have had very good reasons for keeping the girl so ignorant of the world, but Dewar couldn't imagine what they were. "You must tell me about your home," he said, opening his book, "so that I can find it in this Ephemeris. This is a book which lists all the places—all the foci in all the worlds the Well sustains—and it tells where they are."

Freia stared at him like a tousled owl, big-eyed and unblinking, her head between hunched shoulders, her legs drawn up to her chest. The palpable wrongness knotted around her. Dewar's neck prickled. Was she mad? Had she been mad all along, one of those who swing from humor to humor as a weathercock follows the wind? She had utterly altered from the person he'd met in Chenay.

"Freia, tell me something about your home," he urged.

"I can't," she said.

"Why not," he said, very patiently.

"I promised I wouldn't ever."

"If you don't tell me," Dewar said, his voice taking on an edge of impatience, "I cannot take you there."

"You wouldn't," Freia said coldly. "You'd leave me behind again. You'll go without me. You want to find Prospero, you said so. That's what you really want."

Her distrust was insultingly apparent. Dewar's mouth set

in a line. "I won't leave you behind," he said. "And I have apologized. Both times," he pointed out.

"Apologized," she echoed, still cold.

"Yes, apologized! And offered to assist you. There's not a sorcerer in all the worlds who'd give you either apology or assistance, madame. You are fortunate that I am a gentleman as well."

"I don't believe you," she said. "You said you'd take me home. Why did you say that if you didn't know where?"

"I presumed you had the wit to know where you'd been," Dewar snapped. "Clearly I was mistaken." He rose to his feet, and her wide-eyed flinch away from him as he did angered him beyond anything she had said. "If you do not wish to be returned home, I shall return you to the Emperor's hospitality at once, as I regret that I can be of no service to you," he said. He stalked out of the room.

Dewar paced upward through a spiral of rooms to his workroom in the center of the round white house, steaming. Sister she might be, but he had no obligation to pamper a madwoman nor to play riddle-games with a fool. Let her begone, and soon. He set the Ephemeris on the worktable there, unrolled its companion Map, and in a little pocketbook began to calculate a Way to Landuc.

Halfway through the exercise, his anger began to recede. Hadn't she said she'd promised not to tell anyone about her home? Then she couldn't tell him without breaking her promise and suffering the consequences.

His pen slowed, stopped; the nib began to dry.

There must be some way of working around the barrier of the vow. That was the real problem. Possibly her distrust stemmed from the promise's working on her, as they'd gotten along amiably in the past. Dewar sat back on his stool and frowned, his anger deflected by the conundrum of breaking Freia's word without breaking it.

He couldn't tell her he was trying to do so; that would nullify the whole thing. He had to trick her. Dewar riffled the Ephemeris. So many places and things worth mentioning, and many more not: the world was a vast and varied congeries.

The Ephemeris! He could put a spell of memory on the book, give it to her, let her look at it privately, and take it back; then the book would rehearse again her turnings of pages, her pauses, and he'd be shown her home—without her breaking her vow.

Dewar smiled and set about ensorcelling his Ephemeris.

Among the contorted, straining roots of a mighty tree sat Prospero, his Castellan, and his Seneschal. They were not small men, but the mossy roots were thick and high enough to make excellent upholstered benches, or, in the case of the Seneschal, Scudamor, a backrest. He blended with the tannin-rich brown moss and the mulch and earth and wood, and his wide-shouldered torso seemed to grow out of the root, rather than to be superimposed on it. Utrachet the Castellan's face and wiry body still bore marks of his ordeal as a prisoner in Landuc. He sat on a root opposite Scudamor, dangling one foot and twitching it slightly, head cocked to attend Prospero, who sat against the broad mighty trunk of the tree.

Prospero had chosen this place for its power, its privacy, and its connotations. The Spring swelled out from the roots on the other side of the tree, behind them. It seeped along the stone and into the thick carpet of rich moss that flourished with the tree. There were no sounds but those the three made themselves and the whisper of the water.

"Freia's found," Prospero began.

The other two nodded. They had expected no less, but his gravity since his arrival had put them in mind of the worst, and they waited apprehensively for him to continue.

"She's prisoner," Prospero said. "The Emperor hath her sorcerously confined and protected in such a way that I cannot break in and free her."

"Could someone else?" Utrachet asked.

"Nay. Must be broken in the manner it was laid, else break her, and she's watched ceaselessly. I investigated freeing her myself and found 'twas not to be done." He looked from one to the other: gauging them. "The Emperor Avril hath her hostage, and he presented me terms for her release.

These have I come to discuss with you, for we'll all bear the weight of the matter, and I would be certain I do not misvalue some item nor ignore some opportunity. I confess I'm not unbent in assaying the bargain."

"Lord, how can they bargain? She is your daughter," Scudamor said. "What good is she to anyone there? What use to keep her against her will? She cannot love them for it."

"She's my blood, a hold on me, Scudamor."

"You have not been there, Scudamor," Utrachet said. "They are strange. They see value in things beyond belief here. They see the Lady's worth and covet her, though she must be prisoned to be kept."

"She's worth as much as I'm willing to give for her," Prospero said, "and there's the crux of the matter. Hear what Avril would have of me ere she go free from his claws.

"His first demand is that I shall renounce the practice of sorcery save in the petty forms of Summoning, Sending, and Opening of Ways.

"His second demand is that I shall renounce all claim to precedence in Landuc, abdicating my place in the succession, which oath shall bind me and all my after-kin.

"His third demand is that I shall vow never take arms against Landuc again.

"His fourth demand is that I shall pay reparations for the war most recently past, in a sum which I calculate is near double his expense.

"His fifth demand is that I shall swear fealty to him personally.

"His sixth demand is that I shall dwell in the Palace of Landuc on his sufferance.

"His seventh demand is that he shall choose a husband for Freia.

"His eighth demand is that I shall yield to him all titles in all lands where I hold same."

Prospero's voice, as he recited the list, was cool, his manner remote.

Scudamor broke the silence that followed. "Lord, these are difficult things to do."

"He cannot expect all," Utrachet said. "They begin by asking more than they want. What things does he love best among those?"

"Those that would cripple me most," Prospero said. "Sorcery; reparations; vows of fealty. He knoweth naught, I'm certain, of this place. Freia told me she'd said no word of it."

"If they handled her as me," Utrachet said, "she has endured much in silence."

"In the eighth demand his mind's full of my large holdings in Landuc, that I might dispute with him," Prospero said, "for he seized them lawlessly 'pon his accession. For those I care nothing now. I'd more likely pursue the claims of my friends, who have suffered greatly 'neath his heel. But the implication must include here."

"Fealty," Scudamor said, "is to acknowledge him as above you—" The idea was puzzling, self-contradictory. Who could be above Prospero?

" 'Twould sound repercussions here. The nature of such an oath is that it's ever-binding, all-binding. It becometh of the essence of the oathgiver and he cannot scape it without fatality. Forswearing sorcery would mean I'd no longer be able to build this place as I have done, would not complete what I've planned here."

The Seneschal and Castellan looked at one another.

"He playeth high stakes for one girl," Prospero said. "I'm minded to bluff him: deny him all, see what he doth."

"He might kill her," Utrachet said.

"Ah." Scudamor shook his head, visibly grieved at the idea.

" 'Tis the whole of my life, of my realm," Prospero said.

"You wish to refuse him these things," Scudamor said.

"He has no use for Freia, himself," Utrachet said, "he might slay her as some do that foul their prey when they cannot eat it."

"If you gave way in small matters—"

"He'd demand more. Your own lives are at stake here also, gentlemen. Do not forget that. Yours, your descendants, everything here."

"And your descendants," Scudamor pointed out.

" 'Tis little matter. I've learned that I have a son. Utrachet, hast met him. The fellow who fell through the fire at the end of Perendlac, after me."

"I recall," Utrachet said. "A powerful man."

"A boy yet by our reckoning, called Dewar. Rash, impetuous—but hath qualities in him of endurance and deeds as well. Nay, I've no concern about descendants."

Utrachet looked across at Scudamor, and Scudamor looked at the moss between his feet, an expression of distress on his dark face.

"Speak, Scudamor," Prospero said. "I have asked for counsel."

"Lord," Scudamor said slowly, "I cannot think it wise to rely on the future to provide you with an heir. The Lady is ours and although Utrachet and I can understand the necessity of not redeeming her at so great cost, I think the others will be confused by it. For did you not set her here among us and bid us honor her? And she earned honor herself, by taming the gryphon, by teaching us the ways of the wood for hunting, of the tossflowers for weaving, of the healing herbs. She told us about bow-wood—she knows all the world's ways. You have risked much and paid dear to bring the rest of us who went there with you home again, here. It seems strange to leave her at their uncertain mercy. She is ours."

Utrachet's unblinking eyes were on Scudamor, but he watched Prospero sidelong and saw that he struggled with this speech.

"Master," Utrachet said, "I do think there is truth in that, that the Lady belongs here. We know nothing of the future; your son is not here, and you said he is hostile to you. It would be weakness to leave one of our own in their hands, and the strength we might get from doing so would be tainted."

"The weakness to come from buying her free will cripple us," Prospero said. "My son's young yet; I'll win him to me. He'd be a stronger and more able ally than she hath been or could ever be. He is a sorcerer."

"Then could we not rely upon him, when you had him won over, for sorceries, if you could not work them?" Scudamor said. "Not all making is done with sorcery, Master, you have said this yourself. Walls are built with stone and sweat."

Prospero held himself very still.

"You have asked, Master, and we have given our counsel," Utrachet said. "Shall we leave you?"

"Aye," said Prospero. "Go."

They rose together and padded over the leaf mold and moss away from the dark-trunked tree and the Spring.

Ephemeris in hand, Dewar went to the bedchamber—his chamber; he'd exiled himself to sleep on the kitchen hearth. The white bed was empty and the house rang with silence under the susurrus of the sea.

He listened, his heart speeding with fresh annoyance, and then he went quickly through the house, room after room, and found Freia nowhere. She had left, unceremonious and ungrateful. Icy with anger, he returned to the bedchamber, found a hair on the pillow where she'd lain, and coiled it into a ring, whispering a simple spell of seeking. He slipped the ring on his finger. A frail tingle drew on it: toward Freia.

Dewar took the uncoiling way from the round house. The sand outside caught and tangled his feet as if to delay him. He was barefooted; he loped with long strides, as difficult as running in water.

She couldn't go fast or far, not so ill, not in the small time she'd had. He caught up with her among the wind-scooped, sunny-ridged dunes behind the house, which separated the marshes from the sea.

Freia, dressed in the heavy, still-damp clothes she'd worn escaping the Palace, turned as Dewar ran down a steep slope and bounded toward her. She stood tensed, half-crouching, her hands fists. He halted, her attitude warning him.

"Where are you going?" Dewar demanded.

She glared at him. "Away," she said.

"Away! Whither away? You don't know your way home,

you said! You're sick! Are you mad as well? What are you going to do?"

"Nothing to do with you," Freia said.

"Come back with me," Dewar said. He took half a step toward her, lifting a hand, meaning to take her arm. She backed away.

"Don't touch me!"

"Come back. You're tired; you need more rest or you'll be ill again."

"What do you care what happens to me?"

"You're my guest," Dewar replied.

"Your guest! No! You just want to use me to get at Prospero," Freia said accusingly. "I'm a line to him and you think that by trolling me around, bait, you'll land him. Just like that hateful Emperor and Ottaviano and Golias. Well, he won't bite. I'm rotten bait. He doesn't care about me. I'm not worth his time and I'm not worth yours—so let me go."

"I want to help you!"

"You do not! You want to use me to find Prospero, don't you, and you leave me behind every time and I won't go with you!"

They glared at one another. Dewar, fuming, considered and dismissed several gambits.

Freia sidled away from him. "Leave me alone."

"What do you think you're going to do?" he demanded, moving toward her.

"I'll take care of myself," Freia said, stepping back from him.

"Oh? There's nobody here but us, Freia, there's no other person, nothing here but birds and water and fish."

"I can take care of myself." She was shivering; her eyes stared too brightly.

"You cannot. You're sick and you said yourself you don't know your way home."

They were moving in a circle, he trying to catch her, she backing away. "Stop chasing me!"

"Stop running away. This is lunacy! What is wrong with you? I'm trying to help you!"

"I said leave me alone! I don't want your help." Freia spit

the words at him. "You want to find Prospero—then find him yourself. Leave me alone!"

Dewar halted, folding his arms. Freia stopped a few steps away from him. "I'm tempted to take you at your word and let you drown in the marshes. You display the same single-mindedness you showed at Perendlac, and look where that got you!"

"You left me there," Freia said. "You left me."

"Prospero left you too," Dewar retorted.

The words' effect on Freia was instant, as sharp as a twig's snap. Her back went down; anger evaporated and she slumped. "I know," she whispered.

He couldn't resist victory. "It was your own fault. You got yourself into it. You have only yourself to blame."

Freia half-turned away, covering her face with her hands. She said nothing more. Dewar took a cautious step toward her, then another, and caught her wrist. She jerked her arm, trying to pull out of his grip, then swung her free hand and slapped him with all her strength across the face; and in the same instant she burst into tears.

The crack of the blow made Dewar's ears ring; it caught him off-balance and staggered him, and he lifted his own hand to return the favor, glaring down at her with every thought drowned under his rage. Freia cowered, catching her breath in a sob and meeting his gaze with pure terror as her wrist wrenched and twisted in his grip, and Dewar recoiled from her look.

Slowly he lowered his hand, softened his hold on her arm (but did not let go), and whispered, "I'm sorry. Freia—" He felt sick with the outwash of his anger, with self-disgust, and he caught her other arm, hugging her to him. "I'm sorry," he whispered again. She flailed, sobbing, saying incomprehensible words. He held her still and stroked her hair down her rigid back, whispering, "Hush, hush, hush," to her unsteadily.

Now Freia wept convulsively, clutching him with knotted fingers. They stood in the hollow of the dunes under the sun, the dry, sharp-edged grass hissing around them in a rising breeze. Dewar tried to think. She wasn't thinking: that was clear to him now. She was in such a distressed state that she couldn't think, couldn't be rational, and he had to think for her and help her no matter what she said or did. She was hysterical. He had been terrorizing her, treating her as other sorcerers treated their inferiors, domineering and violent. He had been ungentlemanly. She was his sister, his father's daughter, and she had done him no harm. Striking her would be wrong. He must be patient. She was ill; she hardly knew herself, and she knew him not at all.

"Freia, hush."

"Oh . . ." she howled, muffled in his shoulder.

"There. There."

"I'm s-s-sor-ry-y-y . . ."

"Shhh. I understand. I think."

Her breathing was raggedly slowing. Dewar admitted the truth to himself: he *had* left her twice in peril, in Chenay and in Perendlac. He had known her danger, and he had no right to her trust or gratitude. Indeed, if Prospero ever got wind of what Dewar had done, he might well take offense unless Dewar could make up for it somehow, could soothe and comfort Freia now. She gulped air, hiccuping, in his arms.

"S-something—snapped, I'm so sorry," sobbed Freia. "I—sorry—I never hit anyone like that ever; I'm sorry—you're trying to help—I'm sorry—"

"Forgiven. Forgotten. The fault's mine, for teasing you so. Hush." He waited for catharsis to steal over her, for the wild tears to exhaust her, and eventually Freia was calmer.

"Dewar—"

"I'm sorry, Freia—"

She shuddered, gulped again, pushed at his chest. "Let go, I—I'm going to—"

The symptoms were too familiar; he held her shoulders and steadied her as she was sick. Afterward, he wiped her sweaty forehead and her mouth with his handkerchief, scuffed sand over the mess, and led her a few steps toward his house.

"Don't," Freia said, pulling weakly away. "Please don't. Please stop. Please." She was weeping again, not the great wracking sobs but a steady tremor this time.

"Let me help. Freia, it is my fault. I shouldn't have left you. I'm sorry you got hurt. You need help. I want to help you, and I can help you. Let me."

"Don't. Leave me alone. You can't help. You can't. Nobody can help." She shook her head emphatically.

"I can. I know I can if you'll just let me try," he insisted.

Freia tossed her head back and glared at him, streaked and reddened with salt tears and sun. "How do you know you can help?" she demanded. "You don't even know what's wrong!"

"If you'd tell me, I'd know, and then I'd help you," Dewar said reasonably, squelching annoyance again. Her contrariness was enough to provoke a stone.

"You want me to tell you this and tell you that and I don't trust you," Freia said, the hysterical edge coming to her voice again. She yanked her arms away from his hands. "You can't help and you don't believe me and why can't you just *leave me alone?*"

"Because I'm your brother," he shouted back at her.

The color drained from her face and her eyes grew wide and dark, staring up at his face, disbelief fading into shock. He seized her arm, steadied her.

"How—" she whispered.

"Prospero is my father," Dewar said.

He had said it to Lady Miranda, still stunned by the revelation, and sworn her to silence. He had not said it, even to himself, since then.

"But—" Freia couldn't make words fit her tumbling, shattering thoughts. She closed her eyes.

"Now will you let me help you?" Dewar pressed her, exasperated. "What ails you?"

She looked at him again, cold in the hot sun. "I'm pregnant," Freia said.

Prospero's sweeping cloak was the color of the twilight sky, its lining midnight-black. Head low, he galloped on tireless Hurricane through the vast forest called Herne's Riding, hypnotizing himself with the beat of the horse's four hooves on the cold road. The obsessive rhythm crowded out other thoughts, doubts, and the gut urge to turn around and get out of here, to consider himself lucky to have what he did and live without more. He carried his damnation in a rolled tube in the saddlebag—damnation and a fragment of redemption.

He congratulated himself on his forethought in emancipating Freia. He had not intended that the document should be used, but had done it, four years before he'd opened his war, out of a sense of justice; it was the closest he had come to contemplating defeat. Were he to go down, she'd not fall with him, remaining free of the claws of the Crown. Or so he had hoped. Had the disobedient chit but obeyed him, neither of them would have come to the present pass.

The existence of the emancipation invalidated, he thought, the treaty-clause in which Avril claimed the right to bestow Prospero's daughter. That Avril would have thought of it at all, Prospero thought, showed what a base mind the man had, and that he had insisted on it showed him mean and subhuman. Gaston was less than he made himself seem, to serve such a worm.

Hurricane leapt a creek without losing the beat of his gallop.

Thus, to frustrate some of Avril's desire to grind his allies, Prospero had made the lands over to her. She would keep them for him, and he would still have sway in their governance—not that he cared for any but Argylle. The others were all smoke, veils of dust to conceal the gem that was Argylle.

He could not contemplate it further. He returned to counting hoofbeats.

Freia's revelation eclipsed his own. Dewar felt his face go slack with shock, his jaw drop to a graceless gape. Memory tumbled incidents together.

"—rape," his lips shaped voicelessly. No marvel now her distraught thrashing, her desperation. Golias—it had to have been the sham-bastard Golias. Otto had no taste for force, and Gaston was a true Prince and a man of honor.

Dewar looked away, ashamed to have badgered and baited her. "Did the Emperor know? Or Gaston?" he asked. "Are you certain?"

She snorted.

"No."

Freia shook her head.

"Freia." He put his hand on her shoulder. "If you are not sure—"

"Dewar, don't say anything else stupid. Please. I cannot bear it," she said in a taut, high voice. She pressed the heels of her hands to her eyes.

Irked, he began to retort, "I'm sorry for you—"

"I don't want your pity." She pulled back again, distracted from one pain by another.

"You have my compassion and my earnest desire to do you good, if you can bring your pride to accept them. We are bound at least by blood, at best by more."

Freia said, a quaver in her voice, "I find it hard to believe you."

"He said it himself."

"Oh, well, a man would know, wouldn't he."

Dewar took a moment to hear this as sarcasm, and then he flushed. "I assume he has reason to know," he said coldly, "and I am inclined to believe him."

"What has your mother got to say about it?"

"I don't know. I have not seen her in many, many years, and she hates me with all her heart. She is a dangerous and evil woman. And yours?" he added.

Freia shrugged.

Dewar decided it was a poor subject for conversation now. He drew his breath in, let it out slowly. The straightforward task of rescuing Freia from the Emperor had just become a maze. "Come with me," Dewar said gently, "and let us talk somewhere quiet out of the sun, where we may sit and be easy. And it may be you think I have no business with you still, but if you will let me I'll help you."

"Avril," Gaston said, " 'tis less than manly and less than kingly to wittingly seal a false bargain."

"If he returns and says he will covenant with us, then it is of no concern—"

"You have nothing to return to him. His daughter's gone. You'll stoop to fraud? A market-charlatan's pea-and-shell game's more honorable than this," said Gaston.

"So, Gaston, we should let him go free. Scot-free. Not a mark on him. To draw back and plan another strike. We should shake the serpent and drop it on our foot to bite or not as it chooses. We find these sentiments difficult to believe, coming from our Marshal," the Emperor hissed, twisting and staring back at Gaston.

"Cannot uphold your side," Gaston insisted. "The bargain's void ere it's made. An 'a come, tell him she's fled."

"This is not a matter on which we have requested a second opinion, Marshal."

" 'Twill bring ill to the Empire if you press on, Avril. Prospero'd not yield without some plan to repay evil for evil, to you and the Empire. 'Tis well, 'tis needful that he be defeated, but not thus, not with a lie and a false vow." Gaston, not waiting for permission to leave the Emperor's presence, turned away in disgust and strode toward the door. It opened as he approached. Herne stood there, horsy and smelling of his cold dry forest.

"Prospero comes," Herne said, and he showed his teeth in a smile.

## — 37 —

THEY SAT ON OPPOSITE SIDES OF the white-scoured table, and Freia ate nothing as Dewar wolfed down his long-delayed luncheon—little shellfish steamed quickly in a hot pan in the coals and buttered, a salad of sharp greens, toasted bread. The day's stresses and sorcery had left him hungry, though he forbore to point this out to his sister, who sat with her head in her hands.

He finished with hard-skinned fruits from the low bushes around the house, slicing them neatly and eating them by scooping the seeds and pulp into his mouth. Red juices flowed.

"Freia, you must eat something."

"I don't want to."

"Why not?" he probed.

"I'm tired of vomiting."

She had a knack for answers which were unanswerable, thought Dewar, and looked at his fruit with less relish.

"I thank you for your patience with my appetite," he said, rising and going to the kitchen pump. He washed his hands and dried them, watching her sidelong.

Freia said nothing.

Dewar sat down opposite her again and put his hands on hers. "Lady," he said, "tell me your desire."

Her hysteria had faded. "I want to go home," Freia said listlessly. "But truly I should not. He will be so angry at me. I wasn't supposed to leave at all. Now— He was angry before, but he—he won't—like me." She shook her head.

"Why should he be angry with you?" Dewar wondered. She had followed Prospero everywhere, trying to help him. How could the sorcerer Prince take such devotion amiss?

Freia shook her head again, not looking at him, staring at the wooden table. "He won't want me the way I am now. I should just take a knife and gut myself." Her hands became fists.

He pulled her hands away from her head and made her look up at him, sad-eyed. His heart seemed to move in his breast, and she, tired and grief-bitten, in an instant became unbearably precious and dear. Dewar knew dishonored women sometimes chose death. He would not let her do that. "You're not going to die."

"I want to. How could you have any idea—how could anybody—I didn't want—I don't—" She moved away from him jerkily. Her voice rose; she was nearly shouting again, the edge of wildness returning.

"Freia," Dewar said, and he went around the table and sat beside her on the bench, conscious of the cutlery lying casually on the table and dresser and of how fast she could move. He took her hands again, but lightly. "It is your will to return home."

"He won't want me there."

"Your will, Freia. Not his. And don't try to guess his will—"

"He's always saying that, too," she muttered, and pulled her hands a little away from his, but not far; their fingers still touched. "You're much like him."

"What's he like?"

"Much like you," Freia said wearily. "Self-centered, unreliable, kind on a whim, and ill to cross. I suppose all sorcerers are like that."

Dewar frowned. "You're quick to damn, aren't you."

"I guess all Landuc people are like that," Freia mused on in an undertone, half to herself.

"Freia," Dewar said, "if you have nothing good to say about me or anyone else to my face, when I have been expending considerable effort to help you—"

"I don't need to get home to Prospero," she said. "I can take care of myself anywhere. I know the plants, the animals."

"You're not yourself, Freia," he pointed out. "And you'll not be well—"

"I'll be fine; there is an herb there I need to—to be myself, and I know where to find it," she said.

Understanding substantially redirected Dewar's thoughts. He drew a breath and savored it. "Herbs," he said. He was moving onto unfamiliar ground; he had never studied more than rudimentary medicine or surgery, but he had travelled widely and he thought he knew her better than he had. "Perhaps I can help you find the herb you want—to be yourself," he said, using her phrasing delicately.

Freia stiffened. They regarded one another, combatants or allies.

"What's this herb called?" he asked.

"Mayaroot," she said.

"Mayaroot?"

"It's not a root truly, it's a fungus that grows on the roots of old veil-trees in the seaside marshes," Freia said.

"Why do you want it?"

"If you must know," she said, drawing away from him, "to bring a miscarriage."

Dewar nodded slowly. "Are you certain of it? Certain that it will work?"

"Two women—" Freia began, and she stopped herself.

"Trust me," he said, frustrated by this slow eking, word-by-word, of pieces of stories. He seized her shoulders. "I will not abandon you, I swear it. I will help you. I have not brought you so near me to leave you. I will not see you suffer a day longer if I can help you. I'm no herbalist, but I know plants vary in potency. The mayaroot might fail you. There are better remedies. Trust me."

Stiff and withdrawn at first, Freia relaxed as he spoke. "Trust you," she repeated softly.

"Please."

"I trust you."

Dewar moved toward her and embraced her, grateful. "Thank you," he whispered, and whispered it again when he felt her arms go around him, her weight fall against him. With her trust, he could undo what had been done, erase the vile evidence of his own failure and restore her to happiness. He could set all right for her, with her trust.

"Two women," she whispered to the wall, her voice creaking, "they were with child, and they were gathering crabs, and they ate the crabs with mayaroot. It made them sick. It was terrible. They were very sick, and then they bled some days, and they—their pregnancies ended. Another woman—Cledie—had had the crabs unseasoned by the mayaroot, and a few men, and none were ill save those women and a man who ate the mayaroot, and Prospero said it was poison."

Dewar nodded. "I see. Freia, I can take you to an Eddy I know, a city where they have skillful physicians, where pregnancies are ended by women in better—kinder—ways than that, without sickness or long bleeding. You will not be hurt or blamed or abused. You will be made comfortable and no one will harry you as I do. You needn't wander about looking for unreliable fungi. I will take you there if you wish." He hadn't been there in thirty Well-years; he trusted it wouldn't have altered greatly, being a stable, slow-spinning backwater of the Well's stream—and if it had, he'd find her another. There were women everywhere, in every world, and in every world some of them didn't want to bear children.

She turned this over in her thoughts slowly, examining all sides of it. "Dewar," she said, straightening and taking his hands in hers, "please promise me a thing."

He pressed her hands.

"Promise me you will never talk of this with anyone," she said. "I mean anyone, Prospero included—"

"I swear," he said, interrupting her, "by the blood of my body, by my life, that I will not speak to anyone of the rape nor of your abortion, unless you expressly should desire that I do so. Shall I exclude you from the oath?"

That intense, burning look flashed up at him again. "Don't you ever dare throw it up to me."

"I will not mention this to you to shame you, to blame you, or to impugn you. And indeed when it is done it will be done, and the ill of it less than a bastard rapist's bastard brat would bring." His voice softened, lowered; he stroked her hands. "All shall be well, Freia."

"I don't think so. I don't think anything can ever be right again."

"Yes, it will. And you will too. You will. You will."

Dewar calculated a Way to the Eddy-world, a finicky process, and took Freia there through a Way-fire. The place had changed little. He guided her through the busy streets full of lights and sounds and people all moving faster than Freia could comprehend; he led her one place, another, another where they rested, then to a harshly-lit soft-colored building as big as a city in itself; he lied and half-lied and explained for her, for she spoke none of the language, and his tongue and ear were tuned by the Well. Throughout, Freia continued sickly. Dull-eyed, hunched into herself like an ailing animal, flinching at the strange noises and ill from the reeks of sterility and industry, she made no objection when Dewar announced that they would stay a few days longer in the Eddy.

"You need rest," he told Freia. "They said you'll feel more like eating. Do you want something to eat?" He'd brought her back to the rooms he had hired, knowing she would be unable to travel at once. One wall was all windows, looking into a courtyard with a fountain as tall as the five-storey building, the water pouring down and down, rushing and tumbling, raising a fine mist. Sometimes the wind frisked and their window became wet, as with sudden rain.

Freia whispered, "I wish I understood what they were saying. Why do I understand you and not them? Why didn't they understand me?"

"I have passed the Fire of the Well. It is a pity I did not think to send you through it while we were in Landuc; certainly that's one place they wouldn't have looked for us, though the tomb was also good." Dewar smiled, a quick flash of pride. "It's inconvenient, but in a way it's also convenient, madame; no one can ask you awkward questions you don't want to answer."

She nodded and hugged herself.

Dewar sat down on the curly-armed, high-backed sofa beside her. "How are you feeling?" he asked cheerfully. "Better?"

"I don't know yet."

He nodded and examined a book of unreadable text and colorful pictures which had been given to Freia by the brisk, kind woman in blue who had taken charge of her during the oddly swift and painless procedure of removing something which had been added slowly and with painful violence.

"You should eat something," Dewar announced.

"Do you ever not think about food?" she wondered.

Irritated, he said, "Then don't eat, starve yourself."

Freia squeezed her elbows to her sides. She felt unballasted, light-headed and detached from her body. She looked at the incomprehensible book and it reminded her, as all books tended to, of Prospero bent over books, writing in tiny handwriting, and she was suddenly blindingly homesick for the life they had led before he had started his war. If only she could go home and let him feed her golden baked-root soup or (her mouth watered) a fresh-cut piece of liver from a young elk, seared quickly, with pungent tiny thready mushrooms. She licked her lips. And then to curl up in her own bed beside the painted screen with trees and mountains on it, and on the other side the lamplight glowing on Prospero's creamy leaves of close-written parchment—

"Freia?" Dewar said softly.

She shook herself. "Yes?"

"Are you all right?" He was peering at her closely, his forehead furrowed. "You looked odd for a moment."

"I was just thinking of—thinking of—of home," she said, and she thought of the two chairs and the winged table and the trim little boat for going up and down the river, of sun through the trees in the afternoon and mist on the river in the morning.

It had changed since then; Prospero had crowded the place with people, cut down trees, made them into walls, though she had argued with him tearfully. "It must change, Puss," he had told her again and again. "It is time for change." She had altered not a stone of his plans.

Would he listen to her now? She wanted to tell him what had happened and to scream at him for not hearing her call to him when he had left first Perendlac and then Chasoulis, for leaving her in Landuc when she wanted to go home and sit with her head on his knee and tell him everything and hear him say—

"Freia, listen to me."

Freia blinked. Prospero's face swam and blended in Dewar's.

"If you want to go home, you must tell me about the place so that I can find it in my Ephemeris. Tell me what it is called."

"Argylle." Argylle. Prospero had shouted it, calling everyone to him in the confusion of fire and darkness, and he had waited for everyone, all of them, all but her. Argylle.

"Freia, I can't find an entry with that name, or anything like it." Dewar's voice had an edge now. "Tell me other names."

"Other names?"

They stared at one another, she blank, he frowning.

"If you will not cooperate," Dewar said, after a long silence, "then either you will never return home or I will have to find the place myself."

Freia's blankness became another kind of emptiness. "You can't take me there," she said. "You said—"

Dewar held up a hand, turning away, scowling. "Very well. *I* said. *You* have not said anything helpful about finding the place. I have been thinking about this problem since the last time it arose. Have you always lived, or almost always, there?"

"Yes," she whispered.

He nodded. "I shall find it with sorcery, and I shall require your cooperation to the extent of letting some blood in a phial, which I shall use for the work."

"Blood?"

"Moreover, I require apparatus which is not here, and I will not take you to the place where I keep my tools. I shall leave you here, prepare the sorcery, and return." His expression was cold. "If you will not trust me with more information, then you must trust me to leave you while I work."

"You're leaving?" Freia grasped at this and closed her eyes. She had known it would happen again. All the whirling skies and alien lands between here and home—

"Freia," he said, suddenly gentle again, and his arm was on her shoulder. He was pulling on her arm, taking her hand, holding it so tightly it nearly hurt. "I'll be back. I shall not abandon you. You must sleep. Come now, lie down. You're tired," said Dewar, a soft, persuasive voice breaking her reverie again. "You must rest while I'm gone. I'll not be long. You must rest. Sleep now."

Freia let him plump up a pillow, allowed herself to be reclined on the sofa and covered with Dewar's discarded cloak. He was fumbling with her hand again. She drew it up to her cheek, to pillow her head—odd, there was a little bandage on her thumb, soft white cloth.

"I'll be back directly," Dewar said again, patting her shoulder.

Freia nodded and turned on her side, drawing her knees up and closing her eyes as the door closed behind him. She had wished herself home again and again while imprisoned by Ottaviano, Golias, and the Emperor. Now home came to her with practiced ease. She drew the image of the door before her mind's eye and opened it.

The walls were coming along. Freia stopped on the hilltop and looked down at the curve of stones, built on a line she had ploughed with a flower-wreathed stick, guided by Prospero's instructions and a long rope made of braided grasses. The breaks for the gates were more evident now, three of them. The wall went down to the river-edge but did not cross; the bridges Prospero planned would be difficult work, requiring large barges, not yet built, to set the piers in the swift current of the narrow, deep river. The great blocks of stone would come from the Jagged Mountains, from the same ugly quarries that now provided stone for the wall-works, and be dragged and floated to the construction site. She knew as much about it as he did; she had sat mouse-quiet listening hopelessly to his plans for the city and its appurtenances for hours.

Already three mud-trodden ways led in from the gates through bare-trampled ground, meeting at a collection of log-and-daub buildings in the middle; a stone-enclosed, roofed fountain rose there, the main public water supply—as if the river weren't sufficient. Already many of the older wooden buildings, Prospero's first projects for his people, had been replaced by stone; two stood half-constructed. These were Prospero's command-post now, where he dwelt himself and planned his works and war and housed the favored of his folk.

"A young city," Dewar said beside her. A glass ball on a golden chain swung from his hand, its inside stained with a few drops of blood.

"Yes," she said.

There were still trees on the Isle, but now the riverbanks were naked. Bare ground and sloping meadows sprawled where once she had threaded her way through mighty trees and stalked wood-elk and other prey. She would have left it so. Prospero's ideas were not hers.

Dewar was quivering with tension. "Hope he's here," he muttered.

"I don't know where he'd be, but I never did," Freia said. "He never trusted me to tell me," she said, almost to herself, but Dewar heard.

Freia began walking very rapidly, blinking back tears. Please be home, Papa, she pleaded with Prospero in her thoughts. Please, please, please.

A man from a group working on the walls ran toward them, sprinting.

"Utrachet!" Freia recognized him, but hadn't the strength to run toward him.

Dewar fell back a few steps behind her, storing away his glass ball.

"Lady!" Utrachet cried, putting on a last burst and covering a hundred paces at race-speed. "Lady! Lord! Welcome! Is it—" and he broke off.

"Utrachet, I'm so happy to see you," Freia said. His face was scarred, she had seen it so in Dewar's bowl of vision-water, but he was heavier and healthier-looking than he had been. "Utrachet— How, how are things here?"

"Lady, they go on," he said, and looked at Dewar behind her and at her.

"This is—this man is Dewar," Freia said. Recognition came to Utrachet's face, and she added, "You know who he is?"

"Yes; Lord Prospero has spoken of him," Utrachet said. "Welcome, Lord," he added in Lannach, bowing.

"Thank you, Utrachet." Dewar bowed also.

Lord Prospero never mentioned him to *me,* Freia thought. "Is he here?"

"Lord Prospero?"

"Yes."

Utrachet stared at her. "Is he not with you?"

"Oh, Utrachet. Please don't let's have one of these conversations about him," Freia said, tears starting to her eyes. "Of course he's not here. He never is when I need him. Where is Cledie?"

"She has gone, Lady," said Utrachet. "She left the dawn after you did, and did not say whither she went to anyone."

Freia stared, frozen for a moment, and then walked past the Castellan and continued on toward Prospero's walled city.

Utrachet and Dewar looked at one another.

"She has had difficulties," Dewar said.

"We know she was captive," Utrachet said in accented Lannach. "But why is Lord Prospero not with you?"

Dewar frowned. "Has he been looking for, ah, Lady Freia?"

"He went to free her," Utrachet said.

Dewar blinked. "When?"

"Five days past."

"Uh-oh," Dewar muttered. "Free her how? By attack? Covertly? Do you know?"

"You do not?"

"No—"

"Best to wait, then," Utrachet decided, and, looking very worried, turned to begin trotting after Freia. "Come, if you will," he called back over his shoulder.

Prince Gaston must be present, loth the proceedings though he did; the Emperor swore him to silence. Prince Herne was solidly of the Emperor's opinion in the matter. Prince Fulgens had never liked Prospero well, for Prospero's winds sported with his ships and had driven many of the navy onto rocks and shoals over the years of war. The prospect of seeing Prospero shorn of sorcery had the Admiral in an expansive mood, despite the severe winter storms that were setting in.

The Fireduke wished that Prospero might be suspicious of his daughter's absence from the room where the Emperor received him, flanked by officials of his court and the two other Great Dukes and the sorceress Oriana, who was also a party in the deception. Would it not seem unnatural to him? More likely it would appear as more of the Emperor's caution.

The doors were opened by two heavily-armed guards, who stood one on each side. Prospero entered. His cloak covered him shoulder to heel and he carried a metal-shod black staff in one hand. Under his cloak was a leather messenger's cylinder.

Prince Gaston tried to catch Prospero's steel-grey eye, but Prospero watched Oriana and the Emperor, whom he rightly saw as the two most dangerous in the room.

"I'll renounce nothing before another adept," he told the Emperor without preamble, "and thou'rt a fool to think I would, a fool doubly, for anything she learn of me could be to wield 'gainst thee, and anything she wield 'gainst me shall rebound on thee."

"She shall remain," the Emperor said.

"Then needs must accept my word that I shall fulfill my vow, for I'll perform naught before any man, layman or sorcerer. 'Tis as binding as the deed; though thy words are gossamer, mine hold."

"This seems a forthright precaution," Gaston said, "and I support it. It is no matter where the vow is kept, nor exactly when, so long as it be done and done timeously."

"Aye," Fulgens said, "Prospero keeps his vows, all know't, though they work to his own ill." He smiled.

"No need to spawn a second scourge in putting down the first," Herne agreed.

Oriana remained loftily silent.

The Emperor considered it. "So be it," he said. "You shall complete the terms of the agreement at earliest possible time—within, let us say, five days of its making, and shall be bound by them in that interval."

" 'Twill not be done instanter," Prospero said in a level tone which was also, somehow, sarcastic, "for thou commandest nor Time nor Elements. Seven days shall pass ere I may complete the vow, and that's if all go well in journeying—which it may not, for thy Empire's full of wildnesses where all was tamed before thy reign. You that travel little," and he glanced at them contemptuously, "know it not so well as one who does."

"He speaks truth," Oriana said distantly, coldly—perhaps repaying Herne's slight. "A twelve-day's frist be not overgenerous, considering the terms of the contract."

The Emperor, burning with Prospero's insults, began to naysay this, but was interrupted by Prince Gaston.

"Indeed it's true, travelling's not so easy as it was," the Marshal said, "and the old ways are not always reliable. I think twelve days, for journeying to thy bolt-hole and returning, be not unreasonable; and indeed, if it lieth in six days' Road-journey of the capital, 'tis near indeed. As the condemned man may choose his hour, so may you, Prospero; how long will you reasonably require? Considering that you're bound by the vow 'pon agreeing to it, there's no harm in allowing adequate time for its completion."

Fulgens and Herne glanced at one another; Gaston could be fiendishly diplomatic at times.

Prospero said, through clenched teeth, "Your kindness, brother, is warm, and warmly received. Twelve days be not unreasonable, eighteen be somewhat realistic."

"Eighteen," Prince Gaston repeated, firmly. Prospero's stronghold lay far afield, but not too far. Where could it be, that it was hidden from Landuc?

"Eighteen," the Emperor muttered, displeased.

"At which time shall my daughter be delivered me," Prospero said, leaning forward.

"The Crown cannot impede your daughter's liberty," the Emperor said.

Gaston hoped Prospero would demand to see the girl, but Prospero said, "An ill wind thou art, Avril, pure pestilence. Any hurt she hath taken I shall charge to thy account, for that thou'rt so eager to claim benefits, must also claim evils done in thy demesnes—and with them a father's curse on thee." His voice was soft and menacing.

The Emperor said nothing, but stared back at him hatefully, ignoring the coldness on his neck.

Evil comes of evil, thought Gaston. He rubbed a pounding vein in his temple.

"Now let us review these terms," Prince Prospero said, opening his cylindrical leather case.

"Agreement?" Freia repeated. "What agreement?"

"Oh, my Lady," said Scudamor. He and the Castellan looked at one another across the table, then at her where she sat in the seat to the right of Prospero's empty chair. Dewar stood at a window at the other end of the table, gazing out and listening.

"The Emperor Avril made a writing agreement with Lord Prospero when Lord Prospero went to seek you," Utrachet said. He spoke Argos to Freia, the language native to his tongue and Scudamor's, and Dewar understood nothing of what they said, but did understand Freia. He puzzled over this with a piece of his thought.

"I didn't know that. They didn't tell me."

"He did not w—did not like it," Utrachet corrected himself, "but he decided that it was best to go along with it, better than leaving you prisoner and under Landuc's power as you were."

"The writing agreement, yes," Scudamor said. "Lady, you have not seen him?"

She shook her head, their sick expressions frightening her. "No, no, he came once to me, went away, he said nothing of agreements, he only—I suppose he wanted to know I was alive. He said nothing."

Scudamor swallowed. "The Emperor did propose to him an agreement of several points. I have the writing, the same writing copied. It is in the language of Landuc, not ours."

"I can read that," Freia said.

Scudamor nodded and left the room. They said nothing until he returned and handed her a rolled sheet. "This is a copy of what they gave him," Scudamor said, "he made it and left it here."

"Do you know—?" Freia paused in unrolling it.

"He did ask our counsel, Lady, and we gave it," Utrachet said.

Dewar turned from the window and watched her read.

Her eyes widened as she went down the document. Twice she cried "What!" and the second time Scudamor put his head in his hands and whispered, "Aye, Mistress, aye . . ."

"This is, this is horrible!"

"So he thought, but he could make little change in it," Utrachet whispered. "Yet we did fear that to leave one of our own in their hands would be great danger to all, greater danger than any other herein."

"He would have left me," Freia said, going cold.

The room was very still, and then, quickly, Scudamor said, "Nay, Lady, I think not."

"He would have left me," she repeated. "These terms are harsher to him than death. He could not consider me worth so much." She looked at Dewar and her eyes narrowed. "Especially if he knows about you."

"Aye, Lady," whispered Scudamor, looking down unhappily, before Dewar could equivocate.

She held the rolled paper under her icy hands and stared at it. "When did he go?"

"Five days ago."

Freia looked at the paper. Five days previous had been the day she had rid herself of Golias's burden, the hateful seed he had started: a day of evil for evil, fear for fear. "Fitting," she whispered, her lips numb. The shock held her motionless.

"May I see?" Dewar asked softly.

She flicked the treaty; it rolled down the table toward him. He carried it to the window to read.

"I wonder if we can get to him in time," she said.

Utrachet and Scudamor brightened. "Could try," said the latter.

"He has Hurricane," Freia said.

"Yes," said Utrachet.

"Nothing can outrun Hurricane," Freia said. "Nor do I know the way there. Trixie followed him when I went before; she knew. Where is Trixie?"

"I can find the way," Dewar said.

"She fled," Scudamor said, "she came and killed, but

would permit none to harness her, and left after eating."

Freia's face fell further, injury and disappointment in every line.

"I daresay the gryphon could outspeed Hurricane, if you could find her," Dewar said.

"She'll be over the Jagged Mountains by now," Freia said sadly. "Gone feral—not that she was ever truly tame."

"Lord Prospero left other writings," Scudamor said, "which he said were to do with you, and which he had us sign also, Lady. He said 'twould give the Emperor a prick in the arse to see them."

"If you can find them—"

"I'll fetch the copies he did not take," the Seneschal said, and he left the room.

"He's buried them deep in some burrow of his," Utrachet said. "Nests in paper, not leaves. Lady, I will not conceal it, Lord Prospero was much oppressed."

"I cannot believe he agreed to do these things for me. I don't understand any of this. Why couldn't he do as you did and break the bonds? He got away from Malperdy himself. Why couldn't he free me?"

Dewar coughed. "As a sorcerer, madame, I can give you a number of reasons. In Malperdy, the Bounds around Prince Prospero were forged differently than in Landuc, where you were bound yourself to the prison. Otto, who pent him in Malperdy, had not the art to do so well, and so Prospero was able to use his familiar creatures, whatever they are, to free him."

"Where is Caliban?" Freia asked Utrachet.

"Not seen in long and long, Mistress—yet that is not uncommon," Utrachet added.

"At least *you're* still here," Freia said mournfully to the Castellan. He bowed his head.

Dewar waited and went on, "Stonework is a branch of sorcery possibly less familiar to Prospero than to me, as I apprenticed in it. Thus it may be that he does not know the ways in which such Bounds as held you are broken, though he can perhaps see how they are made. I suspect he could have broken them, given much time to study—did he not break Chasoulis's walls, which were Bound by Neyphile?—but such an examination is difficult without time and with interruptions by guards."

"So you think he couldn't," Freia said to him.

"That is what I said."

"I don't believe it," said she.

"Mistress," Utrachet said, "alas, it is true as far as I have seen."

"How can he renounce sorcery?" she cried. "It is all he does. He cannot just forget it."

"There are oaths," Dewar said, "which he can be forced to take, which are strong enough to prevent him from using what he knows, or speaking of it, or meditating on it."

"This is evil, evil," whispered Freia. "I knew no good would come of his war. He wouldn't listen to me."

Scudamor returned and set a wooden box before Freia. "Lady, here are the writings."

She opened the box. "They are in Argos and Lannach," she said.

"Yes," said Scudamor.

Freia read, and they waited, the sorcerer by the window and the Castellan and Seneschal to either side of her.

"Why does he do this?" she whispered.

"What has he done?" Dewar asked.

"He has bestowed things on me, my name here and here— Titles, lands I've never heard of—Argylle," she said, coming to the last, her eyes widening. "How can this be?"

"They are titles?" Dewar asked.

"They say he renounces—whatever it is, each is different—in order to bestow it upon me. So here he says I own lands in a place called Penrun, and in Wallong, and others . . ." She leafed through the sheets. "And here it says Argylle is mine."

"This city, Argylle?" Dewar asked patiently.

"This city?" Freia repeated.

Scudamor, Utrachet, and she all looked at one another.

"It is where you are, Dewar," she said. "All of it. The city—" She made a dismissing gesture. "That's new. At first Prospero called it Garvhaile, but I could never say it properly, and now it is Argylle. But that is not what I don't understand. Why has he done this? He knows I don't want this kind of thing. We argued about it. I won't take these things from him. He can't make me."

"They are titles to lands," Dewar half-asked, "and estates, things of that nature—"

"Yes, I guess that's what they are. If that's what it is when you give somebody something they don't want."

"Then they are deeds of gift of title," Dewar said. "Prospero is a shrewd man, and the Emperor's getting less than he hoped from the bargain, but still much." He came around the table to stand behind her and look over her shoulder.

"Why?"

"In the agreement Prospero has made, he yields up his titles to lands to the Emperor—any he has. But before he went to sign the agreement—see, all is dated and witnessed, and I daresay he is doing the same with some honorable folks of Landuc—he has divested himself of every scrap of earth he could claim and places all in your hands."

Freia stared at the papers.

"You cannot refuse; it's not a question of accepting or refusing. You can ignore the properties, but legally Landuc cannot touch them. They are yours, by perfectly legal gift. Hm, this is rather older. And odder." Dewar paused and picked up a parchment, written in Prospero's perfect penwork.

"That was when he had just begun planning the war. I didn't understand what it was, but he made me sign it and he put a copy into some place he said was important. What is this word?" She pointed to a particularly intimidating one.

"This document declares that you are an emancipated freewoman and that he holds no claim on you or anything you possess. It is a thing that is filed sometimes in Landuc when women are widowed and thus become legally wards of their brothers. If the brothers and the woman can come to some agreement, they will grant her the independence to manage property or money left to her by her husband or in her dowry and renounce claims on it. It is very rare," Dewar added, "and I've never heard of it being done with a daughter. You must ask a man of law if it is legally possible to emancipate a daughter."

"He doesn't own me!"

"That's what this paper says." Dewar sighed.

"I mean he certainly does not own me, and he never did, and he knows it! This is an insult!"

"Not in Landuc. In Landuc it is a scandal," said Dewar, grinning.

"Damn Landuc!" Freia banged the lid of the box closed. "Can you open a Way there? We must stop him from going through with this horrible business the Emperor has forced on him! It will kill him."

"No, it won't," Dewar said, "but it will cripple him, and the Emperor will like that better."

# — 38 —

"FREIA, THERE IS SOMETHING IN THIS place which tickles my curiosity," Dewar said, sitting beside her and selecting a nut from the dish before them.

"I don't know anything," Freia said dully. She was rolling three nuts around the rim of the dish, her head heavy on her hand. He had been playing with odd instruments for several hours now, things with lenses and things with prisms and swinging balances, things with finely-graven marks and his Map and thick Ephemeris. She had been contemplating Prospero's disregard for her, past and present. Neither had much to show for the time so spent.

Dewar cracked his nut in his fist and picked the meat out. In a honeyed voice he went on, "There is some force here which overwhelms my sorcery. Do you know whether Prospero has placed Bounds or barriers hereabouts? I felt Bounds at the city walls, but not strong enough to account for the difficulty I'm encountering."

"He doesn't tell me anything. Perhaps Utrachet or Scudamor would know," she replied bitterly.

Dewar ate his nutmeat and cracked another more neatly. He tidied the shells into a pile as he constructed his next remark. "Lady," he said, "a chance encounter made us comrades, and a chance of genealogy made us siblings. Though we're mostly strangers still, yet I think we've travelled and done enough together that I can ask you to tell me what's troubling you now." He leaned forward to look at her face.

"Everything," she said after a short silence, during which the nuts were allowed to roll to a halt. "I do not understand what Prospero is doing, or why, and he has never told me anything that mattered. He told Utrachet about you, Utrachet said so, yet he never told me. He doesn't trust me," she finished.

"I do not think he has known very long that I exist, and less that I'm his son," said Dewar gently. "How long have you lived here with him?"

"I don't know. Always."

"Well, you have the advantage of me there," Dewar suggested. "I have not had more than an hour or so all told with him, much of that in the war when we were adversaries. Has he taught you sorcery?"

"No," she said. "He wouldn't. He said it would be bad for me to learn that from him. You don't have that problem," she added in her bitter tone.

Dewar understood. She was jealous. Prospero had excluded her from his confidence in the past, and she foresaw further exclusion because Dewar was a sorcerer and she was not.

"He wouldn't let me go with him," she went on in an undertone, "but if it had been you he would have."

"Freia, I do not know him well enough to second-guess him, but I surmise he left you behind to protect you." And rightly too, Dewar thought, if he had emancipated her and endowed her with lands. But he went on, "If he has gone to the trouble of having you with him for a long time, Freia, you shouldn't be afraid that he's going to cut you off. Surely he loves you. He has gone to Landuc to get you back."

She was silent, but he could see that she was troubled still.

Dewar touched her shoulder and then cautiously half-embraced her. "Freia," he said, "do not let such ideas gnaw you. Let us work together as we have before to find him and then, when we have done so, we can begin to figure out what we are to one another."

Freia looked at him sidelong. She didn't want a brother. If they two had dallied in the haystack before going to Perendlac, what would they be now? She had wanted Dewar painfully then; she didn't want him now, her body was sick and shocked still, but she knew that she had ached for him then and that everything she had seen in him was still there.

He had seemed antagonistic toward Prospero and she had thought to mediate between them, to help her father and please herself at once by finding a mate whose interests, talents, and affection could be brought to Prospero's aid.

"I thought you sought Prospero to quarrel with him," she said.

He looked down. "Yes and no," he said. "He had dismissed me suddenly—then did it again—and I misliked his arrogant way of doing so. It seemed to me—and still does—that we've much to discuss. We were adversaries, but without personal feeling, in the war. I've left the war."

"He does that to everyone," Freia said. "All at his beck and call." She looked out the window at the forest, on the other side of the low course of stone that was becoming a wall.

"It befits a sorcerer and a Prince both," Dewar said, "and it pricked me, as I said, but now I would not see the Emperor strip him of his powers. It sets a dangerous example, for one thing."

Freia noted that he did not speak of affection for Prospero. He had none, probably.

"I would not gladly see any colleague so treated," Dewar was saying, "least of all one for whom I have such respect and whose prowess is as great as his nobility. I would like to know more of him." His arm, still across her shoulders, tightened. "Lady, we are allies in purpose. Doubtless you have been taught to trust none, believe none, but I promise you I bear him no ill-will."

"What return do you want for all this? Nobody does anything for kindness," Freia said, turning from the forest to his face.

"You yourself misprove that," Dewar said. "You have imperilled yourself and taken grave hurts for love of your father. Grant me some small share of your own altruism, Lady," he concluded in a near-whisper.

They sat eye-to-eye, breaths mingled, motionless. Finally Freia nodded fractionally.

"Thank you," Dewar replied, and bowed his head slightly.

Freia relaxed. She had been bow-tight.

"I am meeting great difficulty in working sorcery," Dewar said, "for there's something here which overwhelms and turns awry my least effort, just as I could not bring us closer to the place than that wasteland. Do you know of anything which could be the cause?"

"I think I do."

"What is that?"

"I think I'm not supposed to tell you," she said unhappily, biting her lip.

Dewar began to frame arguments and further wooing persuasions of confidence and then altered his plan. "Well. I would not have you flout your father's will. Then I must go from here to get to Landuc, and it will take precious time to do that. Several days, I should think, to leave the reach of this spell which confounds me."

She blooded her lip and Dewar forced himself not to look away.

"Dewar, I am not used to—" she started, but did not conclude the thought. "Let me think. Just do let me think."

"Surely." He lifted her hand and kissed it lightly.

Freia thought, weighing Prospero's safety against Prospero's fury, love against fear. "There is a Spring here," she said. "It is a source of power for him in some ways. He uses it to—to—change things. Sometimes. I don't understand very much of it," she said unhappily, "I wish I did, but he doesn't tell me things like that—you look strange; what's wrong?"

Light of knowledge and realization had broken over Dewar, a pure and intense emotion of recognition and desire. The Third Source was here. Someone had found it before him.

"A Spring, you say," he said, and his voice shook.

"It's just water. I bathed in it once," she said, his expression unnerving her.

"Water," he repeated. Yes. It would be Water. It made perfect symmetrical sense. He had suspected Water, all along, and yet he had never quite found the place. Ottaviano's and Prospero's wars had distracted him from his quest. Facts snapped together, forming new structures of reason and truth. Prospero had deeded the place to his daughter to keep Landuc from destroying it and being destroyed, as destruction must surely follow such a subsumption of Water to its antithesis Fire. Freia untrained might well see it as only water, to drink and bathe in; that was the oddly impenetrable part of her, the part of her that was attuned to the Spring—most of her. This was why he did not understand the speech of these people, nor had anyone in Landuc who had passed the Well's Fire; these were aliens, true outsiders whose essential nature was other than Fire.

"I think I shouldn't have told you that," Freia decided. "I can't do anything right."

"Freia, Freia! Yes, you have done right! I— You see I have been looking for this place. For many, many years. I knew it had to exist; it made itself apparent in disruptions of the other forces, the Well of Fire's and the Stone of Blood's, and I learned to compensate for it but never could locate the source of the difficulty. I theorized that it was some third force incompatible with those two but I could not locate it, though I sought. And here it is, here you are, imbued with it unknowing." He had seized both her hands and was staring into her face intently, and she stared back, riveted by the transformation his excitement had made in him.

"If I had thought it through I would have seen it." He laughed suddenly. "But there's been little time for thinking, really thinking. Freia, Lady, take me to this Spring."

She hesitated. "I think I shouldn't. I think he wouldn't like that." Prospero had warned her again and again not to speak of the Spring, of Argylle, of him, and she had now broken all those promises, and she didn't want to compound her crimes with what she feared he would see as treason outright.

"Please, Freia! I have searched so long, so long, and—"

"He told me not to!" she cried, throwing his hands away from her and jumping up, backing away from him. "You're always wanting more!"

A perfect, taut silence stretched between them. Dewar broke it. "Your pardon, Lady," he said. "Yet your father's—*our* father's—safety hangs on it."

"He couldn't make sorcery beyond here and I don't believe you could either even if I showed you the Spring," Freia retorted. Why had she trusted him? She should not have brought him here; she should have stayed in cold, hateful Landuc until Prospero returned for her. Her stomach cramped. She rubbed it and swallowed a lump in her throat.

Dewar gazed at his hands, not seeing her. "Well," he said then, "I must leave here at once if I'm to get to Landuc or to him in time to keep him from cutting his throat on your behalf, Lady." He had been too vehement. More gently, and she might have shown him the Spring. He suspected she'd not leave him an instant alone now, so that he'd not be able to find it himself.

"I'll go with you. To explain."

"It is your choice. The ride will be fast and hard. I do not constrain you," he said.

"We'll go. Utrachet will give us horses. Come with me," Freia said.

The city was out of sight behind them before Freia thought to look back. Utrachet had given them food for the horses and themselves and water in heavy skins for the desert area.

"Perhaps I'll be able to work in that desert," Dewar had said. He understood now that the desert was where Landuc ended and this place began. It was two days' cruel riding away from the Spring, two days of rationed rest, of pushing the horses to the limits of their endurance and encouraging them to go beyond if they could.

"If only Trixie had stayed," Freia said at one rest stop, as she rubbed down her mare, Epona.

"If, if, if," Dewar retorted curtly, having no patience with conjecture.

Freia said no more.

She knew the shortest way by some instinct and he followed her along the unmarked Road through the vast forest she said was called Threshwood, the core of the Spring's dominion. As they drew near the edge of Threshwood, Dewar began to feel again the beat of the Well, intermittent and weak. They saw no other people; the Road passed only through forests. It was a straightway journey with none of the waits, detours, and encumbering procedures required in Landuc, yet they still took more than two days to reach the hilly, dark-skied semidesert where Dewar would try to open a Way to Landuc with the first trickle of the Well's power. The distance seemed wrong to Freia. She said nothing to Dewar, but it felt farther every time she travelled it. Usually distances shortened with use.

Dewar had collected faggots of wood, which load had slowed them, and with his sister now he piled these and lit them. She rubbed and walked the horses and watered and fed them slowly. The animals were nearly foundered; Freia had called for a halt again and again when her brother would have pushed onward, and now her care was more for the horses than for the sorcery. They paced heavy-hooved with her under the stars. A little food, walking; a little water, walking—the horses followed her dully.

She heard him chanting words and saw the light pulse upward, sparks flying to the night sky. A few heartbeats later he was calling her.

"Freia!"

The horses plodded with her, back to him, through the lumpy hillocks.

"Dewar."

Leaning on his staff, he was soaked with sweat, his cloak, coat, and waistcoat discarded. "Not working," he said. "Can't quite get there."

"They can't go farther, Dewar. They can't. It will just kill them. They must rest."

The two looked at one another. Dewar muttered something and spat in the fire, mopped his face on his sleeve.

"Once when I was hurt," Freia said, "I'd fallen and broken my leg, you see, and I couldn't get home, Papa brought me home with sorcery. I was fainting and I thought I heard him call me, and when I woke he was holding me and we were home."

"A tender tale," Dewar said. "He Summoned you, a Great Summoning."

"Can you do that?"

"It is a basic spell. You mean Summon Prospero."

"Yes."

"If I cannot open a Way to Landuc, in all likelihood I cannot drag Prospero to me with a Great Summoning—against which, in all likelihood, he is well-guarded." He shook his head. "I have no token to Summon him with, anyway, Freia. You don't understand sorcery."

"You mean something that's his. I have something. If I give it to you, will you try?"

"It won't work. Why do you think it will?"

"Maybe he would at least feel it a little and, and—I don't know." She wasn't sure. Her thinking was as blown as the horses. She walked up and down, tugging their reins gently to make them move slowly with her.

Dewar drank greedily from one of the wineskins. He took out a flat loaf of bread, their last, and devoured half, considering. It would be a small gesture, and if he did not try she would think he meant them to fail; she was suspicious of him still, mistrustful. "To please you I'll do it," he said, brushing crumbs from his sleeves. "We'll not move from here before the animals are ready anyway."

"If you don't want to—"

He held up a hand, silencing her. "It's as worthwhile a

way to spend the time as any," he said. "Give what you have to me."

"Here."

The token was a dagger, an elegant weapon tingling with sorcery, with an ebony handle that fit Dewar's hand like a lover's touch, the blade silk-smooth steel gold-damascened with clouds. The pommel was set with a glittering stone like a diamond, but black. "This is a thing of some power, Freia." He turned it over and over, sheathed it again after looking at it in the firelight. The sheath was plain and black, tipped with silver: a gentleman's accoutrement, functional, not ostentatious. Prospero was a man of good taste.

"He carries it often. I thought he might want it. Maybe he forgot it." It was a fixture in her mental picture of him: the gem at his belt, always, the blade drawn to cut a piece of bread at table; to dissect a dead animal and point to its parts, naming them to her; to split and graft a twig; to share an apple. Other things too, that she never saw.

"Maybe. I'll try, Freia." One bundle of wood was left, and he dropped it onto the fire. "Stand back. Well back. It may frighten the horses."

She led them away. As he began to speak and invoke Prospero (the dagger thrummed in his hands, cold though he held them in the very heart of the fire), Freia came and stood just behind him, watching.

The power of the Well's Fire coursed through and through Dewar, and a part of his mind recognized that this time it was going to work, and that part tried to brace itself for success, but most of him was caught up in the beautiful coils of his spell winding around and out and through the world, snaring already-tangled Prospero, snapping back—

The fire exploded; sparks, coals, and half-burned wood sprayed high and wide.

A thunderous voice roared, "Bastard! By Blood and Breath, I'll send thy soul to frigid Hella piecemeal—"

"Papa!"

Dewar ducked beneath the sword blow he barely saw; it whistled; Freia screamed the same note.

"Papa!"

A horse snorted and then a man. Dewar straightened, his own sword in his hand.

Black Hurricane had pranced out of the fire, which was only coals now, nearly consumed. Prospero on his back was staring down at him, the sword which had trimmed a few stray hairs from the top of Dewar's head still hovering ready for murder.

"Your pardon, sir," Dewar said weakly. "I—I didn't think it would actually—work."

"Cub! And I thought thee adept," snarled Prospero. "What manner of play be this, that thou mak'st Summonings with no faith in their potency— Give that me, 'tis mine own—" He sheathed the sword and dismounted, grabbing the dagger from Dewar. "Freia!"

Dewar said nothing as Freia leapt for Prospero, hugging him. The change from incandescent rage to confused relief and then solicitude on Prospero's face was nearly comic to watch.

"Puss, Puss," Prospero was whispering, stroking her hair.

"Papa. Papa. Oh, Papa. I was so worried," she replied, "I'm so happy to see you, Papa—"

Uncomfortable, Dewar looked away, at the shadows of the fire, and up at the stars, and then down into the ruddy coals.

"So thou'rt Avril's man," Prospero said, in a very different tone than he'd used to greet his daughter.

Dewar looked back. Prospero still embraced her; Freia seemed half-swooning with joy. Prospero's stance and voice were defiant and defensive.

"No," Dewar said, puzzled. "Far from it— Oh, no. We're too late," he whispered.

"What mean you, too late? I've given my word; did Gaston prevail 'pon Avril to pack off my girl betimes—"

"Papa, you mustn't go to Landuc," Freia said, coming out of her blissful reverie.

Dewar dragged a hand slowly down his face, half-turning away.

Prospero looked, and felt, heart-sick. "Puss, Freia," he

said, and took her arms, bent down to stare into her face, "tell me what this means, that thou'rt here that erst I left in durance at the Emperor's pleasure. For my fear is that all's worked to great ill. Ease me. Tell me thy tale, be quick."

"This is Dewar," Freia said.

"I know him."

"He came and got me from Landuc," she said.

"He what," Prospero whispered.

"And brought me home, but you weren't there."

"When did he take thee from Landuc?"

"Eight days after you were there. Papa—P—" She began to weep, shaking. "I thought you wouldn't come back," she said.

"What!" he shouted, straightening, rounding on Dewar. "And how cam'st thou in this tale?"

"I had been trailing you for a little time, a few days, trying to catch up to you," Dewar said, "and I came across Ottaviano in Outer Ascolet, by a Ley from Mazhkëanea."

Prospero bared his teeth. "That misbegotten whelp. I hope 'twas none too soon after my passing."

Dewar smiled. "A night or two, and he was in a compliant mood. So that when I had freed him I pried from him a strange story—that Freia was Landuc's captive, and that you her father had gone to set her free; that that ass Avril had finally bargained with a sorceress, Oriana, to confine Freia—all that Otto knew he told me, on pain of being tree-tied again and used for target practice. I set out after you once more, but it took longer than I'd wanted to get to the capitol where Freia was, where I thought you were."

"Ah," said Prospero heavily. "And I was gone."

"Yes, sir. And she there, clearly against her will."

"He broke the glass," Freia said, "climbing up a rope, and made me cut my hand and put blood around the window and did a sorcery to let me out." She slid under Prospero's arm again, at his side, damp-faced.

Prospero inhaled slowly, his face grim. "Three days I tested that damned construction of Oriana's," he said. "And made no breach."

Dewar swallowed, daunted by the coldness in Prospero's

voice. "We left," he said, "and Freia wanted to go home. She was ill. We rested a few days and then I carried her to Argylle."

"Hast been there too, then," Prospero said softly.

"Yes, sir," Dewar whispered, fear tickling his back. They could yet come to a duel. He had violated Prospero's stronghold, had all but abducted his daughter, and the man had a violent temper and the sorcerer an apt command of violence.

"Wench, hadst thou no faith in my return?" Prospero turned on Freia, seizing her arm and shaking her sharply.

Freia flinched. "You didn't come back," she said. "You didn't say— I didn't know!" she cried. "I wanted to go home."

"Couldst not abide my coming?" he shouted at her, shaking her again. "Thou impatient infant! And thou, thou meddling monkey! What have you wrought, you two, but my destruction? Conspired against me to strip me, castrate me—"

"Papa, no!" wailed Freia.

"Prospero, be reasonable!" yelled Dewar over them both.

"My undoing's all thy doing, disobedient chit! Hadst but obeyed my first command to thee and remained safely in Argylle—but nay! Headstrong, self-willed, and full of thy own idea, wouldst not wait, needs must flit hither and yon, straight into the monster's maw, and deliver me into his hands with thyself!"

The sheathed dagger in Prospero's left hand caught Dewar's eye as Prospero gestured with it. Freia was sobbing incoherently, trying to argue, and then surrendering and sitting down abruptly, overcome.

"I—I—I'm—sor-sorry—" came out from her brokenly as Prospero paused in his tirade and caught his breath.

Dewar looked at her and then at Prospero. He had not expected Prospero to receive her thus. Clearly she hadn't either. He looked at her again, weeping silently, her whole body shaking. "All she's been able to think of is returning to you," Dewar said. "You wrong her."

"Impudence, wouldst tutor me? Thy—"

"I didn't come here to be abused, Prospero; no more did she! It is all ill-hap, all ill-timed accidents and misencounters! You missed her at Perendlac, at Chasoulis; you did not *tell* her you'd return to Landuc; how could she know? They told her nothing, assuredly. And I have done as I thought best on her behalf and yours."

"What gives thee interest in my daughter?" demanded Prospero. "How's she known to thee?"

"We met in Chenay, where she saved my life by hauling me from the ditch where you had left me in the snow," Dewar said, "accidentally, you said; regardless, I'd have died without her help. She told me nothing of herself then—purely nothing, and I never thought to see her again until we met at Malperdy, where she'd gone to try to free you. But you'd freed yourself, and we fled together, and parted; met again and made common cause to find you, trading names and little more. Together we tracked you to Perendlac, and there were separated in the battle. We have been comrades, and it surprised us to be siblings too—and through all we've sought no ill to you, Prospero."

Prospero's storm of anger had blown itself out before Dewar's indignant front. His face lined, tired, he studied Dewar in the fading glow of the coals and then looked down at Freia, who had not risen.

"That fickle, teasing slut Fortuna," he said heavily. " 'Tis her I must blame." He folded his arms. "Aye, one missed meeting on another, I see't now. Thou, she, I, haring one behind t'other, a steeplechase of folly leading o'er a cliff. And here's the cliff, and I leapt blindly. Fool I was! Not to demand to speak again to her ere I swore. And false Avril! Damned and damned again, he and the others, who led me to take an oath that cost them nothing. For thou hadst freed her already. Freia—" he knelt, touched her shoulder hesitantly—"I did but seek to spare thee misery, not to torment thee. It so pained thee to see me once, and pained me too, I dared not go again. And I trusted Gaston would ward thee well, I asked it of him, and he said he had taken utmost care of thee; be none of them honorable, I thought him so—yet he said naught!—Freia, believe me, I had not abandoned thee. I was delayed by natural barriers, not by unnatural disinclination to redeem thee. When I knew thou wert captive I spared naught to find thee. Precious child, I rage at myself, not at thee. Thou know'st my ways. Thy heart is all affection, I know't." His voice dove-gentle, Prospero persuaded her into his arms again, and he bowed his head over hers, still bent, and went on. "They have rent me from myself, Puss, and it shall make me half-mad, and thou the lone thing to save from all the wrackage. Pardon a sorcerer's tempest and kiss thy father, for he loves thee."

Freia snuffled and took a pair of deep breaths, then looked up red-eyed and kissed Prospero on right and left cheeks, a favor he accepted gravely and then returned.

"Is the tale that this—that thy—thy brother hath spun me true?" he asked her.

She nodded.

Dewar slowly sat on his heels beside them.

"Thou'rt in sooth a huntress, to seek me so o'er all Landuc," Prospero told her, mustering a small smile. "Bravely done. Now tell me the end of't. He found thee, bore thee home at last—then what?"

Freia nodded and, after swallowing, said hoarsely, "Utrachet and Scudamor said you had been there and gone again. They showed me the papers you left. Then we began to see what was happening—that you didn't know Dewar had gotten me. And we tried to find you in time, Papa—Papa, they can't make you do anything, can they? Can they? It's not right—"

Dewar watched, something tightening in his chest, as Prospero brushed fresh tears from her cheeks and kissed her eyes.

"Poor Puss, thy eyes are weary o' weeping. Ban these tears. An oath's an oath, my girl, and that the Emperor hath falsely sworn shall be to his injury in the end. All know't, but he believeth himself above truth and honor and other human constraints. He that liveth faithlessly shall die the same, and 'twill be a glad day for the earth when his foot weighs no more on't. Aye, I must hold to my word. Greater ill—'tis scarce conceivable—worser things should come of my breaking vow than keeping it. I have done what I could to protect thee, dearest of mine heart."

"I don't want you to give up sorcery," Freia whispered. "It's everything. You shouldn't have to give up everything."

"Well, I shall learn new tricks to fill my days," Prospero said hollowly. "Puss, I cannot think on't much, else it preys on my thought and devoureth it. Prithee speak not of't. I cannot be unsworn. Mine oath is made in blood and fire and shall endure until all the world be unmade around us. I shall aid thee in governance of thy city and live as other men."

"I don't want a city! You know that. I never wanted a city."

"No tears, no sighs. Hush. We shall all have things we do not want, Freia, burthens of undesirability unsurpassed. Thine be lighter than many others'. And canst not deny; 'tis sealed and entered in the Titles of Landuc. Bribery put it there, but nothing can remove it. No tears, I say; hast courage enough to fare into a wilderness, and must have courage to face what thou hast found." He kissed her eyes again.

"Oh, Papa." Freia hugged him around the neck. Dewar shifted his gaze to the fire's dull coals, for a tear glittered on Prospero's beard, and it was not hers.

"There's my true brave maid, my nimble-footed huntress," Prospero said, patting her back.

Freia sniffed once and sat back, half on his lap still. "Let's go home," she said.

"Needs must, Puss," he said gravely. "There's much I must do yet to fulfill my word." He laid his hand on her cheek. "How came you here? Afoot?"

"Horses. Epona and Torrent. We half-killed them, poor creatures. I was walking them," she recalled, and brushed her hair back.

"Find them—Hurricane's got 'em, no doubt—bring 'em here. We'll walk homeward some ways. There's better resting places beyond this waste for man and beast alike."

She nodded, rose, and went into the dark. They heard her whistling for the horses.

Prospero regarded Dewar by the ebbing coal-light. "I know not what to make of thee, boy."

Dewar's mouth twitched; he lifted an eyebrow. "I could take offense, sir."

"Better, then: I know not what to make of thee, son."

Dewar glanced after Freia, back to Prospero's steel-colored gaze: less of steel than cloud in his eyes now. He sought words, but they slipped apart and would not connect to meanings. "You threw a war," Dewar said.

"I'd not put it so," said Prospero gruffly. "I'd say, a man doth not squander what be most precious—life's-blood. Even in another's body."

"Would you have killed me?"

"Aye. Could have done, three times. Thou'rt unseasoned for the task thou hadst elected. I misliked to murder a promising fellow, at first, and learned more of thee as I could, and then bespoke thee. My kindness goes beyond my kin. I'd no stomach to oppose thee, that final day, to break thee and bind thee, and my honor had liever I defeat my enemies with a prince's weapons and not a sorcerer's. Belike canst not compass that, being wholly a sorcerer in thy nurture."

"I have tried to be a gentleman as well," Dewar said.

"Hast been more than gentle to thy sister, and my thanks to thee for't. Hers she tenders slowly, o'er a lifetime. Forgets naught, returns tenfold any boon."

"A lady," Dewar said, smiling a little.

"She'll deny the name hotly. What's thy setting now? May ask?"

"I thought I'd go back with you," Dewar said.

Prospero was silent.

"If you didn't mind."

Silence still.

"It seems to me that there may be some who seek to take advantage of what may look like a sudden opportunity," Dewar tried to fill the silence, "and if they know I'm about, an adept, they'll think twice. I know little of you, sir—of your enemies, your feuds—but I don't engage in trade, and in the past I think I have served those whose causes I supported well, or well enough . . ." He lost the words, and they frittered away in the dark. A horse neighed.

Prospero's eyes were fixed upon Dewar's face. "A bond of friendship sufficed for thee when thou wert aside Ottaviano," he said. "Thou'rt indeed a gentleman—and a sorcerer. An thou'lt be my son and my daughter's brother, must accept that bonds of blood are weightier betimes than friendship's golden links. My daughter's my daughter, for all our life. So should be my son."

"Family," Dewar said, and he bit his lip.

"Or canst go from here on thy own course with all our due affection."

"And leave you alone hereafter."

The other countered gently, "Nay. But join us now, and—and 'twould mean much to me. For thou hast right, that there be harpies and vultures with old cuts to salve with fresh blood, and I fear for her safety in their frenzy more than for mine own. Blood-kin need not be a curse, e'en to a sorcerer. And to a gentleman, well—would any with sense be averse to claim even a prince o'erthrown for parent?" Prospero's voice was wry, his face near-invisible in the poor light.

Dewar heard horses thumping on the dry, hard ground, coming near from the other side of the fire. "A prince is a prince all his life," he said, "even as a son is. I will go with you, the latter to the former."

# Acknowledgments

The author is grateful to:

- Mary Hopkins, Delia Sherman, Betsy Perry, Greer Gilman, Eluki bes Shahar, and Deborah Manning, whose warm friendship was not cooled by the drafts vented upon them;
- Valerie Smith, for sometimes counsel and sometimes tea;
- The National Science Foundation, the Office of Naval Research, the Sloan Foundation, the Department of Brain and Cognitive Sciences, and others who provided funding to the quondam Center for Biological Information Processing at the Massachusetts Institute of Technology, enabling the author to eat and live indoors;
- and most fundamentally, her husband.